VANISHED!

Gwen kept pace with him determinedly. *"Rod!* Thou
. . ." Then whatever she was saying faded away. Rod
turned back toward her, frowning. . .
. . . and found himself staring at the trunk of a tree.

A white trunk, white as a birch, but corrugated like an
oak—and the leaves were silver.

Rod stared.

Then, slowly, he looked up, and all about him; all the
trees were just like the first. They towered above him,
spreading a tinsel canopy between himself and the sun;
it tinkled in the breeze.

THE WARLOCK UNLOCKED

Ace Science Fiction Books by Christopher Stasheff

A WIZARD IN BEDLAM
(coming in February 1986)

THE WARLOCK SERIES
ESCAPE VELOCITY
THE WARLOCK IN SPITE OF HIMSELF
KING KOBOLD REVIVED
THE WARLOCK UNLOCKED
THE WARLOCK ENRAGED
THE WARLOCK WANDERING *(coming in May 1986)*

THE WARLOCK UNLOCKED

CHRISTOPHER STASHEFF

ACE SCIENCE FICTION BOOKS
NEW YORK

To Mary Margaret Miller Stasheff
— Wife and Mother —

THE WARLOCK UNLOCKED

An Ace Science Fiction Book / published by arrangement with
the author

PRINTING HISTORY
Ace Original / March 1982
Eighth printing / January 1986

ISBN: 0-441-87330-8

Ace Science Fiction Books are published by The Berkley Publishing Group,
200 Madison Avenue, New York, New York 10016.
PRINTED IN THE UNITED STATES OF AMERICA

PROLOGUE

Pope John the XXIV said his first Mass with the whole world watching through its 3DT cameras. He said his second at sunrise the next morning, with a handful of devoted clerics watching, in a little chapel adjoining his chambers. Not too many were willing to get up at 5:00 AM, even for a Mass said by the Holy Father.

After a frugal breakfast—he had resurrected the quaint, antique custom of saying Mass on an empty stomach, in spite of what his doctor told him that thimbleful of wine every morning was doing to its lining—the Pope sat down at his desk to face his first day on the job.

Cardinal Incipio gave him just time enough to get settled before entering with an armful of fiche-wafers. "Good morning, Your Holiness."

"Good morning, Giuseppe." Pope John eyed the bulging case, sighed, and pulled over his wafer-reader. "Well, let's get started. What've you got for me?"

"An air of mystery." Cardinal Incipio produced an ancient envelope with a magician's flourish. "I thought you might like to start the morning with a dash of intrigue."

The Pope stared at the nine-by-twelve parchment container. "You've certainly got my attention. What, by all the stars, is *that?*"

"An envelope." Cardinal Incipio handed it to him reverently. "Be careful, Your Holiness; it's rather old."

"An envelope." The Pope took it, frowning. "Enclosures for messages. So *large?* It *must* be old!"

"Very old," Cardinal Incipio murmured, but Pope John wasn't hearing him. He was staring, awed, at the sprawling, handwritten inscription:

To be opened by:
  His Holiness, Pope John XXIV
  On August 23, 3059

Pope John felt a tingling spread from the base of his neck over his upper back and shoulders.

"It's been waiting a very long time," Cardinal Incipio said. "It was left by a Dr. Angus McAran, in 1954." And, when the Pope remained silent, he went on nervously, "It's amazing anyone was able to keep track of it, buried in the vaults like that. But it *was* hermetically sealed, of course."

"Of course." His Holiness looked up. "One thousand, one hundred and five years. How did he know I'd be Pope on this date?"

Cardinal Incipio could only spread his hands.

"Certainly, certainly." The Pope nodded, glowering. "I can't expect you to know. In fact, it *should* be the other way around—but I'm afraid Papal Infallibility is only in matters of doctrine, and even then, only *ex cathedra* . . . Well! No sense sitting here, contemplating in awe!" He took out a pocket-knife and slit the flap. It broke with a skeleton's rattle. Cardinal Incipio couldn't restrain a gasp.

"I know." The Pope looked up in sympathy. "Seems like desecration, doesn't it? But it was meant to be opened." Carefully, gingerly, he slid out the single sheet of parchment the envelope contained.

"What language is it?" Cardinal Incipio breathed.

"Early-International English. I don't need a translator." Even as Cardinal Kaluma, Pope John had still found time to teach an occasional course in comparative literature. He skimmed the ancient, faded handwriting quickly, then read it again very slowly. When he was done, he lifted his eyes and stared off into space, his dark brown face becoming steadily darker.

Cardinal Incipio frowned, worried. "Your Holiness?"

The Pope's eyes snapped to his, and held for a moment. Then His Holiness said, "Send for Father Aloysius Uwell."

The pitcher crashed to the floor. The child darted a quick,

frightened glance at the video pickup hidden in the upper right-hand corner of the room, then turned to start picking up the pieces.

In the next room, Father Uwell nodded, and sighed, "As I expected." He turned to the orderly, waiting at the back of the chamber. "Go clean that up for him, would you? He's only eight years old; he might cut a finger, trying to do it himself."

The orderly nodded and left, and Father Al turned back to the holovision tank with a sad smile. "So many unbreakable materials in this world, and we still prefer our vessels made of glass. Reassuring, in its way . . . and so is the boy's glance at our hidden pickup."

"How so?" Father LeBarre frowned. "Is it not proof that his powers are magical?"

"No more than his making that pitcher float through the air, Father. You see, he made no use of the paraphernalia of magic—no mystic gestures, no pentagrams, not even a magic word. He simply stared at the pitcher, and it lifted off the table and began to drift."

"Demonic possession," Father LeBarre offered half-heartedly.

Father Al shook his head. "He's scarcely even naughty, from what you tell me; if a demon possessed him, it would make him a very unpleasant child indeed."

"So." Father LeBarre ticked off points on his fingers. "He is not possessed by a demon. He does not work magic, either black or white."

Father Al nodded. "That leaves us with one explanation—telekinesis. His glance at the 3DT pickup was very revealing. How could he know it was there, when we did not tell him, and it is well hidden, built into the ceiling? He probably read our minds."

"A telepath?"

Father Al nodded again. "And if he is telepathic, it's quite probable that he's also telekinetic; psi traits seem to run in multiples." He stood. "It is too early for a complete opinion, of course, Father. I will have to observe the boy more closely, inside this laboratory and outside—but at the moment, I would guess that I will find nothing of the supernatural about him."

Finally, Father LeBarre dared a smile. "His parents will be vastly relieved to hear it."

"Now, perhaps." Father Al smiled, too. "But before long, they will begin to realize the problems they will have, rearing a telekinetic and telepathic boy who has not yet learned to control his powers. Still, they will have a great deal of help, possibly more than they want. Telekinetics are rare, and telepaths are even more so; there are only a few dozen in the whole of the Terran Sphere. And in all but two of them, the talent is quite rudimentary. The interstellar government realizes that such abilities may be of enormous benefit, so they take a great interest in anyone found to possess them."

"The government again," Father LeBarre cried, exasperated. "Will they never be done meddling in the affairs of the Church?"

"Beware, Father—the government might think it is you who violates the separation of Church and State."

"But what was more natural than to bring him to the priest?" Father LeBarre spread his hands. "This is a small village; only the magistrate represents the Terran government, and none represents the DDT. The parents were on the verge of panic when objects within their house began to fly through the air in the boy's presence. What was more natural than to bring him to the priest?"

"Natural, and wise," Father Al agreed. "For all they knew, it might have been a demon, or at least a poltergeist."

"And what was more natural than that I should call upon my Archbishop, or that he would call upon the Vatican?"

"Quite so. And therefore I am here—but I doubt not I'll find no taint of the supernatural, as I've said. At that point, Father, the matter ceases to fall within our jurisdiction, and moves to the government's. 'Render unto Caesar. . .'"

"And is this boy Caesar's?" Father LeBarre demanded.

A soft, muted chime spared Father Al from answering. He turned to the comscreen and pressed the "accept" button. The screen blinked clear, and Father Al found himself looking through it into a Curia chamber, hundreds of miles away in Rome. Then the scene was blocked by a brooding face under a purple biretta. "Monsignor Aleppi!" Father Al smiled. "To what do I owe this pleasure?"

"I have no idea," the Monsignor answered, "but it should be a great pleasure indeed. His Holiness wishes to speak to you, Father Uwell—in person."

" 'On September 11, 3059 (Terran Standard Time), a man named Rod Gallowglass will begin learning that he is the most powerful wizard born since the birth of Christ. He dwells on a planet known to its inhabitants as "Gramarye" . . .' Then he gives the coordinates, and that's all. Nothing more but his signature." The Pope dropped the letter on his desk with a look of disgust.

Joy flooded through Father Al; he felt like a harp with the wind blowing through it. His whole life he had waited for it, and now it had come! At last, a real wizard!

Perhaps. . .

"Reactions?" His Holiness demanded.

"Does he offer any proof?"

"Not the slightest," His Holiness said in exasperation. "Only the message that I've just read you. We've checked the Public Information Bank, but there's no 'Rod Gallowglass' listed. The planet is listed, though, and the coordinates match the ones McAran gives. But it was only discovered ten years ago." He passed a faxsheet across the desk to Father Al.

Father Al read, and frowned. "The discovery is credited to a Rodney d'Armand. Could it be the same man?"

The Pope threw up his hands. "Why not? Anything is possible—and nothing probable, when you've so little information. But we checked his PIB bio. He's a younger son of a cadet branch of an aristocratic house on a large asteroid called 'Maxima.' He had a short but varied career in the space services, culminating in his enlistment in the Society for the Conversion of Extra-terrestrial Nascent Totalitarianisms. . ."

"The what?"

"I don't think I could say it again," His Holiness sighed. "It seems to be a sort of government bureau that combines the worst aspects of both exploration and espionage. Its agents are supposed to seek out the Lost Colonies, decide whether or not their government is headed towards democracy and, if it's not, put it onto a path that will eventually evolve a democracy."

"Fantastic," Father Al murmured. "I didn't even know we had such a bureau."

"Any government that's overseeing three-score worlds should have a bureau that just keeps track of all the other bureaus." His Holiness spoke from personal experience.

"I take it, then, that this Rodney d'Armand discovered a Lost Colony on Gramarye."

"Yes, but the Lord only knows which one," the Pope sighed. "You'll notice that the PIB sheet doesn't tell us anything about the inhabitants of the planet."

Father Al looked. Sure enough, any human information on the planet was summed up in one word at the bottom of the page: CLASSIFIED. It was followed by a brief note explaining that the planet was interdicted to protect its inhabitants from exploitation. "I'd guess it's a rather backward culture." Excitement thrilled through Father Al's veins—were they backward enough to still believe in magic?

"Backward, indeed." The Pope peered at another paper on his desk. "We checked our own data bank, and found we did have an entry on the planet—just a very brief report, from a Cathodean priest named Father Marco Ricci, that he'd accompanied an expedition by a group calling themselves the 'Romantic Emigrés.' They found an uncharted, Terra-like world, seeded a large island with Terran bioforms, and established a colony, four or five hundred years ago. Father Ricci requested permission to establish a House of the Order of St. Vidicon of Cathode—your own Order, I believe, Father Uwell."

"Yes, indeed." Father Al tried not to let his disappointment show; the Cathodeans had to be engineers as well as priests. No planet could be *too* backward, if they were there. "Was he granted permission?"

His Holiness nodded. "So it says; but apparently the Curia was never able to convey the news to him. The Interstellar Dominion Electorates fell about that time, and the Proletarian Eclectic State of Terra was established. As you know, one of the first things PEST did was to lose the Lost Colonies. There was no way to communicate with Father Ricci."

"Well, that's hopef . . . I mean, that might create problems."

"Yes, it might." The Pope fixed him with a glittering eye. "We may have another splinter sect there, calling themselves Roman Catholics, but out of touch with us for centuries. No telling what heresies they'll have dreamt up in that time." He sighed. "I'd hoped to have a rest from that sort of thing for a while."

Father Al knew what the Pope meant. Just before he'd been elevated to the Chair of St. Peter, Cardinal Kaluma had conducted the negotiations with the Archbishop of Burbank, a Lost Colony that had been found about twenty years before. They'd managed to keep the Faith fairly well, except for one heresy that had taken firm root: that plants had immortal souls. It turned out to be a fundamental point of doctrine on Burbank, since the whole planet was heavily involved in botanical engineering, with the goal of creating chlorophyll-based intelligence. The talks had become rather messy, and had ended with the establishment of the Church of Burbank. Its first act had been to excommunicate the Church of Rome. His Holiness hadn't been quite so drastic; he'd simply declared that they were incommunicado, and that the Church of Burbank could no longer really be said to be Roman Catholic.

A shame, too. Other than that, they'd been so sane. . .

"I will be discreet, Your Holiness, and only report accurately what I discover."

"Oh?" The Pope fixed Father Al with an owlish eye. "Are you going somewhere?"

Father Al stared at him for a moment.

Then he asked, "Why else would you have sent for me?"

"Quite so," His Holiness sighed, "I admit to the decision. It rankles, because I have no doubt that's what this McAran intended."

"Have we any choice, really?" Father Al asked quietly.

"No, of course not." The Pope frowned down at his desktop. "A letter that's been lying in the vaults for a thousand years acquires a certain amount of credibility—especially when its sender has managed to accurately predict the reign-name of the Pope. If McAran could be right about that, might he not be right about this 'wizard?' And whether the man is really a wizard or not, he could do great damage to the Faith; it has never proven terribly difficult to subvert religion with superstition."

"It's so tempting to believe that you can control the Universe by mumbling a few words," Father Al agreed.

"And too many of those who are tempted, might fall." The Holy Father's frown darkened. "And, too, there is always the infinitesimal chance of actually invoking supernatural powers. . ."

"Yes." Father Al felt a shadow of the Pope's apprehension. "Personally, I'd rather play with a fusion bomb."

"It would do less damage to fewer people." The Pope nodded.

Pope John XXIV stood up slowly, with the dignity of a thundercloud. "So. Take this with you." He held out a folded parchment. "It is a letter in my hand, directing whoever among the clergy may read it, to render you whatever help you require. That and a draft for a thousand Therms, are all the help I can send with you. Go to this planet, and find this man Gallowglass, wherever he is, and guide him to the path of the Lord as he discovers his wizardry, or the illusion of it."

"I'll do my best, Your Holiness." Father Uwell stood, smiling. "At least we know why this man McAran sent his letter to the Vatican."

"But of course." The Pope smiled, too. "Who else would've taken him seriously?"

CHAPTER ONE

There was a crash, and the tinkle of broken glass.

"Geoffrey!" Gwen cried in exasperation, "if I have told thee once, I have told thee twenty times—thou must not practice swordplay in the house!"

Rod looked up from Gerbrensis's *Historie of Gramarye* to see his smaller son trying to hide a willow-wand sword behind his back, looking frightened and guilty. Rod sighed, and came to his feet. "Be patient with him, dear—he's only three."

" 'Tis thy fault as much as his," Gwen accused. "What business has so small a lad to be learning o' swordplay?"

"True, dear, true," Rod admitted. "I shouldn't have been drilling Magnus where Geoff could watch. But we only did it once."

"Aye, but thou knowest how quickly he seizes on any arts of war. Here, do thou speak with him, the whilst I see to the mending of this vase."

"Well, I didn't know it then—but I do now. Here, son." Rod knelt and took Geoff by the shoulders, as Gwen knelt to begin picking up pieces, fitting them together and staring at the crack till the glass flowed, and the break disappeared.

"You know that was your mother's favorite vase?" Rod asked gently. "It's the only glass one she has—and glass is *very* expensive, here. It took Magnus a long time to learn how to make it."

The little boy gulped and nodded.

"She can mend it," Rod went on, "but it'll never be quite as good as it was before. So your Mommy won't ever have it looking as nice as it did before. You've deprived her of something that made her very happy."

9

The little boy swallowed again, very hard, and his face screwed up; then he let loose a bawl, and buried his face in his father's shoulder, sobbing his heart out.

"There, there, now," Rod murmured. "It's not *quite* as bad as I made it sound. She *can* mend it, after all—psi-witches have an advantage that way, and your mother can manage telekinesis on a *very* fine scale—but it *was* very naughty, wasn't it?" He held Geoff back at arm's length. The little boy gulped again, and nodded miserably. "Now, buck up." Rod pulled out a handkerchief and dabbed at Geoff's cheeks. "Be a brave boy, and go tell your Mommy about it." Geoff nodded; Rod turned him toward Gwen, gave him a pat on the backside, then stood back to watch.

Geoff toddled over to Gwen, stood mute and apprehensive until she was done melding the last piece back in place, then lisped, "I sorry, Mommy. Di't *mean* to."

Gwen heaved up a sigh that said chapters, then managed a smile and tousled his hair. "I know thou didst not, my jo. 'Twas happenstance; still, when all's said, thou *didst* break it. 'Tis why I have told thee to keep thy swordplay out of doors. So thou wilt ever keep thy manly arts out of housen from this day forth, wilt thou not?"

Geoff nodded miserably. "Yes, Mommy."

"And thou wilt obey thy mother henceforth?"

"Uh-huh. . . . But, Mommy!" he cried, in a sudden wail of protest, "was *raining!*"

Gwen heaved a sigh. "Aye, and I know, thou couldst not go out of house. Yet still, jo, 'twas then time to draw up thy pictures."

Geoff made a face.

Gwen bent an accusing eye at Rod.

He looked around, frantically, then pointed to himself, with an incredulous look.

Gwen leaped up and marched over to him. "Aye, thee! How many times hast thou said thou wouldst show him the drawing of a moated keep? That, at least, he would draw— once, and again, and a thousand times! Wilt thou not do it?"

"Oh, yeah!" Rod slapped his head. "I didn't really *have*

to do research this morning. Well, better late than never. . ."

They both whirled around at an explosion of wailing, screaming, and angry barking.

Magnus had come in from the boys' room and found the evidence. He stood over little Geoff, waving a heavy forefinger down from the height of his eight years of life-experience. "Nay, 'twas foully done! To break a present to our Mother that I was so long in the crafting of! Eh, little Geoffrey, when wilt thou learn. . ."

And Cordelia had sailed in to Geoff's defense, standing up to her big brother from five years' age and forty inches' height. "How durst thee blame him, thou, who didst bar him from his own room. . ."

"And mine!" Magnus shouted.

"And his! Where he might have played to's liking, with hurt to nought!"

"Be still, be still!" Gwen gasped. "The baby. . ."

On cue, a wail erupted from the cradle, to match Geoffrey's confused bawling.

"Oh, *children!*" Gwen cried in final exasperation, and turned away to scoop up eleven-month-old Gregory, while Rod waded into the shouting match. "Now, now, Geoff, you haven't been *that* naughty. Magnus, stop that! Scolding's *my* job, not yours—and giving orders, too," he added under his breath. " 'Delia, honey, it's very good of you to stick up for your brother like that—but don't be good so loudly, okay? . . . *Sheesh!*" He hugged them all, pressing their faces against his chest to enforce silence. "The things they don't tell you about the Daddy business!"

On the other side of the room, Gwen was crooning a lullaby, and the baby was already quiet again. Rod answered her with a quick chorus of:

"Rain, rain, go away!
Come again some other day!"

"Well, if you really want it, Daddy." Magnus straightened up and looked very serious for a minute.

"No, no! I didn't mean . . . oh, stinkweed!" Rod

glanced at the window; the pattering of the rain slackened, and a feeble sunbeam poked through.

"Magnus!" Gwen's tone was dire warning. "What have I told thee about tampering with the weather?"

"But Daddy *wanted* it!" Magnus protested.

"I did let that slip, in an unguarded moment," Rod admitted. "But it can't be just what *we* want, son—there're other people who actually *like* the rain. And everyone *needs* it, whether they like it or not—especially the farmers. So bring it back, now, there's a good boy."

Magnus gave a huge sigh that seemed to indicate how disgustingly irrational these big people were, screwed up his face for a moment—and the gentle patter of raindrops began again. Cordelia and Geoffrey looked mournful; for a moment there, they'd thought they were going to get to go out and play.

"Odd weather we're having around here lately," Rod mused, wandering over to the window.

"In truth," Gwen agreed, drifting over to join him with Gregory on her shoulder. "I cannot think how he does it; 'twould take me an hour to move so many clouds away."

"Yeah, well, just add it to the list of our son's unexplained powers." He glanced back at Magnus, a chunky boy in tunic and hose with his hand on the hilt of his dirk. His hair had deepened to auburn, and the loss of his baby-fat had revealed a strong chin that puberty might turn to a lantern-jaw—but Rod could still see the affectionate, mischievous toddler. Strange to think his powers were already greater than his mother's—and his father's, of course; Rod had only knowledge and wit, and a computer-brained robot-horse, on his side. But Magnus had the wit already.

They all did. Cordelia was a flame-haired fairy-slender version of Gwen. Golden-haired Geoff had a compact little body that would probably grow up into a unified muscle, where Magnus would probably turn lean and rangy; golden hair that would probably stay that way, though Magnus's was darkening; clear, blue eyes that seemed to show you the depths of his soul, and a square little chin that seemed made for deflecting uppercuts.

And Gregory, who was fair-haired and chubby, though not as much as a baby should be, who was so very quiet and reserved, and very rarely smiled—an enigma at less than a year, and a prime focus for Rod's chronic, buried anxiety.

Each of them gifted enough to drive Job to distraction!

There was a knock at the door.

Gwen looked up, inquiringly.

Rod stepped over to the panel with a sinking stomach. Knocks meant trouble. So much for his quiet day at home!

He opened the door, and found what he'd expected—Toby the warlock, in his mid-twenties now, grinning and cheerful as ever, in the livery of a King's courier. "Good day to thee, High Warlock! How goes it with thee?"

"Hectic, as usual." Rod smiled; he couldn't help it, when Toby was around. "Step in, won't you?"

"Only the moment; I must be up and away." Toby came in, doffing his cap. "A fair day to thee, fair Gwendylon. Thy beauty never fades!"

"Uncle Toby!" shrieked three gleeful voices, and three small bodies slammed into him at speed. Rod put out a hand to prop up the esper, who was crooning, "Ho-o-o, whoa, not so quickly there! How goes it w' thee, Geoffrey-my-bauble? Cordelia, little love, thoul't steal my heart yet! Good Magnus, good tidings!"

"What did you bring me, Uncle Toby?"

"Can I play with your sword, Uncle Toby?"

"Toby! Unc' Toby! Can'y?"

"Now, now, children, let the poor man capture his breath!" Gwen pried her brood off her guest with tact and delicacy. "Thou'lt take ale and a cake, at least, Toby."

"Ah, I fear not, sweet Gwendylon," Toby sighed. "When I said I must be away, I spoke not lightly. Queen Catharine is wroth, and the King waxes somber."

"Oh." Gwen's glance went to Rod, and a shadow crossed her face. "Well, I should not complain. I've had thee home a week, now."

" 'Fraid the work goes with the title, dear," Rod said, commiserating. "Twenty-four-hour call, and all that." He turned to Toby. "What's going on?"

"I know only that I was summoned to fetch thee, with their Majesties' compliments and a request for greatest speed." Toby inclined his head knowingly. "Yet I know the Lord Abbot approaches Runnymede at greatest speed."

"Yeah, there has been something brewing between the Church and the Crown, hasn't there? Well, I'd better let Tuan fill me in on it."

"In Runnymede, then!" Toby raised his hand in farewell. " 'Til next we meet, fair mother!" And his form started to waver around the edges.

"Toby," Gwen said, quickly but firmly, and the young warlock's form stabilized again. "Not in the house, if you please," she explained. "An' you do, the boys'll be popping in and out in all manner of places the rest of the day, and part of the night!"

"Oh! Aye, I had forgot. Well, 'tis gratifying to know they hold me in such regard. Farewell, children!" He doffed his cap, and stepped to the door.

"Uncle Toby!" cried three anguished voices, and they pressed forward to their friend. He slipped a hand into his belt-purse, cast a quick, furtive look at Gwen, then tossed a quick spray of candies at the children and ducked out the door as they scrambled for the booty.

Gwen heaved a sigh. "They'll never eat now! Well, I'd best delay dinner."

"Yeah, but I think you'd better not keep it warm for me." Rod looked up at the thunder-rumble as air rushed in to fill the space where the young warlock had just disappeared. He turned back to Gwen. "From the sound of it, this could go on for some time."

Gwen shook her head. "But *why* do they not call thee when they know such broils are brewing? Why do they always wait 'til the troubles are come?"

"Well, you know Catharine—she always thinks she and Tuan can handle it on their own, until the moment arrives. Then they want me by, just for moral support."

"And skill," Gwen reminded him. "When 'tis all done, 'tis thou who hast averted conflict, not they."

"Yeah, well, you can't expect one of the teams to referee." Rod leaned forward to kiss her. "Bear up without me, darling. I'll be home when I can."

"Papa's going!" Cordelia shrieked, and delight filled the air as the children ran for the back room window that faced the stable, to wave goodbye when Papa left.

Gwen caught Rod's sleeve and glanced back, waiting till all three were out of sight. Then she leaned forward and hissed, "Beware, my lord! I would I could'st go with thee, to guard thy steps."

"Why?" Rod frowned. "Oh! Those idiots and their ambushes . . . Don't worry, dear. Their marksmanship's no better than their intentions."

"Yet how oft have they tried, my husband?"

Rod pursed his lips. "Well, now, let's see . . ." He started counting on his fingers. "There was the cretin who took a potshot at me from the steeple in that village—what was it, about a year ago now?"

"Eleven months," Gwen corrected. "Three weeks ere Gregory was born."

"Eleven months, then. He didn't seem to realize that a crossbow bolt can't possibly go as fast as a robot horse with a built-in radar. And there was that so-called 'peasant,' who jumped out of a hay wagon with a laser—poor chump." He shook his head sadly. "He didn't realize he should've waited until he was away from the hay before he pulled the trigger."

" 'Twas good of thee, to pull him from the flames, and hurl him into the millpond. Still, his lance of light did come but a hair's-breadth from thy body."

"Yeah, but Fess side-stepped in time. And there was that guard at Tuan's castle; Sir Maris is still wearing sackcloth and ashes because the enemy managed to infiltrate his troops. But, that! My Lord, that was a joke! You can see a pike blow coming a mile away! It takes at least a quarter-second to swing a ten-foot pole; all I had to do was dodge, and yank the shaft as it came past." He shook his head, remembering. "He went right past me, into the moat—and Fess wasn't even with me on that one."

"Aye, my lord, but 'tis the only one of these ambushes in which he hath not saved thee—and he may not 'company thee within the castle. Nay, sweet lord, take care!"

"Oh, don't worry." Rod reached out to caress the line of her jaw. "I'll be wary. After all, I have something to come home to, now."

The great black horse looked up as Rod stepped into the stable, and a voice spoke through the amplifier embedded in the bone behind Rod's ear. "I detected a warlock's arrival, Rod, and his departure. Are we off to the castle, then?"

"We are." Rod threw the saddle on Fess's back. "Just a Sunday outing, I think."

"But it is Wednesday, Rod."

"Well, the clergy'll be there, anyway. The Lord Abbot himself."

Static whispered in Rod's ear—Fess's equivalent of a sigh. "What game is the Church beginning?"

"Cards, probably." Rod tightened the girth and took down the bridle. "At least, I'll have to keep a poker-face."

"Are you sure of your hand, Rod?"

"The best." Rod fitted the bridle, grinning. "Full house, Fess."

As they rode out of the stable, the back window of the house exploded into a hail of goodbyes, and the frantic waving of three little hands.

A few minutes later, as his steel horse's gait ate up the miles between his home and the King's Castle at Runnymede, Rod mused, "Gwen's worried about the assassination attempts, Fess."

"I will always guard you, Rod—but I do wish that you would take greater precautions."

"Don't worry—they bother me, too, but in a different way. If our futurian foes are suddenly working so hard to get rid of me, they must have plans for a big push at toppling Tuan's government."

"Why not say 'revolution,' Rod?"

Rod winced. "Nasty word, when it's my side that's in power. But they do seem to be gearing up for a big offensive, don't they?"

"I agree. Could this conference between the Abbot and Their Majesties signal the beginning of such an offensive?"

Rod scowled. "It could, now that you mention it. The totalitarians have pretty much exhausted the 'Peasants' Revolt' motif for the moment, and the anarchists have ridden the 'Barons' Rights' movement into the ground. They've got to try a new theme, don't they?"

"The Church-State conflict has a long tradition, Rod. Henry II of England had a protracted feud with St. Thomas à Becket, Archbishop of Canterbury, because the Church's authority obstructed Henry's attempts to centralize government. The feud ended with Thomas's murder, and Henry's public humiliation; he was forced to grant concessions to the Church. His son, King John, was more obstinate; John's feud with the Pope resulted in England being laid under the Interdict, which meant that no baptisms, weddings, or funerals could be held—no Masses could be said, no confessions heard; none of the sacraments could be performed. To the medieval mind, this was disaster; most of the people of England felt they were being doomed to Hellfire eternally, because of their King's sin. The resulting pressure was so great that John had to publicly repent, and do penance. The Protestant movement in Christianity succeeded partly because the German princes welcomed an excuse to oppose the Holy Roman Emperor. England became Protestant because Henry VIII wished a divorce that the Pope would not grant him. The Inquisition, the Huguenot Rebellion . . . the English Civil War occurred partly because the nation was Protestant, but ruled by a Catholic King. . . . The list goes on. It is small wonder that, when the United States of America was established in the 18th Century, the founding fathers wrote a separation of Church and State into their Constitution."

Rod nodded grimly. "It's a potent force, no question about it—especially in a medieval society, where most of the people take their religion superstitiously. Just the kind of a conflict to topple a government, in fact—if the Church can drum up enough popular support, and an army.''

''With the futurians' propaganda techniques and weaponry, neither should be too great a problem.''

''Not if it gets that far.'' Rod grinned. ''So it's up to us to head it off before it gets to that pass, eh, old circuit rider?''

''So many human battles could be averted by a little common sense,'' Fess sighed.

''Yes, but the King and the Lord Abbot aren't common— and when religion and politics are involved, no one's got much sense.''

CHAPTER TWO

"Travel light, don't you, Father?" the spaceport guard commented.

Father Al nodded. "It is one of the advantages of being a priest. All I need is a spare cassock, a few changes of underwear, and my Mass kit."

"And a surprising amount of literature." The guard riffled through a book from the stack. *"Magic and the Magi . . .* Little odd for a priest, isn't it?"

"I'm a cultural anthropologist, too."

"Well, to each his own." The guard sealed the suitcase. "Certainly no weapons in there—unless you come across a devil or two."

"Hardly." Father Al smiled. "I'm not expecting anything worse than the Imp of the Perverse."

" 'Imp of the Perverse?' " The guard frowned. "What's that, Father?"

"An invention of Edgar Allan Poe's," Father Al explained. "To my way of thinking, it nicely explains Finagle's Law."

The guard eyed him warily. "If you don't mind my saying so, Father, you're not exactly what I expect in a priest—but you're clear." He pointed. "The shuttle gate's over that way."

"Thank you." Father Al took up his suitcase and headed for the boarding area.

On the way, he passed a fax-stand. He hesitated; then, on an impulse, he dropped in his credit card and punched up "McAran, Angus, ca. 1954." Then he leaned back and waited. It must have been a long search; almost five seconds passed before the machine began humming. Then the hard copy emerged slowly—about a meter of it. Father Al pulled it out and devoured it with his eyes.

"McAran, Angus, Ph.D., 1929 - 2020: Physicist, engineer, financier, anthropologist. Patents. . ."

"Excuse me, Father."

"Eh?" Father Al looked up, startled, at the impatient-looking gentleman behind him. "Oh! My apologies. Didn't realize I was in the way."

"Perfectly all right, Father," the man said, with a smile that contradicted the words. Father Al folded the hard copy in thirds, hastily, and moved off toward the boarding area.

He sat down in a floating chair and unfolded the copy. Amazing what the PIB had stored in its molecular circuits! Here was a thumbnail biography of a man who'd been dead more than a thousand years, as fresh as the day he'd died—which was presumably the last time it'd been updated. Let's see, now—he'd patented five major inventions, then set up his own research and development company—but, oddly enough, he hadn't patented anything after that. Had he let his employees take the patents in their own names? Improbably generous, that. Perhaps he just hadn't bothered to keep track of what his company was doing; he seemed to have become very heavily involved in. . .

"Luna Shuttle now boarding."

Drat! Just when it was getting interesting. Father Al scrambled up, folding the copy again, and hurried to tail onto a very long line. The shuttle left once every hour, but everyone who was leaving Europe for any of Sol's planets or for any other star system had to go through Luna. Only half a percent of Terra's population ever left the mother planet— but half a percent of ten billion makes for very long lines.

Finally, they were all crowded onto the boarding ramp, and the door slid shut. There was no feeling of movement, and any sound from the motors was drowned out by the quiet hum of conversation; but Father Al knew the ramp was rolling across a mile of plasticrete to the shuttle.

Finally, the forward door opened, and the passengers began to file aboard the shuttle. Father Al plopped down into his seat, stretched the webbing across his ample middle, and settled down to read his hard copy with a blissful sigh.

Apparently having tired of inventing revolutionary devices, McAran had turned his hand to treasure-hunting, finding fabled hoards that had been lost for centuries; the most spectacular was King John's treasury, but there had also been major finds all the way back to the city of Ur, circa 2000 BC. This pursuit had naturally led him into archaeology, on the one hand, and finance, on the other. Apparently the combination had worked well for him; he had died a very wealthy man.

All very impressive, Father Al admitted, but not when it came to magic. How would the man have been able to identify a wizard, even during his own time? Father Al had searched history assiduously, but had never come up with anyone who could have been a real magic-worker—they were either tricksters, espers, or poor deluded souls, almost certainly. Of course, in the very early days, there were a few who *might* have been sorcerers, tools of the devil. Opposing them, there were definitely saints. And, though the saints were certain, Father Al doubted there had ever really been any "Black Magic" witches; it made very poor business sense for the Devil. But magic without a source in either God or the Devil? Impossible. It would require someone who was an esper, a medium, and had some unnamed power to break the "Laws of Nature" by, essentially, merely wishing for things to happen. That was the stuff of fairy tales; neither science nor religion even admitted its possibility, had even a chink in its wall of reason through which such powers might seep.

Which, of course, was what made it so delightful a fantasy. If any such individual ever did actually come to light, those walls of reason would come tumbling down—and who could tell what new and shining palaces might emerge as they were rebuilt?

"Gentlefolk," said a canned voice, "the ship is lifting."

Father Al bundled up his paper, thrust it in his breast pocket, and pressed his nose against the port. No matter how many times he flew, it still seemed new to him—that wonderful, faerie sight of the spaceport growing smaller, falling away, of the whole city, then the countryside, being dwarfed, then spread out below him like a map, one that dropped away further and further beneath him, till he could see Europe enamelled on the bottom of a giant bowl, its rim the curve of the Earth . . . and that was just on the ballistic rocket flights from one hemisphere to another. The few times he had been in space, it had been even better—the vast bowl dropping further away, till it seemed to turn inside out and become a dome, then a vast hemisphere filling the sky, somehow no longer below him, but beside him, continents mottling its surface through a swirl of clouds. . .

He knew that seasoned passengers eyed him with amusement, or contempt; how naive he must seem to them, like a gawking yokel. But Father Al thought such delights were rare, and not to be missed; to him, it was wrong to ever cease to glory in the wonder of God's handiwork. And, at the moment when he sat most enthralled with the majestic vista on the other side of the port, a question sometimes tickled the back of his mind: Who was the true sophisticate, they or he?

This time, the overcast quickly cut off sight of the faerie landscape below, but turned into a dazzling sea of cotton beneath him, sinking away till it seemed a vast snowfield. Then, just barely, he felt the ship quiver, then begin a low, threshold hum of muted power. The antigravity units had been shut off, and the powerful planetary drive now propelled the shuttle.

Father Al sighed, and sat back, loosening his webbing, gazing out the port as his current problem floated to the surface of his mind again. There was one big question that the PIB bio hadn't answered: How could McAran have known about this man Gallowglass, about something that would happen more than a thousand years after his own death? And that question, of course, raised another: How had McAran known just when to have the letter opened, or who would be Pope at the time?

The boarding ramp shivered to a stop, and Father Al filed out into Luna Central with a hundred other passengers. Gradually, he worked his way through the flow to a datawall, and gazed up at the list of departing ships. Finally, he found it—Proxima Centauri, Gate 13, lifting off at 15:21. He glanced up at the digital clock above—15:22! He looked back at the Proxima line in horror, just as the time winked out, to be replaced by the glowing word, "Departed." Then the gate number blanked, too.

Father Al just stared at it, numbed, waiting for the departure time of the next ship to light up.

Presently, it did—3:35 Greenwich Standard Time. Father Al spun away, fueled by a hot surge of emotion. He identified it as anger and stilled, standing quiet, letting his whole body go loose, letting the outrage fill him, tasting it, almost relishing it, then letting it ebb away till it was gone. Finagle had struck again—or his disciple Gundersun, in this case: "The least desirable possibility will always exert itself when the results will be most frustrating." If Father Al arrived at Luna to catch the Centauri liner at 15:20, of *course* the liner would lift off at 15:21!

He sighed, and went looking for a seat. There was no fighting Finagle, nor any of his minions—especially since they were all just personifications of one of humankind's most universal traits, perversity, and had never really existed. You couldn't fight them, any more than you could fight perversity itself—you could only identify it, and avoid it.

Accordingly, Father Al found a vacant seat, sat down, pulled out his breviary, and composed himself to begin reading his Office.

"Gentleman, *I* was sitting there!"

Father Al looked up to see a round head, with a shock of thick, disorderly hair, atop a very stocky body in an immaculately-tailored business coverall. The face was beetle-browed and almost chinless, and, at the moment, rather angry.

"I beg your pardon," Father Al answered. "The seat was empty."

"Yes, because I got up long enough to go get a cup of coffee! And it was the only one left, as you no doubt saw. Do I have to lose it just because there was a long line at the dispense-wall?"

"Ordinarily, yes." Father Al stood up slowly, tucking his breviary away. "That's usually understood, in a traveller's waiting room. It's not worth an argument, though. Good day, gentleman." He picked up his suitcase and turned to go.

"No, wait!" The stranger caught Father Al's arm. "My apologies, clergyman—you're right, of course. It's just that it's been a bad day, with the frustrations of travel. Please, take the seat."

"Oh, I wouldn't dream of it." Father Al turned back with a smile. "No hard feelings, certainly—but if you've had as rough a time as that, you need it far more than I do. Please, sit down."

"No, no! I mean, I do still have some respect for the clergy. Sit down, sit down!"

"No, I really couldn't. It's very good of you, but I'd feel guilty for the rest of the day, and. . ."

"Clergyman, I told you, sit down!" the man grated, his hand tightening on Father Al's arm. Then he caught himself and let go, smiling sheepishly. "Will you look at that? There I go again! Come on, clergyman, what do you say we junk this place and go find a cup of coffee with a table under it, and *two* seats? I'm buying."

"Certainly." Father Al smiled, warming to the man. "I do have a little time. . ."

The coffee was genuine this time, not synthesized. Father Al wondered why the man had been waiting in the public lounge, if he had *this* kind of expense account.

"Yorick Thal," the stranger said, holding out a hand.

"Aloysius Uwell." Father Al gave the hand a shake. "You're a commercial traveller?"

"No, a time traveller. I do troubleshooting for Doc Angus McAran."

Father Al sat very still. Then he said, "You must be mistaken. Dr. McAran died more than a thousand years ago."

Yorick nodded. "In objective time, yes. But in my subjective time, he just sent me out in the time machine an hour ago. And I'll have to report back to him when I get done talking to you, to tell him how it went."

Father Al sat still, trying to absorb it.

"Doc Angus invented time travel back in 1952," Yorick explained. "Right off, he realized he had something that everyone would try to steal, especially governments, and he didn't want to see what that would do to war. So he didn't file for a patent. He made himself a very secret hideout for his time travel lab, and set up a research company to front the financing."

"There's not a word about this in the history books," Father Al protested.

"Shows how well he keeps a secret, doesn't it? Not quite well enough, though—pretty soon, he found out there were some other people bopping around from advanced technological societies, cropping up in ancient Assyria, prehistoric Germany—all sorts of places. After a while, he found out that they came mostly from two organizations—the Society for the Prevention of Integration of Telepathic Entities, and the Vigilant Extenders of Totalitarian Organizations. He also found out that they were both using time machines that were basically copies of his—without his permission. And they weren't even paying him royalties."

"But you said he didn't file for a patent."

Yorick waved the objection away. "Morally, he figured he still had patent rights—and they could at least have asked. So he formed his own organization to safeguard the rights of individuals, all up and down the time line."

"Including patentholders?"

"Oh, yes. In fact, he calls the organization 'The Guar-

dians of the Rights of Individuals, Patentholders Especially.'
Pretty soon, he had a network of agents running all the way
from about 40,000 BC on up, fighting SPITE and its anarchists, and VETO and its totalitarians.''

Father Al pursed his lips. ''I take it that means he supports
democracy?''

''What other system really tries to guarantee an inventor's
patent rights? Of course, supporting an organization that size
requires a lot of money, so he went into the treasure-hunting
business. He'd have an agent in, say, ancient Greece bury
some art objects; then he'd send a team to dig 'em up in 1960,
when even a child's clay doll would fetch a thousand dollars
from a museum. With coins, he'd have 'em dug up in the
Renaissance, and deposit them with one of the early banks.
It's really amazing what can happen to a few denarii, with
five hundred years of compound interest.''

''Speaking of interest,'' Father Al said, ''it's rather obvious that our meeting was no accident. Why are you interested
in me?''

Yorick grinned. ''Because you're going to Gramarye.''

Father Al frowned. ''I take it you have an agent in the
Vatican, today.''

''No fair telling—but we do have our own chaplains.''

Father Al sighed. ''And what is your interest in
Gramarye?''

''Mostly that SPITE and VETO are interested in it. In fact,
they're doing all they can to make sure it doesn't develop a
democratic government.''

''Why?''

Yorick leaned forward. ''Because your current interstellar
government, Father, is the Decentralized Democratic Tribunal, and it's very successful. It comprises sixty-seven
planets already, and it's growing fast. SPITE and VETO
want to stop it, any way they can—and the easiest way is to
let it grow until its own size destroys it.''

Father Al gave his head a quick shake. ''I don't understand. How can size destroy a democracy?''

''Because it's not the most efficient form of government.

Major decisions require a lot of debating and, if the diameter of the Terran Sphere gets too long, the Tribunes won't be able to learn what the folks at home think about an issue until after it's decided and done with. That means that unpopular decisions get rammed down the throats of the voters, until they start rebelling. The rebellions're put down, but that turns into repression, which breeds even more rebellion. So eventually, the democracy either falls apart, or turns into a dictatorship.''

"You're saying, then, that the size of a democracy is limited by its communications." Father Al gazed off into space, nodding slowly. "It sounds logical. But how does this affect Gramarye?"

"Because most of the people there are latent telepaths—and about 10 percent are active, accomplished, and powerful."

Father Al stared, feeling excitement thrum through his blood. Then he nodded. "I see. As far as we know, telepathy is instantaneous, no matter how much distance separates the sender and the receiver."

Yorick nodded. "With them in the DDT, democracy could expand indefinitely. But they'd have to be willing volunteers, Father. You can't expect much accuracy in your communications if you're using slaves who hate you."

"Quite apart from the fact that the requirement for membership in the DDT is a viable planetary democracy. So the DDT has to see to it that the planet develops a democratic government."

Yorick nodded again. "That's why the DDT has SCENT—to sniff out the Lost Colonies, and see to it that they develop democratic governments. And SPITE and VETO have to see to it that SCENT fails."

Father Al's mouth tightened in disgust. "Is there no place free of political meddling any more? How many agents does SCENT have on Gramarye?"

"One." Yorick sat back, grinning.

"*One?* For so important a planet?"

Yorick shrugged. "So far, they haven't needed any more—and too many cooks might spoil the brew."

Father Al laid his hand flat on the table. "The agent wouldn't be the Rodney d'Armand who discovered the planet, would it?"

Yorick nodded.

"And Rod Gallowglass? Where does he fit into this?"

"He's Rodney d'Armand. The man always feels more comfortable using an alias."

"Insecure, eh?" Father Al gazed off into space, drumming his fingers on the table. "But effective?"

"Sure is. So far, he's thwarted two major attempts by SPITE and VETO together. What's more, he's used those victories to put the current monarchy on the road to developing a democratic constitution."

Father Al's eyebrows shot up. "Extremely able. And he's about to discover some psionic talent of his own?"

"He's about to disappear," Yorick corrected, "and when he reappears in a few weeks, he's going to be a genuine, full-fledged, twenty-four-carat wizard, able to conjure up armies out of thin air. And that's just the beginning of his powers."

Father Al frowned. "And he won't do it by psi talents?"

Yorick shook his head.

"Then what *is* the source of his power?"

"That's *your* field, Father." Yorick jabbed a finger at the priest. "You tell us—if you can catch up with him before he disappears, and go with him."

"You may be sure that I'll try. But why isn't he a psi? Because he comes from off-planet?"

"Only the genuine, Gramarye-born article occasionally turns out to be a telepath—and usually a telekinetic or teleport, too, depending on sex. The women are telekinetic; that means they can make broomsticks fly, and ride on them, among other things."

"The witches of legend," Father Al mused.

"That's what they call 'em. They call the esper men 'warlocks.' They can levitate, and make things, including themselves, appear and disappear, sometimes moving 'em miles between."

"But Rod Gallowglass can do none of these things?"

"No, but he wound up marrying the most powerful witch in Gramarye—and they've got four kids who're showing a very interesting assortment of talents. In fact, they're all more powerful than their mother. When they start realizing that, she'll *really* have trouble."

"Not necessarily, if they've raised them properly," Father Al said automatically (he'd been assigned to a parish for several years). "Odd that they should be more powerful than their mother, when they don't have psionic genes from both parents."

"Yeah, isn't it?" Yorick grinned. "I just love these little puzzles—especially when someone else gets to solve 'em. But it might not be all that strange—there're still new talents that keep cropping up on that planet. I mean, they've only been inbreeding for a few hundred years; they've got a lot of untapped potential."

"Inbreeding . . . yes . . ." Father Al had a faraway look. "The answers would lie with their ancestors, wouldn't they?"

"Buncha crackpots." Yorick waved them away. "Ever hear of the Society for Creative Anachronism, Father?"

"No. Who were they?"

"A hodgepodge collection of escapists, who tried to forget they were living because of an advanced technology, by holding gatherings where everybody dressed up in medieval outfits and performing mock battles with fake swords."

"Ah, I see." Father Al smiled fondly. "They tried to restore some beauty to life."

"Yeah, that was their problem. That kind of beauty requires individuality, and reinforces it—so they weren't too popular with the totalitarian government of the Proletarian Eclectic State of Terra. When PEST came in, it broke up the SCA and executed the leaders. They all requested beheading, by the way . . . Well. The rest of the organization went underground; they turned into the backbone of the DDT revolution on Terra. Most of 'em, anyway; there's a rumor that about a quarter of 'em spent the next few centuries playing a game called 'Dungeons and Dragons.' They were used to being underground.''

''Fascinating, I'm sure,'' Father Al said drily, ''but what does it have to do with Gramarye?''

''Well, a dozen of the richest SCA members saw the PEST coup coming, and bought an outmoded FTL space liner. They crammed aboard with all the rank-and-file who wanted to come along, renamed themselves the 'Romantic Emigrés,' and took off for parts unknown—the more unknown, the better. When they got there, they named it 'Gramarye,' and set up their version of the ideal medieval society—you know, architecture out of the Fourteenth Century, castles out of the Thirteenth, armor out of the Fifteenth, costumes out of any time between the fall of Rome and the Renaissance, and government out of luck. Well, they did have a King, but they paid him a fine medieval disregard. You get the idea.''

Father Al nodded. ''A thorough collection of romantics and misfits—and a high concentration of psi genes.''

''Right. Then they proceeded to marry each other for a few centuries, and eventually produced telepaths, telekinetics, teleports, levitators, projective telepaths. . .''

''Projectives?'' Father Al frowned. ''You didn't mention those.''

''Didn't I? Well, they've got this stuff they call 'witch moss.' It's a telepathically-sensitive fungus. If the right kind of 'witch' thinks hard at it, it turns into whatever she's thinking about. And, of course, the whole population turned latent-esper fairly early on, and they loved to tell their children fairy tales. . .''

''No.'' Father Al blanched. ''They didn't.''

''Oh, but they did—and now you'll find an elf under every elm. With the odd werewolf thrown in—and a few ghosts. Hey, it could've been worse! If they hadn't had this thing against anything later than Elizabethan, they might've been retelling *Frankenstein*.''

''Praise Heaven for small blessings!''

Yorick nodded. ''You'll have trouble enough with what

they've got there already. Be careful, though—new talents keep showing up, from time to time.''

"Indeed? Well, I thank you for the warning. But I'm curious . . . Why did you come tell me all this? Why didn't Dr. McAran just put it all into his letter?''

"Because if he had, the Pope would've thought he was a raving maniac,'' Yorick said promptly. "But since he put down just the bare-bones-vital information, and made an accurate 'prediction' about who would be Pope. . .''

"With a little help from your agent in the Vatican,'' Father Al amplified.

"Don't say anything against him, Father, he's from your Order. Anyway, with that much and no more in the letter, the Pope believed it, and sent you.''

"Ingenious. Also devious. But why bother with the letter at all, since you were coming to meet me anyway?''

"Because you wouldn't have believed me if you hadn't read the letter.''

Father Al threw up his hands in mock despair. "I give up! I never could make headway against a circular argument—especially when it might be valid. But tell me—why did you bother? Why does Mr. McAran care?''

"Because SPITE and VETO keep trying to sabotage us, anywhen they can. It's us versus them, Father—and you and Rod Gallowglass are part of the 'us.' If he loses, we lose—and a few trillion people, all down the ages, lose a lot of individual rights.''

"Especially patentholders,'' Father Al amplified.

"Of course. And by the way, Doc Angus did finally patent it—in 5029 AD.''

"After the secret was finally out?''

Yorick nodded.

"How did he manage to get a patent when its existence was already public knowledge?''

"Did you ever stop to think how difficult it would be to prove when a time machine was invented?'' Yorick grinned. "It's a fun puzzle. Think it over when you've got some time—say, on your way to Gramarye." He glanced at his watch-ring. "Speaking of which, you'd better hurry— SPITE and VETO are already massing for their next big attack on Gramarye. Massing behind a poor dupe of a front man, of course."

"Oh?" Father Al inquired mildly. "Who's the poor dupe?"

"The Church, of course." Yorick grinned. "Good luck, Father."

CHAPTER THREE

"How dare this tatter-robed priest so flout our power!" Queen Catharine stormed.

They were pacing down a hallway in the royal castle, heading for the state audience chamber. Rich oak panelling flashed past; thick carpet soaked up Catharine's angry stamping.

"His robe is scarcely tattered, my dear," Tuan answered. "And he governs all priests in our land."

"An *abbot?*" Rod frowned. "I think I've been overlooking something this past decade. Doesn't he take orders from a bishop?"

Tuan turned to him, perplexed. "What is a 'bishop?' "

"Uh—never mind." Rod swallowed. "How come an abbot of a monastery governs parish priests?"

"Why, because all priests in this land are of the Order of St. Vidicon!" Catharine snapped impatiently. "How is it that the High Warlock does not know this?"

"Uh—just haven't been taking religion very seriously, I guess." Rod hadn't even been going to Mass on Sundays, but he didn't think this was the time to mention it. "So the Abbot's the head of the church, here—and I understand he's not too happy about your appointing all the parish priests in the country. *Now* it makes sense."

"Some, but not overmuch," Tuan said grimly.

"Where was he when the barons still named their own priests?" Catharine stormed. "Oh, he would not go up against them! But now that 'tis accepted that *we* appoint them . . . Uh!"

A cannonball of a body hit her in the midriff, crowing, "Mama, Mama! Chess time! Chess time!"

Catharine's face softened remarkably as she held the small one away from her, kneeling to look into his eyes. "Aye, sweetling, 'tis the hour we usually play. Yet your mother cannot, this morn; we must speak with the Lord Abbot, thy father and I."

"Not fair, though!" the little prince protested. "You couldn't play yesterday, neither!"

"Either," Tuan corrected, tousling the boy's hair. "Aye, Alain, thy mother had need to speak with the Duchess d'Bourbon yestere'en."

"Not that I wished to." Catharine's tone hardened a little. "Yet not even kings and queens can do only what they please, my boy."

She, Rod reflected, had definitely matured.

Alain pouted. "Not *fair!*"

" 'Tis not," Tuan agreed, with an achingly sad smile. "Yet. . ."

"My apologies, Majesties!" A middle-aged lady in a grey coif and gown, with a gleaming white apron, hurried up and dropped a curtsy. "I but turned my gaze away for the half of a minute, and. . ."

" 'Tis no matter, good nurse." Tuan waved away the apology. "If we have not an occasional moment to spare for our son, what worth is our kingdom? Yet thou must not keep us long from matters of state, child, or there will be no kingdom for thee to inherit! Come, now, go with thy nurse—and take this with thee." He felt in his purse and produced a sugarplum.

Alain glared at it accusingly, but accepted it. "Soon?"

"As soon as we are done with the Lord Abbot," Catharine promised. "There, now, go with thy nurse, and we'll be with thee presently." She gave him a kiss on the forehead, turned him around, and gave him a pat on his bottom to speed him. He plodded off after Nurse, looking back over his shoulder.

His parents stood, gazing fondly after him.

"Fine boy," Rod said into the silence.

"He is that," Catharine agreed. She turned to Tuan. "But thou dost spoil him atrociously!"

Tuan shrugged. "True; yet what are nurses for? Still, Madame, remember—he has not yet come under my tutelage."

"That, I want to see," Rod said, nodding. "Papa as swordmaster."

Tuan shrugged. "My father managed it. Stern he was— yet I never doubted his love."

"Your father's a grand man." Rod knew old Duke Loguire quite well. "What does *he* think of your appointing priests for his parishes?"

Tuan's face darkened as he was wrenched back to the topic. He started toward the audience chamber again. "He is not overly joyous about it, but sees the need. Why will not the Lord Abbot?"

"Because it encroaches on *his* authority," Rod said promptly. "But isn't the appointment just a matter of form? I mean, who do the priests take their orders from *after* they're appointed?"

Tuan stopped dead, and Catharine whirled about, both staring at Rod. "Why, that is so," Tuan said slowly. "Barons ruled priests, when barons appointed them—yet since Catharine began that function, our judges have watched to be sure the lords give no orders to clergy." He turned to Catharine, frowning. "Hast *thou* given commands to priests?"

"I had not thought of it," Catharine admitted. "It seemed it were best to leave God to the godly."

"Sounds like a good policy," Rod agreed. "See any reason to change it?"

Tuan beamed. "I would not want to, save when a priest breaks the law—and I must own the Lord Abbot deals more harshly with a soiled cassock than I ever would, save in matters of death."

"Point of conflict?"

"Never," Catharine stated, and Tuan shook his head. "For any offense great enough to be capital, the Abbot's punishment is to strip the cleric of office, and cast him out of the Order—whereupon, of course, our officers seize him.

Nay, I catch thy drift—we've let the Abbot rule all the parish priests, have we not?''

" 'Twas a grievous omission,'' Catharine grated.

"Not really,'' Rod grinned. "It put the clergy solidly on *your* side, against the barons—and their flocks with them. But now. . .''

"Aye, now.'' Tuan's face darkened again; then he shrugged. "Well, no matter; for a priest, there's small choice between Abbot and King, in any event. Aye, if 'twere only a matter of granting him power of appointment, the form, why, let him have it! Since he hath already the substance.''

"If 'twere all,'' Catharine echoed.

"There's more?'' Rod could almost feel his ears prick up. "You've got my attention, I conFESS.''

"The traditional conflict between Church and Crown,'' Fess's voice murmured behind his ear, "revolved over two issues: secular justice versus ecclesiastical, specifically in the matter of sanctuary; and Church holding of vast tracts of tax-exempt land.''

"Aye, and more difficult,'' Tuan said somberly. "He thinks we take too little care of the poor.''

Well, it was reassuring to know that even a computer could miss. "I'd scarcely call that a disaster.''

"Would you not?'' Catharine challenged. "He wishes us to cede all administration of charitable funds unto himself!''

Rod halted. Now, *that* was a Shetland of a different shade! "Oh. He only wants to take over a major portion of the national administration!''

"Only that.'' Tuan's irony was back. "And one that yields great support from the people.''

"Possible beginnings of a move toward theocracy,'' Fess's voice murmured behind Rod's ear.

Rod ground his teeth, and hoped Fess would get the message. Some things, he didn't need to have explained to him! With a theocracy in the saddle, what chance was there for the growth of a democracy? "That point, I don't think you can yield on.''

"I think not." Tuan looked relieved, and strengthened—and Catharine glowed.

Which was not necessarily a good thing.

"We are come." Tuan stopped before two huge, brass-bound, oaken doors. "Gird thy loins, Lord High Warlock."

A nice touch, Rod thought—reminding him that he ranked equally with the man they were about to confront.

The doors swung open, revealing an octagonal, carpeted room lit by great clerestory windows, hung with rich tapestries, with a tall bookcase filled with huge leather-bound volumes. . .

. . . and a stocky, brown-robed man whose gleaming bald pate was surrounded by a fringe of brown hair running around the back of his head from ear to ear. His face was round and rosy-cheeked, and shone as though it were varnished. It was a kind face, a face made to smile, which made it something of a shock to see it set in a truculent frown.

Tuan stepped into the room; Catharine and Rod followed. "Lord Abbot," the King declaimed, "may I present Rod Gallowglass, Lord High Warlock."

The Abbot didn't get up—after all, he was the First Estate, and Rod was the Second. His frown deepened, though he bobbed his head and muttered, "My lord. I know thee by repute."

"My lord." Rod bobbed his head in return, and kept his tone neutral. "Take my reputation with a grain of salt, if you will; my magic is white."

"I hear thy words," the Abbot acknowledged, "but every man must judge his fellows for himself."

"Of course." Determined to be a hard case, wasn't he? But that was it, of course—"determined." He had to work at it; it didn't come naturally.

"Majesties," the Abbot was saying, "I had thought my audience was with thy selves."

"As it is," Tuan said quickly. "But I trust thou wilt not object to Lord Gallowglass's presence; I find him a moderating influence."

The Abbot slipped for a second; relief washed over his face. Then it was gone, and the stern mask back in place; but Rod warmed to the man on the instant. Apparently he didn't mind being made more moderate, as long as their Majesties were, too. It meant he was looking for a solution, not a surrender. Rod kept his eyes on the Abbot's chest.

The monk noticed. "Why starest thou at mine emblem?"

Rod started, then smiled as warmly as he could. "Your indulgence, Lord Abbot. It's simply that I've noticed that badge on every priest on Gramarye, but have never understood it. In fact, I find it unusual for a cassock to have a breast pocket; it's certainly not pictured so, in the histories."

The Abbot's eyes widened—he was concealing surprise. At what? Rod filed it, and went on. "But I can't imagine why a priest would wear a screwdriver in the breast pocket—that *is* what that little yellow handle is, isn't it?"

"Indeed so." The Abbot smiled as he slipped the tiny tool out of his pocket, and held it out for Rod to inspect—but his eyes were wary. " 'Tis only the badge of the Order of St. Vidicon of Cathode, nothing more."

"Yes, I see." Rod peered at the screwdriver, then sat down at Tuan's left. "But I can't understand why a monk would wear it."

The Abbot's smile warmed a little. "On a day when no grave matters await us, Lord Warlock, I will rejoice to tell thee the tale of our founder, St. Vidicon."

Rod cocked a forefinger at him. "It's a date."

"Amen!"

And the ice was broken.

The Abbot laid both palms flat on the table. "Yet now, I fear, we must turn to weighty matters."

Rod felt the temperature lowering noticeably.

The Abbot drew a rolled parchment from his robe, and handed it to Tuan. "It is with sorrow, and all respect, that I must present this petition to Your Majesties."

Tuan accepted the parchment, and unrolled it between himself and Catharine. The Queen glanced at it, and gasped in horror. She turned a thunderous face to the Abbot.

"Surely, Milord, thou canst not believe the Crown could countenance such demands!"

The Abbot's jaw tightened, and he took a breath.

Rod plunged in. "Uh, how's that phrased, Your Majesty?"

" 'In respect of our obligations to the State and Your Majesties,' " Tuan read, " 'we strongly advise. . .' "

"Well, there you are." Rod sat back, waving a hand. "It's just advice, not demands."

The Abbot looked up at him, startled.

Catharine's lips tightened. "If the Crown feels the need of advice. . ."

"Uh, by your leave, Your Majesty." Rod sat forward again. "I fear I lack familiarity with the issues under discussion; could you read some more of it?"

" 'Primus,' " Tuan read, " 'we have painfully noted Your Majesties' encroachment upon the authority of Holy Mother Church in the matter of appointment of. . .' "

"I see. There, then, is the substance of the case." Rod leaned back, holding up a forefinger. "I beg your indulgence, Your Majesties; please excuse the interruption, but I believe we really should settle this issue at the outset. Authority would seem to be the problem. Now, the people need the Church, but also need a strong civil government; the difficulty is in making the two work together, is it not? For example . . ." Rod took a quick look at the parchment for form's sake, and plowed on. "For example, this item about administering of aid to the poor. What fault find you in the Crown's managment of such aid, my lord?"

"Why . . . in that . . ." Rod could almost hear the Abbot's mind shifting gears; he'd been all set for a hot debate about appointment of clergy. "Why, in that, quite plainly and simply, there is too little of it! That is the substance of it!"

"Ah." Rod nodded, with a commiserating glance at Tuan. "So we come down to money, so quickly."

They hadn't, but Tuan picked up a cue well. "Aye, so soon as that. We are giving all that the Crown can spare, Lord

Abbot—and a bit more besides; we do not keep great state here, the Queen and I.''

"I know thou dost not.'' The Abbot looked troubled.

"And there is the cause of it. We do not feel we should eat off gold plate, if our people go hungry. Yet they *do* go in hunger, for there's simply not enough coin flowing to the Crown, for us to be able to channel back more than we do.''

"Thou couldst levy greater taxes,'' the Abbot offered, half-heartedly.

Tuan shook his head. "Firstly, an' we did, the barons upon whom we levy it would simply wrench it out of their villeins, who are the same poor we speak of here; and secondly, because, if the barons did not, the villeins would rise in rebellion. No, Milord Abbot—the taxes are already as high as we may push them.''

"For example,'' said Catharine sweetly, "thou thyself, Lord Abbot, would be first to protest if we levied a tax on all the vast lands of the Church!''

"And little would you gain thereby,'' the Abbot declared stiffly. "The Order's holdings are scarcely a fortieth part of thy whole kingdom!''

"Datum correct,'' Fess immediately hummed behind Rod's ear. And if Fess said it, it *had* to be right—statistics were his hobby.

But it struck Rod as anomalous, that a medieval administrator could be so accurate, without being able to consult the State's records.

"Many of thy barons hold more!'' the Abbot went on. "And of our income from those lands, the bulk is already given out to the poor—so thou wouldst gain quite little by taxing us! Excepting, mayhap,'' he amended, "that thou mightest, thereby, take even *more* from the poor!''

"You see?'' Rod threw up his hands. "The well's dry; you've said it yourself.''

The Abbot looked up, startled, then realized that he had.

"And if both Church and State are already giving all they can,'' Rod pursued, "what more can we do?''

"Put the administration of what funds there are under one

single exchequer," the Abbot said promptly; and Rod's
stomach sank as he realized he'd lost the initiative. "Two
whole trains of people are currently employed in the disburs-
ing of these funds, and the upshot is, a village I know has two
poorhouses, one a hospice of our Order, one paid by the
Crown—and there are scarcely twenty souls who need either!
Such doubling is costly. Moreover, if only one staff worked
at this task, the others' pay could go to the poor—and since
the Brothers of St. Vidicon do this work for only meager bed
and board, assuredly ours would be the less expensive staff to
maintain!"

Rod sat, dumfounded. Of course, it was *possible* that the
Lord Abbot had hit on this idea by himself—but Rod doubted
it.

"Subject refers to duplication of effort," Fess murmured
behind his ear, "a concept in systems analysis. Such con-
cepts are far too sophisticated for a medieval society. Off-
planet influence must be suspected."

Or time-traveller influence. Who was sticking a finger in
the Gramarye pie *this* time, Rod wondered—the future
Anarchists, or the Totalitarians?

Probably the Anarchists; they tended to work on highly-
placed officials. Though there *was* a proletarian issue
here. . .

He'd paused too long. Catharine was saying, caustically,
"Aye, leave an hundred or so loyal servants without
employment, and their wives and families without bread!
Thou wilt thus assure thyself of good custom at thine
almshouses, Lord Abbot!"

The Lord Abbot's face reddened; it was time for Rod to get
back in. "Surely neither system is perfect, Lord Abbot. But,
with two operating, what the one misses, the other catches."
Had he heard of redundancy? "For example, does the
Church still divide its charity-money equally, between all the
parishes?"

"Aye." The Abbot nodded, frowning. "That which the
parish itself doth not raise."

"But parishes in Runnymede have a much greater proportion of desperately needy than the rural parishes,'' Rod explained.

The Abbot blinked, and stared, wide-eyed.

''I don't think the parish priests have even had time to notice it, they're so overworked.'' Rod was a great one for saving the other guy's face. ''But the King's almshouses are there, giving these poor parishioners at least enough for bare subsistence. That's the advantage to having two systems— and the disadvantage to only having one. Who then would catch what the officers missed?''

He'd gone on long enough for the Abbot to recover. ''There's some truth in that,'' he admitted. ''But surely, if there are to be two systems, at least each one should be self-governing. Would it not work at its best that way?''

Rod glanced at the Queen and King. Catharine was considering it—and didn't seem disposed to commit herself.

''Aye,'' Tuan said slowly, ''I confess there's reason to that.''

''But mine cannot be so!'' The Abbot slapped the tabletop and sat back with an air of triumph, obviously pleased with himself for having gotten them back to the topic they hadn't wanted to discuss—and with such a good case for it, too.

''No—it really can't, I suppose.'' As far as Rod was concerned, the timing was just right.

''Nay. While the Crown appoints priests to parishes, I cannot set the man I deem best for the task, to the doing of that task. Does this not lessen the excellence of this double-chain thou speakest of?''

''At least our appointments are better than those of the barons, whose choices obtained ere I was crowned,'' Catharine retorted; but her tone lacked vehemence.

''For which, I must thank Your Majesties.'' The Abbot inclined his head. ''Yet is it not now time to take a further step on the upward road?''

''Mayhap,'' Tuan said judiciously, ''though it's surely not to the Crown's advantage to lessen any further its hold over the roots of government. . .''

"But is it to the interests of thy people?" the Abbot murmured.

Tuan fairly winced. "There, good Milord, thou touchest the quick. Yet thou wilt understand, I trust, that the Queen and I must discuss these matters you have so kindly brought to our attention, at some length."

"That," Catharine warned, "will be a fulsome talk, and hot."

Tuan grinned. "Why, then, here I stand." Suiting the action to the word, he stood. "Wilt thou, then, hold us excused, Lord Abbot? For indeed, we should begin this while we're fresh to it."

"But of course, Your Majesties." The Abbot scrambled to his feet, and even inclined his head a little. "Thou wilt, then, summon me, when thou dost feel further need of, ah, converse, on this matter?"

"Be assured, we shall," Tuan said grandly, "and so, goode 'en."

"God be with thee," the Abbot muttered, sketching a quick cross in the air. Then the doors boomed wide as the two monarchs turned away, arm in arm, and paced out, in a hurry—but more, Rod suspected, to get to a chess game with a small boy, than to discuss affairs of state.

Still, he couldn't let the Abbot suspect that—and he had a curiosity bump to scratch. "Now, Milord—about your founder. . ."

"Eh?" The Abbot looked up, startled. "Oh, aye! I did say, when there would be time."

"All the time in the world," Rod assured him. "The wife doesn't expect me home till late."

Air rang with a small thunderclap, and Toby stood there, pale and wide-eyed. "Lord Warlock, go quickly! Gwendylon hath sent for thee—thy son Geoffrey hath gone into air!"

Rod fought down a surge of panic. "Uh—he does that all the time, Toby—especially after you've just been there. Just lost, right?"

"Would she send for thee if he were?"

"No, hang it, she wouldn't!" Rod swung back to the Abbot. "You must excuse me, Milord—but this's got to be a genuine emergency! My wife's a woman of *very* sound judgement!"

"Why, certes, be on thy way, and do not stay to ask leave of a garrulous old man! And the blessings of God go with thee, Lord Warlock!"

"Thank you, Milord!" Rod whirled away, out the door, with Toby beside him. "Try not to pop in like that, when there's a priest around, Toby," he advised. "It makes them nervous."

CHAPTER FOUR

"Someone's out to get me," Father Al muttered, as he flew through an underground tube in a pneumatic car, along with a dozen of his fellow passengers from Terra. They had just filed out of the liner from Luna and up to the datawall. Father Al had found his entry, and seen that the ship to Beta Cassiopeia was leaving at 17:23 GST, from Gate 11 of the North Forty terminal. Then he'd looked up at the digital clock and seen, to his horror, that it was 17:11, and he was in the South 220 terminal. That meant he was 180 degrees away from his next ship in both horizontal and vertical planes—which meant that he was exactly on the opposite side of the two-and-a-half-mile-wide planetoid that was Proxima Station!

So down, and into the tube. The only saving grace was that he didn't have to pass through Customs, as long as he stayed within the Station. That, and the speed of the pneumatic car—it could cross the two-and-a-half kilometers in three minutes. It could've done the trip in less than a minute, if the computer didn't limit it to 1.5 G acceleration and deceleration at the beginning and end of the trip. Under the circumstances, Father Al would've settled for the quicker time, and taken his chances on ending his existence as a thin paste on the front of the car. It had taken him five minutes to find the tube, and a four-minute wait before the car came.

Deceleration pushed him toward the front of the car, then eased off and disappeared. The doors hissed open, and he was on his feet, turning and twisting between other passengers, threading his way toward the platform. "Excuse me . . . Excuse me . . . I beg your pardon, madame . . . Oh, dear! I'm sorry about your foot, sir. . ."

Then he was through, and standing, hands clasped on his suitcase handle, glaring at the lift's readout. The minutes crawled agonizingly by while a discreet, impersonal voice from the ceiling informed him that Chairlady Spaceways' Flight 110 to Beta Casseiopeia was about to depart from Gate 11; last call for Chairlady Spaceways' Flight 110. . .

The lift doors hissed open. Father Al held himself back by a straining effort of will as the passengers filed out; then he bolted in. That was a mistake; five people crowded in behind him. The doors hissed shut, and he began elbowing his way back to them. "Excuse me . . . I'm sorry, but this really is imperative . . . I'm sorry, sir, but my liner's leaving, and the next one's apt to be quite a while coming. . ."

Then the doors hissed open, and he charged out, with one eye watching to avoid a collision, and the other watching for signs. There it was—Gates 10 through 15, and an arrow pointing to the left! He swerved like a comet reeling around the Sun, leaving a trail of bruised feet, jogged elbows, and shattered tempers behind him.

Gate 11! He skidded to a halt, leaped toward the door—and realized it was chained shut. With a sinking heart, he looked up at the port-wall—and saw a glowing spot already small and diminishing, the St. Elmo's-Fire phosphoresence that surrounded a ship under planetary drive, growing smaller and dimmer as his ship moved away.

For a moment, he sagged with defeat; then his chin came up, and his shoulders squared. Why was he letting it bother him? After all, it wouldn't be *that* long before the next flight to Casseiopeia.

But the datawall said otherwise; the next flight to Beta Cass. wasn't leaving for a week! He stared at it in disbelief, Yorick's warning to hurry echoing in his ears. Rod Gallowglass was going to disappear, and Father Al had to make sure he disappeared with him!

Then a nasty suspicion formed at the back of his mind. Admittedly, it was too soon to say—three times is enemy action, and he'd only been delayed twice; but Rod Gallowglass was about to discover some sort of extraordinary power within himself, and probably had some major flaw in his personality, as almost everyone had—well-hidden and well-rationalized, to be sure, but there nonetheless. That flaw could be a handle to grasp his soul by, and twist him toward evil actions—again, well-hidden and well-rationalized, not recognized as evil; but evil nonetheless. He could be a very powerful tool in the hands of Evil—or a great force for Good, if someone were there to point out the moral pitfalls and help him steer clear of them.

Definitely, it helped Evil's chances if Father Al missed contact with Rod Gallowglass.

And it was so easy to do—just make sure he missed his ship, and arrived on Gramarye too late! All Hell had to do was to help human perversity run a little more than its natural course. Perhaps the captain of the liner had been in a bad mood, and hadn't been about to wait a second longer than was necessary, even though one of the booked passengers hadn't arrived yet . . . Perhaps the spaceport controller had had an argument earlier that day, and had taken it out on the rest of the world by assigning the ship from Terra to the South 220 terminal, instead of the North 40; so Finagle had triumphed, and the perversity of the universe had tended toward maximum.

Father Al turned on his heel and strode away toward the center of the terminal.

Father Al arrived in the main concourse and strolled down the row of shops, searching. The Church did all it could to make the Sacraments available to its members, no matter how far from Terra they might be—and especially in places where they might need its comfort and reinforcement most. There was one Order that paid particular attention to this problem; surely they wouldn't have ignored a major way-station on the space lanes. . .

There it was—a curtained window with the legend, "Chapel of St. Francis Assisi" emblazoned on it. Father Al stepped through the double door, gazed around at the rows of hard plastic pews, the burgundy carpet, and the plain, simple altar-table on the low dais, with the crucifix above it on a panelled wall, and felt a huge unseen weight lift from his shoulders. He was home.

The Franciscans were very hospitable, as they always were. But there was a bit of a problem when he explained what he wanted.

"Say Mass? *Now?* With respect, Father, it's six o'clock in the evening."

"But surely you have evening Masses."

"Only on Saturday evenings, and the vigils of holy days."

"I'm afraid it really is necessary, Father." Father Al handed the Franciscan his letter from the Pope. "Perhaps this will make the situation more clear."

He hated to pull rank—but it was satisfying to watch the Franciscan's eyes widen when he looked at the signature. He folded the letter and handed it back to Father Al, clearing his throat. "Yes. Well . . . certainly, Father. Whatever you'd like."

"All I need is the altar, for half an hour." Father Al smiled. "I don't think there'll be any need for a sermon."

But he was wrong. As he began to say Mass, passersby glanced in, stopped, looking startled, then came quietly in, found a pew, and knelt down. When Father Al looked up to begin the Creed, he stared in amazement at a couple dozen people in front of him, most of them well-dressed travellers, but with a good sprinkling of spaceport mechanics and dirtside crew—and a few gentlemen with three-day beards, whose coveralls were patched, greasy, and baggy at the knees. It was curious how any major spaceport always seemed to develop its own skid row, even if it was millions of AU's from any habitable planet. It was even more surprising how many Catholics cropped up out of the plastic-work at the drop of an altar bell.

Under the circumstances, he felt obliged to say something—and there was one sermon he always had ready. "My brothers and sisters, though we are in a Chapel of St. Francis, allow me to call to your minds the priest in whose honor my own Order was founded—St. Vidicon of Cathode, martyr for the faith. In the seminary, he had a problem—he kept thinking in terms of what did work, instead of what should work. He was a Jesuit, of course.

"He also had a rather strange sense of humor. When he was teaching, his students began to wonder whether he believed more firmly in Finagle than in Christ. Too many young men were taking his jokes seriously, and going into Holy Orders as a result. His bishop was delighted with all the vocations, but was a bit leery of the reasons—so the Vatican got wind of it. The Curia had its doubts about his sense of humor, too, so they transferred him to Rome, where they could keep an eye on him. As an excuse for this surveillance, they made him Chief Engineer of Television Vatican.

"The term is confusing today, of course; 'television' was like 3DT, but with a flat picture; 3DT was originally an abbreviation for 'three-dimensional television.' Yes, this was quite a few centuries ago—the Year of Our Lord 2020.

"Well. Father Vidicon was sad to leave-off teaching, but he was overjoyed at actually being able to work with television equipment again . . . and he didn't let his nearness to the Pope dampen his enthusiasm; he still insisted on referring to the Creator as 'the Cosmic Cathode . . .' "

"Praise God, from Whom electrons flow!
Praise Him, the Source of all we know!
Whose order's in the stellar host!
For in machines, He is the Ghost!"

"Father Vidicon," Monsignor reproved, "that air has a blasphemous ring."

"Merely irreverent, Monsignor." Father Vidicon peered at the oscilloscope and adjusted the pedestal on Camera Two. "But then, you're a Dominican."

"And what is *that* supposed to mean?"

"Simply that what you hear may not be what I said." Father Vidicon leaned over to the switcher and punched up color bars.

"He has a point." Brother Anson looked up from the TBC

circuit board he was diagnosing. "*I* thought it quite reverent."

"You would; it was sung." Monsignor knew that Brother Anson was a Franciscan. "How much longer must I delay my rehearsal, Father Vidicon? I've an Archbishop and two Cardinals waiting!"

"You can begin when the camera tube decides to work, Monsignor." Father Vidicon punched up Camera Two again, satisfied that the oscilloscope *was* reading correctly. "If you insist on bringing in Cardinals, you must be prepared for a breakdown."

"I really don't see why a red cassock would cause so much trouble," Monsignor grumbled.

"You wouldn't; you're a director. But these old plumbicon tubes just don't like red." Father Vidicon adjusted the chrominance. "Of course, if you could talk His Holiness into affording a few digital-plate cameras. . ."

"Father Vidicon, you know what they cost! And we've been the Church of the Poor for a century!"

"Four centuries, more likely, Monsignor—ever since Calvin lured the bourgeoisie away from us."

"We've as many Catholics as we had in 1390," Brother Anson maintained stoutly.

"Yes, that was right after the Black Death, wasn't it? And the population of the world's grown a bit since then. I hate to be a naysayer, Brother Anson, but we've only a tenth as many of the faithful as we had in 1960. And from the attraction Reverend Sun is showing, we'll be lucky if we have a tenth of *that* by the end of the year."

"We've a crisis in cameras at the moment," the Monsignor reminded. "Could you refrain from discussing the Crisis of Faith until the cameras are fixed?"

"Oh, they're working—now." Father Vidicon threw the capping switch and shoved himself away from the camera control unit. "They'll work excellently for you now, Monsignor, until you start recording."

Monsignor reddened. "And why should they break down then?"

"Because that's when you'll need them most." Father Vidicon grinned. "Television equipment is subject to Murphy's Law, Monsignor."

"I wish you were a bit less concerned with Murphy's Law, and a bit more with Christ's!"

Father Vidicon shrugged. "If it suits the Lord's purpose to give authority over entropy into the hands of the Imp of the Perverse, who am I to question Him?"

"For the sake of Heaven, Father, what has the Imp of the Perverse to do with Murphy's Law?" Monsignor cried.

Father Vidicon shrugged. "Entropy is loss of energy within a system, which is self-defeating; that's perversity. And Murphy's Law is perverse. Therefore, both of them, and the Imp, are corrolary to Finagle's General Statement: 'The perversity of the universe tends toward maximum.' "

"Father Vidicon," Monsignor said severely, "you'll burn as a heretic someday."

"Oh, not in this day and age. If the Church condemns me, I can simply join Reverend Sun's church, like so many of our erstwhile flock." Seeing the Monsignor turn purple, he turned to the door, adding quickly, "Nonetheless, Monsignor, if I were you, I'd not forget the Litany of the Cameras before I called 'roll and record.' "

"*That* piece of blasphemy?" the Monsignor exploded. "Father Vidicon, you *know* the Church has never officially declared St. Clare to be the patron of television!"

"Still, she did see St. Francis die, though she was twenty miles away at the time—the first Catholic instance of 'television,' 'seeing-at-a-distance.' " Father Vidicon wagged a forefinger. "And St. Genesius *is* officially the patron of showmen."

"Of *actors*, I'll remind you—and we've none of those here!"

"Yes, I know—I've seen your programs. But do remember St. Jude, Monsignor."

"The patron of the desperate? Why?"

"No, the patron of lost causes—and with these antique cameras, you'll need him."

The door opened, and a monk stepped in. "Father Vidicon, you're summoned to His Holiness."

Father Vidicon blanched.

"You'd best remember St. Jude yourself, Father," the Monsignor gloated. Then his face softened into a gentle frown. "And, Lord help us—so had we all."

Father Vidicon knelt and kissed the Pope's ring, with a surge of relief—if the ring was offered, things couldn't be all *that* bad.

"On your feet, Father," Pope Clement said grimly.

Father Vidicon scrambled to his feet. "Come now, Your Holiness! You know it's all just in fun! A bit irreverent, perhaps, but nonetheless only levity! I don't *really* believe in Maxwell's Demon—not quite. And I know Finagle's General Statement is really fallacious—the perversity's in us, not in the universe. And St. Clare. . ."

"Peace, Father Vidicon," His Holiness said wearily. "I'm sure your jokes aren't a threat to the Church—and I'm not particularly worried by irreverence. If Christ could take a joke, so can we."

Father Vidicon frowned. "Christ took a joke?"

"He accepted human existence, didn't He? But I've called you here for something a bit more serious than your contention that Christ acted as a civil engineer when He said that Peter was a rock, and upon that rock He'd build His Church."

"Oh." Father Vidicon tried to look appropriately grave. "If it's that feedback squeal in the public address system in St. Peter's, I'll do what I can, but. . ."

"No, I'm afraid it's a bit more critical." The hint of a smile tugged at the Pope's lips. "You're aware that the faithful have been leaving us in increasing droves these past twenty years, of course."

Father Vidicon shrugged. "What can you expect, Your Holiness? With television turning everyone toward a Gestalt mode of thought, they've become more and more inclined toward mysticism, needing doctrines embracing the Cosmos and making them feel vitally integrated with it; but the Church still offers only petrified dogma, and logical reasoning. Of course they'll turn to the ecstatics, to a video demagogue like Reverend Sun, with his hodge-podge to T'ai-Ping Christianity and Zen Buddhism. . .''

"Yes, yes, I know the theories." His Holiness waved Father Vidicon's words away, covering his eyes with the other palm. "Spare me your McLuhanist cant, Father. But you'll be glad to know the Council has just finished deciding which parts of Chardin's theories *are* compatible with Catholic doctrine."

"Which means Your Holiness has finally talked them into it!" Father Vidicon gusted out a huge sigh of relief. "At last!"

"Yes, I can't help thinking how nice it must have been to be Pope in, say, 1890," His Holiness agreed, "when the Holy See had a bit more authority and a bit less need of persuasion." He heaved a sigh of his own, and clasped his hands on the desktop. "And it's come just in time. Reverend Sun is speaking to the General Assembly Monday morning—and you'll never guess what his topic will be."

"How the Church is a millstone around the neck of every nation in the world." Father Vidicon nodded grimly. "Priests who don't pass on their genes, Catholics not attempting birth control and thereby contributing to overpopulation, Church lands withheld from taxation—it's become a rather familiar bit of rhetoric."

"Indeed it has; most of his followers can recite it chapter and verse. But this time, my sources assure me he intends to go quite a bit farther—to ask the Assembly for a recommendation for all U.N. member nations to adopt legislation making all these 'abuses' illegal."

Father Vidicon's breath hissed in. "And with so large a percentage of the electorate in every country being Sunnite. . .''

"It amounts to virtual outlawing of the Roman Catholic Church. Yes." His Holiness nodded. "And I need hardly remind you, Father, that the current majority in the Italian government are Sunnite Communists.''

Father Vidicon shuddered. ''They'll begin by annexing the Vatican!'' He had a sudden nightmarish vision of a Sunnite prayer meeting in the Sistine Chapel.

''We'll all be looking for new lodgings,'' the Pope said drily. ''So you'll understand, Father, that it's rather important that I tell the faithful of the whole world before then, about the Council's recent action.''

''Your Holiness will speak on television!'' Father Vidicon cried. ''But that's wonderful! You'll be. . .''

''My blushes, Father Vidicon. I'm well aware that you consider me to have an inborn affinity for the video medium.''

''The charisma of John Paul II, with the appeal of John the XXIII!'' Father Vidicon asserted. ''But what a waste, that you'll not appear in the studio!''

''I'm not fond of viewing myself as the chief drawing-card for a sideshow,'' His Holiness said sardonically. ''Still, I'm afraid it's become necessary. The Curia has spoken with Eurovision, Afrovision, PanAsiavision, PanAmerivision, and even Intervision. They're all, even the Communists, willing to carry us for fifteen minutes. . .''

''Cardinal Beluga is a genius of diplomacy,'' Father Vidicon murmured.

''Yes, and all the nations are worried about the growth of Sun's church within their borders, with all that it implies of large portions of their citizenry taking orders from Singapore. Under the circumstances, we've definitely become the lesser of two evils, in their eyes.''

''I suppose that's a compliment,'' Father Vidicon said doubtfully.

''Let's think of it that way, shall we? The bottleneck, of course, was the American commercial networks; they're only willing to carry me early Sunday morning.''

''Yes; they only worry about religion when it begins to affect sales,'' Father Vidicon said thoughtfully. ''So I take it Your Holiness will appear about two p.m.?''

''Which is early morning in Chicago, yes. Other countries

have agreed to record the speech, and replay it at a more suitable hour. It'll go by satellite, of course. . ."

"As long as we pay for it."

"Naturally. And if there's any failure of transmission at our end, the networks are *not* liable to give us postponed time."

"Your Holiness!" Father Vidicon threw his arms wide. "You wound me! Of *course* I'll see to it there's no transmission error!"

"No offense intended, Father Vidicon—but I'm rather aware that the transmitter I've given you isn't exactly the most recent model."

"What can you expect, from donations? Besides, Your Holiness, British Marconi made excellent transmitters in 1990! No, Italy and Southern France will receive us perfectly. But it would help if you could invest in a few spare parts for the converter that feeds the satellite ground station. . ."

"Whatever that may be. Buy whatever you need, Father Vidicon. Just be certain our signal is transmitted. You may go now."

"Don't worry, Your Holiness! Your voice shall be heard, and your face be seen, even though the Powers of Darkness rise up against me!"

"Including Maxwell's Demon?" His Holiness said dourly. "And the Imp of the Perverse?"

"Don't worry, Your Holiness." Father Vidicon made a circle of his thumb and middle finger. "I've dealt with *them* before."

" 'The good souls flocked like homing doves,' " Father Vidicon sang, "or they will after they've heard our Pope's little talk." He closed the access panel of the transmitter. "There! Every part certified in the green! I've even dusted every circuit board . . . How's that backup transmitter, Brother Anson?"

"I've replaced two I.C. chips so far," Brother Anson answered from the bowels of the ancient device. "Not that they were bad, you understand—but I had my doubts.''

"I'll never question a Franciscan's hunches." Father Vidicon laced his fingers across his midriff and sat back. "Did you check the converter to the ground station?"

" 'Converter?' " Brother Anson's head and shoulders emerged, covered with dust. "You mean that huge resistor in the gray box?"

Father Vidicon nodded. "The very one."

"A bit primitive, isn't it?"

Father Vidicon shrugged. "There isn't time to get a proper one, now—and it's all they've given me money for, ever since I was 'promoted' to Chief Engineer. Besides, all we *really* need to do is to drop our 50,000-watt transmitter signal down to something the ground station can handle."

Brother Anson shrugged. "If you say so, Father. I should think that would kick up a little interference, though."

"Well, we can't be *perfect*—not on the kind of budget we're given, anyhow. Just keep reminding yourself, Brother, that most of our flock still live in poverty; they need a bowl of millet more than a clear picture."

"I can't argue with that. Anyway, I did check the resistor. Just how many ohms does it provide, anyway?"

"About as many as you do, Brother. How'd it test out?"

"Fine, Father. It's sound."

"Or will be, till we go on the air." Father Vidicon nodded. "Well, I've got two spares handy. Let the worst that can happen, happen! I'm more perverse than Murphy!"

The door slammed open, and the Monsignor was leaning against the jamb. "Father . . . Vidicon!" he panted. "It's . . . catastrophe!"

"Murphy," Brother Anson muttered; but Father Vidicon was on his feet. "What is it, Monsignor? What's happened?"

"Reverend Sun! He discovered the Pope's plans, and has talked the U.N. into scheduling his speech for Friday morning!"

Father Vidicon stood, galvanized for a second. Then he

snapped, "The networks! Can they air His Holiness early?"

"Cardinal Beluga's on three phones now, trying to patch it together! If he brings it off, can you be ready?"

"Oh, we can be ready!" Father Vidicon glanced at the clock. "Thursday, 4 pm. We need an hour. Any time after that, Monsignor."

"Bless you!" the Monsignor turned away. "I'll tell His Holiness."

"Come on, Brother Anson." Father Vidicon advanced on the backup transmitter, catching up his toolkit. "Let's get this beast back on line!"

"Five minutes till air!" the Monsignor's voice rasped over the intercom. "Make it good, reverend gentlemen! Morning shows all over the world are giving us fifteen minutes—but not a second longer! And Reverend Sun's coming right behind us, live from the U.N.!"

Father Vidicon and Brother Anson were on their knees, hands clasped. Father Vidicon intoned, "Saint Clare, patron of television. . ."

". . . pray for us," finished Brother Anson.

"Saint Genesius, patron of showmen. . ."

"One minute!" snapped the Monsignor. "Roll and record!"

". . . pray for us," murmured Brother Anson.

"Rolling and recording," responded the recording engineer.

"Saint Jude, patron of lost causes. . ."

". . . pray for us," Brother Anson finished fervently.

"Slate it!" Then, "Bars and tone!"

They could hear the thousand-cycle test tone in the background, whining. Then it began beeping at one-second intervals.

"Ready mike and cue, ready up on one!"

"Five!" called the assistant director. "Four! Three!"

"Black! Clip tone!" the Monsignor cried. "Mike him! Cue him! Up on One!"

Television screens all over the world lit up with the grave but faintly-smiling image of the Pope. "Dearly beloved in Christ. . ."

The picture flickered.

Father Vidicon darted a glance at the converter. Its tally light was dead. Beside it, the light glowed atop the back-up converter.

"Quick! The big one died!" Father Vidicon yanked open the top of the long gray box and wrenched out the burned-out resistor.

"There are a few points of theology on which we can't agree with Reverend Sun," His Holiness was saying. "Foremost among these is his concept of the Trinity. We just can't agree that Reverend Sun is himself the third Person, the 'younger son' of God. . ."

Brother Anson slapped the spare resistor into Father Vidicon's palm.

". . . nor is the sharing of a marijuana cigarette a valid form of worship, in the Church's eyes," the Pope went on. "But the Council does agree that. . ."

The screen went dark.

Father Vidicon shoved the spare into its clips and threw the routing switch.

The screen glowed again. ". . . have always been implicit in Catholic doctrine," His Holiness was saying, "but the time has come to state their implications. First among these is the notion of 'levels of reality.' Everything that exists is real; but God is the Source of reality, as He is the Source of everything. And the metaphor of 'the breath of God' for the human soul means that. . ."

"Yes, it's gone." Father Vidicon yanked the burned-out resistor out of the back-up. "The manufacturers must think they can foist off all their defectives on the Church." Brother Anson took the lump of char and gave him a new resistor. "That's our last spare, Father Vidicon."

Father Vidicon shoved it into its clips. "What're the odds against three of these blowing in a space of ten minutes?"

"Gunderson's Corollary," Brother Anson agreed.

Father Vidicon slapped down the cover. "We're up against perversity, Brother Anson."

The tally blinked out on the main converter as the little red light on the back-up glowed into life.

"We're out of spares," Brother Anson groaned.

"Maybe it's just a connection!" Father Vidicon yanked open the cover. "Only four minutes left!"

"Is it the resistor, Father?"

"You mean this piece of slag?"

". . . the oneness, the unity of the cosmos, has always been recognized by Holy Mother Church," the Pope was saying. "Christ's parable about the 'lilies of the field' serves as an outstanding example. All that exists is within God. In fact, the architecture of the medieval churches. . ."

A picture of the Cathedral of Notre Dame appeared on the screen. The camera zoomed in for a close-up of the decorative carving. . .

. . . and the screen went blank.

"It died, Father Vidicon," Brother Anson moaned.

"Well, you fight fire with fire." Father Vidicon yanked out the dead resistor. "And this is perversity. . ." He seized the lead from the transmitter in his left hand, and the lead to the ground station in his right.

Around the world, screens glowed back into life.

". . . and as there is unity in all of Creation," the Pope went on, "so there is unity in all the major religions. The same cosmic truths can be found in all; and the points on which we agree are more important than the ones on which we disagree—saving, of course, the Godhood of Christ, and of the Holy Spirit. But as long as a Catholic remembers that he is a Catholic, there can certainly be no fault in his learning from other faiths, if he uses this as a path toward greater understanding of his own." He clasped his hands and smiled gently. "May God bless you all."

And his picture faded from the screen.

"We're off!" shouted Monsignor. "That was masterful!"

In the transmitter room, Brother Anson chanted the *Dies Irae*, tears in his eyes.

The Pope moved out of the television studio, carefully composed over the exhaustion that always resulted from a television appearance. The Monsignor dashed out of the control room to drop to his knees and wring the Pope's hand. "Congratulations, Your Holiness! It was magnificent!"

"Thank you, Monsignor," the Pope murmured, "but let's judge it by the results, shall we?"

"Your Holiness!" Another Monsignor came running up. "Madrid just called! The people are piling into the confessionals—even the men!"

"Your Holiness!" cried a cardinal. "It's Prague! The faithful are flocking to the cathedral! The commissars are livid!"

"Your Holiness—New York City! The people are streaming into the churches!"

"Your Holiness—Reverend Sun just cancelled his U.N. speech!"

"Your Holiness! People are kneeling in front of churches all over Italy, calling for the priests!"

"It's the Italian government, Your Holiness! They send their highest regards, and assurances of continued friendship!"

"Your Holiness," Brother Anson choked out, "Father Vidicon is dead."

They canonized him eventually, of course—there was no question that he'd died for the Faith. But the miracles started right away.

In Paris, a computer programmer with a very tricky program knew it was almost guaranteed to glitch. But he prayed to Father Vidicon to put in a good word for him with the Lord, and the program ran without a hitch.

Art Rolineux, directing coverage of the Superbowl, had eleven of his twelve cameras die on him, and the twelfth started blooming. He sent up a quick prayer to Father Vidicon, and five cameras came back on line.

Ground Control was tracking a newly-launched satellite when it suddenly disappeared from their screens. "Father

Vidicon, protect us from Murphy!'' a controller cried out, and the blip reappeared on the screens.

Miracles? Hard to prove—it always could've been coincidence. It always can, with electronic equipment. But as the years flowed by, engineers and computer programmers and technicians all over the world began counting the prayers, and the numbers of projects and programs saved—and word got around, as it always does. So, the day after the Pope declared him to be a saint, the signs went up on the back walls of every computer room and control booth in the world:

"St. Vidicon of Cathode, pray for us!"

"Thus Saint Vidicon died, in an act of self-sacrifice that turned perversity back upon itself." Father Al turned his head slowly, looking directly into the eyes of each person in his little congregation, one by one. "So, my brothers and sisters, when you are tempted to commit an act of perversity, pray to St. Vidicon to intercede with Almighty God, and grant you the grace to turn that perversity back upon itself, as St. Vidicon did. If you are a masochist, and are tempted to find someone to whip you, be even more perverse—deny yourself the pleasure you long for! If you are tempted to steal, find a way of defrauding the bank's computer into giving you money from your own account! If you're tempted to try to ruin an enemy, pay him a compliment instead—he'll go crazy wondering what you're plotting against him!"

One of the businessmen shifted uncomfortably in his seat.

Father Al took a deep breath. "Thus may we take the energy of the urge toward perversity, and turn it to the strengthening of our souls, by using its energy to perform good works."

The congregation looked a bit confused, and he didn't blame them—it wasn't exactly the most coherent sermon he had ever delivered. But what could you expect, on an ad-lib basis? He did notice a look of surprise on a few of the derelicts' faces, though, followed by thoughtful brooding. At least not all the seed had fallen on rocky ground.

He hurried on to the Creed, then pronounced the intention

of the Mass. "Dear Lord, if it pleases You, allow the soul of Your servant, the sainted Vidicon of Cathode, to lend his strength in defense of this member of the Order founded in his name, by battling the forces of perversity that ring Your Holy Church, turning them against themselves, to the confounding of those who seek its downfall, and who war against holiness and freedom of the soul. Amen."

From there on, it was pretty straightforward, and he could relax and let himself forget the troubles of the moment while he became more and more deeply involved in the Sacrament. As always, the spell of the Mass wove its reassuring warmth around him; soon all that existed were the Host and the wine, and the silent, intent faces of the congregation. A surprising number of them turned out to be in shape for Communion; but, fortunately, one of the Franciscans was standing by in the sacristy, and came out to unlock the tabernacle and bring out a ciborium, so no one went away empty.

Then they were trooping out, singing the recessional, and Father Al was left alone, with the usual sweet sadness that came from knowing the Mass was indeed ended, and that he must wait a whole twenty-four hours before he could say it again.

Well, not quite alone. The Franciscan came over to him, with a whispering of his rough robe. "A moving Mass, Father—but a strange sermon, and a strange intention."

Father Al smiled wanly. "And stranger circumstances that brought them forth, Father, I assure you."

He had almost reached the departure port again when the public address system came to life, with the howling of a siren behind the voice. "All passengers please clear the area. Conditions of extreme danger obtain; a ship is returning to port with damage in its control system. All passengers please clear the area immediately."

It went on to repeat the message, but Father Al was already on his way back toward the main terminal. He only went as far as the rope, though—the red emergency cord that attendants were calmly stringing across the corridor, as though it were a daily event. But one look at their eyes assured Father Al that this was rare, and dreaded. *"My Lord!"* he prayed silently. *"I only sought aid for myself, not danger to others!"* And he found the nearest viewscreen.

Emergency craft were moving into position, amber running-lights flashing. Snub-nosed cannon poked out of their noses, ready to spray sealant on any ruptures in the hull of ship or station. A hospital cruiser drifted nearby.

And, in the distance, a dot of light swelled into a disc—the returning ship.

The disc swelled into a huge globe, filling a quarter of the velvet darkness, pocked with the parabolic discs of detectors and communicators. Then the swelling stopped; the huge ship drifted closer, slowing as it came. The emergency craft maintained a respectful distance, wary and alert, as the liner loomed over them, till it filled the whole sky. Then the front of the hull passed beyond the range of the viewscreen. Father Al listened very carefully, but heard nothing; he only felt the tiniest movement of the station about him as the behemoth docked in the concave gate awaiting it. He breathed a sigh of relief; no matter what trouble they'd detected, the control system had functioned perfectly for docking.

He turned away, to see the attendants removing the velvet rope, with only the slightest tremor in their hands. "Excuse me," he said to the nearest. "What ship was that, docking there?"

The steward looked up. "Why, it was the liner for Beta Casseiopeia, Father. Just a minor problem in the control system—they could've gone on with it, really. But our line doesn't believe in taking chances, no matter how small."

"A wise policy," Father Al agreed. " 'The Universe'll get you, if you don't watch out.' "

The attendant smiled thinly. "I'm glad you understand."

"Oh, perfectly. In fact, it's something of a fortunate coincidence for me; I was supposed to be on that liner, but my ship from Terra arrived a bit late."

The attendant nodded. " 'Fortunate' is right. The next ship for Beta Cass. doesn't leave for another week."

"Yes, I know. You will let them know they've another passenger waiting, won't you?"

Six hours later, the engineers had found and replaced a defective circuit-grain, and Father Al slid into his couch, stretching the webbing across his body with a sigh of relief, and prayers of thanks to St. Vidicon and God.

No reason to, really; it was probably all just a coincidence. No doubt St. Vidicon had sat by smiling in amusement all the time, and the ship would've returned to port even without Father Al's Mass. But a little extra praying never hurts, and it had kept him occupied.

Besides, in the realm of the supernatural, one never knew. Rod Gallowglass might really be important enough to merit the personal attention of the Imp of the Perverse. Father Al just hoped he'd reach Gramarye in time.

CHAPTER FIVE

The jets cut out, and the great black horse landed at full gallop. He slowed to a canter, stubby wings folding back into his sides, and then to a trot.

"Elben Pond, Toby said," Rod muttered, glaring at the dark sheet of water barely visible through the trees. "Here's Elben Pond. Where are they?"

"I hear them, Rod," Fess answered.

A few seconds later, Rod could, too: two small voices crying, "Geo-ff! Geo-ffrey!" And a full one calling, "Geoffrey, my jo! Geoffrey! Whither art thou?"

"Geof-frey, Geof-frey!" Cordelia's voice came again, with sobs between the cries. Then Fess was trotting into a small clearing, with the little lake gleaming at its edge, and Cordelia's head poked out of the shrubbery as Rod swung down. "Papa!" And she came running.

"Oh, Papa, it's turrible! It's all Magnus's fault; he disappeared Geoffrey!"

"Did *not!*" Magnus howled, agonized, as he came running up, and his mother seconded him as she landed on her knees next to her daughter.

"Cordelia, Cordelia! Magnus did not *do* it, he only *said* it!"

"You sure his just saying it couldn't make it happen?" Rod looked up at her over Cordelia's head. "Magnus may be the only warlock who's ever been able to teleport someone else, except for old Galen—but Magnus did do it, when he got into that argument with Sergeant Hapweed."

"Aye, and it took old Galen himself to fetch him back! Oh, we've sent for him—but truly, I misdoubt me 'tis that! Magnus would not lie on a matter of such gravity."

65

"No, he wouldn't." Rod transferred Cordelia to her mother's arms and caught Magnus against him. The boy resisted, his body stiff, but Rod stroked his head and crooned, "There, now, son, we know you didn't do it! Maybe something you said makes you think so—but *I* know you can't do a thing like that without meaning to!"

The eight-year-old trembled; then his body heaved with a huge sob, and he wept like a thundercloud, bellowing anguish. Rod just hung on and kept stroking the boy's head and murmuring reassurances until his sobs slackened; then he held Magnus gently away, and said quietly, "Now, then. Tell me what happened, from beginning to end."

Magnus gulped and nodded, wiping at his eyes. "He was trying to play my games, Papa, the way he always does—and you've *told* me not to let him climb trees!"

"Yes; he might be too scared to levitate, if he fell from twenty feet up," Rod said grimly. "So he was tagging along in his usual pesty way—and what happened?"

"Magnus told him . . ." Cordelia burst out; but Gwen said, "Hush," firmly, and clapped a hand over her daughter's mouth.

"Let thy father hear it for himself."

"And?" Rod prompted.

"Wull—I told him to go jump in the lake. I didn't know he'd *do* it!" Magnus burst out.

Rod felt a cold chill run down his spine. "He always does everything you tell him; you should know that by now. So he jumped in."

"Nay! He never did get to 't! Ten feet short o' the water, he faded!"

"Faded?" Rod gawked.

"Aye! Into thin air! His form grew thinner and thinner, the whiles I watched, till I could see the sticks and leaves through him—like to a ghost!"

Cordelia wailed.

Rod fought down the prickling that was covering his head and shoulders. "And he just—faded away."

Magnus nodded.

Rod gazed out at the pond, frowning.

"Dost thou think . . ." Gwen's voice broke; she tried again. "Dost thou think we should drag the waters?"

Rod shook his head.

"Then . . . what?" She was fighting against hope.

"Fess?" Rod murmured.

"Yes, Rod."

"You watched me being sent through that time-machine in McAran's lab once, right?"

"Yes, Rod. I remember the seizure vividly. And I see your point—Magnus's description does match what I witnessed."

Gwen clutched his arm. "Dost thou think he has wandered in time?"

"Not *wandered*," Rod corrected. "I think he's been sent."

"But I ran right after him, Papa! Why would it not have sent me, too?" Magnus protested.

"Yeah, I was wondering about that." Rod rose. "The most logical answer is that whoever turned the machine on, turned it off right after poor little Geoff blundered into it . . . But maybe not. Son, when you told Geoff to go jump in the lake, where were you standing, and where was he?"

"Why . . . I stood by yon cherry tree." Magnus pointed. "And Geoff stood by the ash." His arm swung toward a taller tree about ten feet from the first. "And he called, 'Magnus, me climb, too!' and started toward me." Magnus gulped back tears, remembering. "But I spake to him, 'No! Thou knowest Mama and Papa forbade it!' And he stopped."

Rod nodded. "Good little boy. And then?"

"Well, he began to bleat, in that way he hath, 'Magnus! You climb, *me* climb! Me big!' And I fear I lost patience; I cried, 'Oh, go leap in the lake!' And, straightaway, he fled toward the water."

"From the ash." Rod turned, frowning, toward the tree, drawing an imaginary line from it straight toward the lake, and cutting it off ten feet short of the water. "Then?"

"Why, then, he began to fade. I own I was slow; I did not

think aught was out o' place for a second or two. Then it struck me, and I ran hotfoot after.''

Rod drew an imaginary line from the cherry toward the pond. The two lines did not intersect, until their end-points. ''Fess?''

''I follow your thought, Rod. The machine's focus was no doubt ten feet or so further back from the water's edge. Geoff's momentum carried him further while he was beginning to shift.''

Rod nodded and started for the ash tree.

''What dost thou do?'' Gwen cried, running after him.

''We've got the theory; now I'm testing it.'' Rod turned right at the ash and started toward the water.

''Thou seekest to follow him, then!'' Gwen kept pace with him determinedly. ''And if thou dost?''

''Then he'll have company. You stay with the other three, while we find our way back—but don't hold dinner.''

''Nay! If thou dost . . . Rod! Thou . . .'' Then whatever she was saying faded away. Rod turned back toward her, frowning. . .

. . . and found himself staring at the trunk of a tree.

A white trunk, white as a birch, but corrugated like an oak—and the leaves were silver.

Rod stared.

Then, slowly, he looked up, and all about him; all the trees were just like the first. They towered above him, spreading a tinsel canopy between himself and the sun; it tinkled in the breeze.

Slowly, he turned back to the meter-wide trunk behind him. So that was why Geoff had faded, instead of just disappearing—the machine's computer had sensed solid matter at the far end, and hadn't released him from its field until he was clear of the trunk. Rod nodded slowly, drew his dagger, and carefully cut a huge ''X'' in the trunk; he had a notion he might want to be able to find it again.

Apropos of which, he turned his back to the trunk, and looked about him carefully, identifying other trees as landmarks—the one with the split trunk over to the left, and the twisted sapling to his right. . .

And the gleam of water straight ahead!

And just about the same distance away as Elben Pond had been. The machine had set him down in the spot that exactly corresponded to the pick-up point.

But when? When had there been silver-leafed, white-trunked oaks on Gramarye?

When *would* there be?

Rod shook off the tingling that was trying to spread over his back from his spine. He had more important things to think about, at the moment. He stepped away toward the shoreline, calling, "Geoff! Geoffrey! Geoff, it's Papa!"

He stopped dead-still, listening. Off to his left, faintly, he heard tiny wails, suddenly stopping. Then a little head popped up above underbrush, and a small voice yelled, "Papa!"

Rod ran.

Geoff blundered and stumbled toward him. Silver leaves rang and chimed as they ran, with a discordant jangle as Rod scooped the little body up high in his arms, stumpy legs still kicking in a run. "Geoff, m'boy! Geoff!"

"Papa! Papa!"

After a short interval of unabashedly syrupy sentimentality, Rod finally put his second son down, but couldn't quite bring himself to take his hand off Geoff's shoulder. "Thank Heaven you're safe!"

"Scared, Papa!"

"Me too, son! But it's all right, now we're together—right?"

"Right!" Geoff threw his arms around his father's leg and hugged hard.

"Well! Time to go . . . *what's that?*"

Something blundered into the underbrush and stopped with a clashing of leaves. Then it set up a frightened wail.

A voice faded in after it. ". . . thou dare—Cordelia! Thou'st done . . . Oh, child! Now *two* of thee are lost!"

"Uh—three!" Rod called, peering over the underbrush to

see Magnus come barrelling out of the tree-trunk. "Come on, Geoff! Family-reunion time!"

"Not lost, Mama!" Cordelia crowed triumphantly. "We're *all* here!"

"And all lost," Rod agreed as he came up. "Here he is, Gwen."

"Oh, *Geoffrey!*" Gwen fell to her knees and threw her arms around her boy.

Rod let her have *her* few minutes of sickening sentimentality while he set his arms akimbo and glared down at Magnus. "You know, this wasn't exactly the world's smartest idea."

"If one of us's lost, we should all be lost!" Cordelia declared.

"So said she to Mama," Magnus stated, "and methought her idea had merit."

"Oh, you did, did you?" Rod growled, glaring; but he couldn't hold it, and grappled them to him, one against each hip, hugging them hard. "Well, maybe you've got a point. The family that strays together, stays together—even if we *are* all in danger."

"Danger?" Magnus perked up. "What danger, Papa?"

Rod shrugged. "Who knows? We don't even know what kind of country we're in, let alone what lives here."

"It's all *new!*" Cordelia squealed in delight.

"Well, that's one way of looking at it." Rod shook his head in amazement. "And to think I used to be a cynic!"

"Where are we, Papa?" Magnus was looking around, frowning.

"It's beginning to get through to you, too, huh? Well, I *think* we're still in Gramarye, but way in the future—way, *way* in the future. It couldn't be the past, because Gramarye never had trees like this—before the colonists came, it was all Carboniferous."

"Carbo-*what?*"

"Just giant ferns, no trees."

"Art thou certain?"

"Well, that's what the rest of the planet still has—but let's check it, anyway . . . Fess?" Rod waited for the robot to answer, then frowned. ''Fess? Fess, where are you? Come in, hang it!''

There was no answer.

''Can Fess 'talk' across time, Papa?'' Magnus asked quietly.

''Well, we tried it once, and it worked—but Doc, uh, Dr. McAran was lending us a time-machine's beam, then.'' Rod didn't finish the thought, but a cold lump of dread began to swell in his belly.

''But isn't there a time-machine still running, here?''

Rod *would* have to beget brainy kids! ''Don't miss much, do you? Uh, Gwen, dear? I think it's time we were getting back.'' *Or trying to*.

Gwen looked up, startled. ''Oh, aye!'' She scrambled to her feet. ''I had clear forgot about time! Why, Gregory must be squalling with hunger!''

''I have a feeling you should have weaned him sooner,'' Rod mused.

The telepathic mommy picked it up from her kids. ''What is this foreboding . . . ? Oh.'' She looked up at Rod. ''Magnus fears the gate may be closed.'' Her face firmed as she accepted it.

Rod felt a surge of admiration, and gratitude that he'd lucked into this woman. ''There is that possibility, dear. Let's check it out, shall we?''

Without a word, Gwen clasped little Geoff's hand and followed after her husband.

Rod went slowly, holding Cordelia's hand and letting Magnus stalk by his side, searching for the bent sapling on the one hand, and the split trunk on the other. There, and . . . there. And there was the big oak with the ''X'' on it.

He caught Magnus's hand. ''Take your mother's hand, son. I think we'd better be linked up, just in case this works.''

Silently, Magnus caught Gwen's hand.

Slowly, Rod paced toward the tree.

He stopped when the bark was grooving his nose, and didn't seem disposed to melt nicely out of the way.

''Thou dost look silly, Papa,'' Cordelia informed him.

"I never would have guessed," Rod muttered, turning away. His eyes found Gwen's. "It didn't work, dear."

"No," she answered, "I think it did not."

They were silent for a few minutes.

"Art thou certain 'twas here, Papa?" Cordelia asked hopefully.

Rod tapped the tree-trunk. "X marks the spot. I should know—I put it there, myself. No, honey—whoever opened this particular door for us, has shut it."

"At least," Gwen pointed out, "I will not have to wait dinner for thee."

"Yes." Rod smiled bleakly. "At least we're all here."

"No, Papa!" Cordelia cried. "*Not* all here! How *could* you forget Gregory!"

"Believe me, I haven't," Rod assured her, "but I think whoever trapped us here, did."

"*Trapped* us?" Magnus's eyes went round.

"Don't miss much at all, do you?" Rod gave him a bitter smile. "Yes, son, I think somebody deliberately set out to trap us here—and succeeded admirably." His gaze travelled up to Gwen. "After all, it makes sense—and it's about the only theory that does. There's a storm brewing, between the Church and the Crown, back on Gramarye—*our* Gramarye, that is. And I've got some pretty strong hints that somebody from off-world's been pushing the Church into it. So what happens? Church and Crown have a meeting this afternoon, a confrontation that should've blown the whole thing sky-high—and what do I do but foul up the plan by getting them both to see reason! No, of *course* whoever's behind it would want me out of the way!"

Magnus frowned. "But why us, Papa?"

"Because you're a very powerful young warlock, mine offspring, as anyone on Gramarye knows. And, if they're going to all this trouble just to foist off a war between the Church and the State, you can darn well bet they don't intend to have the State win! So the smart thing to do is to remove the State's strongest weapons—me, and your mother, and you. Don't forget, they lost one because of you, already, when you were only two. And Geoffrey's three already, and Cordelia's all of five! They've got no way of telling *what* any of you might be able to do." *Nor do I, for that matter.* "So, as long as you're setting the trap, why not catch all five of the birds-of-trouble while you're at it?"

"But Gregory, Papa?"

Rod shrugged. "I'm sure they'd've preferred it if your mother'd carried him in here, too—but since she didn't I don't expect they're going to lose much sleep over it. He's not even a year old, after all. Even if he had every power in the book, what could he *do* with them? No, I don't think they were about to keep the gate open just to try and get Gregory, too—especially if it meant that the five of *us* might escape! Speaking of Gregory, by the way—who's with him?"

"Puck, and an elf-wife," Gwen answered. "And, aye, fear not—she knows the crafting of a nursing-glove."

Rod nodded. "And anything else she needs to know about him, I'm sure Brom will be glad to supply."

"He takes so great an interest in our children," Gwen sighed.

"Ah—yes." Rod remembered his promise not to tell Gwen that Brom was her father. "Comes in handy, at a time like this. In fact, I wouldn't be surprised if he flits in from Beastland, just to take charge of Greg personally—and Baby couldn't be safer inside a granite castle guarded by a phalanx of knights and three battlewagons. No, I think he'll be safe till we get back."

" 'Until?' " Magnus perked up. "Then thou'rt certain we can return, Papa?"

Well, Rod *had* been, until Magnus mentioned it—but he wasn't about to say so. There were times when it came in handy, being telepathically invisible, even to members of his own family.

Damn few, though. And there were so *many* times when it was a curse, almost made him feel excluded. . .

He shrugged it off. "Of course we can get back! It's just a problem—and problems are made to be solved, right?"

"Right," all three children shouted, and Rod grinned in

spite of himself. They were handy to have around, sometimes. Most times.

"Tell us the manner of it!" Magnus demanded.

"Oh . . . I dunno . . ." Rod let his gaze wander. "We
don't exactly have enough information to start building
theories. We don't even know where we are, in a manner of
speaking, or what materials and tools are available—which
might be handy to know, 'cause it might come down to
building our own time-machine. For that matter, we don't
even know if there're even any people!"

"Then let us go discover it!" Magnus said stoutly.

Rod felt the grin spreading over his face again. "Yeah,
let's go!" He whipped out his dagger. "Blaze trees as we go,
kids—we might want to be able to find our way back here.
Forward *march!*"

CHAPTER SIX

"I trust you had a pleasant journey, Father Uwell."

"As usual, Your Grace." Father Al dug gratefully into a pile of asparagus that appeared to be fresh. "Aboard ship, it was very pleasant—ample time for meditation. It was getting *to* the ship that was the problem."

Bishop Fomalo smiled thinly. "Isn't it always? I believe my secretary said you were from the Vatican." The Bishop knew that full well; that's why he'd invited Father Al to dinner. Not to impress him, but because that was the only half-hour open in the Bishop's schedule.

Father Al nodded, chewing, and swallowed. "But I have no official standing, Your Grace. An informal trouble-shooter, you might say."

The Bishop frowned. "But we have no troubles in my diocese—at least, none that would merit the Vatican's attention."

"None that you know of." Father Al tried a sympathetic smile. "And it's debatable whether or not it's in your diocese."

Bishop Fomalo seemed to relax a little. "Come, now, Father! Certainly the Vatican knows which solar systems my diocese includes."

"Lundres, Seredin, and Ventreles—I believe those are the colonists' names for the stars. I'm afraid I don't know the catalog numbers."

"I'd have to look them up, myself," the bishop said, with a thin smile. "There are colonies on the third and fourth planets of Lundres, one on the fourth planet of Seredin, and one on the second planet of Ventreles."

"But they haven't begun to branch out to the moons and asteroids yet?"

"No, the planets are enough for us, for the time being. After all, Father, we scarcely total a million souls."

"So little as that? My, my. I trust that doesn't indicate a disaster?"

"Scarcely." The bishop tried to repress a smile. "But when you begin with a colony of a few thousand, Father, it does take a while to build up a sizable population, even with sperm and ova banks to keep the genetics stable."

"Yes, of course. I hope you'll pardon my ignorance, Your Grace—I've never been so far from Terra before. And distance is the factor—with so few people spread over so many light-years, it must be an Herculean task to stay in touch with them."

"It is difficult," the bishop admitted, "especially with so few vocations. But we do have hyperadio now, and of course we've had a dozen pinnaces with FTL drives all along."

"Of course." But Father Al's eyes suddenly gleamed.

The bishop shifted uncomfortably in his chair. "About this trouble you mentioned, Father—on which colony is it?"

"A Lost Colony, Your Grace, about two-thirds of the way between Seredin and Ventreles, and thirteen light-years away."

The Bishop relaxed again. "Well, that is out of my diocese. What colony is this?"

"Its people call it 'Gramarye,' Your Grace."

"Troubling." The bishop frowned. "The word refers to sorcery, does it not?"

"Well, magic, certainly, and it does have occult connotations. The term's also used to refer to a book of magical spells."

"I can see why the Vatican would be concerned. But how is it I've never heard of this Lost Colony, Father?"

"Why, they wished to stay lost," Father Al said, lips puckering in a smile. "As far as I've been able to make out, they deliberately set about cutting themselves off from the rest of humanity."

"An ominous symptom." The bishop's frown deepened. "All manner of heresies could break out in such a situation. And they've been there for several centuries?"

Father Al nodded. "The colony was founded just before the Interstellar Dominion Electorates fell to the Proletarian Eclectic State of Terra's coup."

"At least they were founded under a democratic interstellar federation. I take it they saw the totalitarian rule of PEST coming, and went off to try to keep democracy alive?"

"Not really; they established a monarchy."

"Why, I wonder?" The bishop rubbed his chin. "How did the Vatican learn of them?"

Father Al heard the indignant echo under the words; what business did he, an outsider, have coming in here, telling the bishop there was a nearby trouble spot he hadn't known about? "You might say the information was leaked to us, by an agency associated with the interstellar government." Which was true; but the Decentralized Democratic Tribunal didn't know about the association.

"I see." The bishop's face cleared. "It's good to know there are still some concerned citizens. Was your source Catholic?"

"I believe his name's Irish, but that's all I know."

"That's indication enough." The bishop sat back in his chair. "I assume he gave you the coordinates. How will you get there?"

"Well, ah. . ."

The bishop's eyes widened. "No, Father. All my boats are fully scheduled, for the next three months. If we were to transport you, one of the colonies would have to miss its consignment of missalettes."

"I think the clergy could manage to find the correct readings, Your Grace. Besides, don't you keep at least one of your craft on standby, in case of breakdowns?"

"Yes, but what if there *were* a breakdown? Good heavens, Father, two of our colonies can't even produce their own altar wine yet!"

"But surely. . ."

"Father!" The bishop's eyebrows drew down in a scowl. "I hate to be so blunt, but—the answer is an unequivocal 'No!' "

Father Al sighed. "I was afraid you'd say that—but I was hoping to avoid having to do this." He drew a long white envelope from the inside pocket of his cassock. "Pardon this archaic form of communications, Your Grace—but we weren't sure what level of technology we'd encounter on Gramarye. I assure you, it's just as personal as a message cube." He handed the envelope to the bishop.

Frowning, the bishop slid out the letter and unfolded it. He read with a scowl. "Aid the bearer of this letter, Father Aloysius Uwell, in any way he may request. In all matters pertaining to the planet 'Gramarye,' he speaks with my voice." He blanched as he saw the signature. "Pope John the XXIV!"

"And his seal," Father Al said apologetically. "So you see, Your Grace, I really must have transportation to Gramarye."

CHAPTER SEVEN

They cut a particularly big blaze on a huge old willow overhanging the shore, then set off to the left, along the lakeside, heading north. After a half-hour's walk, they came out of the silver wood into an emerald-green meadow.

"Oh, *look!*" Cordelia gasped, pointing. "The prettiest cow in the world!"

Rod looked, and swallowed, hard. The "cow," even if it didn't have any horns, was definitely the biggest, toughest, meanest-looking old bull he'd ever seen. "No, Cordelia, I don't think that's. . ."

"*Cordelia!*" Gwen gasped, and Rod whirled, just as a miniature witch on a branch of a broomstick shot past his nose.

"Too *late!*" Gwen clenched her fists in frustration. "Oh, you dare not take your eyes from them for a *second! Milord, she is dangered!*"

"I know," Rod ground out, keeping his voice low, "but we don't dare charge out there, or we might spook it . . . No, put down that branch! I've got to stalk it . . . No you don't, young man!" He made a frantic grab for Magnus's collar, and yanked him back. "I said *I'll* stalk it! One child in danger is enough, thank you! Gwen, hold onto 'em!" And he stepped out into the meadow, drawing his sword.

Geoffrey began to cry, but the sobs cut off quickly—Gwen's hand over his mouth, no doubt. She was right; they didn't dare make a sound. Rod moved very slowly, though every cell of his body screamed at him to hurry.

Especially since Cordelia was coming in for a landing! Not right under the bull's nose, thank Heaven—but only a few feet away! She plumped right down on the grass, though—at least she had the sense not to go running up to it.

"Here, Bossy!" He could hear her voice clearly, over a hundred feet of meadow grass—that might as well have been a thousand miles! "Sweet moo-cow, come here!"

And the bull was turning its head towards her!

And now the rest of its body! It was moving! It was ambling towards her! Rod braced himself for a frantic mad dash. . .

And it nuzzled her outstretched hand.

Rod stood rigid, unable to believe it. But it was real—it liked her! It was gentle! It was nibbling grass from her hand! A father itself, no doubt—and sure enough of its own masculinity not to be insulted by her mistake as to its gender. Thank Heaven!

Not that he was about to stop trying to get to her—but carefully, now, very carefully; it was being gentle, let's not upset the cattle car! And move around to come at it from the side—if it charged him, Rod didn't want Cordelia in the way.

But there was no need to worry about that—she was going to be on top of the situation. Because the bull was folding its legs, and lying down beside her, in pure invitation! And she was climbing on! He choked back her name, and the impulse to shout it; don't spook the bull!

But it was climbing to its feet, and trotting away across the meadow—with his little girl on its back! "Cor-deeel-iaaaa!"

She heard him; she waved—and turned the bull somehow, set it trotting back towards him! Rod breathed a sigh of relief, then stiffened again. This was only an improvement, not a solution—she was still on its back!

He pulled away, backing up toward his family, until his left hand brushed Gwen's arm. The boys could teleport out, if they had to, and there was a nice-sized boulder right next to Gwen—small enough for her to "throw" by telekinesis, but large enough to knock the bull cold. He saw her glance flick over to it, and knew she was thinking along the same line.

But about twenty feet away, the bull started getting skittish. It slowed, and slewed around sideways, prancing to a stop, then pawing the turf.

"Oh, come, sweet cow, come!" Cordelia pleaded. "Thou'rt so lovely, I wish to show thee to my family! *Please* do come!"

"Now, now, dear don't push him—uh, it. *We* can come over—can't we, dear?" And Rod stepped forward.

The bull stepped back.

Rod halted. "I . . . don't think he likes me. . ."

"Mayhap he is wise enough not to trust males," Gwen suggested. "*I* shall try." And she took a step forward.

The bull stepped back again.

"Try it without the boys." Rod caught Geoff's and Magnus's hands, and Gwen stepped forward again.

The bull held its place—warily, but holding.

Gwen took another step, then another, and another.

Great. Just great. Now Rod had *both* his womenfolk at peril!

Then the boys shouted with delight, and both little hands wrenched out of his. "*Hey!*" Rod made a frantic grab—but he landed on his face, as two small *booms* told him they'd teleported. He scrambled back to his feet, just in time to see them reappear at the far end of the meadow, way over against the trees on the other side, along with. . .

That was the attraction—another little boy!

But what a boy—or at least, what an outfit! His doublet was dark green, with a golden surcoat; its sleeves belled out to brush the ground. His hose were buff, and fitted like second skins—and was that the glimmer of gold in his hair? Not a coronet, surely!

Whatever he was, he was moving very slowly toward a shaggy-looking horse that seemed to be waiting for him, head up and turned toward him, ears pricked forward. But it was bare-backed.

Wild?

Magnus whooped a greeting, and the boy looked up. The horse tossed its head angrily, and sidled closer. Magnus ran toward the new boy, with Geoff hurrying after.

Rod squeezed his eyes shut, gave his head a quick shake in disbelief, and looked again. It *was!* The horse's body had grown longer—say, long enough for a couple of more riders!

Rod decided he didn't like its looks. He lit out running, sword in hand.

The boys had gotten past the opening wariness, and were shaking hands. Now the new boy was pointing to the horse—and Magnus was nodding eagerly—and the horse was kneeling down!

Then Gwen cried out in fright, and Rod whirled. She was running after him, waving frantically at the boys. Behind her, Cordelia was shrieking and kicking her heels against the bull's sides. It rumbled, and lumbered into motion.

The boys screamed behind him—high, hoarse, with raw, absolute terror! Rod spun about again, running. The horse was running flat-out toward the lake, and the boys were yanking and tugging, trying to pull themselves loose from its back.

Rod swerved, and fear shot a last ounce of adrenalin into his veins. He tore through the grass, shouting.

The horse hit the water with a huge splash; fountains of foam shot high. When they cleared, its back was bare; it reared up, wheeling about and plunging down at three small heads in the water, mouth gaping wide—and Rod saw carnivore's teeth!

He bellowed rage, and leaped.

Spray gushed about him as he hit, directly under the horse. It surged down, jaws gaping wide; he leaned to the side and slashed, back-handed, straight into its jaws. It screamed, rearing back, and lashed out at him with razor-edged hooves. Fire raked his side; then a thundering bellow shook the earth, and a juggernaut knocked him back, floundering. Water closed over his face; daylight glimmered through water. He fought his way back, broke surface, and stood—to see the horse twenty feet farther from shore, scrambling back upright, wheeling about in time to catch the bull's second charge.

The great dun beast slammed into the chestnut stallion. It folded over the bull, gleaming hooves slashing, needle-teeth ripping. The bull bellowed in anger and pain, and dove down. Blood sheened the water as both animals went under.

Rod didn't stay to wait for the curtain call. He floundered over to his boys, shot a hand down under water to grapple Geoff's collar and yanked him back above the surface, spluttering and wailing.

"Papa!" Magnus yelled. "Elidor! He can't swim!"

Rod wallowed over to the sinking princeling, bellowing, "Get to shore!" Water whooshed in as Magnus disappeared, shooting Elidor briefly to the surface. Rod caught him under the arms in a cross-body carry and backed toward shore, towing both boys. He stumbled and fell as he hit shallow water, scrambled back up, and hauled the two boys out onto the grass. And he kept hauling, yanking them up, one under each arm, and ran. He stopped when he fell, but Gwen was there by that time, with Magnus beside her, to catch Geoff in her arms. "Oh, my boy, my foolish lad! We near to lost thee!"

Rod followed suit, yanking Magnus to him, hugging him tight to reassure himself the boy was still there. "Oh, thank Heaven, thank Heaven! Oh, you fool, you little fool, to go near a strange animal like that! Thank the Lord you're alive!"

A high, piercing scream shattered the air.

They whirled, staring.

For a moment, the horse and bull shot out of the water, the horse leaping high to slash down at the bull with its teeth, catching it where neck joined shoulders. But the bull twisted, catching the horse's hind leg in its own jaws. Even a hundred feet away, they could hear the crunch. The horse screamed, and the bull bellowed, rearing up to drive down with its forelegs, slamming its opponent back under the water with the full force of its weight. It sank, too, but the water churned like a maelstrom, and the blood kept spreading.

Gwen shuddered and turned the children's heads away. " 'Tis a horrid sight, and one that only thy father need watch, that he may warn us to flee if need be." Then she noticed the blood dripping from Rod's doublet. "Milord! Thou'rt wounded!"

"Huh?" Rod looked down. "Oh, yeah! Now I remember. Unnnngh! Say, that's beginning to hurt!"

"Indeed it should," Gwen said grimly, unlacing his doublet. "Cordelia, seek out St. John's Wort and red verbena! Boys, seek four-leafed clovers! Quickly, now!"

The children scampered to search. Elidor stood, blinking in confusion.

"Four-leafed clovers, lad," Gwen urged. "Surely thou mayst seek them, no matter how little herb-lore thou knowest! Quickly, now!"

Elidor stared at her indignantly; then fright came into his eyes, and he ran to join Magnus and Geoff.

"Strange one, that," Rod said, frowning. "Ow! Yes, dear, the skin's broken."

" 'Tis not pretty," Gwen said, tight-lipped. She tore a strip from the hem of her skirt.

"Here, Mommy!" Cordelia was back, leaves in hand.

"Good child," Gwen approved. A flat rock lifted itself, a few feet away, and sailed over to land at her feet. She plucked Rod's dagger and dropped to her knees, pounding the herbs with the hilt.

"Here, Mama!" Magnus ran up, two four-leafed clovers in hand, with the other boys right behind him.

"Any will aid. I thank thee, lads." Gwen added them to the porridge, then gave Rod's ribs a swipe with his doublet and plastered the herbs on the wound.

"St. John's Wort, red verbena, and four-leafed clovers," Rod winced. "Not exactly the usual poultice, is it?"

"Nay, nor wast thou ripped by a usual beast." Gwen wound the improvised bandage around his torso.

Rod tried to ignore the prickling in his scalp. "As I remember, every one of those herbs is supposed to be a sovereign against fairies."

"Indeed," Gwen said, carefully neutral. "Well, I have never seen such as these two beasts afore—yet I mind me of certain tales from my childhood. There, now!" She fastened the bandage and handed him his doublet. "Walk carefully a week or so, mine husband, I pray thee."

A long, piercing shriek echoed over the meadow. Before it died, a rumbling, agonized bellow answered it.

They spun about to face the lake. The maelstrom subsided; the waters grew calm. Finally, they could make out the body of the bull drifting toward shore.

"Children, be ready!" Gwen warned.

"No, I don't think so." Rod frowned, and stepped carefully toward the lake. About twenty feet away, he could see a thick stew of blood and chunks of flesh drifting away toward the east. A passing crow noticed, too, circled back, and flew down for a sample. Rod shuddered and turned away. "I don't think we'll have to worry about the horse, either."

" 'Tis courtesy of thy good rescue," Elidor said solemnly. "An thou hadst not come to our aid, this land had lacked a sovereign. A King's thanks go with thee!"

Rod looked down, startled. Then he darted a questioning glance at Gwen. She looked as startled as he felt, but she was nodding in confirmation.

Well, maybe she could read the kid's mind, but he couldn't. "Are you the King of this land, then?"

"I am." Elidor was wet to the skin; his fine clothes were torn and bedraggled, and he'd lost his coronet somewhere along the fray—but he straightened his shoulders, and bore himself regally. "By courtesy of my mother the Queen, though I never knew her, and of Eachan, my father the King, dead these three years, I am King of Tir Chlis."

Rod's face composed itself, hiding a stewpot of emotions—incredulity, sorrow for the boy, a yearning to take him in his arms . . . and the realization that this could be a huge stroke of good fortune for a family of wanderers, marooned in a strange world. "It is my honor to greet Your Majesty. Yet I cannot help but notice your age; may I inquire who cares for you now?"

"A thousand thanks for kind rescue, brave knight and fair lady!" gasped an anxious voice.

Rod looked up, startled.

A gross fat man, a little shorter than Rod, with a gleaming bald pate surrounded by a fringe of hair around the back of his head, and a ruddy complexion, waddled toward them, swathed in an acre of white ankle-length robe topped with a brocade surcoat, and belted by a four-inch-wide strap. Behind him trooped thirty courtiers in bell-sleeved skirted coats and hose, and two peasants with a brace of belling hounds.

The courtiers all had swords, and the fat man had a lot of sweat and a look just short of panic. "Gramercy, gramercy! If aught had happened to mine nephew through my lack of vigilance, I had never come out of sackcloth and of ashes! Yet how didst thou know to set a bull of the Crodh Mara 'gainst the Each Uisge?"

"Ag whisky?" Rod was watching Elidor; the boy had drawn in on himself, staring at the fat man with a look that held wariness, but a certain longing, too . . . "Uh, well . . . to tell you the truth. . ."

"We but knew the old grannies' tales," Gwen cut in hurriedly. "The water-bull and the water-horse—all else followed from reason." Her elbow tapped Rod lightly in the short ribs.

They were the wounded ones; the stab of pain cut through the murk of sentiment. "Uh, yes, of course! Opposite forces cancel out."

"Indeed, an thou sayst it." The fat man's brows were knit. "Though I do not claim to understand. Thou must be a warlock most accomplished."

Typed again! Rod winced. There must be something about him . . . "A great part of wizardry is luck. By good fortune, we were here when we were needed." He took a chance. "Your Lordship."

Fatso nodded, but his gaze strayed to Elidor, as though to assure himself the boy was all right. "Fortunate indeed, else I had lacked a nephew—and this land, a King." There was something of longing in his eyes, too.

He tore his gaze away from Elidor and turned back to Rod, forcing a little smile, "Forgive me; I forget the courtesies. I am Duke Foidin, Regent to His Majesty, King Elidor.'' He extended a beringed hand, palm down.

Gwen beamed, but there was uncertainty in her eyes. Rod tried to convert his puzzled frown to a polite smile, but he kept his hands on his hips, and inclined his head. ''Rodney d'Armand, Lord Gallowglass.'' Some prick of caution kept him from using his real title. ''And my Lady Gwendylon—and our children.''

''I rejoice at thine acquaintance, Lord and Lady . . . Gallowglass?'' The Duke seemed a little puzzled. '' 'Tis a title unfamiliar. Thou art, then, travellers from another land, far from thine own estates?''

''Very far,'' Rod agreed. ''A foul sorcerer's curse has sped us here, far from our homeland; but we shall return with all due expedition.''

''Nay, not so quickly!'' the Duke cried. ''Thou must needs let us honor thee—for thou hast saved a King!''

Somehow, Rod didn't want to spend a night under the man's roof. '' 'Tis courteously said—but time does press upon us. . .''

''Certes, not so much as that!'' Wet and bedraggled, Elidor stepped up to his uncle's side—but still with that look of wariness about him. ''Surely thou'lt not deny the hospitality of a King!''

He was trying so very hard to be regal! Rod was about to cave in—but Gwen did, first. ''Well, a night's rest, then—we are sore wearied.''

But Rod was watching the Duke. The man's face lit up at Elidor's approach, and his hand hovered over the boy's shoulder, but didn't quite touch; Rod saw the longing in his face again, quickly masked, then a hint of a darker emotion that flashed upon his features, and was gone—but left Rod chilled. Somehow, he didn't think he'd want to be around if the Duke lost his temper.

Then Elidor smiled bravely up at his uncle, and the man's face softened. Troubled, he nodded reassuringly at the boy, forcing a smile; the hand hovered again, then fell to his side.

He turned the smile up to Rod. "Thou art in accord with thy Lady, then? Thou'lt guest within our castle this night, that we may honor thee?"

Gwen's elbow brushed his side again, and Rod winced again, too. She hadn't had to do that! The Duke seemed nice enough, or seemed to be honestly trying to be—but somehow, Rod didn't want to leave Elidor alone with him just yet. "Indeed we shall. We are honored to accept your invitation."

"Most excellent!" The Duke's face split into a huge, delighted smile. "Then come, in joy! To Castle Drolm!"

He whirled away, the hovering hand finally descending to clap Elidor's shoulder, and clasp the boy against his side. Elidor seemed to resist a little, and the Duke's hand immediately sprang free. *Insecure,* thought Rod, as he and his family were borne forward by the tide of the entourage that followed the Duke, roaring a victorious war-song.

"Papa," Cordelia piped up through the din, "I don't like going to that man's house."

"Don't worry, dear," Rod reassured her. "We can always get out again—fast."

CHAPTER EIGHT

"The excitement, the glory of it!" Brother Chard burbled. "Just think, Father, we may be the first clergy to contact these poor, benighted people in centuries!"

"Quite so, Brother." Father Al couldn't help smiling at the young pilot's enthusiasm. "On the other hand, we may arrive to find them quite well-equipped with their own clergy; one never knows." He gazed at the viewscreen, letting his subconcious read ecclesiastical symbols into the random swirls of color that hyperspace induced in the cameras.

"Roman Catholic clergy, in a society devoted to magic? Scarcely, Father! Just think, a whole new world of lost souls to save! We must try to get some estimate of the population, so that I can come back to His Grace with some idea as to how many missionaries we'll be requiring! How long before we get there?"

"Why ask me?" Father Al hid a smile. "You're the pilot."

"Oh! Yes, of course!" Brother Chard peered at his instrument panel. "Let's see, ten light-years . . . It should be about six more days." He turned back to Father Al. "Sorry the quarters are so cramped, Father."

"It's easy to tell you've never spent much time inside a confessional. Don't worry, Brother, the quarters are positively luxurious. Why, we even have a separate cabin for sleeping! . . . Ungh!"

His body slammed into his shock webbing, as though the ship had suddenly rammed a wall. Then it took off like a bear with a fire on its tail, slapping Father Al back into his couch. His vision darkened, and he fought for breath, waiting for the bright little stars to stop drifting across his field of view. They didn't, but they did dim and fade, and the velvet blackness with them. Through its last tatters, he saw Brother Chard leaning forward groggily, groping toward his control console.

"Wha . . . what happened?"

"See for yourself." The monk pointed at the viewscreen. Father Al looked, and saw the velvet darkness and bright little stars again; but this time, they stayed still. "We're back in normal space?"

Brother Chard nodded. "And travelling at sub-light-speed. Very high, but still below C. We're lucky the difference in velocity didn't smear us against the forward bulkhead."

"It would have, without the webbing. What went wrong?"

Brother Chard peered at a readout screen, punching keys. "No significant damage; everything's padded as well as we were . . . There! The isomorpher quit!"

"Quit? Just . . . quit? Why?"

"That is a good question, isn't it?" Brother Chard loosed his webbing, smiling grimly. "Shall we go have a look, Father?"

They climbed into pressure suits, cycled through the tiny airlock one at a time, clipped their safety lines to rings on the ship's skin, and clambered aft to the drive unit. Brother Chard slipped out a wrench and loosened the access hatch. He slid through head-first; Father Al followed, groping for the rungs set into the hull, gaze rivetted to the mirror-surfaced unit before him. "Doesn't appear to be a break in the shielding."

"No," Brother Chard agreed. "At least we can rule out any effects from stray radiation. Though you never know; if we can't find anything else, we'll have to go over it with a microscope." He turned a knob, and the silver egg split open, the top half lifting up like a clamshell. A steady background of white noise faded in on Father Al's helmet speaker. He frowned. "It *is* sick, isn't it?"

"Yes; we should be hearing a 1650 Hz tone." Brother Chard looked up. "I didn't know you knew electronics, Father."

Father Al shrugged. "Cathodeans pick up a lot from each other, especially during the seminary bull-sessions. I wouldn't claim to be an FTL mechanic, but I know basically how the isomorpher works."

"Or how it doesn't. Well, let's see where the circuit broke." Brother Chard pulled out a set of probes and started poking at the isomorpher's insides. Father Al crouched beside him in the crawl space, silent and intent, watching the meter on the forearm of Brother Chard's suit, atop the pocket that held the probes.

Finally, the monk looked up. "No break, Father. Current's flowing through the whole beast."

"Then you've got a grain that's passing current, but not doing anything with it. May I try?"

Brother Chard stared at him; then, reluctantly, he moved back. "Certain you know what you're doing, Father?"

"Enough to know how to find out which grain is gone." Father Al slipped the probes out of his sleeve pocket. "We just test each pair of terminals, and when the needle goes into the red, we've found the trouble-spot, haven't we?"

"Yes, that's all," Brother Chard said drily. "Check your chronometer, Father; I think we'll have to go back for a recharged air cycler in about an hour."

"Oh, I don't think it'll take us that long." Father Al started probing.

Brother Chard was silent; when his voice came over the headphones, it was strained. "I hope you're right, of course, Father—but it could take a week. If only we had a diagnostic computer aboard!"

"Well, a pinnace can't carry everything," Father Al said philosophically. "Besides, Brother Chard, I have a certain faith in the perversity of electronic circuitry."

"You mean a faith in perversity, period, don't you, Father? I've heard some of the stories you Cathodeans tell about Finagle; sometimes I think you've fallen into heresy, and made a god of him!''

"Scarcely a god—but we might promote him to the status of demon, if he were real—which, fortunately, he's not. But the perversity he personifies is real enough, Brother.''

"True,'' Brother Chard admitted. "But the perversity's in us, Father, not in the Universe.''

"But so much of our universe is man-made, Brother, so many of the things around us, the things that keep us alive! And it's so easy for us to build our own perversity into them—especially really complicated pieces of electronics!''

"Such as an isomorpher?''

"Well, yes. But computers, too, and 3DT cameras, and any number of other gadgets. Have you ever noticed, Brother, how they'll sometimes stop working for no apparent reason, then suddenly start again?''

"Now and then. But when you dig into them, Father, you can always find a reason.''

"When *you* dig into them, perhaps. Not when I do. But then, I seem to have an anti-mechanical personality; any chronometer I carry, starts gaining about five minutes a day as soon as I touch it. On the other hand, there're people machines seem to like; let one of them walk in and lay his hand on the widget, and it works perfectly.''

"A little far-fetched, isn't that, Father?''

"Perhaps. But I'm fetching as far as I can, right now.'' *Fetching aid from my patron, I hope. St. Vidicon, no matter how far away you may be, please come to my aid now! Intercede with the Almighty for me, that this isomorpher may begin working again, long enough to get us to Gramarye and to get Brother Chard safely home again!* "That might do it.'' Father Al withdrew his probes. "By the way, Brother Chard, you did disengage the isomorpher before we came out here, didn't you?''

"Of course, Father. There's just a trickle of current flowing through it now.''

"Good. Can you fire it up fully from in here?''

"I could.'' The ghost of a smile tugged at Brother Chard's

lips. "But I wouldn't recommend it. The ship might not go into H-space, but we might."

"Hm." Father Al turned away toward the access hatch. "Then let's go back to the bridge, shall we? We'll try it from there."

"But you can't think it'll work again, Father! We haven't even found the trouble yet."

"Perhaps not." Father Al turned back with a smile. "But I think we may have fixed it."

"That's impossible!"

"Brother Chard, you should be ashamed of yourself! *All* things are possible—with God."

"And St. Vidicon of Cathode," Brother Chard muttered; but he closed the isomorpher's shell, anyway, and followed Father Al.

On the way back to the airlock, Father Al finally let himself feel the dread at what might happen if the isomorpher *couldn't* be fixed. They'd be stranded light-years away from any inhabitable planet, with only a month's supply of food and water. The air cycler would keep working for several years and, with strict rationing, the food might last an extra month; but no matter how you looked at it, even if they accelerated the ship to nearly the speed of light, by the time it came near enough to civilization for its beacon to summon aid, it would be carrying only two mummies.

Dread clutched at Father Al's belly; fear soured his throat. He took a deep breath, closed his eyes. *Thy will, Father, not mine. If it suits Thy purpose that I die in this place, then let it be as Thou wilt have it.*

Serenity filled him; the fear ebbed away. Smiling, he ducked into the airlock.

They loosened their helmets and webbed themselves into their couches. Brother Chard fed power into the engines, then engaged the isomorpher and fired it up.

The stars disappeared in a swirl of colors.

Father Al heaved out a huge sigh. "Praise Heaven!" *And I thank you, St. Vidicon, for interceding with Him for me.*

Brother Chard just sat staring at the viewscreen. "I don't

believe it. I see it, but I don't believe it.''

"Faith, good Brother," Father Al chided gently. "With faith, all things are possible." He took out his breviary and began reading his Office.

CHAPTER NINE

The Duke's Hall was huge, panelled in a grayish wood with silver highlights, and adorned with old weapons, bent and battered shields in a variety of coats-of-arms, and the skins of animals with the heads still on—not the most appetizing decoration in the world, Rod reflected, as he looked up into the eyes of a twelve-point stag while he chewed a mouthful of venison.

He noticed that Magnus was chewing his food very carefully, and wondered why. *Have to ask him about that, later.* Still, it seemed like a good idea. Seemed like a good idea to be careful about everything, with Duke Foidin for a host. In accordance with which thought, he made sure that he served himself only from platters that at least two other courtiers were eating from. He noticed Gwen was doing the same, and pointedly hadn't sipped her wine.

The Duke noticed, too. "Do you not find my vintage sweet, Lord Gallowglass?"

Rod swallowed and smiled. "Religious rule, Duke. We never touch intoxicating spirits." *We have too many for friends.*

That drew startled looks from the whole table. A low mutter of gossip started up.

"Be ye paynim, then?" the Duke inquired, a little too carelessly.

" 'Paynim?' . . . Oh, Moslems! No, not at all. Are you?"

"Sir!" The Duke drew himself up, affronted, and all the courtiers stared, aghast. "What mockery is this? Are we not in Christendom?"

Okay, so they were. At least Rod knew what the local

religion was. "No offense, Milord. But as you know, we're far-travellers; I honestly did not know that you're of the same religion as ourselves."

Foidin relaxed. "Ah, then, ye do be Christian folk. Yet how's this? I've never heard of a Christian would refuse wine."   .

Rod smiled. " 'Other lands, other rules,' m'lord. At least, in our land, the Church allows wine at Mass. I've heard of some Christians who won't even go *that* far."

"Strange, most truly strange," Foidin murmured. "Are many of your folk warlocks, like yourself?"

Careful, boy. "Not too many. It requires the Gift, the talent, and a great deal of study and training."

"Ah." The Duke nodded. "Even as it doth here. I' truth, there be not four warlocks of any power in this land—and one of them's a vile recreant, who seeks to steal the person of the King, and usurp my regency!"

"No!" Now was the time to keep him talking—but Foidin wasn't the type to give any information away. What was he trying to pull?

Elidor nerved himself up. "Nay, Uncle! Lord Kern. . ."

"Hush; be still, Majesty." Foidin patted Elidor's hand with a paternal touch and gave him a steely glance. "Thou'st had time a-plenty to speak with these good folk; do now allow your old Uncle a modicum of conversation."

Elidor met that steely gaze, and subsided.

"Well, I can't say I'm terribly surprised." Rod turned back to his food. "Wherever there's wizardry, there'll always be warlocks who misuse their power."

"Aye, and so he doth!" Foidin fairly jumped on it. "Indeed, his villainy surpasseth all imagining; he would seek to lay the whole of the land under the rule of magic!"

The table was noticeably silent. Elidor was reddening like a volcano, about to erupt.

Gwen caught his eyes and moved her hand, just a little, in a calming gesture. He stared at her, surprised; then he glanced up at his uncle, and back to his food.

"Indeed," Gwen cooed, "Tir Chlis is fortunate to have so goodly a man as thyself, to defend it from such a knave."

Nice try, Rod thought, but he was sure the Duke knew about flattery.

He did; he battened on it. He fairly expanded. "Why, gently said, sweet lady—and true, quite true! Aye, the greater part of this land now dwells in peace and prosperity, under m . . . His Majesty's beneficient rule."

"Mmf!" A courtier across the table suddenly pressed a napkin to his mouth; bit his tongue, probably.

The Duke noticed, and frowned.

"Then thou must presently free the unhappy remainder," Gwen said quickly.

"Ah, but 'tis not easily done, fair lady." The Duke waved a forefinger sadly. "Knowest thou that vasty range of mountains, in the northeast?"

"Nay; we came by magic." Gwen smiled sweetly. "We know only the meadow where thou didst find us, and the stretch of riverbank that curls on northward to the spot where we appeared."

Northward? Rod could've sworn they'd *hiked* northward—which meant their entry-point lay southward!

"So newly-come as that!" The Duke was too surprised. Who was pumping whom, here? "Yet let me assure thee, the mountains lie there, in the northeast, blocking off a poor eighth-part of this land; and 'tis there Lord Kern hath fled, to try to build a robber-force to steal the King away. I cannot go against him through those mountains, for he's blocked the only pass that's large enough for armies, with foul sorcery."

"Yet he is thereby blocked himself!" Gwen crowed, delighted.

The Duke looked surprised, but he hid it quickly. "Ye-e-e-s, there is that, sweet lady—for if he lifts his sorcery, my armies would be upon him in a moment!"

The courtier across the table was having trouble swallowing again.

"Yet there is coastline near him," the Duke went on, "and

he hath attempted to land a force within our safe domain."

"Thou hast repulsed him, then?"

"I have." The Duke preened a little. "My ships are of the best, most especially when I command 'em."

The courtier grabbed for his wine-cup.

"Thus have matters stood for three long years." The Duke spread his hands. "He cannot come out, nor can I go in, to free those miserable wretches who live beneath his yoke. Yet time will ripen my good designs, and rot his fell ones; my armies daily increase, as do my ships; and, when the time hath come, I'll strike at him by sea and grind him to the dust! Then will this land be whole again, to deliver up to Elidor when he doth come of age."

The boy-King looked frightened at that last remark. Gwen caught his eyes briefly, then looked back at the Duke. "Simply planned, but nobly, Milord. And thou art wise to bide thy time; disaster visits he who strikes before the iron's hot!"

"Well said, well said." The Duke sat back, nodding, pleased. "Thou art most rare of ladies. I am not accustomed to such intelligence in one so beautiful."

Rod felt his hackles rising; but Gwen's foot touched his under the table, and he forced a smile. "And we are fortunate to have so wise and prudent a host—and one who sets so goodly a table, as well!"

The Duke waved carelessly. "My table's yours, whenever thou dost wish it. Yet dost thou wish to dine at my most noble banquet?"

Rod stared, caught short.

"Come, sir." Gwen smiled roguishly. "Wouldst thou have us think thou hast not laid forth thy finest for the rescuers of thy King?"

"Assuredly, I have," the Duke said heartily. "Yet I spoke not of game and pasties, but of battle."

"Oh." Rod nodded slowly. "You speak of this gallant expedition to free the northeast corner of Tir Chlis."

"Aye, indeed." The Duke's eyelids drooped, and tension seemed to emanate from him, as from a lion who sees the antelope step near. "As I have told thee, in that broil I'll face magics as well as spears. 'Twould soothe me, then, to have stout warlocks by my side. How say you, Lord Gallowglass? Wilt thou dine at my table, and aid King Elidor?"

"That's . . . a most attractive offer." Rod found Gwen's eyes. "To tell you the truth, nothing of the sort had occurred to me. We *had* been planning to get back home as fast as we could."

" 'Tis a long and weary journey, I doubt not," Gwen pointed out. "And, to tell the truth, we know not even where our homeland lies, nor how far it is."

"We *could* use a rest," Rod agreed, "and some time to find out where we are." He glanced back at the Duke, and saw Elidor staring at him, suddenly tense.

But Magnus was sitting next to Rod, looking absolutely chirpy. Elidor noticed him, and relaxed a little.

"It *is* a very attractive offer," Rod said to the Duke. "But you'll understand, Milord, that w . . . *I* must consider it fully. I'll give you my answer over breakfast."

"I shall await it eagerly," the Duke said, smiling. "Yet we have lingered long at table, and the hour doth grow late. No doubt thou'rt wearied."

"Kind of," Rod admitted. "A soft bed would feel good."

"Then let us have no more of talk." The Duke clapped his hands, and a functionary in a glittering tunic stepped forward. "Show these good people to their chambers!" The Duke stood. "Myself am minded also of my rest; the day has been demanding. Elidor—Majesty! Wilt thou come with me?"

Elidor rose slowly, still wary—and almost, Rod would have said, hopefully.

His uncle seized his shoulder; Elidor winced, and bit back a cry. "To bed, to bed!" the Duke sang jovially. "Good night to all!"

CHAPTER TEN

"Amphibians?" Father Al stared at the screen of the electron-telescope, unbelieving.

"I've noticed a couple of true lizards, but they're small." Brother Chard shook his head. "I'm sorry, Father. We've been around this planet four times in four separate orbits, and that's the highest form of life on any of the continents."

"So there's only that one large island with humans; the rest of the planet is carboniferous." Father Al shook his head. "Well, if we needed anything to assure us that we're dealing with a colony instead of native sentients, we've found it. Could you call up the recordings of that island, Brother Chard?"

The monk pushed buttons, and a large island appeared in the main viewscreen, a huge, uncut emerald floating in a blue sea. "Close in on that one large town, if you please," Father Al murmured. A tiny hole in the greenery, a little north and west of the center of the island, began to grow; the shorelines disappeared beyond the edges of the screen. The dot swelled into an irregular, circular clearing, and other dots began to appear around it.

"Really the only settlement large enough to be called a town," Father Al mused.

The roofs filled the screen now, with the spire of a church and the turrets of a castle reaching up toward them, from the crest of a hill off to the eastern edge of the town.

"It's medieval architecture, Father—early Tudor, I'd guess."

"Yes, but the castle's got to be Thirteenth Century; I'd swear it was almost a reproduction of Chateau Gaillard. And the church is late Gothic; Fourteenth Century at the earliest."

"Church! It's a cathedral! Why does it look so familiar?"

"Possibly because you've seen pictures of the cathedral of Chartres. The original colonists don't seem to have been terribly original, do they?"

Brother Chard frowned. "But if they were going to copy famous buildings from Terra, why didn't they make them all from the same period?"

Father Al shrugged. "Why should they? Each century had its own beauties. No doubt some liked the Fifteenth Century, some the Fourteenth, some the Thirteenth . . . If we kept looking, Brother, I'm sure we'd find something Romanesque."

Brother Chard peered at the screen as the camera zoomed in to fill it with an overhead view of a single street. "Apparently they applied the same principle to their clothing; there's a bell-sleeved tunic next to a doublet!"

"And there's a doublet *with* bell-sleeves." Father Al shook his head. "I can almost hear their ancestors saying, 'It's my world, and I'll do what I want with it!' "

Brother Chard turned to him with a sympathetic smile. "You're going to have a bit of a problem with transportation, aren't you?"

"I never did learn to ride a horse." Father Al felt his stomach sink. "Appalling great brutes, aren't they?"

Brother Chard turned back to the viewscreen. "Are you searching for just one man down there, Father? Or a community?"

"One lone individual," Father Al said grimly. "I can't just punch up a directory and scan for his name, can I?" He thought of Yorick and had to fight down a slow swell of anger; the grinning jester could've prepared him for this!

"Under the circumstances," Brother Chard said slowly, "I don't really suppose there's much point in following the usual protocol about landing."

"Better try it, anyway, Brother," Father Al sighed. "You wouldn't want to be imprisoned on a technicality, now would you?"

"Especially not by all the King's horses and all the King's men." Brother Chard shrugged. "Well, it can't do any harm. Who could hear our transmission down there, anyway?" He set the communicator to "broadband" and keyed the microphone. "This is Spacecraft H394P02173 Beta Cass 19, the Diocese of Beta Casseiopeia's *St. Iago,* calling Gramarye Control. Come in, Gramarye Control."

"We hear you, *St. Iago,*" a resonant voice answered. "What is your destination?"

Father Al almost fell through his webbing.

"Did I hear that correctly?" Brother Chard stared at the communicator, goggle-eyed. He noted the frequency readout and reached forward to adjust the video to match it. An intent face replaced the overhead view of the town street, a thin face with troubled eyes and a dark fringe of hair cut straight across the forehead. But Father Al scarcely noticed the face; he was staring at the little yellow screwdriver handle in the breast pocket of the monk's robe.

"What is your destination, St. Ia . . . Ah!" The face lit up, and the man's gaze turned directly toward them as they came into sight on his screen. Then he stared. *"St. Iago,* you are men of the cloth!"

"And your own cloth, too." Father Al straightened up in his couch. "Father Aloysius Uwell, of the order of St. Vidicon of Cathode, at your service. My companion is Brother Chard, of the Order of St. Francis Assisi."

"Father Cotterson, Order of St. Vidicon," the monk returned, reluctantly. "What is your destination, Father?"

"Gramarye, Father Cotterson. I've been dispatched to find a man named Rod Gallowglass."

"The High Warlock?" Father Cotterson's voice turned somber.

"You'll pardon my surprise, Father, but how is it you've retained knowledge of technology?" asked Father Al. "I was told your ancestors had fled here to escape it."

"How would you have known that?"

"Through a prophet, of a sort," Father Al said slowly.

"He left a message to be opened a thousand years after he wrote it, and we've just read it."

"A prophecy?" Father Cotterson murmured, his eyes glazing. "About *Gramarye?*"

He was in shock; one of his prime myths had just focused on himself. The pause was fortunate; Father Al needed a little time to reflect, too.

High Warlock? Rod Gallowglass?

Already?

As to the rest of it, it was perfectly logical—there had been a Cathodean priest among the original colonists; and where there was one Cathodean, science and technology would be kept alive, somehow.

How? Well, that was nit-picking; it had any number of answers. The question could wait. Father Al cleared his throat. "I think we have a great deal to discuss, Father Cotterson—but could it wait till we're face-to-face? I'd like to make planetfall first."

Father Cotterson came back to life. He hesitated, clearly poised on the horns of a dilemma. Father Al could almost hear the monk's thoughts—which was the worst danger? To allow Father Al to land? Or to send him away, and risk his return with reinforcements? Father Al sympathized; myths can be far more terrifying than the people underlying them.

Father Cotterson came to a decision. "Very well, Father, you may bring down your ship. But please land after nightfall; you could create something of a panic. After all, no one's seen a ship land here in all our history."

Father Al was still puzzling that one over, three hours later, when the land below them was dark and rising up to meet them. If no spaceship had landed for centuries, how had Rod Gallowglass come to be there? Yorick had said he was an off-worlder.

Well, no use theorizing when he didn't have all the facts. He gazed up into the viewscreen. "About 200 meters away from the monastery, please, Brother Chard. That should give you time to lift off again, before they can reach us. Not that I think they *would* prevent you from leaving—but it never hurts to be certain.''

"Whatever you say, Father,'' Brother Chard said wearily.

Father Al looked up. "You're not still saddened at discovering they don't need missionaries, are you?''

"Well. . .''

"Come, come, Brother, buck up.'' Father Al patted the younger man on the shoulder. "These good monks have been out of contact with the rest of the Church for centuries; no doubt they'll need several emissaries, to update them on advances in theology and Church history.''

Brother Chard did perk up a bit at that. Father Al was glad the young monk hadn't realized the corollary—that those "emissaries'' might find themselves having to combat heresy. Colonial theologians could come up with some very strange ideas, given five hundred years' isolation from Rome.

And Rod Gallowglass could spark the grandaddy of them all, if he weren't properly guided.

The pinnace landed, barely touching the grass, and Father Al clambered out of the miniature airlock. He hauled his travelling case down behind him, watched the airlock close, then went around to the nose, moving back fifty feet or so, and waved at the nose camera. Lights blinked in answering farewell, and the *St. Iago* lifted off again. It was only a speck against dark clouds by the time the local monks came puffing up.

"Why . . . did you let him . . . take off again?'' Father Cotterson panted.

"Why, because this is my mission, not his,'' Father Al answered in feigned surprise. "Brother Chard was only assigned to bring me here, Father, not to aid me in my mission.''

Father Cotterson glared upward at the receding dot, like a spider trying to glare down a fly that gained wisdom at the last second. The monk didn't look quite so imposing in the flesh; he was scarcely taller than Father Al, and lean to the point of skinniness. Father Al's respect for him rose a notch; no doubt

Father Cotterson fasted frequently.

Either that, or he had a tapeworm.

Father Cotterson turned back to Father Al, glaring. "Have you considered, Father, how you are to leave Gramarye once your mission is completed?"

"Why. . ." said Father Al slowly, "I'm not certain that I will, Father Cotterson." As he said it, the fact sank in upon him—this might indeed be his final mission, though it might last decades. If it didn't, and if the Lord had uses for him elsewhere, no doubt He would contrive the transportation.

Father Cotterson didn't look too happy about the idea of Father Al's becoming a resident. "I can see we'll have to discuss this at some length. Shall we return to the monastery, Father?"

"Yes, by all means," Father Al murmured, and fell into step beside the lean monk as he turned back toward the walled enclosure in the distance. A dozen other brown-robes fell in behind them.

"A word as to local ways," Father Cotterson said. "We speak modern English within our own walls; but without, we speak the vernacular. There are quite a few archaic words and phrases, but the greatest difference is the use of the second person singular, in place of the second person plural. You might wish to begin practice with us, Father."

"And call thee 'thee' and 'thou?' Well, that should be easy enough." After all, Father Al had read the King James Version.

"A beginning, at least. Now tell me, Father—why dost thou seek Rod Gallowglass?"

Father Al hesitated. "Is not that a matter I should discuss with the head of thine Order, Father Cotterson?"

"The Abbot is absent at this time; he is in Runnymede, in conference with Their Majesties. I am his Chancellor, Father, and the monastery is in my care while he is gone. Anything that thou wouldst say to him, thou mayst discuss with me."

A not entirely pleasant development, Father Al decided. He didn't quite trust Father Cotterson; the man had the look of the fanatic about him, and Father Al wasn't quite certain which Cause he served.

On the other hand, maybe it was just the tapeworm.

"The prophecy I told thee of," Father Al began—and paused. Decidedly, he didn't trust Father Cotterson. If the man was the religious fanatic he appeared to be, how would he react to the idea that the High Warlock would become even more powerful?

So he changed the emphasis a little. "Our prophecy told us that Rod Gallowglass would be the most powerful wizard ever known. Thou dost see the theological implications of this, of course."

"Aye, certes." Father Cotterson smiled without mirth—and also without batting an eye. "Wrongly guided, such an one could inspire a Devil's Cult."

"Aye, so it is." Father Al fell into the monk's speech style, and frowned up at him. "How is it this doth not disconcert thee, Father?"

"We know it of old," the monk replied wearily. "We have striven to hold our witchfolk from Satan for years. Rest assured, Father—if no Devil's Cult hath yet arisen on Gramarye, 'tis not like to rise up now."

" 'Witchfolk?' " Suddenly, Father Al fairly quivered with attention to the monk's words. "What witchfolk are these, Father?"

"Why, the warlocks and witches in the mountains and fens, and in the King's Castle," Father Cotterson answered. "Did not thy prophecy speak of them, Father?"

"Not in any detail. And thou dost not see thy High Warlock as any greater threat to thy flock?"

"Nay; he ha' been known nigh onto ten years, Father, and, if aught, hath brought the witchfolk closer to God." Father Cotterson smiled with a certain smugness, relaxing a little. "Thy prophet seems to have spake somewhat tardily."

"Indeed he doth." But Father Al wondered; the lean monk didn't seem to have noticed anything unusual about Rod Gallowglass. Perhaps there was a big change due in the High Warlock's life-style.

"At all odds, if thou hast come to guide our High Warlock, I fear thou hast wasted time and effort," Father Cotterson said firmly. "I assure thee, Father, we are equal to that task." They came to a halt at the monastery gates. Father Cotterson pounded on them with a fist, shouting, "Ho, porter!"

"I am sure that thou art," Father Al murmured as the huge leaves swung open. "Yet the prime task given me, Father, is to seek out the truth regarding our prophecy. If nought else, my mission is well-spent simply in the learning so much of a flock we had thought lost—and better spent in finding that they are not lost at all, but exceedingly well cared for."

Father Cotterson fairly beamed at the compliment. "We do what we can, Father—though we are sorely tried by too little gold, and too few vocations."

"I assure thee, Father, 'tis the case on every world where humanity doth bide." Father Al looked about him as they came into a wide, walled yard. "A fair House you hold, Father, and exceedingly well-kept."

"Why, I thank thee, Father Uwell. Wilt thou taste our wines?"

"Aye, with a right good will. I would fane see summat of this goodly land of thine, Father, and thy folk. Canst thou provide me with means of transport, and one to guide me?"

The thaw reversed itself, and Father Cotterson frosted up again. "Why . . . aye, certes, Father. Thou shalt have thy pick of the mules, and a Brother for guide. But I must needs enjoin thee not to leave this our House, till the Lord Abbot hath returned, and held thee in converse."

"Indeed, 'tis only courtesy, Father," Father Al said easily.

"Yet most needful," Father Cotterson said, in a tone of apology that had iron beneath it. "Our good Lord Abbot must impress upon thee, Father, how strictly thou must guard thy tongue outside these walls. For these people have lived for centuries in a changeless Middle Ages, look you, and any hint of modern ways will seem to them to be sorcery, and might shake their faith. And, too, 'twould cause avalanches of change in this land, and bring ruin and misery to many.''

"I assure thee, Father, I come to verify what is here, not to change it," Father Al said softly.

But something in the way Father Cotterson had said it assured Father Al that, if he waited for the Abbot, he might spend the rest of his life waiting. After all, he had taken an oath of obedience, and the Abbot might see himself as Father Al's lawful superior, entitled to give binding orders—and might resent it if Father Al chose to honor the Pope's orders over those of an Abbot. His resentment might be rather forcibly expressed—and, though Father Al valued times of quiet contemplation in his cell, he preferred that the cell be above ground, and that the door not be locked from the outside.

". . . *per omnia saecula saeculorum,*" Father Cotterson intoned.

"Amen," responded fifty monks, finishing the grace.

Father Cotterson sat, in his place at the center of the head table, and the other monks followed suit. Father Al was seated at Father Cotterson's right hand, in the guest's place of honor.

"Who are servitors tonight?" Father Cotterson asked.

"Father Alphonse in the kitchen, Father." One of the monks rose and stripped off his robe, revealing a monk's-cloth coverall beneath. "And myself, at the table."

"I thank thee, Brother Bertram," Father Cotterson answered, as the monk floated up over the refectory table and hung there, hovering face-down above the board. Father Alphonse bustled out of the kitchen with a loaded tray and passed it to Brother Bertram, who drifted down to the monk farthest from the head table and held the platter down for the monk to serve himself.

Father Cotterson turned to Father Al. "Is this custom still maintained in all chapters of the Order, Father—that each monk becomes servitor in his turn, even the Abbot?"

"Well . . . yes." Father Al stared at Brother Bertram, his eyes fairly bulging. "But, ah—not quite in this manner."

"How so?" Father Cotterson frowned up at Brother Bertram. "Oh—thou dost speak of his levitation. Well, many of our brethren do not have the trick of it; they, of necessity, walk the length of the tables. Still, 'tis more efficient in this fashion, for those that can do it."

"I doubt it not." Father Al felt a thrill course through him; his heart began to sing. "Are there those amongst thee who can move the dishes whilst they remain seated?"

"Telekinesis?" Father Cotterson frowned. "Nay; the gene for it is sex-linked, and only females have the ability. Though Brother Mordecai hath pursued some researches into the matter. How doth thy experiments progress, Brother?"

A lean monk swallowed and shook his head. "Not overly well, Father." The salt-cellar at the center of the table trembled, rose a few inches, then fell with a clatter. Brother Mordecai shrugged. "I can do no better; yet I hope for improvement, with practice."

Father Al stared at the salt-cellar. "But—thou didst just say the trait was sex-linked!"

"Aye; yet my sister is telekinetic, and we are both telepaths; so I have begun to attempt to draw on her powers, with the results thou dost see." Brother Mordecai speared a slab of meat as Brother Bertram drifted past him. "She, too, doth make the attempt, and doth draw on mine ability. To date, she hath managed to levitate three centimeters, when she doth lie supine."

Father Cotterson nodded, with pursed lips. "I had not known she had made so much progress."

"But . . . but . . . " Father Al managed to get his tongue working again. "Is there no danger that she will learn of the technology thou dost so wish to keep hidden?"

"Nay." Brother Mordecai smiled. "She is of our sister Order."

"The Anodeans?"

Father Cotterson nodded, smiling. "It doth warm my

heart, Father, to learn that our Orders are maintained still, on other worlds."

"Yet 'tis indeed a problem of security," another monk volunteered. "Our old disciplines seem to wear thin, Father Cotterson, in the closing of our minds to the espers without our Order."

Father Cotterson stiffened. "Hath one of the King's 'witch-folk' learned of technology from our minds, Father Ignatius?"

"I think not," the monk answered. "Yet, the whiles I did meditate on mine electrolyte vies an hour agone, I did sense an echo, an harmonic to my thoughts. I did, of course, listen, and sensed the mind of a babe in resonance with mine. So 'tis not an immediate threat; yet the child will, assuredly, grow."

"Might not his parents have been listening to his thoughts!"

"Nay; I sensed no further resonance. And yet I think it matters little; the babe's mind held an image of his mother, and 'twas the High Warlock's wife."

Father Cotterson relaxed. "Aye, 'tis small danger there; Lady Gallowglass cannot have escaped learning something of technology, and must assuredly comprehend the need of silence on the issue."

"I take it, then, thou hast found ways of shielding thy minds from other telepaths?" Father Al burst in.

"Indeed." Father Cotterson nodded. " 'Tis linked with the meditation of prayer, Father, in which the mind is closed to the outside world, but opened toward God. Yet it doth seem we'll have to seek new ways to strengthen such closure. Brother Milaine, thou'lt attend to it?"

A portly monk nodded. "Assuredly, Father."

"Research is, of course, common amongst we who are cloistered within this monastery," Father Cotterson explained.

Father Al nodded. " 'Twould not be a House of St. Vidicon, otherwise. Yet I assume such activity is forbidden to thy parish priests."

"Nay; 'tis more simply done." Father Cotterson started

cutting his ounce of meat. "Monks trained for the parishes are taught only their letters and numbers, and theology; only those who take monastic vows are trained in science and technology."

"A practical system," Father Al admitted, "though I mislike secrecy of knowledge."

"So do we, Father." Father Cotterson's eyes burned into his. "Knowledge ought to be free, that all might learn it. Yet 'twas only through subterfuge that Father Ricci, the founder of our Chapter, did manage to retain knowledge of science when he did come to Gramarye; and assuredly, he'd have been burned for a witch had he attempted to teach what he knew. Those who originally did colonize this planet were intent on forgetting all knowledge of science. We'd likely suffer burning ourselves, if we did attempt to disclose what we know—and 'twould throw the land into chaos. The beginnings of science did batten the turmoil of Europe's Renaissance, on Terra; what would knowledge of modern technology and science do to this medieval culture? Nay, we must keep our knowledge secret yet awhile."

"Still, the High Warlock may ope' us a path for the beginnings of teaching it," Father Ignatius offered.

"Indeed he may." Father Cotterson's eyes gleamed with missionary zeal.

"Saint Vidicon," Father Al murmured, "was a teacher."

"As are we all—are we not?" Father Cotterson fairly beamed at him. "Are we not? For how can we gain new knowledge, and not wish immediately to share it with others?"

This, Father Al decided, was the kind of fanaticism he could agree with.

Father Cotterson turned back to his monks. "Apropos of which, Brother Feldspar, how doth *thy* researches?"

Brother Feldspar chewed his meat thoughtfully. "Dost thou not wish more salt on this fowl, Father?"

"Indeed I do, but. . ."

The salt-cellar appeared in front of Father Cotterson with a whoosh of displaced air.

He sat back sharply, eyes wide, startled.

The company burst into laughter.

After a second, Father Cotterson relaxed and guffawed with them. "A most excellent jest, Brother Feldspar! Yet I must caution thee against thy proclivity for practical jokes."

"Yet without it, Father, how would I ever have begun to seek methods of teleporting objects other than myself?"

"Truth," Father Cotterson admitted. "Yet I think thou didst make intermediate bits of progress in thine experiments that thou didst not inform us of. Beware, Brother; we might credit someone else with thy results! For a moment, I thought Brother Chronopolis had made progress."

"Sadly, no, Father," Brother Chronopolis smiled. "The theory is sound, and I do think we *could* manufacture a quantum black hole—but we fear to do it on a planet's surface."

Father Al tried not to stare.

"Indeed," Father Cotterson commiserated. "I shudder to think of the effects of so steep a gravity-gradient, Brother; and I've no wish to find myself atop a sudden new volcano! Nay, I fear the experiment will have to wait till we've access to space flight."

Brother Chronopolis turned to Father Al. "Father, when thou dost depart Gramarye. . ."

"Well, I could not perform the experiment myself." Father Al smiled. "I do be an anthropologist, not a physicist. Yet where I can provide aid, I will rejoice to do so."

"The rest is for the Abbot to consider," Father Cotterson said firmly.

Manufacture quantum black holes? The DDT's best scientists still thought they couldn't exist! Either the Gramarye monks were very mistaken—or very advanced. There was a way to find out . . . Father Al said casually, "Hast thou made progress in molecular circuitry?"

The whole room was silent in an instant; every eye was fastened to him. "Nay," breathed Brother Chronopolis, "canst thou make a circuit of a molecule?"

Well. They were very far behind, in *some* things. "Not I,

myself. Yet I do know that 'tis done; they do fashion single crystalline molecules that can perform all the functions of. . ." What was that ancient term? Oh, yes . . . ". . . an whole integrated-circuit chip."

"But thou knowest not the fashion of it?"

"I fear I do not."

" 'Tis enough, 'tis enough." Brother Feldspar held up a quieting palm. "We know it can be done, now; 'twill not be long ere we do it."

Somehow, Father Al didn't doubt that for a minute.

"A most excellent evening, indeed," Father Cotterson sighed as he opened the oaken door and ushered Father Al in. "Thy presence did stimulate discussion wonderfully, Father."

" 'Twas fascinating, Father—especially that account of the nun who doth surgery without opening the body."

"Well, 'tis only the mending of burst blood vessels, and the massaging of hearts thus far," Father Cotterson reminded him. "Yet it doth hold great promise. I trust this cell will be to thy satisfaction, Father."

"Luxurious," Father Al breathed, looking around at the nine-by-twelve room with bare plaster walls, a straw mattress on an oaken cot-frame, a wash-stand and a writing-desk with a three-legged stool. "True wood is luxury indeed, Father!"

"To us, 'tis the least expensive material," Father Cotterson said with a smile. "I'll leave thee to thy devotions, then, Father."

"God be with thee this night, Father," Father Al returned, with a warm smile, as Father Cotterson closed the door.

Then Father Al darted over to it, carefully pressing his ear against the wood. Faintly, he heard a key turn in a lock—and all his earlier forebodings came flooding back. Disappointment stabbed him; he'd found himself liking the monks' company so well that he'd hoped his suspicions were unfounded, then had become almost certain it was only his own paranoia.

Not that locking him in his cell proved they intended to

imprison him, and not let him see the rest of Gramarye. In fact, the Abbot might be delighted to have him visit Rod Gallowglass.

But he also might not.

So Father Al charitably decided to avoid putting him to the test. Accordingly, he waited two hours, after which all the Brothers must certainly have been snoring on their cots. Then he took out his vest-pocket tool-kit, picked the huge old lock, and slipped down darkened hallways, as silently as a prayer. He drifted through the colonnade like a wraith of incense, found a ladder and a rope, and slipped silently over the wall.

They were such wonderful monks. It was so much better to remove temptation from their path.

CHAPTER ELEVEN

"All sleep, except Elidor," Magnus said, glowering.

He sat on the edge of a massive four-poster bed opposite a fireplace as tall as Rod. Tapestries covered cold stone walls; Rod paced on a thick carpet.

"He was . . ." Cordelia burst out; but Gwen clapped a hand over her mouth, and stared at Magnus. He looked up at her, surprised, then nodded quickly, and closed his eyes, sitting very straight. He held it for a few minutes, then relaxed. "I'm sorry, Mama; I was carried away."

"No great harm is done," Gwen assured him. "They heard only that one sentence, and they cannot do so much with that."

"Spies?" Rod frowned. "How many of them *were* there?"

"Only the two," Gwen assured him. "One there, behind the knight on the tapestry o'er the hearth—thou seest that his eye is truly a hole? And one behind the panel next the door, where there's a knot dropped out."

Rod nodded. "Milord Foidin likes back-up systems—no doubt so he can check them against each other, and make sure no one's lying. Well, it kinda goes along with the rest of his devious personality; I think he's in the process of inventing the police state." He turned to Magnus. "How long are they out for?"

"Till dawn," Magnus assured him, "or after."

Rod shook his head in amazement. "How does he do it so *fast?*"

Gwen shook her head, too. "I know not how he doth it at all."

"Oh, that's easy! It's just projective telepathy. You just think 'sleep' at 'em, right, son?"

"Not really, Papa." Magnus frowned. "I just *want* them to sleep."

Rod shook his head again. "You must 'want' awfully loudly . . . Well! Can you tell what Duke Foidin's thinking?"

"I shall!" Cordelia said promptly.

"No, thou shalt not!" Gwen pressed her hands over her daughter's ears. "Thou shalt not soil so young a mind as thine; that man hath filth and muck beneath the surface of his thinking that he doth attempt to hold back, but ever fails!"

"Oh." Rod raised his eyebrows. "You've had a sample already?"

"Aye, of the things he doth yearn to do to the folk in his part of Tir Chlis, but doth never, out of cowardice, and, be it said to his slight credit, some lingering trace of scruple. This I read in him, whilst he did speak of Lord Kern's 'foul rule!' "

Rod nodded. "If you could get him talking about one thing, all the related thoughts came to his mind, just below the surface."

"Thou hast learned the fashion of it well, mine husband. Almost could I believe thou hast practiced it thyself!"

"No, worse luck—but I've learned a lot about the human mind, from books." He surveyed his children. "I hope none of you were peeking into the Duke's mind."

All three shook their heads. "Mama forbade us," Magnus explained.

"One of those little telepathic commands that I couldn't hear." Rod sighed philosophically. "Speaking of things I can't hear, what's the Duke doing right now?"

Gwen's eyes lost focus. "Speaking to Elidor. . ." Her voice suddenly dropped in pitch, in a parody of the Duke's. "I was so *very* glad to find thee well, unharmed—believe, 'tis true!" Her voice rose, imitating Elidor's. "I do believe it, Uncle."

"Then believe it, also, when I tell thee that thou must not wander off again, alone! 'Tis too dangerous for an unfledged lad! There be a thousand perils in this world, awaiting thee! I own I have been harsh with thee, from time to time—yet only when thou hast tried mine patience overly, and ever have I repented of mine anger after! Stay, good lad, and I'll promise thee, I'll try to be more moderate.''

Very low: "I'll bide, good Uncle.''

''Wilt thou! There's a good lad! Be sure, 'tis chiefly my concern for thee that moves me to this protest! Oh, I will not hide from thee my hatred for Lord Kern, nor have I ever sought to hide it—or my abiding fear that he may somehow seize thee from me, and use thee to gain power over me! For thou dost like him more than me, now dost thou not? . . . Dost thou not! . . . Answer!''

''He and his wife were kindly,'' Elidor muttered.

''And was I not? Have I never treated thee with kindness? Nay, answer not—I see it in thine eyes. Thou dost remember only cuffs and blows, and never all the sweetmeats I did bring thee, nor the games that we did play! Nay, thou didst not wander off for mere adventure this day, didst thou? Thou didst seek to join Lord Kern! Didst thou not? Now answer to me! . . . What, wilt thou not?'' Gwen's whole body shook; she shuddered, and her eyes focused on Rod again. Trembling, she said, ''He doth beat the lad. Most shrewdly.''

Rod's face darkened. ''The animal! . . . No, son!'' He clamped a hand on Magnus's shoulder; the boy's body jolted, his eyes focussing again. ''You can't just teleport him away from the Duke; you'd raise a hue and cry that'd keep us penned in this castle for days. Poor Elidor'll have to last it out until we can find a way to free him.''

''He did not seem so bad a man, when first we met him,'' Cordelia said, troubled.

''He probably wouldn't be, if he weren't a Duke, and a regent.'' Rod ran his fingers through his hair. ''A burgher, say, where he could split the responsibility with a committee—or a clerk in an office. Without the pressure, his kind side'd be able to come through. But in the top position, he knows down deep that he can't really handle the job, and it scares him.''

"And when he's fearful, he will do anything to safeguard himself," Magnus said somberly.

Rod nodded. "Good insight, son. Anyway, that's how I read him. Unfortunately, he *is* the regent, and he's out of control—even his own control."

"Thus his power doth corrupt him," Gwen agreed, "and all his hidden evils do come out."

"Evil he is," Magnus said with a shudder. "Papa, we must wrest Elidor from out his power!"

"I agree," Rod said grimly. "No kid ought to have a man like that in charge of him. But we can't just bull in there and yank him loose."

"Wherefore not?" Cordelia's chin thrust out stubbornly.

"Because, sweetling, a thousand guardsmen would fall on us ere we'd gone fifty paces," Gwen explained.

"Papa can answer for ten of them—and thou and Magnus can answer for the rest!"

"Nay, I fear not." Gwen smiled sadly. "There are some things that surpass even witches' power."

"I *could* defeat a thousand!" Magnus protested.

Rod shook his head. "Not yet, son—though I'm not sure you won't be able to, when you're grown. A thousand men, though, you see, they come at you from all sides, and by the time you've knocked out the ones in front, the ones behind have stabbed you through."

"But if I took them all at one blow?"

Rod smiled. *"Can* you?"

Magnus frowned, looking away. "There must be a way. How doth one do it, Papa? Without magic, I mean."

"Only with a bomb, son."

Magnus looked up. "What is a 'bomb?' "

"A thing that makes a huge explosion, like a lightning-blast."

Magnus's face cleared. "Why, *that* I can do!"

Rod stared at him, feeling his hair trying to stand on end. He might be able to do it—he just might. No one knew for sure, yet, just what the limits were to Magnus's powers—if there were any. "Maybe you could," he said softly. "And how many would die in the doing of it?"

Magnus stared at him; then he turned away, crestfallen. "Most, I think. Aye, thou hast the right of it, Papa. We cannot withstand an army—not with any conscience."

"Stout lad," Rod said softly, and felt a gush of pride and love for his eldest. If only the kid could pick it up, straight from his mind!

Instead, he had to content himself with clasping Magnus's shoulder. "Well, then! How *will* we do it? First, we need some information. What did you get from him while you had him talking, dear?"

"She had a bonfire of craving," Cordelia said. "That, we could not shut out!"

Rod went so still that Magnus looked up at him, startled.

"Nought but what one would expect from so foul a man," Gwen said quickly. "Indeed, I doubt a lass doth cross his threshold that he doth not so desire!"

"But what doth he want them for, Mama?" Cordelia piped.

"That's one of the things we don't want you hearing from his mind, darling," Rod said grimly.

"Papa, cool thy spirit," Gwen cautioned.

"I will, for the time being. But when I can get him alone, I think Duke Foidin and I will have a very interesting exchange."

"Of thoughts?" Magnus frowned.

"Interpret it as you will, son. But, speaking of thoughts, dear. . . ?"

"Well!" Gwen sat down on the bed, clasping her hands in her lap. "To begin with, Lord Kern was the old King's Lord High Warlock."

Rod stared.

Gwen nodded. "And I do not ken the meaning of it, for none at that table could hear thoughts—of this, I'm certain. Still, the Duke is sure Lord Kern wields magic, and knows of several others—but none so strong as Kern."

"No wonder he wants us! But what kind of magic do they do here, if they aren't espers?"

Gwen shook her head. "I cannot tell; there were no clear events. Beneath the surface of his mind, there was but a feel of many mighty deeds unrolling."

"There was making many men at once to disappear," Magnus chipped in, "and summoning of dragons, and of spirits."

"And calling up the fairies! Oh! 'Twas pretty!" Cordelia clapped her hands.

"An' swords, Papa!" Geoff crowed in excitement. "Swords that cut through all, and could fight by th'selves!"

Rod stared.

Then his gaze darkened, and he turned slowly, glowering down at each child in turn.

They realized their mistake, and shrank back into themselves.

"Mama only said not to listen to the Duke's mind," Magnus explained. "She said nothing of the other folk."

Rod stilled.

Then he looked up at Gwen, fighting a grin.

" 'Tis true," she said, through a small, tight smile. "In truth, it may have been a good idea."

"There *were* some with nasty, twisted thoughts," Magnus said eagerly, "but I knew that was why Mama did not wish us to 'listen' to the Duke, so I shunned those minds, and bade Cordelia and Geoffrey to do the same."

"Thou'rt not to command," Cordelia retorted, "Papa hath said so! . . . Yet in this case, I thought thou hadst the right of it."

Rod and Gwen stared at each other for a moment; then they both burst out laughing.

"What, what?" Magnus stared from one to the other; then he picked it up from his mother's mind. "Oh! Thou art *that* pleased with us!"

"Aye, my jo, and amazed at how well thou dost, without fully understanding what or why I bade thee," Gwen hugged Geoff and Cordelia to her, and Rod caught Magnus against his hip. "So! Magic works here, eh?" It raised a nasty, prickling thought; but Rod kept it to himself.

"It seems it doth, or there is something that doth pass for it. The old King sent Lord Kern away, to fight some bandits in the northeast country; then the King died. But Duke Foidin's estate's nearby, and the Duke was the King's first cousin—so, even though he was out of favor with the King, he and his army were able to seize young Elidor and, with him, the strings of government. His army was the largest, three-quarters of the royal force being with Lord Kern; so when he named himself as regent, none cared to challenge him." Her voice sank. "It was not clear, but I think he had a hand in the old King's death."

The children sat silent, huge-eyed.

"It fits his style," Rod said grimly. "What's this nonsense about a spirit having closed the pass?"

"No nonsense, that—or, at least, the Duke doth in truth believe it. Yet the spirit was not summoned by Lord Kern; it's been there many years. The High Warlock's force went to the northwest by sea."

"Hm." Thoughts of Scylla and Charybdis flitted through Rod's mind. "Be interesting to find out what this 'spirit' really is. But what keeps Lord Kern from filtering his troops through smaller passes?"

"The Duke's own army, or a part of it. Once he'd seized Elidor, he fortified the mountains; so, when Lord Kern turned his army southward, he was already penned in. Moreover, the ships that landed him, the Duke burned in their harbor. He has at most ten ships in his full-vaunted 'Navy'—but they suffice; Lord Kern has none."

"Well, he's probably built a few, by this time—but not enough. So he's really penned in, huh?"

"He is; yet Duke Foidin lives in fear of him; it seems he is *most* powerful in magic."

"But not powerful enough to take the spirit at the pass?"

Gwen shook her head. "And is too wise to try. Repute names that spirit *most* powerful."

"*Must* be a natural hazard." Rod had a fleeting vision of a high pass with tall, sheer cliffs on either side, heaped high with permanent snow. An army doesn't move without a *lot* of noise; an avalanche . . . "Still, Duke Foidin no doubt lives in dread of Lord Kern's finding a way to fly his whole army in. Does he really think we'd work for him?"

"He doubts it; though what had he to lose in trying? Yet he's not overly assured by 'our' victory o'er the *Each Uisge;* he doth not trust good folk."

"Wise, in view of his character."

"Yet even if we'll not labour for him, he doth want us." Gwen's face clouded. "For what purpose, I cannot say; 'twas too deeply buried, and too dark."

"Mm." Rod frowned. "That's strange; I was expecting something straightforward, like a bit of sadism. Still, with that man, I suppose *nothing'd* be straightforward. I'd almost think that's true of this whole land."

"What land is that, Rod?" Gwen's voice was small.

Rod shrugged irritably. "Who knows? We don't exactly have enough data to go on, yet. It *looks* like Gramarye—but if it is, we've got to be *way* far in the future—at least a thousand years, at a guess."

"There would be more witches," Gwen said softly.

Rod nodded. "Yes, there would. And where'd the *Each Uisge* come from, and the *Crodh Mara?* Same place as the Gramarye elves, werewolves, and ghosts, I suppose—but that would mean they'd have risen from latent telepaths thinking about them. And there weren't any legends about them in Gramarye—were there?"

"I had never heard of them."

"None had ever told us of them," Magnus agreed.

"And the elves have told you darn near every folk-tale Gramarye holds. But a thousand years is time for a lot of new tales to crop up . . . Oh, come on! There's no point in talking about it; we're just guessing. Let's wait until we have some hard information."

"Such as, mine husband?"

"The year, for openers—but I don't feel like asking anyone here; there's no point letting them know just how much we don't know, other than to excuse our lack of local knowledge. We don't even know enough to know whose side we're on."

"Elidor's," Magnus said promptly.

"He is the rightful sovereign," Gwen agreed.

"Fine—but who's on his side? Lord Kern?"

Magnus nodded. "He slipped away from the Duke's men, and was fleeing in hopes of reaching Lord Kern, for protection. This was in his mind whilst the Duke did whip him."

Rod nodded. "If only he hadn't stopped to play with the pretty horsey, hm?"

"He did not play, Papa! He knew he stood no chance without a mount!"

"Really?" Rod looked up. "Then he's got more sense than I pegged him as having."

Magnus nodded. "Thou hast told me I have 'roots of wisdom,' Papa; so hath he."

"We must defend him," Gwen said quietly.

"We cannot leave him to that Duke!" Cordelia said stoutly.

Rod sighed and capitulated. "All right, all right! We'll take him with us!"

They cheered.

CHAPTER TWELVE

"Ow! Cur . . . I mean, confound it!" Father Al fell back onto a grassy hummock, catching his poor bruised foot in both hands. It was the third time he'd stubbed it; Gramarye had uncommonly sharp rocks. They couldn't poke holes through his boots, but they could, and did, mash the toes inside.

He sighed, and rested his ankle over the opposite thigh, massaging it. He'd been hiking for six hours, he guessed—the sky to the east was beginning to lighten with dawn. And all that time, he'd been wandering around, trying to navigate by the occasional glimpse of a star between the bushy trees, hoping he was heading away from the monastery, and not around in a circle back toward it. He had no idea where he was going, really—all that mattered right now was putting as much distance as possible between himself and his too-willing hosts before daybreak. They'd given him one of their brown, hooded robes, but it was torn by thorns in a dozen places; his face and hands were similarly scratched, and he could've sworn he'd heard snickering laughter following him through the underbrush from time to time. All in all, he'd had better nights.

He sighed, and pushed himself to his feet, wincing as the bruised left one hit the ground. Enough hiking; time to try to find a place to hole up for the day. . .

There was a flutter of cloth, and a thump. He whirled toward it, sudden fear clutching his throat.

She was a teen-ager, with fair skin and huge, luminous eyes, and lustrous brown hair that fell down to her waist from a mob-cap. A tightly-laced bodice joined a loose blouse to a full, brightly-colored skirt. . .

. . . And she sat astride a broomstick that hovered three feet off the ground.

Father Al gawked. Then he remembered his manners and regathered his composure. "Ah . . . good morning."

"Good . . . good morning, good friar." She seemed shy, almost fearful, but resolved. "May . . . may I be of aid to thee?"

"Why . . . I do stand in need of direction," Father Al answered. "But . . . forgive me, maiden, for I have been apart from this world almost since birth, and never before have I seen a maid ride a broomstick. I have heard of it, certes, but never have seen it."

The girl gave a sudden, delighted peal of laughter, and relaxed visibly. "Why, 'tis nothing, good friar, a mere nothing! Eh, they do keep ye close in cloisters, do they not?"

"Close indeed. Tell me, maiden—how did you learn the trick of that?"

"Learn?" The girl's smile stretched into a delighted grin. "Why, 'twas little enough to learn, good friar—I but stare at a thing, and wish it to move, and it doth!"

Telekinesis, Father Al thought giddily, *and she treats it as a commonplace.* "Hast thou always had this . . . talent?"

"Aye, as long as I can remember." A shadow darkened her face. "And before, too, I think; for the good folk who reared me told me that they found me cast away in a field, at a year's age. I cannot but think that the mother who bore me was afrighted by seeing childish playthings move about her babe, seemingly of their own accord, and therefore cast me out naked into the fields, to live or die as I saw fit."

Inborn, Father Al noted, even as his heart was saddened by her history. Prejudice and persecution—was this the lot of these poor, Talented people? And if it was, what had it done to their souls? "Ill done, Ill done!" He shook his head, scowling. "What Christian woman could do such a thing?"

"Why, any," the girl said, with a sad smile. "Indeed, I cannot blame her; belike she thought I was possessed by a demon."

Father Al shook his head in exasperation. "So little do

these poor country people know of their Faith!''

"Oh, there have been dark tales,'' the girl said somberly, "and some truth to them, I know. There do be those harsh souls possessed of witch-power who have taken to worshipping Satan, Father—I have met one myself, and was fortunate to escape with mine life! Yet they are few, and seldom band together.''

"Pray Heaven 'twill never be otherwise!'' And Father Al noted that most of these 'witches' were *not* Satanists, which pretty well assured that their Talent was psionic. "Thine own charity shows the goodness of thine own sort, maiden—thy charity in seeking to aid a poor, benighted traveller; for I'd wager thou knew I had lost mine way.''

"Why, indeed,'' the girl said, "for I heard it in thy thoughts.''

"Indeed, indeed.'' Father Al nodded. "I had heard of it, yet 'tis hard to credit when one doth first encounter it.'' In fact, his brain whirled; a born telepath, able to read thoughts clearly, not just to receive fuzzy impressions! And that without training! "Are there many like thee, maiden?''

"Nay, not so many—scarce a thousand.''

"Ah.'' Father Al smiled sadly. "Yet I doubt me not that Holy Matrimony and God shall swell thy numbers.'' And up till now, there had only been two real telepaths in the whole Terran Sphere!

"May I aid thee in thy journey, Father? Whither art thou bound?''

"To find the High Warlock, maiden.''

The girl giggled. "Why, his home is half the way across the kingdom, good friar! 'Twill take thee a week or more of journeying!''

Father Al sagged. "Oh, no . . . uh, nay! 'Tis a matter of some import, and I mind me there is need for haste!''

The girl hesitated, then said shyly, "If 'tis truly so, good friar, I could carry thee thither upon my broom. . .''

"Couldst thou indeed! Now bless thee, maiden, for a true, good Christian!''

She fairly seemed to glow. "Oh, 'tis naught; I could carry

CHAPTER THIRTEEN

Opening a lock was women's work; it took telekinesis. The boys could make the lock disappear, but they couldn't open it.

"Let Cordelia attempt it. She must be trained, must she not?" Gwen ushered her daughter over to the door and set her in front of the lock. "Remember, sweeting, to ease the bolt gently; assuredly the Duke hath posted guards on us, and they must not hear the turn."

"Uh, just a sec." Rod held up a hand. "We don't *know* they've locked us in."

Gwen sighed, reached out, and tugged at the handle. The door didn't budge. She nodded. "Gently, now, my daughter."

Rod took up a position just behind the door. Cordelia frowned at the lock, concentrating. Rod could just barely hear a minuscule grating as the lock turned, and the bolt slid back. Then Gwen stared, and the door shot open silently.

Rod leaped out, caught the left-hand guard from behind with a forearm across the throat, and whacked his dagger-hilt on the man's skull. He released his hold and whirled, wondering why the other guard wasn't already over him. . .

And saw the man down and out, with Geoff crawling out from between the guard's ankles; Magnus standing over the man's head, sheathing his dagger; and Gwen beaming fondly as she watched.

Rod gawked.

Then he shook his head, coming out of it. "How'd you keep him quiet?"

"By holding the breath in his lungs," Magnus explained. "Can I fetch Elidor now, Papa?"

131

Rod rubbed his chin. "Well, I don't know. You could teleport him away from whatever room he's in—but are you sure you could make him appear right here?"

Magnus frowned. *"Fairly* certain. . ."

" 'Fairly' isn't good enough, son. You might materialize him inside a wall, or in between universes, for that matter." Why did that thought hollow his stomach? "No, I think we'd better do this the old-fashioned way. Which way is he?"

"Thither!" Magnus pointed toward the left, and upward.

"Well, I think we'll try the stairs. Let's go."

"Ah, by your leave, Papa." Gwen caught his sleeve. "If thou shouldst meet some guardsman, or even one lone courtier, 'tis bound to cause some noise."

Rod turned back. "You have a better idea?"

"Haply, I have." Gwen turned to Cordelia. "Do thou lead us, child, skipping and singing. Be mindful, thou'rt seeking the garderobe, and have lost thy way."

Cordelia nodded eagerly, and set off.

"Thus," Gwen explained, "he who doth encounter her will make no outcry; 'twill be a quiet chat."

"Even quieter, after we catch up with him." Rod gazed after his daughter, fidgeting. "Can't we get moving, dear? I don't like letting her go out alone."

"Hold, till she hath turned the corner." Gwen kept her hand on his forearm, watching Cordelia. The little girl reached the end of the hall and turned right, skipping and warbling. "Now! The hall is clear before her; let us go."

They went quickly, trying to match unseen Cordelia's speed, wading through the darkness between torches. Near the end of the hall, Gwen stopped, with a gentle tug at Rod's arm. The boys stopped, too, at a thought-cue from their mother. "She hath encountered a guardsman," Gwen breathed. "Softly, now!"

Rod strained his ears, and caught the conversation:

"Whither goest, child?"

"To the garderobe, sir! Canst tell me where it is?"

"A ways, sweet lass, a ways! There was one near thy chambers."

Oh. So *all* the guards knew where they were quartered. Very interesting.

"Was there, sir? None told us!"

"He curses in his mind, and she has turned him!" Gwen hissed. "Go!"

Rod padded around the corner on soft leather soles. Three torchlight-pools away, Cordelia stood facing him, hopping from foot to foot with her hands clasped behind her back. The guardsman stood, a hulking shadow, between the child and Rod, his back to Papa. Rod slipped his dagger out of its sheath and leaped forward.

"Did not others, clad as I am, stand beside thy door to tell thee the way?"

"Why, no, good sir!" Cordelia's eyes were wide with innocence. "Should there have been?"

"There should, indeed!" The guardsman began to turn. "Nay, let me lead thee b . . . *Ungh!*"

He slumped to the floor. Rod sheathed his dagger.

Cordelia stared down at the guardsman. "Papa! Is he . . ." Then her face cleared with a smile. "Nay, I see; he but sleeps."

"Oh, he'll have a headache in the morning, honey—but nothing worse." Rod glanced back over his shoulder as Gwen and the boys came running up. "Well played, sweeting!" Gwen clasped Cordelia's shoulders. "I could not ha' done it better. On with thee, now!"

Cordelia grinned, and skipped away, lilting the top part of a madrigal.

"If this's what she's doing when she's five," Rod muttered to Gwen, "I'm not sure I want to see fifteen."

"If thou dost not, there are many lads who will," Gwen reminded him uncharitably. "Come, my lord, let us go."

Five guardsmen, three courtiers, four varlets and a lady-in-waiting later, Gwen stopped them all at a corner. "There lie Elidor's chambers," she breathed in Rod's ear. "Two guard the door, three keep watch in the antechamber, and a nursemaid sleeps on a pallet beside his bed."

Rod nodded; Foidin definitely wasn't the sort to take

chances. "This is why I took care of the ones we met en route—so Magnus'd be well-rested. How many can you handle, son?"

"Four, at the least." The boy frowned. "Beyond that, their sleep might be light."

Rod nodded. "That'll do. Now, here's a routine your mother and I used to run. . ."

A few minutes later, Magnus frowned, concentrating; a minute later, there was a clatter and a pair of thumps, followed by a sigh in chorus, as the two door-guards sank into slumber. Rod peeked around the corner, saw them both sitting slouched against the wall, and nodded. "Okay, Geoff. Go to it!"

The three-year-old trotted eagerly around the corner and knocked on the door. He waited, then knocked again. Finally a bolt shot back, and the door swung open, revealing a scowling guardsman. He saw Geoff, and stared.

"Elidor come out 'n' play?" the little boy piped.

The guardsman scowled. "Here, now! Where'd thou come from?" He grabbed, but Geoff jumped back. The guardsman jumped after him, and Geoff turned and scooted.

He sailed around the corner under full steam, with the guardsman a foot behind him, bent double, hand reaching, and another guard right behind him. Rod and Gwen kicked their feet out from under them, and they belly-flopped on cold stone with a shout. Magnus and Cordelia yanked their helmets off, and Rod and Gwen struck down with reversed daggers. A grace note of nasty double *chunks!* sounded, and the guardsmen twitched and lay still, goose eggs swelling on the backs of their heads.

"They'll sleep for an hour or two, at the least." Gwen handed Magnus's dagger back to him.

"Hoarstane? Ambrine?" A hoarse voice called from around the corner.

Everyone froze. Rod's pulse beat high, with the hope that the third guard might follow the first two.

Unfortunately, he was a little too wary. "Hoarstane!" he snapped again. There was silence; then the guardsman snarled again. Metal jangled as he turned away, and the door boomed shut; then a bolt snicked tight.

"Back in, and the door locked." Rod shook his head. "Well, we hadn't expected any more. You said you could handle four, son?"

Magnus nodded. "Without doubt." His eyes lost focus; he became very still.

Rod waited. And waited. Four, he reminded himself, were bound to take a little time.

Finally Magnus relaxed and nodded. "All sleep, Papa."

"Okay. You go get Elidor ready, while we get the door open."

Magnus nodded, and disappeared.

He'd started doing it when he was a baby, but Rod still found it unnerving. With people who were only friends, such as Toby, okay—but his own son was another matter. "Well, teamwork starts at home," he sighed. "After you, ladies."

They tiptoed up to the door. Rod kept a firm hold on little Geoff's hand, to make sure he didn't try to teleport away to join Magnus. Gwen watched with fond pride as Cordelia stared at the lock, and they heard the sound of the bolt sliding back. The door swung open.

They stepped into a scene out of "Sleeping Beauty." The third guardsman sat slumped in a chair, chin on chest, snoring. Beyond him, a half-open door showed a nanny in a rocker, dozing over her needlework. Rod stepped forward and pushed the door the rest of the way open. Elidor looked up from belting on his sword. His hair was tousled, and his eyes bleary from slumber, red and puffy; Rod had a notion he'd cried himself to sleep.

"Almost ready, Papa." Magnus picked up a cloak and held it out.

Elidor stepped over; Magnus dropped it over his shoulders.

"God save Your Majesty." Rod bowed. "I take it Magnus has informed you of our invitation?"

"Aye, and with right good heart do I accept! But why art thou willing to take me from mine uncle's halls?"

"Because my sons have taken a liking to you." You couldn't exactly tell a King that he triggered every paternal response you had. "If you're ready, we shouldn't linger."

"Ready I am!" The King clapped a hat on and headed for the door. Rod bowed him through, and waited as Magnus stepped through behind him.

He found Elidor staring at the snoring guard. "Magnus had told me of it," the boy whispered, "but I scarce could credit it."

"You're moving in magic circles." Rod gave him a firm nudge on the shoulder. "And if you don't keep moving, we'll wind up back where we started."

Elidor paced on forward, pausing for a bow to answer Gwen and Cordelia's curtseys. Rod took the opportunity to dodge on ahead.

Magnus stepped up beside him, as pilot, and they padded silently through dim, torch-lit halls. Whenever Magnus stopped and nodded to Cordelia, she skipped on ahead, singing, to engage whatever unsuspecting person happened to be walking the halls at this late hour, in conversation, until Magnus could knock them out. After the fifth guardsman, Rod noticed the man was twitching in his sleep. "Getting tired, son?"

Magnus nodded.

So did Rod. "I'll take over for a while."

Fortunately, there weren't too many more; the old-fashioned method is a little risky.

Elidor just followed along, his eyes getting wider and wider till they seemed to take up half his face.

Finally they crossed the outer bailey—it was really the only one; the castle had grown till it absorbed the inner. Rod's commando tactics couldn't do much about the sentries on the wall, so Magnus padded along, alert and ready; but the sentries were watching the outside, so they came to the main gatehouse without incident.

There they stopped, and Gwen gathered them into a huddle. "Here's a pretty problem," she whispered. "A sentry stands on each tower, a porter by the winch, and six guardsmen in the wardroom—and thou art wearied, my son.''

Magnus *was* looking a little frayed around the edges. ''I can still answer for two, Mama, mayhap three.''

''That leaves six.'' Rod frowned. ''What're they armed with, Gwen?''

Gwen gazed off into space for a moment. ''All bear pikes, save the Captain; he wears a sword.''

''Could you and Cordelia bop them with their own pike-butts?''

''Aye, but they wear their helmets.''

''So.'' Rod rubbed his chin. ''The problem is, getting them to take off their helmets.''

''Why, that can *I* do!'' Elidor declared, and marched off towards the guardroom before anyone could stop him.

Rod looked up after him, startled, glanced back at Gwen, then turned and sprinted after Elidor. What was the kid trying to do, blow the whole escape?

But the boy moved fast, and he was hammering on the door before Rod could catch him. It swung open, and Rod ducked into the nearest shadow and froze. He could see through the open door, though, as Elidor marched in.

The guardsmen scrambled to their feet. ''Majesty!'' The Captain inclined his head. ''What dost thou abroad so late o' night?''

Elidor frowned. ''I am thy King! Art thou so ill-bred as not to know the proper form of greeting? Uncover, knaves, and bow!''

Rod held his breath.

The soldiers glanced at the Captain, whose eyes were locked with Elidor's. But the boy-King held his chin high, glance not wavering an inch. Finally, the Captain nodded.

The guardsmen slowly removed their helmets and bowed.

Their pikes leaped to life, slamming down on the backs of their heads with the flats of their blades. They slumped to the floor with a clatter.

All except the Captain; he didn't have a pike near. He snapped upright, terror filling his face as he stared at his men.

Then the terror turned to rage.

Rod leaped forward.

"Why, what sorcery is this?" the Captain snarled, coming for Elidor and drawing his sword.

The boy stepped back, paling—and Rod shot through the door and slammed into the Captain. He went down with a clatter and a *"whuf!,"* the wind knocked out of him; but his sword writhed around, the point dancing in Rod's face. Rod yanked the sword to one side, rolling the man half-over, and dived in behind him, arm snaking around the Captain's throat. He caught the larynx in his elbow, and squeezed. The Captain kicked and struggled, but Rod had a knee in his back, so all he could do was thrash about.

But Elidor was loose. He darted over to pluck the Captain's helmet, yanked his dagger out, and clubbed down with all his strength, just the way he'd seen Rod do. The Captain heaved, and relaxed with a sigh.

Rod let go and scrambled out. "Well done, Your Majesty! You've got the makings of a King, all right."

"There's more to that than battle," the boy said, frowning.

"Yes, such as wisdom, and knowledge. But a lot of it's the ability to think fast, and the willingness to act, and you've got those. And style and courage—and you've just demonstrated those, too." Rod clapped him on the shoulder, and the boy seemed to visibly expand. "Come on, Your Majesty. I wouldn't say the rest of our party is dying to find out what happened, but they'll be vastly reassured to actually *see* us intact." He ushered the boy out the door.

"Six down and three to go," he whispered as they came up to Gwen and the children in the alcove.

Gwen nodded. " 'Twas well thou followed Elidor. Well, if thou wilt hide thee near the porter, I think I can distract him for thee."

Rod set his palms against his buttocks and leaned back, stretching. "Okay, but give me a minute. I'm beginning to feel it, too."

A few minutes later, he waited just outside the doorway

leading to the giant windlass that controlled the drawbridge. The porter paced the floor inside, humming to himself— trying to stay awake, probably.

Suddenly the rope that held the windlass slipped loose, and the ratchet chattered as the great drum began to turn.

The porter shouted and leaped for the crank-handle.

Rod leaped for the porter, plucked off his helmet, and clubbed him.

A few minutes later, he rejoined Gwen. "All secure. I take it I should run back there and drop the bridge."

"Aye, and raise the portcullis. Yet attend a moment." She turned to Magnus. "Son?"

Magnus was gazing off into space. A few seconds later, he relaxed and turned to her. "The sentries on the towers are asleep."

Gwen nodded at Rod.

He sighed, and trudged back to the windlass. Being a telepath must certainly save a lot of hiking.

The portcullis rose, the drawbridge fell, and Rod almost did, too. He straightened up, aching in every joint; it was getting to be a long day.

"My lord?" Gwen's head poked around the doorway. "Wilt thou join us?"

"Coming," he grumbled, and shuffled toward the doorway. How could she still look so fresh and cheery?

They went across the drawbridge, as fast as Geoffrey and Rod could manage. Fifty feet from the castle, Gwen stopped the party, and shooed them into the shadow of a big rock. She ducked her head around it, staring back at the castle. Curious, Rod peeked around the other side.

He saw the drawbridge slowly rise.

Startled, he darted a glance at Gwen. A wrinkle showed between her eyebrows; her lower lip was caught between her teeth. She was showing the strain—and so she should! That slab of wood had to weigh half a ton!

Cordelia was watching alertly, glancing from Gwen to the drawbridge and back. Finally, Gwen nodded, and Cordelia's face screwed up tight for a second. Then Gwen relaxed with a sigh. "Well done; thou hast indeed secured the winch. Now slip the ratchet on the portcullis, sweeting—yet not altogether; thou dost not wish it to come a-crashing down."

Cordelia frowned darkly for a few minutes, staring at the castle; then Rod heard a muted, deep-toned clang. Cordelia looked up at her mother, and nodded. " 'Tis down."

"Well done." Gwen patted Cordelia's shoulder, and the little girl beamed. Mama turned to Magnus. "Now wake the sentries, that they may think they've only dozed, and that nothing is amiss."

Magnus gazed off into space a moment—it was a long moment, for he *was* tiring—then looked up at Gwen and nodded.

"Well enough." Gwen nodded, satisfied. " 'Twill be at least an hour ere the others awake, and we'll be long gone; let them search." She turned to Rod. "Yet we had best lose no time."

"Agreed," Rod affirmed. "Make sure the sentries are looking the other way for a few minutes, will you? Otherwise, they can't help seeing us on this slope."

"Hmf." Gwen frowned. "I *had* forgot that. Well . . ." She held the frown for a few minutes, then nodded. "They think they hear voices calling, towards the north. Lose no time."

Rod nodded, and darted out across the slope, swinging Geoffrey up to his shoulders. The family followed. A hundred yards farther on and fifty feet lower, they stopped, panting, in the shade of a huge oak tree, sentinel for a crop of woodland.

"Whither away?" Gwen demanded.

Rod caught his breath and pointed southwest. "That way, toward the grove where we came in. After all that talk about the High Warlock's holdout in the northeast, they'll expect us to head for him. They won't think we've got any reason for going back."

"Have we?"

Rod shrugged. "Not that I know of—except that I don't

like travelling in totally unfamiliar territory at night, especially when I'm on the run.''

Gwen nodded. '' 'Tis as wise a course as aught else. Follow Father, children.''

CHAPTER FOURTEEN

Father Al clung to the broomstick for dear life, knuckles white and forearms aching with the strain. At first, flight on so slender a craft had been a heady, delightful thing, almost like flying under his own power; but the sun had risen, and he'd happened to glance down. The world whizzed by below, treetops reaching up to snag at his robe. His stomach had turned over, then done its best to shinny up his backbone to safety. Since then, the ride had been a qualified nightmare. He just hoped the tears in his eyes were due only to the wind.

"Yon," the girl called back to him, "ahead, and below!"

He craned his neck to see over her shoulder. About a hundred meters ahead, a large cottage nestled within a grove, a half-timbered house with a thatched roof, and two outbuildings behind it. Then the ground was rushing up at them, and Father Al clung to the broomstick as he clung to his hope of Heaven, commanding his body to relax. His body didn't listen. The world rolled upward past them, then suddenly rolled back down. He clamped his jaw and swallowed, hard, just barely managing to keep his stomach from using his tongue as a springboard.

Then, incredibly, they had stopped, and solid earth jarred upward against his soles.

"We are come." The witch-girl smiled back at him over her shoulder. Then her brows knit in concern. "Art thou well?"

"Oh, most excellent! Or I will be, soon." Father Al swung his leg over the broomstick and tottered up to her. "A singular experience, maiden, and one I'll value till the end of my days! I thank thee greatly!" He turned, looking about him for a change of subject. "Now. Where shall I find the High Warlock?"

"Oh, within." The girl pointed at the cottage. "Or if he is not, surely his wife will know when he may return. Shall I make thee acquainted with them?"

"Dost thou know them, then?" Father Al asked in surprise.

"Indeed; most all the witchfolk do." She dismounted, picked up her broomstick, and led him toward the house. "They are gentle souls, and most modest; one would scarcely think that they were numbered 'mongst the Powers of the land." They were almost to the door, which was flanked by two flowering bushes. "Their bairns, though, are somewhat mischiev. . ."

"Hold!" one of the bushes barked. "Who seeks to pass?"

Father Al swung round to the bush in astonishment. Then, remembering what the girl had been saying, he realized one of the children was probably hiding inside the leaves, playing a prank. "Good morn," he said, bowing. "I am Father Aloysius Uwell, come hither to call upon the High Warlock and his family."

"Come hither, then, that I may best examine thee," the voice demanded. Rather deep voice, for a child; but the witch-girl was giggling behind him, so Father Al abided by his earlier guess—one of the children. And important to play along with the prank, therefore—nothing endears one to a parent like being cordial to the child. He sighed, and stepped closer to the bush.

"Why dost thou linger?" the voice barked. "Come hither to me now, I say!"

It was coming from behind him.

Father Al turned about, reassessing the situation—there were at least two children involved. "Why, so I do—if thou wilt hold thy place."

The girl giggled again.

"Am I to blame if thine eyes art so beclouded that thou mistakest quite my place of biding?" The voice was coming out of a bush a little to Father Al's left, farther from the house. "Come now, I say!"

Father Al sighed, and stepped toward the bush.

"Nay, here!" the voice cried from another bush, farther off to his left. "Besotted shave-pate, canst thou not tell my bearing?"

"I would, if I could see thee," Father Al muttered, and ambled patiently toward the new bush. Giggling, the girl moved with him.

"Nay, hither!" the voice commanded again, from yet another bush, off to his right and farther from the house. *"Wilt* thou come, I say!"

About then, Father Al began to get suspicious. The voice was plainly leading them away from the house, and he began to think this was no childish prank, but the work of some guardian who didn't trust strangers. "Nay, I'll go no farther! I've come where thou hast said, not once, but several times! If thou dost wish that I should move another step, now show thyself, that I may *see* which way to step!"

"As thou wilt have it," the voice grumbled; and, suddenly, the form of a broad and portly man rose up and came around the bush. Its head was shaven in the tonsure, and it wore a brown monk's robe with a small yellow-handled screwdriver in the breast pocket.

Father Al stared.

The girl burst into a peal of laughter.

"Dost thou not know me, fellow?" the monk demanded. "Wilt thou not kneel to the Abbot of thine own Order?"

"Nay, that will I not," Father Al muttered. Father Cotterson had said the Abbot was on his way back to the monastery, half a kingdom away—what would he be doing here, near a High Warlock's house, at that? Father Al's suspicions deepened, especially since he recognized an element out of folklore. So he began to whistle loudly, untied his rope belt, and took off his cassock. The witch-girl gasped and averted her eyes; then she looked back at him, staring.

"Friar!" the Abbot cried, scandalized. "Dost thou disrobe before a woman?!!? . . . And what manner of garb is it thou wearest beneath?''

"Why, this?" Father Al sang, improvising a Gregorian chant. " 'Tis nought but the coverall all Cathodeans wear, which warms me in winter, and never doth tear.'' He went back to whistling, turning his cassock inside-out.

The Abbot's voice took on a definite tone of menace. "What dost thou mean by this turning of thy coat? Dost thou seek to signify that thou'lt side with the King against me?''

Interesting; Father Al hadn't known the old Church-State conflict was cropping up here. "Why, nay. It means only that . . ." (he put the monk's robe on again, wrong side out, and wrapped it about him) " . . . that I wish to see things as they truly are.''

And before his eyes, the form of the abbot wavered, thinned, and faded, leaving only a stocky, two-foot-high man with a pug-nosed, berry-brown face, large eyes, brown jerkin, green hose, green cap with a red feather, and a smoldering expression. "Who ha' told thee, priest?" he growled. His gaze shifted to the witch-girl. "Not thou, surely! The witch-folk ever were my friends!''

The girl shook her head, opening her lips to answer, but Father Al forestalled her. "Nay, hobgoblin. 'Tis books have taught me, that to dispel glamour, one hath but to whistle or sing, and turn thy coat.''

"Thou'rt remarkably schooled in elfin ways, for one who follows the Crucified one," the elf said, with grudging respect. "Indeed, I thought that thee and thy fellows scarce did acknowledge our existence!''

"Nor did I." In fact, Father Al felt rather dizzy—in spite of what Yorick had told him; he was frantically trying to reevaluate all his fundamental assumptions. "Yet did tales of thee and thy kind all fascinate me, so that I strove to learn all that I could, of worlds other than the one I knew.''

" 'Worlds?' " The elf's pointed ears pricked up. "Strange turn of phrase; what priest would think that any world existed, but this one about us?''

Somehow, Father Al was sure he'd made a slip. "In Philosophie's far realms. . ."

"There is not one word said of things like me, that do defy all reason," the elf snapped. "Tell me, priest—what is a star?"

"Why, a great, hot ball of gas, that doth . . ." Father Al caught himself. "Uh, dost thou see, there is writing of seven spheres of crystal that surround the Earth. . ."

" 'Earth?' Strange term, when thou most assuredly dost mean 'world.' Nay, thou didst speak thy true thought at the first, surprised to hear such a question from one like me— and, I doubt not, thou couldst tell me also of other worlds, that do swing about the stars, and heavenly cars that sail between them. Is it not so? I charge thee, priest, to answer truly, by thy cloth—dost thou not believe a lie to be a sin?"

"Why, so I do," Father Al admitted, "and therefore must I needs acknowledge the truth whereof thou speakest; I could indeed tell thee of such wonders. But. . ."

"And didst thou not ride hither in just such a car, from such another world?" The elf watched him keenly.

Father Al stared at him.

The elf waited.

"Indeed I did." Father Al's brows pulled down. "How would an elf know of such matters? Hast thy High Warlock told thee of them?"

It was the elf's turn to be taken' aback. "Nay, what knowest thou of Rod Gallowglass?"

'That he is, to thee, indeed a puissant warlock—though he would deny it, had he any honesty within him—and doth come, as I do, from a world beyond the sky. Indeed, he doth serve the same Government of Many Stars that governs me, and came, as I did, in a ship that sails the void between the stars."

" 'Tis even as thou sayest, including his denial of his powers." The elf regarded him narrowly. "Dost thou know him, then?"

"We never have met," Father Al evaded. "Now, since

that I have told thee what thou didst wish to know, wilt thou not oblige me in return, and say to me how it can be that elves exist?''

"Why," the elf said craftily, "why not the way that witches do? Thou hast no difficulty understanding why *she* lives." He nodded toward the witch-girl.

"That is known to me; she is like to any other lass, excepting that God gave to her at birth some gifts of powers in her mind; and I can see that, when first her ancestors did come to this world, those who chose to come had each within him some little germ of such-like powers. Thus, as generations passed, and married one another again and yet again, that germ of power grew, until some few were born who had it in good measure."

" 'Tis even as Rod Gallowglass did guess," the elf mused. "Nay, thou art certainly from the realm that birthed him. But tell me, then, if such a marrying within a nation might produce a witch, why might it not produce an elf?''

"It might; it might indeed." Father Al nodded thoughtfully. "Yet were it so, my whistling, and the turning of my coat, would not dispel thy glamour, as was told in Terran legend. Nay, there is something more than mortal's magic in thee. How didst thou come to be?''

"Thou dost see too well for easy liking," the elf sighed, "and I do owe thee truth for truth. I do know that elves are born of forest and of earth, of Oak, and Ash, and Thorn; for we have been here as long as they. And well ought I to know it, for I am myself the oldest of all Old Things!''

The phrase triggered memories, and *Puck of Pook's Hill* came flooding back to Father Al's mind from his childhood. "Why, thou'rt Robin Goodfellow!''

"Thou speakest aright; I am that merry wanderer of the night.'' The elf grinned, swelling a little with pride. "Nay, am I so famous, then, that all beyond the stars do know of me?''

"Well, all worth knowing." Father Al silently admitted to a bit of bias within himself. "For surely, all who know the Puck must be good fellows.''

"Dost thou mean that I should trust thee, then?" Puck

grinned mischievously. "Nay, not so—for some have known me to their own misfortune. Yet I will own thou dost not have the semblance of a villain. Nay, turn thy coat aright, and tell me wherefore thou dost seek Rod Gallowglass."

"Why . . . 'tis thus. . ." Father Al took off his robe, and turned it right side out again, getting his thoughts in order. He pulled it on, and began, "A wizard of a bygone age foresaw that, in our present time, a change would come to thy High Warlock, a transformation that could make him a mighty force, for ill or good—a force so mighty as to cast his shadow over all the worlds that mortal folk inhabit. This ancient wizard wrote this vision down, and sealed it in a letter, so that in our present time, it might be opened and read, and we could learn, in time to aid Rod Gallowglass."

"And bend him toward the good, if thou canst?" Puck demanded. "Which means, certes, *thy* notion of the 'good.' "

"And canst thou fault it?" Father Al stuck out his chin and locked gazes with Puck, hoping against hope as he remembered the long hostility between Christian clergy and faeryfolk, and the diminishing of the faeries' influence as that of the Christ had grown. And Puck glared back at him, no doubt remembering all that, too, but also reassessing the values the clergy preached.

"Nay, in truth, I cannot," the elf sighed finally, "when thou dost live by what thou preachest. Nor do I doubt thy good intention; and elves have something of an instinct, in the knowing of the goodness of a mortal."

Father Al let out a long-held breath. "Then wilt thou lead me to thy Warlock?"

"I would I could," the elf said grimly, "but he hath quite disappeared, and none know where."

Father Al just stared at him, while panic surged up within him. He stood stock-still against it, fighting for calm, silently reeling off a prayer from rote; and eventually the panic faded, leaving him charged for otherworldly battle. "Admit me to his wife and bairns, then; mayhap they hold a clue they know not of."

But Puck shook his head. "They have vanished with him,

friar—all but one, and he's so young he cannot speak, nor even think in words.''

"Let me gaze upon him, then." Father Al fixed Puck with a hard stare. "I have some knowledge gleaned, sweet Puck; I may see things that thou dost not.''

"I doubt that shrewdly," Puck said sourly, "yet on the chance of it, I'll bring thee to him. But step warily, thou friar—one sign of menace to the child, and thou'lt croak, and hop away to find a lily pad to sit on, and wilt pass the rest of thy days fly-catching with a sticky tongue of wondrous length!''

He turned away toward the cottage. Father Al followed, with the witch-girl.

"Dost thou think that he could truly change me into a frog?" Father Al asked softly.

"I do not doubt it," the girl answered, with a tremulous smile. "The wisest heads may turn to asses', when the Puck besets them!''

They passed through the door, and Father Al paused, amazed at the brightness and coziness of the house, the sense of comfort and security that seemed to emanate from its beams and rough-cast walls, its sturdy, homely table, benches, chests, two great chairs by the fire, and polished floor. If he looked at it without emotion, he was sure it would seem Spartan—there were so few furnishings. But it was totally clean, and somehow wrapped him in such a feeling of love and caring that he was instantly loath to leave. Somehow, he knew he would like the High Warlock's wife, if he should be lucky enough to meet her.

Then his gaze lit on the cradle by the fire, with the two diminutive, wizened old peasant-ladies by it—elf-wives! They stared up at him fearfully, but Puck stepped up with a mutter and a gesture, and they drew back, reassured. Puck turned, and beckoned to the priest.

Father Al stepped up to the cradle, and gazed down at a miniature philosopher.

There was no other way to describe him. He still had that very serious look that the newborn have—but this child was nearly a year old! His face was thinner than a baby's ought to be; the little mouth turned down at the corners. His hair was black, and sparse. He slept, but Father Al somehow had the impression that the child was troubled.

So did the witch-girl. She was weeping silently, tears streaming down her cheeks. "Poor mite!" she whispered. "His mind doth roam, searching for his mother!"

"Even in his *sleep?*"

She nodded. "And I cannot say where he doth seek; his thoughts veer off beyond my ken."

Father Al frowned. "How can that be?" Then he remembered that the child was too young to have gained the mental framework that gives the human mind stability, but also limits. He found himself wondering where that little mind could reach to—and if, in a grown man, such searching would produce insanity.

He looked back at the child, and found its eyes open. They seemed huge in the tiny face, and luminous, and stared up at him with the intensity of a fanatic. Father Al felt an eldritch prickling creep over his scalp and down his back, and knew to the depths of his soul that this was an extremely unusual baby. "Child," he breathed, "would that I could stay and watch thine every movement!"

"Thou mayest not," Puck said crisply.

Father Al turned to the elf. "Nay, more's the pity; for my business is with the father, not the child. Tell me the manner of his disappearance."

Puck frowned, like a general debating whether or not to release classified information; then he shrugged. " 'Tis little enough to tell. Geoffrey—the third bairn—disappeared whilst at play. They called the High Warlock back from council with the King and Abbot, and he drew from his eldest son the place exact where the child had vanished, then stepped there himself—and promptly ceased to be. His wife and other bairns ran after him, dismayed, and, like him, disappeared."

Father Al stared at the elf, while his mind raced through a dozen possible explanations. It could've been enchantment, of course, but Father Al wasn't quite willing to surrender rationality that completely just yet. A space-warp or time-warp? Unlikely, on a planet's surface—but who could say it was impossible?

Then he remembered Yorick, and his claim to be a time-traveller. It could be, it could be. . .

He cleared his throat. "I think that I must see this place."

"And follow them?" Puck shook his head with a sour smile. "I think that five lost are enough, good friar."

Father Al hadn't really thought that far ahead, but now that Puck mentioned it, he felt a creeping certainty. "Nay, I think that thou has said it," he said slowly, "for where'er thy High Warlock has gone, it could be just such a journey that could wake in him the Power that he knows not of. And I must be there, to guide him in its use!"

"Art thou so schooled in witchcraft, priest?" Puck fairly oozed sarcasm.

"Not in witchcraft, but in the ways of various magics." Father Al frowned. "For, look you, elf, 'tis been my life's study, to learn to know when a mortal is possessed of a demon and when he's not; and to prove how things that seem to be the work of witchcraft, are done by other means. Yet in this study, I've of necessity learned much of every form of magic known to mortals. Never have I ever thought *real* magic could exist; yet that letter that I told thee of warned us that Rod Gallowglass would gain real magic power. Still do I think his strength will prove to be of origins natural, but rare; yet even so, he'll need one to show him its true nature, and to lead him past the temptations toward evil that great power always brings."

"I scarcely think Rod Gallowglass needs one to teach him goodness—an should he, I doubt me not his wife is equal to the task." But doubt shadowed Puck's eyes. "Yet I'll bring thee to the place. Thence, 'tis thy concern."

The witch-girl stayed behind, to help with the baby if she could. Puck led Father Al down a woodland path—and the priest kept an eye on the direction of the sun, whenever it poked through the leaves, to make sure he was being led in a definite direction. Finally, they came out into a meadow. A hundred meters away, a pond riffled under a light breeze, bordered by a few trees. A huge black horse lifted its head, staring at them; then it came trotting from the pool.

" 'Tis the High Warlock's charger, Fess," Puck explained. "An thou dost wish to follow after his master, thou first must deal with him." And, as the horse came up to them: "Hail, good Fess! I present to thee a goodly monk, whose interest in thy master doth to me seem honest. Tell him who thou art, good friar."

Well! Father Al had heard that elves had an affinity for dumb animals—but this was going a bit far! Nonetheless, Puck seemed sincere, and Father Al hated to hurt his feelings . . . "I am Father Aloysius Uwell, of the Order of St. Vidicon of Cathode . . ." Was it his imagination, or did the horse prick up its ears at the mention of the good Saint's name? Well, St. Vidicon had influence in a lot of odd places. "I am hither come to aid thy master, for I've been vouchsafed word that he might find himself in peril, whether he did know of it or not."

The horse had a very intent look about him. Father Al must've been imagining it. He turned to Puck. "Canst thou show me where the High Warlock did vanish?"

"Yon," Puck said, pointing and stepping around Fess toward the pond. "Indeed, we've marked the place."

Father Al followed him.

The great black horse sidestepped, blocking their path.

" 'Tis as I feared," Puck sighed. "He'll let no one near the spot."

Suddenly, Father Al was absolutely certain that he *had* to follow Rod Gallowglass. "Come now! Certes no horse, no matter how worthy, can prevent . . ." He dodged to the side, breaking into a run.

The horse reared up, pivoted about, and came down, its forefeet thudding to earth just in front of the priest.

Puck chuckled.

Father Al frowned. "Nay, good beast. Dost not know

what's in thy master's interest?'' He backed up, remembering his college gymnastics.

Fess watched him warily.

Father Al leaped into a run, straight at the great black horse. He leaped high, grasping the front and back of the saddle, and swung his legs up in a side vault.

Fess danced around in a half-circle.

Father Al hit the ground running—and found himself heading straight for Puck. The elf burst into a guffaw.

Father Al halted and turned around, glowering at Fess. ''A most unusual horse, good Puck.''

''What wouldst thou expect, of the High Warlock's mount?''

''Apparently somewhat less than he doth expect of me.'' Father Al hitched up his rope belt. ''But I know better now.'' He set himself, watching Fess with narrowed eyes; then he raced straight at the horse, and veered to the left at the last second. Fess danced to the left, too, but Father Al was already zagging to the right. Fess reversed engines with amazing speed, getting his midsection solidly in front of the priest—and Father Al ducked under his belly.

Fess sat down.

Puck roared with laughter.

Father Al came reeling out of the fray, staggering like a drunk. ''I think . . . a change of tactics . . . might be in order.''

''So I think, too.'' Puck grinned, arms akimbo. ''Therefore, try sweet reason, priest.''

Father Al frowned down at him, remembering Puck's legendary fondness for helping mortals make fools of themselves. Then he shrugged and turned back to Fess. ''Why not? The situation's so ridiculous, why should a little more matter?'' He stepped up to the beast. ''Now, look thou, Fess—thy master's sore endangered. It may be that I may aid him.''

Fess shook his head.

Father Al stared. If he didn't know better, he would've thought the horse had understood him.

Then he frowned—just a coincidence, no doubt. "We had a letter. It was writ a thousand years agone, by a man long dead, who foretold us that, in this time and place, one Rod Gallowglass would wake to greater power of magic than mortals ever knew."

The horse moved to the side, tossing its head as though it was beckoning.

Father Al stared. Then he squeezed his eyes shut, gave his head a quick shake; but when he looked again, the horse was still beckoning. He shrugged, and followed, ignoring Puck's chortle.

Fess was standing by a patch of bare dirt, scratching at it with a hoof. Father Al watched the hoof, then felt a shiver run through him as he saw what the horse had drawn. There in the dirt, in neat block letters, lay the word "WHO?"

Father Al looked up at the horse, facts adding themselves up in his head. "The High Warlock's horse—and you came with him, from off-planet, didn't you?"

The horse stared at him. Why? Oh. He'd said, "off-planet." Which marked him. "Yes, I'm from off-planet, too—from the Vatican, on Terra. And you. . ." Suddenly, the priest shot a punch at the horse's chest.

It went "bongggggg."

Father Al went, "Yowtch!" and nursed bruised knuckles.

Puck went into hysterics, rolling on the ground.

Father Al nodded. "Very convincing artificial horsehide, over a metal body. And you've a computer for a brain, haven't you?" He stared at the horse.

Slowly, Fess nodded.

"Well." Father Al stood straight, fists on his hips. "Nice to know the background, isn't it? Now let me give you the full story."

He did, in modern English. Fess's head snapped up at the name of Angus McAran; apparently he'd had some contact with the head time-spider before. Encouraged, Father Al kept the synopsis going through his meeting with Yorick, at mention of whose name, Fess gave a loud snort. Well, that had sort of been Father Al's reaction, too.

"So if McAran's right," Father Al wound up, "something's going to happen to Rod Gallowglass, wherever he's gone, that's going to waken some great Power that's been lying dormant in him all along. Whatever the nature of that power, it might tempt him toward evil—without his even realizing it. After all, some things that seem right at the moment—such as revenge—can really lead one, bit by bit, into spiritual corruption, and great evil."

The horse tossed its head, and began to scratch with its hoof. Father Al watched, holding his breath, and saw the words appear: POWER CORRUPTS. He felt relief tremble through him; he was getting through! "Yes, exactly. So you see, it might be to his advantage to have a clergyman handy. But more than a clergyman—I'm also an anthropologist, and my life's study has been magic."

Fess's head came up sharply.

Father Al nodded. "Yes. I suppose you might call me a theoretical magician; I can't work a single spell myself, but I know quite a bit about how a man with magical Power might do so. There's a good chance I might be able to help him figure out how to use his new Power to bring himself and his family back here!"

But Fess lowered his head and scratched in the dirt again: AND A GREATER CHANCE THAT YOU, TOO, WOULD BE LOST.

Father Al thrust out his chin. "That is my concern. I know the risk, and I take it willingly. It's worth it, if I can help this poor fellow and his family—and possibly avert a spiritual catastrophe. Have you considered the possible heresies that might arise, if a man should suddenly seem to have *real* magical powers?"

The horse's eyes seemed to lose focus for a few seconds, and Father Al was impressed; not many computers would have any theology on storage in their memory banks. Then Fess's eyes came back into focus again, and Father Al said quickly, "So I have some vested interest in trying to help your master, you see. Properly instructed, he *could* be a mighty asset to the Church on this planet. But left to himself, he might fall into the temptations that power brings, find a way to return here from wherever he's gone, and become the leader of a heresy that could rock the Terran Sphere. We dare not leave him there.''

The horse lowered his head again, scratching with his hoof: HIS SAFE RETURN IS ALL.

Father Al frowned, puzzling it out, wishing the robot had been equipped with speech. Then he nodded, understanding. "I see. It makes no difference to you if he comes back a heretic or a saint, as long as he comes back. But don't you see, with my knowledge of the workings of magic to aid him, his chances of returning are increased? *Much* increased, if you'll pardon my boasting.''

The synthetic eyes stared intently into Father Al's, for a few minutes that seemed to stretch out into aeons. Then, finally, the great horse nodded, and turned away, beckoning.

"I scarce can credit it!" Puck cried. "Thou hast persuaded him!''

Father Al breathed a huge sigh of relief. "I scarcely can believe it, either. It's the first time in my life I've ever made any headway with a computer.'' He sent up a quick, silent prayer of thanks to St. Vidicon, and followed Fess.

The black horse stopped, and looked back expectantly. Father Al trotted to catch up, and came to a halt to see a line of stones laid in the grass—the threshold of a Gate to—where?

The great black horse stood to the side, waiting.

Father Al looked up at him, took a deep breath, and squared his shoulders. "Wish me luck, then. You may be the last rational being I see for a long, long time.'' And, without giving himself a chance to think about it, he stepped forward. Nothing happened, so he took another step—and another, and another. . .

. . . and suddenly realized that the trees had silver trunks.

CHAPTER FIFTEEN

Gwen stopped suddenly. "Hist!"

"Sure," Rod said agreeably. "Why not?"

"Oh, be still! I catch a trace of something I like not!"

"Pursuit?" Rod turned serious.

Gwen shook her head, frowning. " 'Tis Duke Foidin, and in converse; yet I have only a sense of that which he doth speak with, and it's somewhat threatening." She looked down at her children. "Dost thou sense aught more?"

Silently, they shook their heads. " 'Tis not altogether human, Mama," Magnus contributed.

Out of the corner of his eye, Rod noticed Elidor trembling. He caught the boy's shoulder. "Steady, there, lad. You're with us, now." He turned back to Gwen. "Of course, the wise thing to do would be to sneak on by."

Gwen nodded.

Rod turned away. Silently, they picked their way between white trunks in a dazzle of moonlight reflected off silver leaves. After about ten minutes, Gwen hissed, "It doth grow stronger."

Rod didn't falter. "So they're on our line of march. We'll worry about avoiding them when we know where they are."

Then, suddenly, they were out of the trees, at the top of a rise. Below them, in a natural bowl, rose a small hill. Light glowed around it, from glittering, moving figures.

"The faery knowe!" Elidor gasped.

"Hit the dirt!" Rod hissed. The whole family belly-flopped down in the grass. Rod reached up, and yanked Elidor down. "No insult intended, Majesty," he whispered. "It's simply a matter of safety." He turned to Magnus. "You said the thought-pattern wasn't quite human?"

Magnus nodded. "And therefore could I not comprehend it, Papa."

"Well, you hit it right on the nose." Rod frowned, straining his ears. "Hold it; I think we can *just* make out what they're saying."

Duke Foidin and his knights were easy to pick out by their dimness. They stood almost at the bottom of the bowl, off to Rod's left. The being facing him was taller by a head, and fairly seemed to glow. It had to be the most handsome male that Rod had ever seen, the fluidity of its movement, as it shifted from foot to foot continually, indicating musculature and coordination beyond the human. And he was brilliant; he fairly seemed to glow. His extravagant costume had no color; it had only varying degrees of light. A silver coronet encircled his brow, tucking down behind pointed ears.

"The King of Faery?" Rod hissed to Elidor.

The boy shook his head. " 'Tis a coronet, not a crown. A duke, mayhap, an they have such."

The faery duke's arms chopped against each other. "Be done! All this we've hearkened to aforetime, and found small reason in. This is no cause for we of Faery to embroil ourselves in mortal war."

"Yet think!" Duke Foidin protested, "the High Warlock doth champion the White Christ!"

"As have kings done these last two thousand years," the faery replied.

Two thousand? It should've been more like eight hundred, from the medieval look of this land.

"The priests were threat to us at first," the faery conceded, "yet so was Cold Iron, which came not overlong before them—and we endure. The priests have learned they cannot expunge us, nor we rid ourselves of them."

Duke Foidin took a deep breath. "Then I offer price!"

The faery sneered. "What could a mortal offer that a faery would desire?"

"Mortal wizards," Foidin said promptly, "two—a male and female?"

"Should we seek to breed them, then? Nay; we have some

use for human captives, but wizards would be greater trouble than use, for they'd ever seek to learn our secrets.''

"Children."

The faery stilled.

A stream of pure rage shot through Rod, almost seeming to come from someplace, someone, else, scaring him by its intensity. He'd heard the fairy tales about changelings, aged elves left in mortal cradles for the pretty babes the fairies had carried off. The tradition had it that fairies liked mortal slaves, and definitely preferred to raise them, themselves.

And, somehow, Rod thought he knew which children Foidin had in mind.

Foidin saw the faery duke was interested. "And an infant, not yet a year of age; I'll have it soon."

Rod almost went for him, right then and there. The snake was talking about Gregory!

But Gwen's hand was on his arm, and he forced himself to relax. No, of course not; Foidin didn't know Gregory existed. He wasn't even in this world.

" 'Tis the only mortal thing we value," the faery said slowly, "yet scarcely worth the fighting for. We've ways of gaining mortal children, at far less cost than war."

And he turned on his heel, and strode away.

Duke Foidin stared after him, unbelieving, rage rising. "Thou knavish wraith!" he fairly screamed. "Will nothing move thee?"

The faery duke stopped, then slowly turned, and the air seemed to thicken and grow brittle, charged to breaking. "Why should we of Faery care what mortals do?" His voice grew heavy with menace. "Save to avenge an insult. 'Ware, mortal duke! Thou mayest gain the war which thou dost seek, but with the folk of Faery seeking *thy* heart's blood! Now get thee hence!"

Duke Foidin stood, white-lipped and trembling, aching to lash out, but too afraid.

"Mayhap thou dost doubt our power." The faery duke's voice suddenly dripped with honey. "Then let us show thee how easily we gain all that thou didst offer." And his left hand shot up with a quick circling motion.

Suddenly, unseen cords snapped tight around Rod's body, rolling him over and pinning his arms to his sides and his legs to one another. He let out one terror-stricken, rage-filled bellow; then something sticky plastered itself over his mouth. He could still see, though—see Gwen and the children, even Elidor, bound hand and foot, and gagged, as he was, fairly cocooned in shining cords. Grotesquely ugly sprites leaped out of the grass all about them, stamping in a dance and squealing with delight. Their shaggy clothes looked to be made of bark; they had huge jughead ears, great loose-lipped mouths, and bulbous, warty noses dividing platter-eyes. The biggest of them was scarcely three feet high.

"They ever come, the prying big 'uns!" they cried.

"They never spy the sentry-Spriggans!"

"Well caught, spriggans!" the faery duke called. "Now bring them here!"

The spriggans howled delight, and kicked Rod up to the top of the rise, then shoved him over. Sky and grass whirled about him and about as he rolled down the hill, with spriggans running along, whooping, rhythmically pushing him, as a child rolls a hoop. Panic hit, fear for Gwen and the kids— and behind it, a feeling of some sympathetic Presence, its anger beinning to build with Rod's.

He brought up with a thump against the Duke's feet. Gwen slammed into his back, softening the bumps as the children knocked into her.

Foidin stared down at them, horrified. "Elidor!"

"The King?" The faery duke looked up, interested. "Of great account! We've never had a mortal king to rear!"

Foidin's gaze shot up at him, shocked. Then he glared down at Rod, pale and trembling. "This is thy doing! Thou hast brought the King to this! But . . . how? What? How hast thou brought this thing to pass? I left thee safe, behind stout locks and guards!"

Rod mumbled through his gag.

The faery duke nodded contemptuously. "Allow him speech." A spriggan hopped to pull Rod's gag.

"Yeeeowtch!" The sticky plaster hurt, coming off. He worked his mouth, glaring up at the Duke. "You should know, Milord Duke, that locks and guards cannot hold a warlock, if he does not wish it. Your lock did open without a human hand to touch it; your guards all sleep."

"It cannot be!" the Duke fairly screeched, white showing round the borders of his eyes. "Only magics most powerful can bring such things to pass!"

Rod smiled sourly. "Be more careful of your guests—and hope this faery duke doth hold me fast. For now we have a score to settle, you and I." He felt the touch of the helping spirit again, but its rage was growing—and so was his. "You would have sold all my family, to gain this faery's aid! Be sure that never do I have a chance to come at thee alone— for I'll not trouble to use my magic! And this child . . ." It seemed, now, as though it weren't himself talking, suddenly, but the Presence. ". . . who was this babe you would have sold? How shall you gain possession of it?"

The Duke turned away to hide a sudden look of fear, trembling.

"Turn not away!" Rod barked. "Face me, coward, and give answer—what child was this?"

"Indeed, do stay," the faery duke murmured. "Or wilt thou so straightaway abandon this thy King?"

"The King!" Foidin gasped, whirling back. "Nay, as- suredly, thou shalt not keep him—for if thou dost, my power fails!" He stared at the faery duke, drawn and palsied, nerving himself up to it—then his hand flashed to his sword.

The faery duke snapped his fingers contemptuously, and Foidin doubled over a sudden stabbing pain. "Aieeengggh!"

Gwen seized the moment; Rod's sword shot out of its scabbard to slash his bonds, then whirled to cut Gwen's. Out of the corner of his eye, he saw Magnus's little blade shearing his ropes; then he sailed into the faery duke, knocking him back by sheer surprise, over Rod's knee, Rod's dagger at his throat. "Release my family, milord—or feel cold iron in your veins."

But Magnus had slashed his siblings' bonds, and he and

Geoff were holding off a band of spriggans, who were throwing stones but retreating steadily before the boys' swords. Gwen and Cordelia crouched, waiting, as the faery band ran forward with a shout, glowing blades whipping through the air. "Now!" Gwen cried, and a hail of stones shot toward the faeries, bruising and breaking. Some screamed, but most pressed on—and the thrown stones whirled back to strike at them again.

Duke Foidin saw his chance to curry favor, and whipped out his blade. "Nay, Theofrin," he grunted around his pain, "I will aid thee!" And he leaped forward, blade slashing down at Rod.

Rod had no choice; his sword snapped up to guard, and Theofrin whiplashed out of his arms as though they were rubber. The Duke's blade slid aside on Rod's, but the faery duke Theofrin seized Rod's sword arm, snatched him high, whirled him through the air, and tossed him to the ground as though he'd been a bag of kindling. Rod shouted, and the shout turned into a shriek as he hit and felt something move where it shouldn't. His shoulder screamed raw pain. Through its haze, he struggled to his knees, right arm hanging limp— and saw Theofrin stalking towards him, elf-sword flickering about like a snake's tongue.

Beyond him, Duke Foidin and his men frantically parried faery blades; his try for favor hadn't worked. One courtier howled as a faery blade stabbed through him, and whipped back out; blood spurted from his chest, and he collapsed.

And Theofrin's blade danced closer. Rod whipped out his dagger—what else did he have left? Theofrin sneered, and lunged; Rod parried, but the faery duke had overreached, and Rod flicked his dagger-blade out to nick the faery's hand. The faery shrieked at the touch of cold iron, and clasped his wounded hand, the elfin sword dropping to the ground. Rod staggered to his feet, and waded forward. Theofrin's face contorted with a snarl; his own dagger whisked out, left-handed.

"Papa!" Magnus's scream cut through the battle. Rod's head snapped up; he saw his eldest on the ground, spread-eagled, struggling against invisible bonds. A tall, thin faery stood above him, face lit with glee, as he chopped downward with his sword.

Adrenalin shocked through him, and Rod charged. Theofrin stepped to block his path. Rod barrelled into him, dagger-first, and the faery duke skipped aside with a howl of rage, the cold-iron dagger barely missing his ribs. Then Rod's shoulder caught his son's adversary in the midriff, and the sword-cut went wide, slicing his dangling right hand. Rod bellowed with the pain, but caught the hilt and wrenched the sword free. He howled again; it was cold, burning his flesh like dry ice; but he clung to it, lunging after the faery, stabbing. The sword cut into the faery's belly, and it folded with a scream, sprawling on the ground. Rod didn't stay to see if it were dead; he whirled back to his son, and saw the blood flowing from Magnus's shoulder as he struggled up on one elbow, the invisible bonds gone with the faery whose spell had forged them. "Magnus!" Rod clasped the boy to him. "What've they done to you!"

"Just . . . a cut . . ." the boy choked out. His eyes had lost focus. "Couldn't break his spell, Papa . . . Strange . . . too strong . . ." Then he collapsed across Rod's arm.

Panic shot through Rod as he stared at his eldest son, dread clawing up into his throat. It couldn't be—so full of life! He couldn't be. . .

"Dead?"

A metal point pricked his throat. Rod looked up, and saw Theofrin grinning down, with glowing, gloating eyes. "Dead, as thou shalt be! Yet not too quickly. I'll have thine entrails forth for this fell insult, mortal, and pack hot coals in their place, whilst yet thou livest! Thy wife shall be our drudge and whore, thy children slaves, with torques about their necks!" His mouth twisted in contempt. "Warlock, dost thou name thyself? An thou hadst been such, there'd have truly been a battle royal! Hadst thou been Lord Kern, now, our faery ropes would have crumbled ere they touched thee; our spriggans would have turned to stone! Cold iron in a thousand guises would have filled the air about thee, and thine every step would have waked the sound of church bells!''

Then Rod heard Gwen scream in rage. He darted a glance toward her, saw her kneeling with Cordelia and Geoffrey clasped against her. She had caught three fallen swords with her mind, and they wove a deadly dance about her, warding off a dozen faery courtiers; but the faeries' blades all flickered closer, closer. . .

''They are not done with her, quite yet,'' Theofrin said. ''They'll play with her a while longer, then beat down her witch-swords. Then will they play with her again, and her witchling with her. When that is done, if they feel merciful, they may then slay them.'' His eyes gleamed with a chill, self-satisfied light.

Rod glared up at him, terror for his family boiling into anger. He shot that energy into a craving wish for steel to fill the air, for church bells to ring—anything, to banish this fell faery!

And up beneath his rage it mounted, that sense of a kindly, outraged presence, a spirit other than his, reassuring him, but smashing out with all Rod's rage in one huge hammer blow.

Distantly, a bell began to toll.

Closer at hand, another bell began to peal.

Then another joined it, and another, north, east, south, and west—and more, and more, till the bells in every village church for miles around must have been clamoring.

He'd done it! He'd broken through his barrier, through to Gwen—and she'd set the bells to ringing!

The faery duke looked up, horrified; his glow seemed to dim. Then he threw back his head and let out a howl of rage. It echoed from every side as his court picked it up, till the whole of the glen was one huge scream.

Then, still screaming, they flew. A door swung open in the mound, and the faery folk lifted off the ground and whisked away toward it, like dry leaves borne on a whirlwind.

The duke tarried a moment, glaring down at Rod. ''I know not by what magics thou hast wrought this, wizard—yet be assured, I shall avenge it!'' Then he shot up off the ground and towards the mound, with a long, drawn-out scream of wrath, that dwindled and cut off as the mound's door shut. For minutes more, there was screaming still, muted and distant, inside the knowe; then all was quiet. Moonlight showed a peaceful glen, silver leaves tinkling in the breeze; only a circle of flattened grass remained, to show where the fairies had danced.

And the Duke Foidin, and his henchmen. The Duke stood staring at the fairy mound; then, slowly, his eyes moved over the glen, till they fastened on Rod. He stared; then a leering grin broke his face, and he moved forward.

Slowly, Rod laid Magnus's body down and rose to his feet, albeit shakily, dagger at the ready.

Gwen turned and saw. Then she shifted her gaze, seeking and finding Rod's fallen sword. It lifted itself from the ground and shot to his side, point toward Duke Foidin, circling in the air. Through the numbed sorrow that filled him, Rod felt the comfort of her support. "Whoever dies, milord, thou shalt be first."

The Duke and his train stopped, grins vanishing. Foidin's eyes flicked from the floating sword to Rod's dagger, then to Rod's dangling arm, but back to the sword. He licked his lips, and swallowed. "Deliver up mine ward and nephew."

"He comes with me," Rod grated.

The Duke's face darkened; he glanced back at his men, who glanced at one another. Hands felt for sword hilts, but they darted uneasy glances at Rod.

Gwen whispered to Cordelia, and the little girl stared at the sword. Gwen transferred her gaze to a three-foot-high boulder fifty feet from the Duke. It shuddered, then rocked, then began to topple, to roll—over and over, faster and faster, right at the Duke and his men.

The courtiers broke, and fled. The Duke stayed an instant longer, to cast a venomous glance at Rod; then he ran, too.

Rod glared after them.

Little Elidor breathed out a shaky sigh.

The little sound broke Rod's trance; he dropped to the ground beside Magnus's still form. "Gwen! Quickly!"

And she was there. She stared at her son, horrified.

Rod's thumb was on the inside of Magnus's wrist. "There's still a pulse. . ."

"Quickly, children!" Gwen snapped. "Four-leafed clovers, red verbena, and St. John's Wort!" Leaning forward, she ripped open Rod's doublet and stripped the bandage from his wound. " 'Twill do, until they find afresh! He needs it now!" She tore the poultice free; Rod winced, and watched as she flipped the fresh side down with one hand as she yanked Magnus's doublet loose with the other. She pressed the poultice down. "Ah, if only chanting spells could work!"

It seemed reasonable—or at least, in harmony with everything else that'd been happening here. A strange sort of dizziness took hold of Rod, and with it came again that sense of a stern but kindly presence. His lips opened, and he found himself chanting,

"Red blood rise, to fill Life's way;
Close the wounds of weapons fey!
The elfin power hath lost its sway;
Warrior, rise, to greet the day."

Gwen shot him a startled glance.

His right arm gave a terrific wrench, and something popped. Rod clasped his shoulder with a gasp of pain. "Hahhhh . . . aieeee!" He gulped air, and swallowed hard. The glen swam before his eyes, then steadied, and the pain ebbed to a dull ache.

"My lord! What tortures thee?"

"Nothing—now." Rod massaged his shoulder, marvelling. He moved his arm; it was stiff, and ached, but it worked. "Never mind me! How's Magnus?" He looked down, and saw the color returning to the boy's face. Gwen stared, then slowly peeled back the poultice. Beneath it, only a faint red line marked the sword-cut. Rod could scarcely hear her whisper: "He is healed!" Her head snapped up; she stared into Rod's eyes. "Where didst thou learn that charm?"

Rod shook his head slowly. "Just came to mind . . . Uh—it *was* you who rang the church bells, wasn't it?"

Her gaze held his; she slowly turned her head from side to side.

They knelt in silence, gazes locked.

Then Rod looked away. "There *was* a feeling—a sense of some . . . something . . . helping. . ."

"A spirit?" Gwen demanded softly.

Rod shrugged. "Good a name for it as any. . ."

Magnus groaned.

They both bent over him, holding their breath.

He levered himself up on his elbows, frowning and blinking. "Papa . . . sorry. . ."

"Sorry? For what?"

"For that . . . I had to cry for aid. 'Twas . . . full puissant magic, do you see. The strength alone, I might have met, but . . . 'twas strange, unlike to any I had dealt with aforetime."

Rod met Gwen's gaze. "That makes sense; whatever kind of magic these elves use, it's probably not psionic. What kind of place *is* this, anyway?"

"One, I think, where magic truly reigns. Thou didst heal thy son with a spoken chant, didst thou not?"

"Well, yes—but the words just focused the power that did the healing."

Gwen's eyes widened. "Hast *thou* such power?"

"Well, it was in me at the time." Rod frowned. "That 'spirit' that I told you of. Or maybe it *was* me . . . Well, it doesn't matter." He looked back down at Magnus. "Just how well *are* you, son?"

"I do feel stiff—but strong as ever." Before they could stop him, Magnus rolled to his knees and stood. He took a few tentative steps, then nodded. "I do feel wearied, Papa—but I am well."

Rod let out a huge, shaky sigh of relief. "Well, whatever

magic it was that did it, I'm all in favor of it!''

"Yet what was it, indeed?" Gwen wondered. "Or . . . whose?''

"I'm not so sure I want to know the answer to that," Rod said slowly. "Come on, let's get moving. As soon as Duke Foidin gets back to his castle, we're going to have an army on our heels."

CHAPTER SIXTEEN

Not only had the trees changed—so had the time of day. It had been morning when Father Al stepped past Fess, over the line of stones; now it was night, with rays of moonlight sifting down through the tinsel leaves. He caught his breath at the beauty of the woodland glade. *Yes. There could be magic here.*

Then he remembered his mission, and looked about him to see if he could find evidence of the Gallowglasses. The mold of the forest floor was thoroughly churned up; a number of people had been walking about, surely. Bending closer, he was able to distinguish the prints of small feet and large ones; the Gallowglasses and their children, surely. He straightened up and looked about him; immediately he saw two tracks going away from him: a small one and a broad one. He weighed the evidence and decided the small track was a preliminary foray, while the broad one would be the whole family moving together. It was an easy enough trail to follow—last year's fallen, moldering leaves were scuffed up; twigs were broken; and small plants had been trodden down. He wasn't too far behind them, then—certainly no more than 24 hours. And if he hurried . . . He set off, following the moonlit trail.

He'd gone about twenty paces before he happened to glance up and see a blaze on a treetrunk.

He halted, grinning with delight. How considerate of them, to leave him so clear a way to follow! Not that they'd meant it for that purpose, of course—how could they have known someone would come after them? No doubt they'd wanted to make sure they could find their way back to the point they'd come from; presumably, it was the only place where this world was linked to their own.

World?

He looked about him, and silently revised that opinion. Silver trees had never grown on Terra, nor on any planet he'd ever heard of. Scarcely conclusive proof, that, but still . . . The chilling thought crept in that he might not even be in his own universe and, for the first time, it occurred to him that he should perhaps be concerned about getting back home.

Curiously, he wasn't. If God wanted him to return to Gramarye, or Terra, no doubt He would make the means available. And if He didn't, well, Father Al had long ago decided to do whatever work God sent him, wherever it should be. Dying on the planet of his birth mattered little, compared with doing God's will.

So he turned ahead and sauntered away between the forest trees, following the trail of blazes, and whistling—and not just out of good spirits.

He came out onto the bank of a stream, and looked to either side, to see which had trees with—What the blazes! Nothing! Not a single trunk was marked!

Of course—they would be returning back along the river bank; *they'd* know which direction they'd gone in. The stream itself was enough of a trail. They only needed to know at which tree to turn back into the wood.

Here was a knotty problem. Which way had they gone? Left, or right? Upstream, or down?

"Well met by moonlight, handsome stranger."

She rose up out of the water, dark hair shimmering over her shoulders to cloak her breasts—and that was all that did. Her eyes were large, and slanted; her nose was small, but her mouth was wide, with full, red lips, and her skin was very pale. "How fortunate am I," she purred, "that hath found a gentleman to company me." She waded toward him, up out of the water. As she rose, watercress draped itself about her hips in a token tribute of modesty. Father Al managed to wrench his gaze back to her face, feeling the responses in his body that reminded him that priests are human, too. He swallowed thickly, turned his lips inward to wet them, and muttered. "Greetings, Lady of the Waters."

"No lady I," she murmured, "but a wanton, eager to do the bidding of a mortal man." She twined her arms about his neck and pressed up against him.

It ran counter to every demand his body screamed, but Father Al pulled her arms loose, gently but firmly, and pressed her hands together in front of his chest, forcing her body away from his. She stared at him in surprise. "How now! Do not deny that thou dost want me!"

"I do," Father Al admitted, "but 'twould be wrongful." He glanced down at her fingers, and noticed the tiny, vestigial webs between them.

"Wrongful, because thou art a mortal, and I a nymph?" She laughed, revealing small, perfect, very white teeth. "Come, now! It hath been often done, and always to the man's delight!"

Delight, yes—but Father Al remembered some old tales, of how a water-maid's seduction had led to death—or, failing that, to a steadily-worsening despair that had surely torn apart the mortal lover's soul. He clung to the memory to give him strength, and explained, "It must not be—and the fact that I am human and you are not has little enough to do with it; for see you, lass, if thou dost give out favors of thy body where thou art lusted for, but are not loved, thou dost break thine own integrity."

"Integrity?" She smiled, amused. " 'Tis a word for mortals, not for faery folk."

"Not so," Father Al said sternly, "for the word means 'wholeness,' the wholeness of thy soul."

She laughed, a dazzling cascade of sound. "Surely thou dost jest! The faery folk have no immortal souls!"

"Personalities, then." Father Al was miffed at himself for having forgotten. "Identity. The sum and total of thyself, that which makes thee different, unique, special—not quite like any other water-nymph that ever was."

She lost her smile. "I think thou dost not jest."

"Indeed, I do not. Thy identity, lass, thy true self, hidden away and known only to thyself, is what thou really art. 'Tis founded on those few principles that thou dost truly and most deeply believe in—those beliefs which, when manners and graces and fashions of behaving are all stripped away, do still remain, at the bottom and foundation of thy self.''

"Why, then," she smiled, "I am a wanton; for in my deepest self, my chiefest principle is pleasure sexual." And she tried to twine her arms about his neck again.

Well, Father Al had heard *that* one before, and not just from aquatic women, either. He held her hands firmly, and held her gaze, looking deeply into her eyes. " 'Tis an excuse, I trow, and will not serve. Some male hath wronged thee deeply, when thou wast young and tender. Thou didst open thy heart to him, letting him taste thy secret self, and didst therefore open, too, thy body, for it seemed fully natural that the one should follow the other."

She stared at him, shocked, then suddenly twisted, trying to yank herself free. "I'll not hear thee more!"

"Assuredly, thou wilt," he said sternly, holding her wrists fast, "for this young swain, when he had had his fill of thee, tore himself away, and tore a part of thy secret self with him. Then went he on his merry way, whistling, and sneering at thee—and thou wast lost in sorrow and in pain, for he had ripped away a part of thine inner self that never could be brought and mended back."

"Mortal," she fairly shrieked, "art thou crazed? I am a *nymph!*"

Father Al had heard that one before, too. "It matters not. There was never a thinking creature made to tear her secret self to bits, and toss the pieces out to passers-by; thus thou wouldst slowly shred thy secret self away, till nought was left, and thou didst not truly exist—only a walking shell would then be left. And this doth happen whenever thou dost open thy body to one who loves thee not, and whom thou dost not love. That breaks the wholeness of thy secret self, for we are made in such a wise that our inner selves and bodies are joined as one, and when the one doth open, the other should.

So if thou dost open thy body while keeping thy secret self enclosed, thou dost break the wholeness of thy self.''

"A thousand times have I so done," she sneered, "yet I am whole within!"

"Nay, thou'rt not. Each time, a tiny piece of thee hast gone, though thou didst strive to know it not.''

"Nay, not so—for 'tis my nature to give my body and retain my self untouched! I am a *nymph!*''

"This is a thin excuse that thou didst first concoct, when first thy secret self was torn. Thou then didst say, 'It matters not; I am untouched. This is my nature, to give of my body and not of my soul; mine only true desire is pleasure.' And to prove it to thyself, thou didst seek to couple with every male that happened by—yet each time, thou wast more torn, and didst need to prove it more—so thou didst seek out more to pleasure thee, quite frantically—though in thy depths, thou knew it pleasured thee not at all. For in truth, 'twas only an excuse.''

"And what of thee?" she demanded angrily. "Why dost thou rant thus at me? Why dost thou make me stay to listen, when I would turn away? Is not this thine own excuse, for the hot lust that doth throb within thee at the sight of me?''

Touché, Father Al thought. "It is indeed. Yet hath mine excuse done harm to thee? Or me?''

She frowned prettily, searching his eyes. "Nay . . . none to me. Yet I think that it doth harm to thee—for what is natural to thyself would be to grapple me, and couple here in wildness and in frenzy.''

"Thou dost read me shrewdly," Father Al admitted. "Yet though 'tis 'natural,' lass, it is not right—for thereby would a part of me be ripped away, even as a part of thee would.'' He sighed. "It is a male conceit that a woman's self may be rended by a one-night's coupling, while the man's is not— but 'tis only a conceit. We, too, are made all of one piece, body and soul so shrewdly welded together that we cannot give of the one without giving of the other. And we, too, can be rended by a first coupling with a one who loves us not, and may seek to deny that hurt by seeking to lie with every maid we may. Thus is the legend born of prowess male, and many a young man's soul is rended by the promiscuity that comes of thus attempting to prove himself a legend—which is to say, a ghost. But if young men would speak the truth, they would own that there is little enough pleasure in it—for loveless coupling, at the moment when pleasure should transform itself to ecstasy, truly turns itself to ashes, and the taste of gall.''

''I think,'' she said slowly, ''that thou dost speak from hurt that thou hast known.''

He smiled ruefully. ''All young men commit the same mistakes; all step upon the brush that covers o'er the pitfall, no matter how loudly their seniors blare the warnings in their ears. I was once young; and I was not always of the Cloth.''

Her eyes widened in horror. She leaped back, looking him up and down in one quick glance, and pressed her hands to her mouth. ''Thou art a monk!''

He smiled. ''Hadst thou only seen that I was male?''

She nodded, eyes huge.

''If thou hadst looked, thou wouldst have known that I did not walk the stream-banks in search of pleasure.''

''Nay, that follows not,'' she said with a frown, ''for I have known—Nay, never mind. Yet if thou didst not hither come for sport, why *hast* thou come?''

''Why, I do seek an husband, wife, and children three,'' Father Al said slowly. ''They would have come out from this wood some time ago, mayhap whilst sunlight shone. Wouldst thou have seen them?''

''Indeed I did,'' the nymph said slowly, ''they woke me from my daytime sleep—the wee ones made some noise, thou knowest.''

''I do indeed.'' Father Al had delivered sermons at family churches. ''Canst thou say which way they went?''

She shook her head. ''I did not look so long. One quick glance sufficed to show a woman with them—and she was quite beautiful.'' The nymph seemed irritated by the memory. ''I saw no prospect of a satisfaction there, though the man and boys were comely—so I sought my watery bed again.''

''Out upon it!'' Father Al glared up at the leaves, clenching a fist. ''How can I tell which way to go?''

''If 'tis a matter of so great an import to thee,'' the nymph said slowly, ''mayhap that I can aid. Do thou sit here, and wait, and I will quickly course the stream, and seek for sign of them.''

''Wouldst thou, then!'' Father Al cried. ''Now, there's a wench for thee! Why, thank thee, lass! The blessings of. . .''

''I prithee, hold!'' The nymph held up a hand. ''Name not thy Deity, I beg thee! Do thou abide; I'll search.'' She ducked under the water, and was gone.

Father Al stared after her a moment; then he sighed, and lowered himself carefully to the river bank. Not so young as he had been—but still too young for comfort in some ways, eh? He wondered if his hectoring had done any good, if the nymph would even remember it. Probably not; the young never seemed to learn where sex was concerned, and she was eternally young. Nice of her to offer to help, though—or had it just been a convenient excuse for getting away from a garrulous old man?

With that thought in his head, he sat there on tenterhooks, tense in waiting, wondering if the nymph would even return.

Then, suddenly, the water clashed in front of him, and the nymph rose up, pushing her hair back from her face. ''They come, good monk. Back up the stream-bank they do wander.'' She pointed downstream. ''Though why, I cannot say.''

''A thousand blessings on thee!'' Father Al cried, surging to his feet. The nymph gasped in horror, and disappeared in a splash.

Father Al stared at the widening ripple-rings, biting his tongue in consternation at his *faux pas*. Well, no doubt she'd realize he'd just been carried away, and would credit him with good intentions.

Then he turned away, the nymph receding to the back of

his mind, and plunged into the underbrush that lined the bank, heading back into the trees and downstream, excitement rising high within him at the thought of finally meeting the Gallowglasses.

CHAPTER SEVENTEEN

They dodged through the silver woods, trusting to Gwen's sense of direction, until they came out on the lake-shore. Rod sighed with relief. "Okay, into the water. If they're tracking us with hounds, we want to break the trail." He was about to jump in when he noticed his family all hanging back. "Hey, what's the matter? Jump in!"

"My lord," Gwen said delicately, "it doth occur to us to remember the *Each Uisge*. . ."

"What of it? It's dead!"

"Aye; but it may not have been alone. We know so little of this land. . ."

Rod felt a sudden dislike of water, himself. "Uh . . . how about it, Elid . . . uh, Your Majesty? Are there other unfriendly beasties in the water?"

"Oh, aye!" Elidor said promptly. "There do be Fuathan of all sorts and shapes! Shellycoats, peallaidhs, fideal, urisks, melusines. . ."

"Uh, I think that's enough," Rod interrupted. "We'll take our chances with the hounds."

They moved along the lake-shore. It was quicker going; the trees didn't come down right to the water's edge; they generally had a path at least two feet wide.

"We do seem to have come into a country with a rather strange population," Rod admitted to Gwen.

"We do indeed," she agreed. "The Faery, and some of the spirits Elidor doth mention, I have heard of—yet some are total strangers. Can we be in Gramarye, Rod?"

Rod shrugged. "Sure. Given a population of latent telepaths, who can persuade witch-moss to adopt any shape

179

they're collectively thinking of, and a thousand years to work in, who can say *what* would show up?''

''Yet I cannot think the elves would disappear,'' Gwen pointed out, ''and some magics that the faery duke did speak of, no witch or warlock in all Gramarye possesseth.''

''True,'' Rod admitted, ''both points. The spriggans' ropes *are* something new—and so is making them crumble to dust *before* they touched Lord Kern—if the faery duke wasn't just making that up. Still, I could see a way telekinesis might do that. But, turning faeries to stone? No. That's *really* new—if he meant it literally.''

''Yet if we be on Gramarye,'' Gwen said softly, ''where do we be?''

''Nice question.'' Rod looked up at the starry sky above the lake. ''Could be anywhere, dear. McAran's time machine was a matter-transmitter as well as a time-shifter. I suppose we could be on any world, around any star in the universe.'' He frowned, squinting up at the sky. ''Though, come to think of it, there's something familiar about those constellations . . .'' He shook his head. ''Can't place it. But I *know* I've seen that stellar layout before!''

''Yet 'tis not the sky of Gramarye,'' Gwen said softly.

Rod was silent for a moment. Then, slowly, he shook his head. ''No, dear. It's not.''

They walked silently for a few minutes, looking away from the sky and down toward the ground, hand in hand. The children picked up Gwen's thoughts, and crowded close for comfort. Elidor watched, not understanding, alone and to the side.

Gwen reached out and gathered him in. ''Well, 'tis not so great a blow as all that; I've had suspicions. There're far too few folk here with any Power, for it to ha' been our Isle of Gramarye.''

''Yes,'' Rod said somberly. ''We haven't run into so much as a telepath. Not that I'm used to having people read *my* thoughts . . .'' He looked up at Gwen, frowning. ''Strange, isn't it? When I first came to Gramarye, the Queen's witches could read my mind—but by the time I met you, no one could.''

"Oh, really?" said a mellow baritone behind him. "That's interesting!"

Rod whirled about.

A friar in a brown robe with a black rope belt picked his way through the trees toward them. Moonlight gleamed off his tonsure. "Can you think of anything that could cause that effect?"

"Not offhand," Rod said slowly. "And you'll pardon my noticing that you don't quite speak like the rest of the local population."

"Not surprising; I'm from out of this world." The friar thrust out a hand. "Father Aloysius Uwell, at your service."

"I hope so." Rod searched the man's face. He was definitely on the fat side, with brown hair and a library pallor, wide, frank eyes, and a firm mouth; and something immensely likeable about him. Rod warmed to him, albeit reluctantly. He took Father Uwell's hand. "Good to meet you." Then he noticed the tiny yellow screwdriver in the priest's breast pocket. "You're a Cathodean!"

"Is that so surprising?" Father Uwell smiled. "I told you I wasn't of this world."

"Or the next?" But Rod couldn't help smiling. "What world *are* you from?"

"McCorley, originally—but I've been on Terra, at the Vatican, for the last twenty years. Except for jaunts to trouble-spots, of course—such as Gramarye."

"Gramarye?" Rod's eyebrows shot up. "So you came in the same way we did?"

"Yes, and it wasn't very easy, I don't mind telling you! Here I've been outbound from Terra for most of a month, just to meet you—and when I get to Gramarye, I find you've just left! Not very hospitable of you, sir."

"Uh, yeah, well, I'm sorry, but your reservation got mislaid. Pardon my curiosity, but I wouldn't think the Vatican would even have *heard* about me, let alone have been interested in me!"

"We hadn't, until the Pope opened a letter that's been waiting in the vaults for a thousand years or so."

"A thousand *years?*" Rod did some quick subtraction.

"Who knew about me in 2000 AD?" Then it hit him. "Oh. No. Not McAran."

"Ah, I see you've met! Yes, it was from a Dr. Angus McAran. He informed the Pope that Rod Gallowglass, of Gramarye—and he gave the coordinates—was potentially the most powerful wizard ever born."

Gwen gasped.

The kids stared.

Rod squeezed his eyes shut and gave his head a quick shake. "Oh, no, not again! That skinny old b . . ." He remembered the children and took a deep breath. " 'Fraid it's a wild goose chase, Father. I've never shown the faintest trace of any magical ability."

"He did say 'potential,' " Father Uwell reminded, "and I find this sudden telepathic blockage of yours quite interesting—oh, yes, I do believe telepathy works, especially since I've visited Gramarye."

Rod smiled. "Met some of our witches, huh?"

Father Al winced. "Just one—and an elf. I'd really rather call your 'witches' espers, if you don't mind. 'Witch' is a supernatural term, and there's nothing metaphysical about psionic powers. Oh, and by the way, I saw your youngest."

"Gregory!" Gwen's gaze rivetted on the priest. "How doth he, good Father?"

"Quite well, I assure you madame," Father Al said kindly. "Two old elf-wives are watching over him, and the witch-girl who brought me to your house is helping them now. And Puck himself is guarding the door."

Rod smiled, feeling a weight lift off his shoulders. "Well, with him there, no enemy could even get close to the door."

"Doth he fret?" Gwen said anxiously.

"Not visibly." Father Al frowned. "In fact, he's very quiet. But the witch-girl read his thoughts, and told me that his mind searches for you ceaselessly—even when he's asleep. Well did you name him—'Gregory,' the watcher, the sentinel."

But Gwen wasn't listening any more; her eyes had lost

focus as her mind probed. Suddenly she gasped. "I do feel his touch!"

"Across *time?*" Rod cried. Then he frowned. "Wait a minute—McAran had a technique like that, where the mind travelled through time to a host-body. But how could a baby learn it?"

"He's too young to know about time," Father Al suggested. "Perhaps, to him, all moments are the same."

"There are words!" Gwen cried, eyes huge.

"Words?!!? But the kid doesn't know how to talk!"

"Nay . . . 'tis Fess." Gwen's brows knit. "Do not ask me the manner of it."

Rod slammed a fist into his palm. "Transmitting on my thought-frequency—and Gregory's my baby, so his frequency resonates with mine! He's picking up Fess's thoughts, and Gregory's telepathic waves are acting as a carrier wave for Fess! What's he saying, Gwen?"

She frowned. " 'Tis too faint to make much of . . . There is something said of a machine, and of Brom O'Berin and Dr. McAran . . . And something of the Abbot and the King, also. I think . . . 'tis that the Abbot unaccountably turned back, returning to Their Majesties full wroth. He thought he had been duped . . . their bargain was broken . . . the Abbot doth storm away, back to his monastery . . . Tuan hath sent out the summons to his barons, to send him levies of knights and men, and doth gird himself for war . . ." Her voice broke. "Husband—they may come to battle, and our babe lies there defenseless!"

"Not defenseless, not with Puck guarding his door," Rod reassured her quickly. "And you can be sure, if Puck's there, Brom O'Berin's getting hourly reports. If there's any threat to the kid, he'll whisk him away to Elfland so quickly that Gregory won't even know he's been moved!"

"Dost thou truly think he will?" Tears filled Gwen's eyes.

"Of course! After all, he's the kid's gr . . . *god*father! Believe me, you can trust him. But cut the talking, dear—reassure the poor baby, while the contact lasts."

"Aye . . ." Gwen's gaze seemed to turn inward; she sat alone, hands in her lap, mind reaching out to enfold her baby's.

Father Al coughed politely. "Ah, may I inquire—who is 'Brom O'Berin?' "

"The King of the Elves," Rod said absently, then quickly, "Uh, that's semi-classified information! Do you still honor the Seal of the Confessional, Father?"

"We do, though we don't use that term any more." Father Al smiled, amused. "And what you've just let slip is protected by it. Would it reassure you if I called you, 'my son?' "

"No, that's not necessary." Rod smiled, warming even more to the priest. "Brom's also the Royal Privy Counselor, you see—so there is a need for secrecy."

"Hm." Father Al frowned. "Then should your children hear it?"

"The kids?" Rod glanced at the grassy bank; the children lay tumbled on it, asleep. "It *has* been a long day, hasn't it? No, I don't think they heard, Father."

"So I see." Father Al smiled fondly.

Rod cocked his head to one side, watching him. "Little sentimental, aren't you? I mean, considering they're supposed to be little warlocks and a little witch."

Father Al stared at him, startled. "Come now, sir! These children's souls are perfectly normal, from all that I can see! There's nothing supernatural about psionic powers!"

"Sure about that?" Rod eyed him sideways. "Well, it's your field, not mine. Uh—you *are* a specialist, aren't you?"

Father Al nodded. "A cultural anthropologist, really, but I specialize in the study of magic."

"Why?"

Father Al blinked. "How's that again?"

"Why would the Church of Rome be interested in magic?"

The priest grinned broadly. "Why, to prove it doesn't exist, for one thing—and that takes some meticulous work on occasion, believe me; there've been some extremely clever hoaxes. And, of course, the rare actual esper can very easily be mistaken for a sorcerer. Beyond that—well, the whole concept of magic has a strange domination over men's souls, in many cultures; and the soul is our concern.''

"Meaning that if any real magic ever does show up, you want to know how to fight it.''

"If it's demonic, yes. For example, exorcism has a long history. But the Church didn't really begin to become interested in magic until the 25th Century, when provable espers began to become visible. They weren't Satanists, nor possessed by evil spirits; that didn't take long to establish. On the other hand, they weren't saints either—that was even more obvious. Good people, most of them, but no better than the average, such as myself.''

"So,'' Rod said, "you had to decide there was a 'magic' force that had nothing to do with the supernatural.''

Father Uwell nodded. "Then we were off the hook, for the time being. But some of the Cathodeans began to wonder how the Church should react if it ever ran into some sort of *real* magic that was neither witchcraft nor miracle.''

Rod frowned. "Just what'd you have in mind? I mean, if esper powers don't fit that description, what does?''

"Oh, you know—fairy-tale magic. Waving your hands in the air, and chanting an incantation, and making something happen by a ritual process, *not* by the power of your mind.''

"Saying 'Abracadabra' and waving a magic wand, huh? All right, I'll bite—how *should* the Church react?''

Father Uwell shrugged. "How should I know? We've only been discussing it for five hundred years.''

Rod eyed him sideways. "I should think that'd be time enough to arrive at a few tentative conclusions.''

"Oh yes, hundreds of them! That's the problem, you see—we have a notion about how we should respond if we ever do encounter a case of real magic—but so far, we haven't.''

"O-o-oh.'' Rod nodded. "No one to test your theories on, huh?''

"Exactly so. Of course, we've looked for a real magician;

we've investigated hundreds of cases. But most of them proved to be espers who didn't know what they were; and there were a few cases of demonic possession, of course. The rest were hoaxes. So if we ever do find a real 'wizard,' we *think* we'll know how to react, but . . ."

"How?"

Father Uwell shrugged. "The way we should've reacted to the introduction of science, and eventually did—that it's something neither good nor evil, but does raise a deal of questions we have to try to answer."

Rod tilted his head back, lips forming the syllable quite a while before he said it. "Oh. So if a real wizard should happen to come waltzing along, you want to be there from the very beginning, so you can figure out what questions he's raising."

"And bat them to the theologians, to find answers for." Father Uwell nodded. "And there is the danger that a neophyte wizard might start meddling with the supernatural, without realizing what he's doing. If that did happen, someone should be there to steer him back into safe territory."

"And if he doesn't steer?"

"Persuade him, of course."

"And if he doesn't stop?"

Father Uwell shrugged. "Batten down the hatches and get braced for the worst—and try to figure out how he does what he does, so that if he lets loose some really evil power, we can counter it."

Rod stood very still.

Then he nodded, slowly. "So. It does behoove the Church to study magic."

"And we have. We've worked out a great deal, theoretically—but who's to say if any of it's really valid?"

Rod shook his head. "Not me, Father. Sorry, but if you're looking for a wizard, you haven't found him. I've never worked a trick in my life, that didn't have a gadget behind it. I did bump into McAran once, coming through a time machine—but I wasn't a wizard then, either. And he knew it!"

The priest thrust his head forward. "A time machine. He could've used it to take a look at your personal future."

Rod stood stock-still for a moment.

Then he shook his head vigorously. "No. Oh, no. No. There's no way I *could* turn into a wizard—is there?"

"Well, there is the question of your suddenly becoming telepathically invisible—but that's more a matter of psi phenomena than of magic. Still, it indicates you may have some powers you don't know about. Has something improbable ever happened, when you wanted it to happen, for no visible reason?"

Rod frowned, shaking his head. "Never, Father. Can't think of a single."

"Mine husband," Gwen reminded, "the bells . . ."

Rod looked up, startled. Then he turned back to the priest, slowly. "That's right. Just a little while ago, I wanted church bells to ring, very badly—wished it with all my might, actually—I was trying to break through to Gwen, hoping she'd read my mind and start ringing them telekinetically."

"And they rang," Gwen said softly, eyes wide, "though I did not do it."

"Nor the kids either," Rod said grimly. "You don't suppose . . . ?"

"Oh, I do—but it's only a supposition. One incident isn't quite enough to construct a theory. Excuse me—you did say your wife is telekinetic?"

"Among other things." Rod nodded. "And our little girl, too. The boys teleport. That's the usual sex-linked break-down on Gramarye, for espers. But Magnus is telekinetic, too, which breaks the rules—and he's got some powers we're not sure about at all."

"It runs in the family, then."

"Runs? It never even slows down to a trot!"

"Yes, I see." Father Uwell frowned. "I'd heard about this all, of course, but . . . Doesn't it strike you as strange that your children should breed true, in esper powers, when only one of their parents is an esper?"

Rod stared. Gwen's eyes lit.

"I'd assumed it was a dominant trait," Rod said slowly.

"Which it well might be, of course. But how do you explain your son's additional powers?"

"I don't." Rod threw up his hands. "I've been trying for eight years and I still can't. How's 'mutation' sound to you?"

"About the same way 'coincidence' does—possible, but also improbable, and therefore suspect."

"So." Rod steadied his gaze on the chubby, gently-smiling face. "You think he might've inherited it from both sides."

Father Uwell spread his hands. "What can I say? It's possible—but three bytes of data are scarcely a full meal."

"About what I expected." Rod nodded. "So. Keep on observing, and hope for the best, eh?"

"If you don't mind."

"Oh, not at all! Me, mind? Just because we're hiking through unknown territory, where there might be an enemy on every side? Just because we've got supernatural beasties with long, sharp teeth coming out of roadside pools? No, I don't mind at all, Father—but you should. I mean, it's not exactly going to be a church picnic, if you'll pardon the phrase."

"Certainly," the priest said, smiling. "And as to the danger—well, we'll have to take it as it comes, eh?"

"Sure will." Rod couldn't help smiling; there was something *very* likeable about this brown-robe. Not to mention reassuring; it never hurt to have another adult male in the party, even if he wasn't exactly a warrior. "But there might be a way to limit that. You just came in from Gramarye, you say."

Father Uwell nodded.

"Is the door still open?"

The priest blinked. "Why, as far as I know, it was never shut."

"What!!?!"

Father Uwell nodded. "I understand there's been quite a loss of game in the area, and several peasants are complaining about missing livestock. No other people have 'fallen in,' though. There's a great black horse on patrol there, and he won't let anyone near.''

''Fess!'' Rod slapped his thigh. ''He's still standing there, waiting for us to come out!''

''Trying to figure out how to *get* you out, I think. At least, that's the only reason he let me past.''

Rod frowned. ''You don't mean he talked to you.''

''No, but I wouldn't have been surprised if he had. I came to your house, and, not finding you home, I set out to the woods nearby, with Puck for a guide. As I went toward the pond, your horse galloped up to block me. I dodged to the side, but he dodged with me. I ducked under his belly, but he sat on me. I tried to vault over him, and he swivelled around so that I jumped off exactly where I'd jumped on. I finally decided I was dealing with an unusual specimen.''

Rod nodded. ''You should only know *how* unusual.''

''I have some idea; when I struck him, he clanged. So I tried to reason with him.

''He eventually escorted me to the point at which you'd disappeared. I walked ahead—and found myself surrounded by silver leaves! I whirled about, and found myself facing a great white-trunked tree with a big 'X' carved on it. I tried to step back into it, but I thumped roundly against the bark and sat back on my cassock. I fancy I must have looked rather ridiculous.''

''So did I,'' Rod said grimly. ''Don't worry about it, Father. So. The gate's still open, but it only works one-way, eh?''

The priest nodded. ''It would require a transmitter on this end, I fancy.''

Rod's head snapped up, staring.

Then he hit his forehead with the heel of his hand. ''Of course! What's the matter with me? They just set up a transmitter, and didn't worry about who was going to stumble in here, as long as all of *us* did!'' He shook his head, feeling the anger boil. ''Can you believe how callous those futurians are? What do they care if a hundred peasants get torn away from their families, just so long as they get the ones they're after!''

''I take it you have enemies,'' Father Uwell said carefully.

''You might say that, yes.'' Rod smiled sardonically. ''Enemies with time machines—so I was thinking of Doc Angus's time machine, which *can* pass any amount of material, and which *can* pull you back out of whenever it lands you. I forgot that the man at the controls has to *want* to pull you back.''

''Which your enemies obviously don't,'' Father Uwell agreed. ''So they gave you a one-way ticket here, you might say.''

''You might, yes. So getting home will be something of a problem, won't it? Well, you're welcome to poke around in my subconscious all you want, Father, if that'll help get us out of here—but frankly, I can't offer much hope.''

''We'll worry about that when the time comes,'' the priest said, with a faint smile. ''But how *were* you planning to get home?''

Rod looked at Gwen. ''Well, at the moment, our best bet looks to be one Lord Kern, who's got the title of High Warlock.''

''*Your* title.'' Father Uwell frowned. ''Interesting.''

''Is it? But it seems that magic works, here; I'm sure you'll find Lord Kern oodles of fun, if we ever get to him. There are definitely faery folk here, I'll tell you that—we just escaped from a bunch of them. *They* had some interesting tricks, too.''

''Really?'' Father Uwell's eyes fairly glowed. ''You must tell me about them—when you have time. But as to Lord Kern—how do you plan to persuade him to help you?''

Rod shrugged. ''I expect Gwen and I'll have to fight on his side in a little war, first, to earn it—unless he's grateful enough just for our helping his child-King ward escape to him. Father Uwell, meet His Majesty, King Elidor . . .'' He turned toward the boy—and frowned. ''Elidor? Gwen, where did he go?''

"Elidor . . . ?" Gwen's eyes slowly came back into focus.

"Oh! I'm sorry, dear!" Rod's mouth tightened in self-anger. "I didn't mean to break you off from Gregory. I didn't know you were still in contact."

"I was not." Gwen bowed her head, forlorn. "I but sat in reverie, some while after the touch of him faded . . ." She straightened up, forcing a smile. "I must bear it; surely his touch will come again. What didst thou wish, mine husband?"

"Elidor. Where'd he go?"

"Elidor?" Gwen glanced about quickly. "My heaven, I had forgot! Elidor! Where . . ."

"Mama!"

It was small, bald, and wizened, with great luminous eyes and pointed ears. Its mouth was wide, with loose, rubbery lips, and its nose was long and pointed. It wore a rusty-brown tunic and bias-hosen, with cross-gartered sandals.

Gwen screamed, clasping her hand over her mouth.

Rod's eyes bulged; all he could manage was a hoarse, strangled caw.

The noise woke the children. They sat bolt-upright, eyes wide and staring, darting glances about for the danger.

Then they saw the kobold.

Cordelia screamed, and flew into her mother's arms, burying her head in Gwen's breast and sobbing. Geoffrey darted to her, too, bawling his head off.

But Big Brother Magnus clamped his jaws shut around a neigh of terror, plastered his back against a tree, then drew his sword and advanced slowly, pale and trembling.

Rod snapped out of his horrified daze and leaped to Magnus's side, catching his sword-hand. "No, son! Touch him with cold iron, and we'll never see him again!"

"Good," Magnus grated. "I have small liking, to gaze upon such an horror. I beg thee, free my hand, Papa."

"I said *no!*" Rod barked. "That's not just an average haunt who happened by, son—it's a changeling!"

Magnus's gaze shot up to Rod's, appalled. "A *what?*"

"A changeling. Theofrin's faeries must've been following us, waiting for their chance—and while you three were asleep, and Gwen was preoccupied with Gregory's thoughts, and I was talking with Father Al . . ." His lips tightened, again in self-anger. ". . . no one was watching Elidor; so they kidnapped him, and left this thing in its place." He took a quick glance at his own three, to reassure himself they were all there. They were, thank Heaven.

"We must not afright it," Gwen said grimly.

"Your wife is right," Father Al murmured, stepping behind a tree. "We must not scare it away, and the sight of me might do just that. I see you know what a changeling is. Do you know that it holds a correspondence to the child who was kidnapped?"

Rod scowled. "You mean you can use it to work a spell that'll recover Elidor?"

Father Uwell nodded. "And it's our only link to him. If it leaves, we'll have no way of regaining him."

"All right." Rod nodded. "I'll bite. How do we use the changeling to get Elidor back?"

"Well, first you take an egg . . ." He broke off, frowning. "What's that chiming?"

"Just the breeze in the trees; the leaves rustle strangely here."

The priest shook his head. "No, beyond that—the tinkling. Do you hear it?"

Rod frowned, turning his head. Now that the priest mentioned it, there *was* a sound of chiming bells. "Yeah, come to think of it. Strange. What do you suppose it is?"

"Given the terrain and what you've told me about the inhabitants, it could be any of several things, none of which would exactly welcome the sight of a priest. I'd recommend you trace the sound to its source. I'll follow, but I'll stay back out of sight."

"Well, it's your field, not mine," Rod said dubiously. "Come on, kids! And stay close to your mother and me." He glanced back at Magnus. "Uh, bring . . . Elidor?"

"Aye, Papa."

Gwen caught Geoff's and Cordelia's hands, and looked back at the changeling. "Come, then!" She shuddered as she turned away from it. Cordelia clung to her, trembling.

They wound though the silver forest, hands clasped, following the tinkling sound. It began to fall into a tune; and, as it became louder, Rod began to hear a thin piping of reeds, like very high-pitched oboes, underneath it, and, lower in pitch, a flute. Then the trees opened out into a little clearing, and Gwen gasped.

Faery lights wavered over the grove, mostly gold, but with occasional flickers of blue and red. Looking more closely, Rod saw that the air was filled with fireflies, so many that their winking lights lent a constant, flickering glow that supplemented the moonlight, showing a ring of delicate, dark-haired women, supple and sinuous, in diaphanous shifts, dancing to the tune played by a three-foot-tall elf with a bagpipe, and another who sat atop a giant mushroom with a set of panpipes. The ladies, too, couldn't have been more than three feet high—but behind them, beaming down fondly, sat a woman of normal size.

Of more than normal size—in fact, of epic proportions. She would've tipped the scales at three hundred pounds, and kept on tipping them. She wore a mile or so of rose-colored gown, the skirts spread out in a great fan in front of her. A high, square-topped headdress of the same cloth exaggerated her height, with folds of veil framing her face. It was a quiet face, and calm, layered in fat but surprisingly little, compared to her body. Her eyes were large and kind, her nose straight, and her mouth a tuck of kindness.

Rod glanced out of the corner of his eye; the changeling was hanging back in the shadows. Then he turned back to the ample beldame, and bowed. "Good evening, Milady. I am Rod Gallowglass; whom have I the pleasure of addressing?"

"I am called the Lady Milethra, Grand Duchess of Faery," the dame answered with a smile. "Thou art well come among us, Lord Gallowglass."

Rod hiked his eyebrows; she knew his title. He decided not to remark on the subject. "Uh, in my company are my wife, the Lady Gwendylon, and our children—Magnus, Cordelia, and Geoffrey.''

Gwen dropped a curtsey, and Cordelia mimicked her. Magnus bowed, and Geoff needed prompting.

The Grand Duchess nodded graciously. ''Well come, all. A fine crop of young witch-folk, Lord Gallowglass—and please inform your clerical acquaintance that his tact in remaining unseen is appreciated.''

'' 'Clerical acquaintance . . . ?' Oh . . . Father Uwell. I will, Your Grace. If you'll pardon my saying so, you're remarkably well-informed.''

''Prettily said,'' she answered, with a pleased smile. ''Yet 'tis not so remarkable as all that; little escapes mine elves' notice.''

The piper grinned up mischievously at Rod, then went on with his piping.

''Ah—do I take it Your Grace, then, knows of our recent loss?''

''Thou speakest of my godson, Elidor.'' The Lady folded her hands, nodding. ''Indeed, I do know of it.''

A fairy godmother, yet! And was Rod in for a roasting, or a basting? ''Your pardon for our lapse of vigilance, Your Grace.''

She waved away the apology with a lacey handkerchief. ''There is nought to pardon; with Eorl Theofrin's spriggans out to seize the lad, there was little thou couldst do to protect him. Indeed, I am grateful to thee for saving him from the *Each Uisge;* mine elves would have been sore tried to vanquish that monster.''

Which meant they might've had to sweat. ''Uh—I take it Eorl Theofrin is the faery lord who had us in his power not too long ago?''

''The same. Now, as bad fortune hath it, Elidor is within his power again, where I may not run to save him. Since thou hast aided him in this wise once already, may I ask thee to aid him so again?''

''With all heart!'' Gwen said quickly.

''Well, yeah, sure,'' Rod said, more slowly. ''But I confess to some puzzlement as to why you should wish to employ us in this, Your Grace. Doesn't a Grand Duchess kind of outrank an Eorl?''

"I do, indeed—yet there is the practical matter of force. Eorl Theofrin's forces far outweigh mine—and my rank, of itself, suffices only if there is one of paramount rank to whom to appeal.''

"And Oberon's out of the country, at the moment?''

The Grand Duchess's eyebrows rose. "Thou dost know the name of the Faery King? Good, good! Aye, he is afield, in the land of the English, for some time. Some trifling quarrel with Titania, it is, over some tedious Hindu lad . . . Ever did I mistrust that shrewish and haughty demoiselle . . . Enough!'' She turned back to Rod with determination. "There is some hope of welding an alliance 'twixt some other of the Faery Lords; yet few would wish to move against Theofrin, and all dread the illnesses that a war 'twixt the Faery demesnes would work upon the land, ourselves, and the mortals.''

"And it would take a while to get them all working together.''

"Even so; and the longer Elidor remains under Theofrin's hand, the harder 'twill be to pry him loose. Yet mortals stand removed from our quarrel.''

Rod nodded. "We're a third force that can upset the balance, right?''

"Even so. Most mortals' power would be too little to counter a faery's; yet there are some spells which, if wielded by a warlock or witch, can own to far more power than any slung by one faery 'gainst another.''

Rod frowned. "I don't quite understand that. If mortals are magically so much weaker, how could our spells be so strong?''

"Why,'' said the Grand Duchess, with a disarming smile, '' 'tis because ye have souls, which we lack.''

"Oh.'' Now that Rod thought of it, there *was* that old tradition about fairies having no souls. He swallowed hard, wondering what shape his own was in.

"Not so bad as all that," the Grand Duchess assured him.

"Well, that's a relief to hear . . . *Hey!* I didn't say that aloud! How'd you know what I was thinking?"

"How not?" The Grand Duchess frowned. "Ah, I see—no other mortals can hear thy thoughts! Rest assured, 'tis nothing inborn; 'tis only that, deep within thee, thou dost not *wish* them too."

Gwen was staring at him with joy that was rapidly giving place to suspicion.

Rod swallowed. "But why wouldn't I? Never mind, let's not go into that just now! Uh—I take it the Faery folk have more thought-reading power?"

"Nay; but we have spells we may use, when we wish it—quite powerful ones. Since that thou art somewhat new to this world, I did wish it."

"Oh." Rod felt as though he ought to feel outraged that she hadn't given him official notice at the beginning of the interview; but he was scarcely in a position to bargain. He wanted Elidor *back!*

"As do I," the Grand Duchess agreed. "Yet I confess I am mystified as to why it should matter to thee; he is no kin of thine."

Good question. Rod spoke the first answer that came to mind. "I seek to return to my own place and time, Your Grace. I think I'm going to need magical help to do it; and getting Elidor to Lord Kern ought to win me a return favor. From you, too, come to that."

The Grand Duchess leaned forward, peering closely at him. Gwen was staring at him, thinking about getting angry.

"Aye, there is some of that in thy mind," the Grand Duchess said slowly, "yet there is more of a . . . guilt."

Rod winced.

The Grand Duchess nodded. "Aye, 'tis that—that thou didst take him under thy protection, then failed him. Yet beneath that lies sympathy, sorrow for a poor orphaned child among folk who love him not—and under that lies fear for thine own bairns." She sat back, satisfied.

Gwen, however, was another matter. She was watching Rod narrowly. Then, slowly, she nodded, too.

Rod felt something snap around his knee. He looked down, and saw it was Geoffrey, hugging his daddy's leg and peering out wide-eyed at the great big lady.

Rod turned back to the Grand Duchess. "Okay—so I'm trustworthy." He reached down and patted Geoff's head. "What do we do?"

"Eorl Theofrin and all his court do ride nightly from Dun Chlavish to Dun Lofmir," she answered. "If the child's mother were alive, it would be she, closest to him, who would have to do the worst of it; in her absence, 'tis thy wife's place."

Gwen nodded. "I am ready."

Suddenly, Rod wasn't so sure *he* was; but the Grand Duchess was plowing on. "Do thou hide in the furze by the side of the track, where it tops a rise, for there will they be going slowest. When Elidor's horse comes nigh, thou must seize him, drag him down, take off his cloak and doublet, turn them inside out, and set them on him again. Then mayest thou lead him hence, with none to hinder thee."

Gwen frowned. "This will take some time, Your Grace; I have dressed little ones aforetime."

"I know thou hast; and buying thee the time must be thy husband's place."

"Oh?" Rod raised an eyebrow. "And how am I to do *that,* Your Grace?"

"Why, that is thy concern; thou art the man of war, not I." The Grand Duchess sat back placidly, hands folded in her lap. "Yet what e'er thou dost, be minded—bear wood of ash, and rowan berries in thy cap, and keep cold steel about thee."

Rod started to ask why, then decided against it. "Well enough—if I can't think up a diversion by now, I should be drummed out of the Heroes' Union. But tell me, Your Grace—do you have any idea *why* Eorl Theofrin stole Elidor back?"

"Why, 'twould be a triumph for him, to number a king

CHAPTER EIGHTEEN

"Worked, too, didn't it?" Rod said, with a sardonic smile.

"That *is* a problem with goodness," Father Uwell sighed. "It can be used against you. Not that the evil ones don't overbalance themselves occasionally, too . . . Here she comes!"

Cordelia swooped down over the treetops, skimmed low over the meadow grass, and brought her broomstick in for a two-point landing. She hopped off, and reported to Gwen, "There is the mound we saw last night, Mama, and another like it perhaps a mile away. And a track connects them."

Gwen nodded. "The one we saw last night would be Lofmir, then; they would dance at the end of the ride." She turned to Rod. "What land dost thou seek, husband?"

Rod shrugged. "Well, a rise, with a good thicket just beside the trail, as the Grand Duchess said—preferably with a nice high cliff-top right behind it. And plenty of room across from the cliff."

Cordelia nodded. "There is a rise beneath a hill's brow, and the ground falls away on the other side in a long, long slope."

Rod grinned. "Perfect! Okay, scout—lead us to it."

Cordelia hopped back on her broom.

"Uh, hold it, there." Rod caught the straw. "We've got to keep our heads down."

"But, Papa," Magnus protested, " 'twould be so easy just to fly there!"

"Yeah, and easy for Duke Foidin's sentries to spot us, too—or are you forgetting it's daylight now? It was taking enough of a chance, having Cordelia fly reconaissance—and you'll notice I chose the smaller body for the purpose.''

" 'Tis as when we came,'' Magnus grumbled. "We had to walk because Papa could not fly.''

"Hey, now!'' Rod frowned. "No looking down on your old man, mind! Or do I have to prove I can still get in one good spank before you can teleport?''

Magnus glowered truculently up at him, but Rod just held a steady glare, and the kid finally began to wilt.

"It *was* unkind,'' Gwen said softly.

Magnus let go, and looked down at the grass. "I'm sorry, Papa,'' he mumbled.

" 'S'okay.'' Rod clapped him on the shoulder. "We didn't fly then for the same reason, son—don't attract attention until you know whether or not the territory's friendly—and always keep a few surprises handy. Let's go, folks.''

They set out across the meadow, Cordelia skimming the top of the grass with Geoff hitchhiking behind her, Magnus floating along in their wake to keep pace with the grownups. Father Uwell looked startled at first, but he adapted quickly. "I admire your discipline,'' he murmured to Rod.

Rod watched the kids warily, then dropped back a few paces. "Just a matter of getting through to them while they're young enough to hang onto, Father.''

"Yes, surely,'' the priest agreed. "Tell me—*could* you punish him now, if you wanted to?''

Magnus perked his ears up.

"I'd rather not say,'' Rod muttered.

Father Uwell followed the direction of his gaze, and nodded. "I see. Sometimes it helps, being telepathically invisible, eh?''

Rod gave him a very dirty look.

The priest rolled his eyes up, studying the sky.

"What're you looking for,'' Rod demanded, "constellations?''

"Oh, no. I noticed those last night, as soon as I came to a clearing.''

"Really?'' Rod perked up. "Recognize any?''

"Oh, all of them, of course."

"Of *course?*" Rod frowned. "What is this—your home world?"

"No, but I've spent half my life here." The priest cocked his head to the side. "You've never been to Terra?"

Rod stared.

"I take it you haven't."

Rod gave his head a quick shake. "Well, yes, once or twice—but I didn't exactly have time to study the stars. Uh—isn't the scene here a little rural for Terra?"

"The whole planet *is* rather overgrown with cities," Father Uwell agreed, "so, obviously, it's not the same Terra."

Rod stopped.

So did the priest. "You hadn't guessed?"

"Well, yes and no." Rod gestured vaguely. "I mean, I knew we were several thousand years in the future. . ."

Father Uwell shook his head.

Rod just watched him for a minute.

Then he said, "What do you mean, 'no?' "

"The stars are the same as they were when I left," the priest answered. "The whole sphere's rotated a little—I'd guess we're somewhere on the North American continent, whereas I'm used to the Italian sky—but there's no star-drift, no distortion of the constellations. We're just about 3059 AD."

"I can't accept that," Rod snapped.

"I think the Pope said that to Galileo, once," Father Uwell sighed. "But I see a peasant, over there; why don't you ask him?"

Rod looked up. A laborer was out early with his sickle, mowing hay. Rod glanced at his family, decided he could catch up quickly enough, and trotted over to the peasant. He stopped suddenly, remembering where they were. He turned back toward Gwen, and whistled. She looked up, saw the peasant—and all three children dropped to the ground and started walking.

Unfortunately, the peasant had noticed. When Rod got to

him, he was still rubbing his eyes. "Good morrow," Rod called. "Eyes troubling you?"

The peasant looked up, blinking. "I have not waked quite, I think. Were yon children *flying?*"

Rod glanced over at the kids, then back. "No, you're still dreaming."

"Art thou certain?"

"Of course I'm sure! I'm their father. Say, would you happen to know the date?"

The man blinked again. "Date?"

"Uh, the year will do." Rod took a deep breath. "See, we're from out of town, and we want to make sure we count the years the same way you do."

"I see." He didn't. "Well . . . 'tis the Year of Our Lord 3059. . . . Art thou well?"

Rod realized he was staring. "Uh, just asleep on my feet. I hate it when the day starts so early."

"Assuredly," the man said, wondering, "how *can* it begin, but with sunrise?"

"A good point," Rod admitted. "Well, thanks for the information. Have a good day!" He turned, and trotted back to Gwen and the kids. As he came up to them, he glanced back; the laborer was still staring at them. Rod grabbed Magnus's shoulder. "Son, give that guy a quick cat-nap, will you? I want him to think he dreamed us."

Rod surveyed the site from the hill-top, and nodded. "Good. Very good. Gwen, there's your thicket . . ." he pointed to a stand of furze on the near side of the trail. . . ". . . and here's my station, on the slope."

"Where shall we be, Papa?" Magnus asked eagerly.

"Up here, with Father Uwell, for protection."

"*Their* protection?" The priest smiled, amused. "Or mine?"

"Ours," Rod answered, "Gwen's and mine. And Elidor's."

"Mama," Geoffrey piped up, "hungry."

"Me too, come to think of it." Rod's stomach growled. He shrugged. "Okay, kids—go find breakfast."

The children whooped and ran, tumbling down the hillside.

"What will they find?" Father Uwell asked.

Gwen shook her head, smiling. "Only Heaven may know, Father."

"Care to ask?" Rod prompted.

Father Uwell shook his head, smiling. "I'm afraid my pipeline doesn't go beyond the Vatican."

"Yes—the place with the constellations." Rod frowned.

"Have you absorbed it?" the priest said gently.

"Pretty much. You updated, Gwen?"

She nodded. "I was aware of Father Uwell's thoughts."

It didn't faze him. Rod gave him points. "So, Father. . ."

"Please." The priest held up a hand. "We're apt to be together awhile. My friends call me 'Al' "

"Right. Well, Father Al, what do you make of it?"

The priest frowned for a second; then he shrugged and smiled. "We're on Terra, but it's not the Terra we know— and, by the constellations, it can't be any other planet."

"Alpha Centauri A?" Rod said, trying feebly.

The priest shook his head. "No, my friend. Four point three seven light years makes a noticeable difference in the constellations. Besides, I've been on its habitable planet, and it looks nothing like this—you might say the terraforming still hasn't quite taken hold."

"No, it hasn't." Rod had been there, too; it was nice, if you liked wide, empty spaces. "So it's Terra, and there's no way out of it." He swallowed as he realized the double meaning.

Father Al caught it, too. "If humankind can make a way in, they can make a way out," he said firmly, "but we'll have to learn a new set of ground rules."

"Yes," Rod said grimly. "Let's stop skirting around it and say it, Father—we're in another universe."

"Of course." Father Al seemed mildly surprised. "You've adapted to the concept very well."

Rod shrugged. "I'm getting used to the place." He turned to Gwen. "How you feel about it, dear?"

She shrugged. "Is it harder to get home over the void between universes, than over a thousand years?"

"I dunno," Rod said, "but I bet we'll find out. Here comes brunch, Father."

The children came toiling back uphill. Magnus held a few partridge, Geoff proudly bore a rabbit skewered on his sword, and Cordelia had her apron full.

"Rowan, Papa." She held up some red berries as she came to Rod. "You forgot."

"You're right, dear—I did." Rod accepted the berries ruefully and turned to the priest. "Know what an ash tree looks like, Father?"

They woke about sunset. The children scouted up dinner, and rolled the leftovers in a fresh rabbit-skin for Elidor. "For," said Gwen, "he'll surely have had the sense to eat no fairy food."

"We hope," Rod said grimly. "If he has, it'll take more magic than ours to pry him loose from Theofrin."

"Have no fear," Magnus assured them, "he hath neither eaten nor drunk. His godmother hath told him tales."

Rod looked down, startled. "You're still tuned in on him?"

Magnus nodded.

"Hmm." Rod rubbed his chin, gazing southward along the track. "Okay, son—when you 'hear' him getting close, give an owl-hoot. Any questions?"

Everyone shook their heads.

Except Father Al. "I have several—but I think I'll have to observe, and work out the answers for myself."

Rod gave him a withering glance. "I wasn't talking about theology."

"Neither was I."

"That does it." Rod clapped his hands. "Battle stations,

everyone—and keep an eye peeled for spriggans.''

They took their assigned positions, and waited. And waited.

Rod took a stout hold on his ash staff and reminded himself that midnight was the witching hour. Probably a long wait yet. . .

An owl hooted.

Rod looked up, startled. The real thing, or Magnus? But it hooted again, and it was coming from across the track, high up. He glanced up at the sky, saw only stars, moon, and the light-gray of clouds.

Magnus.

Then he began to hear it—tinkling, like tiny cymbals, and a weird skirling of pipes. Over it all ran a wavering drone, like an army of bees, but soaring from one end of the scale to the other.

Then came the clatter of harness.

Rod glanced up at the thicket above him, but there was no movement. Of course not—Gwen was an old campaigner in her own right.

Then the vanguard appeared.

They wound around a hill at the southern end of the track, a host of small, bright, dancing figures, followed by tall, impossibly slender, elongated horses, coats sheening golden by moonlight. And the riders! They caught Rod's breath. Extravagantly dressed, in a rainbow of colors—tall, slender, and beautiful. And glowing. Each of them.

And one tiny rider, in the center of the company, slouched over, head low—Elidor!

Rod rolled to his feet. Time to get moving.

He set off across the hillside, angling downward, then hiking back upward, as though he were trying to keep a straight line and failing. He let his gait wobble and started singing, slurring his voice as much as he could.

He heard a multiple whoop of glee behind him and choked down the surge of panic, forcing himself to keep his feet steady.

He heard hisses behind him. '' 'Tis a toss-pot!'' ''Nay, 'tis a long road home he'll have tonight!" "Do thou afright him from the front!"

Suddenly a huge dun-colored dog rose up before him, growling, mischief dancing in its eyes.

Rod jerked to a stop, trying to stay in character. " 'Ere, now! 'Owzh it wizh 'ee, Bowzher?"

"Nay, look behind thee!" a voice giggled, and he whirled about, stumbled, caught himself on his staff, and found himself staring straight into the dancing eyes of a snake, reared to strike. He let out a shriek and stumbled back, into the multiple arms of a giggling thing with a mouth like a slice of melon. He screamed and thrashed about, but its hold tightened—and touched his staff.

It shrieked, yanking an arm back, and fell over around the wound, screaming like a burn victim. "His staff! 'Tis ash, 'tis ash! Oh, mine arm, mine arm!"

"*Ash! Ash! Ash!*" whispered through the crowd of faeries; and they drew back, leaving a wide space around Rod. Many more came flitting over from the caravan, leaving only the lordly faery folk on their horses; and they were watching closely.

So far, so good. Rod stumbled to his feet, doing his best to tremble. "Nay, good shtaff, pertect me! Ay, poor old Josh! Th' fairy-folk've come to claim thee!"

A dancing light appeared in front of him, coalescing into the form of a beautiful woman. She smiled, as though amused at a hidden joke, and beckoned.

Staring, he took a few stumbling steps toward her.

She drifted away from him, beckoning again. Exactly what it was, he didn't know; some kind of will-o'-the-wisp, no doubt. But why were they springing her on him? He played along, though, stumbling after her, faster and faster. "Nay, pretty shing! Tarry now; let me shee thee!"

The surrounding watchers giggled, and it wasn't a pleasant laugh. Out of the corner of his eye, Rod noticed the faery gentry staring, fairly glued to the scene. Then he saw the reason why; the phantom was floating out over a sudden drop-off. They couldn't touch him, because of the ashen staff; but they could lure him to his death. Then he noticed Elidor suddenly disappear from his saddle, and knew it was time to escalate. He tripped and fell sprawling. An angry moan of disappointment went up all about him; he was a few inches short of the drop-off; but he opened his hand and let the staff roll away, and the moan slid up to a shriek of delight. Then they were on him, pinching and tickling; his skin itched in a thousand places, and his ears were filled with gibbering giggles.

But he had to hold attention, and hold it completely, to buy Gwen time. It was the moment for taking off the mask. He set his hands against the earth and shoved with all his might, surging to his feet and scattering elves left and right. The spriggans howled with glee and lurched in.

Rod whipped out his sword.

A moan of terror swept through the mob. They scuttered back away, wailing, "Cold iron! Cold iron!"

"He is no drunkard!" screamed a spriggan.

"Nay, but a sober warrior in his prime!" Rod called back. "Take me now, if you can!" And he wrenched his doublet open, showing a necklace of rowan berries.

The host moaned in fear, and pressed backward—but Rod saw, beyond them, the faery horsemen galloping toward him, with Eorl Theofrin at their head.

The Eorl drew up thirty feet away, calling, "Whoever hath advised thee, mortal, hath ill-advised thee! Thou art marked for faery vengeance now!"

"I was already," Rod jeered, "last night. Recognize me?"

Theofrin stared. "Cold bones! It is the wizard!"

He whipped about in his saddle, staring back at the trail. "The mortal king! The boy is gone!"

Five riders wheeled their horses about and went plunging toward the track.

Gwen stepped up on the trail, holding Elidor's hand. His doublet and cloak showed seams and lining.

The elf-horse beside him reared, screaming and pawing the air. Then it leapt up and whipped away, blown on a sudden gust of northern wind.

The five riders shrieked in frustration, jumping their mounts high to meet the gust. So did all the faery host, leaping into the air with a scream, and the breeze swept them away round the hill to the south, like autumn leaves.

Only Eorl Theofrin remained, his horse neighing and dancing as though it stood on hot coals. He himself winced and hunched his shoulders against pain, but managed to pull a crossbow from its place on his saddle, cranking the string back. "Thou hast cheated me full, wizard! Yet ere I succumb to pain and fly, I'll break thee for thy life!"

There wasn't a rock big enough to hide behind for a thousand paces. Rod stood his place, sword lifted, fighting a surge of panic. What that bolt could do, he didn't know—but he knew it was deadly. His one chance was to try to block it with his sword—but crossbow bolts moved *very* fast.

Theofrin leveled the bow.

Dimly, Rod was aware of that kindly, stern Presence with him again, reassuring, urging.

Fervently and with his whole being, he wished the faery lord would go follow one of his own phantoms off a cliff—and wherever else it led him, all night long.

Theofrin suddenly dropped his bow, staring off to his left.

Rod stared, too. He glanced over toward where the Eorl was looking, then quickly back to Theofrin. He'd seen nothing.

"Nay, pretty maiden," Theofrin crooned, "come nigh to me!" And his horse began to move forward. "Nay, dost thou flee?" Theofrin grinned. "I'll follow!" And his horse leaped into a gallop.

Straight over the cliff.

And on up into the sky—it was a faery steed, after all—with Theofrin caroling, "Nay, come nigh! Nay, do not flee! I'll do thee no harm, but show thee great delights! Ah, dost thou fly still? Then I'll follow thee, while breath doth last!"

Rod stared after him, stupefied, until Theofrin was only a lighted speck off to the east, that sank below a horizon-line of trees, and was gone.

"My lord!"

He turned. Gwen came running up, clasping Elidor's hand firmly. "My lord, I saw it all! Thou art untouched?"

"Uh . . ." Suddenly, Rod became aware of aches all over. "I wouldn't say that. Those pinches *hurt!* But nothing lasting—I hope."

"There shouldn't be, if Terran folk-tales hold true here." Father Al came puffing up. "But if he'd hit you with that crossbow-bolt, it might've been another matter."

"Oh?" Rod looked up, dreading the answer. "What kind of effects do those things produce, Father?"

The priest shrugged. "Oh, epilepsy, rheumatism, a slipped disc, partial or full paralysis—it would be the same as any elf-shot, I assume."

"Oh, really." Rod felt his knees turn to water. "Gee, isn't it too bad he had to leave so suddenly."

"Yes, I was wondering about that." The priest frowned. "What was he chasing?"

Rod shook his head. "Hanged if I know, Father. All I know is, I was wishing with all my might that he'd go follow one of his own will-o'-the-wisps over a cliff—and he did."

"Hm." Father Al's face instantly went neutral. "Well. Another datum."

Rod frowned; then he leveled a forefinger at the priest. "You're suspecting something."

"Well, yes," the priest sighed, "but you know how foolish it is to state a thesis prematurely."

"Yeah." Rod *should* know——Fess'd told him often enough. He sighed and straightened up. "Okay, Father— play 'em close to your chest. I'll just be real careful what I wish, from now on."

"Yes." The priest nodded grimly. "I'd do that, if I were you."

CHAPTER NINETEEN

A soft tinkling sounded.

The whole company stilled.

Reed pipes overlaid the tinkling; a flute underscored them.

Rod turned to Gwen. "I think we've got company."

"Godmother!" Elidor cried.

They turned to watch as he scooted over the grass to the wealth of woman beneath the firefly canopy. He leaped into her lap, arms outflung, and she gathered him in, pressing him against her more-than-ample bosom, resting her cheek on his head and crooning softly to him.

"Ever feel superfluous?" Rod asked.

"And never was so glad to feel so," Gwen affirmed. "Yet I think there is some business for us here. Come, my lord." She gathered her children's hands, and marched forward.

Rod sighed, caught Magnus's shoulder, and limped after her, while Father Al did a fast fade.

Gwen dropped a curtsey, and Cordelia imitated her. The boys bowed, and Rod bent forward as much as he could.

The Grand Duchess noticed. "Does it pain thee so greatly, High Warlock?"

Elidor looked up, startled.

"Not *that* High Warlock," Rod assured him. "And, well, I've felt this way before, Your Grace—say, the day after the first time I went horse-back riding. It won't last, will it?"

"Nay; 'tis only soreness," she assured him. "Yet trust me, 'tis suffering well-endured; though hast given him good rescue, as I knew thou wouldst."

"I'm glad somebody did. Well, you've got him safe,

now—so, if you'll forgive us, we'll be on our way. Come on, kids.''

The Grand Duchess looked up, startled. ''Thou wilt not take him to Lord Kern?''

Gwen caught Rod's sleeve. ''Assuredly, an thou wishest it. . .''

''Uh, Gwen. . .''

''. . . yet will the royal lad not be safer with his god-mother?'' Gwen finished.

The Grand Duchess smiled sadly. ''Safer, aye; but he'll not die 'mongst mortal men—both sides need him. And duty doth summon him.''

Elidor clung to her, and buried his face in her bosom.

''Nay, sweet chick,'' she crooned softly, ''thou dost know that I speak aright. Nay, nay, I would liefer keep thee all thy life beside me—but therein would I wrong mine old friends, the King and Queen thy parents, who bade me see that thou wouldst grow into a King; and the folk of thy land, who need thee grown. And lastly would I wrong thee, for I'd abort thy destiny. Come now, sweet chuck, bear up; sit tall, and give thyself a kingly bearing.''

Slowly, the little boy sat up, sniffling. He looked at her forlornly, but she pinched his cheek gently, smiling sadly, and he smiled in spite of himself, sitting up more firmly. Then he turned to face the Gallowglasses, straightening and lifting his chin, once again a Prince.

''See thou, he is to be a King of men,'' the Grand Duchess said, low, ''and therefore must he learn what men are, and not from written words alone. He must live and grow among them, good and bad alike, that when he comes to be a king, he'll recognize them both, and know their governance.''

Gwen nodded sadly. ''And therefore canst thou not keep him here, to hide him from the troubles of these times. But might thee not, at least, conduct him to Lord Kern?''

The Grand Duchess sighed. ''I would I could; but know this of us faery folk: we are bound to our earthly haunts. Some among us, like myself, can claim demesnes of miles' width, and freely move within them; but few indeed are they who move wherever they please, and to none of those would I entrust this lad—or any folk, of whom I cared.''

"But you would trust us." Rod could feel it coming.

The Grand Duchess nodded.

Gwen looked up at him, pleading.

"Oh, all right!" Rod clapped his hands. "Keeping track of children is mostly your job, anyway. Sure, Your Grace, we'll take him along."

The children cheered.

Elidor looked surprised; then he smiled, a slow, shy smile.

Magnus ran forward, caught Elidor's arm, and yanked him off the Grand Duchess's lap. "We'll keep thee close, coz! Yet mark thou, stay within mine eye this time!"

"I will stay near," Elidor promised.

"As near as one of mine own." Gwen gathered him in.

"Of course," Rod said, "it would help if we had someone to point us on our way."

"Elidor will show you." The Grand Duchess was clasping her hands tightly, and her smile seemed a little strained. "He hath conned his charts, and doth know the shape of every track and pathway in his land."

"Well, that'll help," Rod said dubiously, "but real hills and lakes don't match a map all *that* well. It'd be better to have someone who's been there, too."

The Grand Duchess shook her head firmly. "The sprites cannot leave their lands or waters, as I've told thee."

"Tell us, then," Gwen asked, "what we must do to see him safely to Lord Kern."

The Grand Duchess nodded, her eyes lighting. "Thou must first rid the Tower of Gonkroma of its Redcap."

CHAPTER TWENTY

"I don't really see what chasing some sort of elf has to do with getting safely to Lord Kern," Rod called.

Gwen said something back, but the roaring wind drowned out her answer.

"Come again, dear?" Rod called. "Louder, please; it's hard to hear, when I'm behind you, and the wind's whistling in my ears."

He was riding pillion on a makeshift broomstick.

"I said," Gwen called, "that I know no reason, but do trust her judgement."

"That's what it seems to come down to, here," Rod sighed, "faith. Wasn't that the medieval ethic, Father?" He looked back over his shoulder. Father Al was clinging to the broomstick for dear life, and was definitely looking a little green around the gills; but he swallowed, and nodded manfully. "Something like that, yes. It's a little more complicated, though."

"Well, I like to deal in over-simplifications. You sure you're okay, now?"

"Oh, fine, just fine! But are you sure your wife can carry all three of us for so long?"

"If I can bear four children," Gwen called back, "I can bear two men."

"There's some truth in that," Rod acknowledged. "After all, she's managed to bear with me for almost ten years now." He turned to the children, floating beside him. "Geoff, you be sure and tell us if you start feeling sleepy, now!"

"Fear not," Gwen called. "They napped well ere we left the Grand Duchess."

"Yes, thanks to Magnus. But Geoff, make sure you tell me if you start feeling tired—after all, Cordelia can give you a lift for a few minutes."

"For an *hour*," Cordelia caroled, swooping her broomstick in a figure-eight, "and not even feel it!"

"Hey, now! Straighten out and fly right! We've got a long way to go; no time or energy for fancy stuff!"

"Killjoy!" Magnus snorted. "Night flying's *fun!*"

"This, from the expert who thought I was wrong wanting to fly this time," Rod snorted.

"Well, Papa, you said yourself it'd attract too much attention."

"Yeah, but we've got a hundred miles to go before dawn; we don't have much choice this time. Besides, we're not too apt to be noticed at night; and if we are, by the time Duke Foidin can get troops after us, we'll be out of reach. And we're certainly going faster than any courier he can send!" He peered over Gwen's shoulder. "How's Elidor holding out, dear?"

Gwen glanced down at the small shape huddled against her, between her arms. "Almost beginning to enjoy it, I think."

"He *is* the stuff of which kings are made," Father Al gulped.

Rod decided the priest could use a distraction. "Figured out how magic works here, Father?"

"Oh, it seems to be fairly straightforward. I postulate three forces: Satanic, Divine, and impersonal. Most of what I've seen today, and tonight, falls in the 'impersonal' category."

Rod frowned. "What's 'impersonal?' "

"Essentially, it's the same force espers use. Everyone has it, to some degree. An esper has so much of it that he can work 'magic' by his own power; but everyone 'leaks' their little bit, and it goes into the rocks, the earth, the water, the air, absorbed into molecules. So it's there, ready to draw on; and, in a universe such as this, a few gifted individuals have the ability to tap that huge reservoir, and channel its force to do whatever they want."

Rod nodded. "Sounds right. Seen anything here that would disprove that?"

"No, but I think I'm going to have to come up with a corollary theory for the faery folk."

"You do that. Any idea why the whole world is still medieval, even though it's 3059 AD?"

"Well, at a guess, I'd say it's because technology never advanced much."

"Fine." Rod smiled. "So how come technology didn't advance?"

Father Al shrugged. "Why bother inventing gadgets, when you can do it by magic?"

That gave Rod pause. He was quiet for the rest of the flight.

Well, most of the time, anyway. "No, Cordelia—you may *not* race that owl!"

"You *sure* you're not getting tired, Geoff?"

"Magnus, leave that bat alone!"

The land rose beneath them, rippling into ridges and hills, then buckling into mountains. Finally, as dawn tinged the sky ahead and to the right, Elidor's finger stabbed down. "Yonder it lies!"

Rod peered ahead around Gwen and saw the ruins of a great, round tower, perched high on a crag. "Be fun getting up to that."

Magnus veered close and pointed downward. "I see a ledge of rock beside it, that trails away behind for a good hundred yards."

"Yeah, but then it blends back into the side of the mountain. How do I get to it in the first place?"

"Why, I will land thee on it, when thou dost wish," Gwen called back. "But, husband, we have flown half the night, and even I begin to weary. Would we not do well to rest ere we advance?"

"Yes, definitely." Rod looked around. "Where's a good place to rest?"

"There, and a safe one." Father Al nodded down toward a

valley, but did *not* point. "That little village, with the small steeple. There's a patch of woods near it, to hide our descent."

Rod looked down. "Well, it looks snug enough. But will we be welcome? As I recollect, mountaineers aren't generally too hospitable to outsiders."

"Oh, the parish priest will let us in," Father Al assured him. "I have connections."

Rod shrugged. "Good enough for me. Wanna let me off this thing, dear?"

"Aye, if thou wilt wait till I do land." Gwen tilted the broomstick down. Father Al gulped, and held on tight.

They found a clearing just big enough, and brought everyone in, in orderly fashion. Little Geoff fell the last two feet and pushed himself up out of the meadow grass, looking groggy. Rod ran over to him. "I *told* you to tell me when you were getting tired! Here, son, why don't you ride a little, now?" He hoisted the boy up onto his shoulders, and turned to Gwen. "Now—which way's the village?"

They found it, webbed in the birdsong of early morning. The parish priest was just closing the back door as they came up.

"Good morning, Father!" Father Al called cheerily, in spite of his rubber legs.

The old priest looked up, blinking. He was bald, and his long beard was grey. He was slim with a lifetime of fasting, and rock-hard as his mountains. "Why . . . good morrow, Father," he returned. " 'Tis early, for travellers to come walking."

"We've been on the road all the night; 'tis a matter of some urgency," Father Al replied. "I am these goodfolks' protection from the powers that walk at night; yet even I must sleep sometime. Canst thou spare us hospitality for a few hours?"

"Why . . . assuredly, for the Cloth," the old priest said, bemused. "Yet there is only my poor small room, behind the chapel. . ."

"No matter; we'll sleep in the nave, if thou dost not object, under the Lord's protection. We'll need every ounce we can get.''

"Father," the old priest said severely, "one ought not to sleep in Church.''

"Tell that to the goodfolk who must listen to my sermons.''

The old priest stared for a moment; then he smiled. "Well said, well said! Avail thyselves of what little thou canst find, then—and pardon my poor hosting. I must bless three fields and see to a woman whose hands pain her.''

"Arthritis?" Rod asked, coming up behind Father Al.

"Nay, only a swelling of the joints, and pain when she moves her fingers. Elf-shot, belike. A drop of holy water, a touch of the crucifix, and a short prayer will set her to rights.''

Rod stared.

Father Al got the thoughtful look again. "Hast thou ever known the treatment to fail, Father?"

"Aye; there do be stronger spells. Then must I ask the Bishop to come—or take my poor souls to him, if they can walk.''

"And the blessing of the fields—are the crops in danger?"

"Oh, nay!" the old priest laughed. "I can see thy mind; but do not trouble thyself, Father; thou hast journeyed long, and hast need of thy rest. Nay, 'tis only the usual blessing, without which the fields will yield scarcely half their corn.''

"Of course." Father Al smiled. "Well, it doth no harm to be certain. Thou wilt send for me if thou dost need me, though?''

"Be assured that I will—but be also assured that I'll have no need. Be welcome in my home, and make thyselves free of what little thou'lt find in the larder. Have no fear for me—the Lord will provide.''

"And He probably will," Father Al noted as they watched the old man leave, with an almost-youthful stride. "After all, magic works, here.''

"Small magics," Rod agreed, "daily ones. It seems the

village priest is the mundane magician, here. How does *that* fit into your theories, Father?''

"Perfectly. As I mentioned, I posit three sources of Power, and one of them is Divine—though I have a notion that some of his spells work more by 'secular,' impersonal magic than by God's Power. Some trace of magical ability could well be a requirement for admission to the seminary.''

"Probably," Rod agreed. "But the old man's abilities notwithstanding, I think it might be in order to keep our hands off his food, if we can." He turned to his son. "Magnus, Geoff's about tuckered. How much grub do you think you could scare up by yourself?''

Magnus pulled a hare out from behind his back. "I was hungry, Papa.''

"So was I.'' Cordelia held out an apronful of birds' eggs and berries.

"Nice thing about kids—they never lose track of the important things," Rod noted, to Father Al. "What do you say I take the skillet, Gwen? You're looking pretty tired, yourself.''

"Aye, but I wish to eat before noon." Gwen caught up the hare and brushed past him into the "rectory." "Come, Cordelia.''

"Well, I guess we get to decide the fate of the world." Rod sat down on the step as the door closed behind the ladies. "Magnus, keep your brother busy until breakfast, so he doesn't fall asleep.''

"Doing what, Papa?''

"Oh, I dunno . . . go play tag with a wolf, or something. Uh, cancel that," he added quickly, as he saw Magnus's eyes light up. "No sense in cruelty to animals. Go cut a couple of willow wands and drill him on fencing—he's a little slow on the riposte.''

"As thou dost wish, Papa." Magnus turned away, crestfallen. "Come, Geoffrey.''

"And stay where I can see you!''

Magnus gave a martyr's sigh. "We will.''

"Would you really have worried more about the wolf than about them?" Father Al asked, sitting beside Rod.

"Not completely," Rod admitted, "but I've seen Magnus drive a wolf to distraction. He disappears just before the wolf gets him, and reappears behind it. Then the wolf turns around to charge him again, and he disappears in the nick of time, bobbing up behind it again. When I caught him, he had it chasing its own tail."

Father Al shook his head in wonder. "I think I begin to understand why you adjusted to a world of magic so easily."

"Kids do keep your mind limber," Rod admitted.

"Limber enough to understand why technology never went beyond the hammer and anvil here?"

"Oh, there's not much question there. Why do you need to develop fertilizers when the average parish priest can do the same thing with a blessing?"

Father Al nodded. "I'll have to worm the wording of the prayers out of him, to see whether it's the prayer that does it, or the charm."

"So you can know which Power is working?"

Father Al nodded. "Increasing crop yields isn't exactly what we mean by 'small miracles happening everywhere.'"

"Like medical technology? It sounds as though he can cure arthritis, though he doesn't know it by that name. Our own doctors can't do much better. I'd imagine the same kind of thing's happening in all areas of technology."

Father Al nodded again. "Smiths producing case-hardened alloys by singing to the metal as they pound it; carriages riding smoothly, cushioned by spells instead of steel leaves, perhaps even spell-propelled; ships communicating with shore by crystal balls . . . Yes, why bother inventing anything?"

"But," said Rod, "magicians being rare, the average man couldn't afford battle-spells; so martial power remained an aristocratic monopoly. Which meant. . ."

"That the political system remained essentially feudal." Father Al's smile grew hard. "Though, with wizards providing kings with efficient communications, and even intelligence abilities, there's a chance centralized governments may have evolved.''

"But never terribly absolute," Rod noted. "The barons could get wizards, too. So they'd think of themselves as 'Christendom' as much as separate countries."

"Not much nationalism," Father Al agreed. "But how would the New World have been colonized?"

Rod shrugged. "No problem; Columbus came over shortly after the Wars of the Roses, and the Vikings set up a colony before him. With wizardry to help them, they shouldn't've had as much trouble with the 'skralings.' ''

"The Amerinds, yes. I notice that most of these people are nowhere nearly as pale as Northern Europeans of the period."

"Probably hybrids. And with their shamans' magic added in, you'd have quite an assemblage of magic. But that indicates a big emphasis on trade, which means mercantilism. How come there's no rise of the middle class?"

"There probably was, to a point. But the kings and barons would've entrusted fund-raising to their wizard-advisers, who, being probably of common birth, could participate in trade for them. No, I'd guess the 'merchant princes' *were* princes. And trade not being their means to rise, they wouldn't push its development as hard."

Rod spread his hands. "But—fifteen hundred years! Could a society really last that long, without changing?"

"Well, there was ancient Egypt—and the Chinese Empire. Dynasties changed, and styles; technology even improved a little, from time to time—but the society remained the same. And, come to think of it, India, before the Mongols . . . You know, Europe may have been the exception, not the rule, with its changing society."

Rod shook his head in wonder. "All because they started being able to make magic work! What do you think was the dividing point—the alchemists?"

" 'Dividing point?' Oh, you mean when this universe split off from ours. It didn't have to, you know—both universes *could* have started at the same time, and evolved independently.''

"Could have," Rod admitted, "but there're just too many resemblances between this universe and ours. The language is even close enough to Gramarye's so that I didn't have any problem understanding."

"Hmf. A good point." Father Al frowned. "Who knows? Perhaps both theories are true. It may be that the model for multiple universes isn't just one branching tree, with universes splitting off from one another at major historical events, but a forest—several root universes, each one branching at decision-points."

"Maybe—but this one looks to have branched off from ours."

"Or ours from it—we're not necessarily the center of Creation, you know." Father Al grinned wickedly.

"A point," Rod admitted. "So what was it—the alchemists?"

"Perhaps. There was much talk of wizardry before that, of course—but the alchemists *were* the first ones to approach the topic rationally. And the astrologers, of course."

Rod nodded. "So some alchemist-astrologer, probably totally forgotten in our own universe, happened to have the Power, and figured out some rules for its use. He probably wouldn't have let anyone else in on the secret—but once he proved it could be done, others would figure out how. When would this have happened—Fourteenth Century?"

Father Al nodded. "Sounds about right—I haven't seen any gunpowder here. That would be the latest point it *could've* happened, at least."

"And styles have continued to change, and they've kept pieces of all of them—but the social set-up hasn't." Rod nodded. "Makes sense. A little on the sick side, but sense. Where did the elves come from?"

Father Al shrugged. " 'Summoned' from another universe, or extremely thorough illusions made by a wizard, and kept 'alive' by the popular imagination. But they may have been there all along, and were only chased out of our universe by the combination of Cold Iron and Christianity, which gradually eroded the people's belief in them. There's some evidence for that last one—the Grand Duchess told us that the faery folk are tied to their own particular piece of countryside. That would seem to indicate that they grew out of the land itself, or rather, out of its life-forms. We aren't the only beings that set up minute electromagnetic fields around themselves.''

Rod nodded slowly. ''Ye-e-e-s. And in our universe, it would have been the 19th Century that finally undid that completely, as it laid Europe under a grid of railroad tracks, and sent telegraph wires all over the countryside, disrupting local field-forces.''

''Well, there were still tales told in the *20th* Century—its early years, at least. But radio and television would have finished the job—those, and concrete. They *are* basically nature sprites, after all.''

The door swung open behind them. ''We dine, gentlemen.''

''Well, enough of the fate of this world.'' Rod slapped his knees and stood up. ''Let's get to the important stuff, Father.''

The boys cheered and beat them to the door.

They waked to the ringing of the noon bell. The old priest had returned, and the boys scampered out to find lunch. The old man was amazed at the table they set for him. ''Cold hare, wild strawberries, grouse eggs, and trout simmering—thy children are most excellent hunters, Milord!''

''Why?'' Rod asked around a mouthful. ''Game getting scarce?''

''Aye, for some years. There were folk here who lived by trade through the mountains; and, when it ceased, they had need to scour the countryside for victuals. Many have wandered away, but there are still so many that our few farms can scarce feed them all.''

''Well, if it moves and is edible, my boys'll find it. What

stopped the trade, Father—Duke Foidin's garrisons?''

"That, and the Redcap who lives in the Tower. Not even a peddler can make his way past it, now.''

"Oh.'' Rod glanced at Father Al. "What does he do to them?''

"And what manner of sprite is he?'' Father Al chipped in.

The old priest shuddered. "He doth take the form of an aged man, squat and powerful, with long snaggled teeth, fiery eyes, long grizzled hair, and talons for nails. He doth wear iron boots and beareth a pikestaff. As to what he doth to travellers, he hath no joy so great as the re-dying of his cap in human blood.''

"Oh.'' Suddenly, cold roast hare didn't taste quite so good. "Can't anyone do anything to stop him?''

The old priest gave a short laugh. "What wouldst thou have? Armies cannot stand against him! 'Tis said that reading him Scripture, or making him look upon a cross, will rout him—but how canst thou force him to listen or look?''

"Good question.'' Rod turned to Father Al. "Any ideas?''

"One.'' The priest nodded. "If religious symbols will repel him when he perceives them, a stronger symbol should banish him by its touch.''

The old priest chuckled. "Certes, Father—but where wilt thou find the man to chance the doing of it?''

"Papa will,'' Geoff piped.

The old priest chuckled again, till his eyes met Rod's, and the chuckle died. Then he paled. "Nay, thou wilt not attempt it!'' He looked from Rod to Father Al, then to Gwen, and sat very still. Then he scrambled up, turning toward the door.

"Father,'' Father Al said quietly, "I shall require thine altar stone.''

The old priest stopped.

Then he turned about, trembling. "Thou mayest not! The Mass must be said on the bones of the saints, embedded within the altar stone! How shall I say Mass without it?''

"We shall return it this evening.''

"Wilt thou?'' The old man strode back, pointing to Father

Al with a trembling forefinger. "Wilt thou come back at all? Redcap can stand against armies; how wilt two of thee best him?"

"Three," Gwen said quietly. "I have some powers of mine own, Father."

"In fact, it's a family affair," Rod corroborated. "You'd be surprised at what my kids can do, without getting in range."

The old priest darted glances from one to another, as though they were mad. "Give over, I beg thee! And these poor wee bairns—do not subject them to such hazard!"

"We couldn't leave them behind if we wanted to," Rod said grimly.

"We will triumph, Father," Gwen said gently. "We have but lately set the *Crodh Mara* to defeat the *Each Uisge,* and have, together, put a faery lord's court to flight."

"Yet the faery lords are not Redcap! They do not *delight* in murder and bloodshed! No! Do not go! But if thou must, thou shalt go without mine altar stone!"

Father Al sighed and pulled a rolled parchment out of his robe. Rod saw fold lines on it, and guessed it had been in an envelope before Father Al got to Gramarye. The Terran monk said, "I had hoped to avoid this, but . . . look upon this writ, Father."

The old man stared at him, frightened. Then, reluctantly, he took the parchment and unrolled it. He read it, gasped, and grew paler the more he read. At last he rolled it back up with trembling hands and lifted his head, eyes glazed. "It . . . it cannot be! He . . . he is in Rome, halfway 'cross the world! Rarely doth he speak to those of us in this far land, and then only to Archbishops! How doth it chance . . . Aiiieee!" He dropped the parchment, clasping his head in his hands. "What have I done? What sin lies on my soul, that *he* should write to *me?*"

"No sin, Father, surely!" Father Al cried in distress, clasping the old man's arm. "In truth, I doubt he doth know that thou dost live! He doth address this Writ to any who

should read it, should I choose to show it them, having need
of their aid!''

"Aye, oh! Aye." The old man lifted a haggard face. "Yet
what mischance doth befall, that *I* should be the one from
whom thou dost require aid? Why doth this chance befall to
me? Nay, surely have I failed in my duty to my God and to my
flock!''

"Thy humility doth thee credit," Father Al said gently,
but with the firmness of irony underlying it. "But thy common sense doth not. This lot doth fall to thee only because thy
flock doth live near to the Tower of Gonkroma, whither I and
my friends must go to challenge Redcap."

Slowly, the old man's eyes focused on Father Al. He
nodded, and his face began to firm up. "Aye. 'Tis even as
thou dost say." He straightened his shoulders and rose.
"Well, then, if it must be so, it must—and I do not doubt it; I
cannot read his hand, yet I've seen the picture of his Seal in
books."

"And now thou dost see the impression of the Seal itself.
Wilt thou render up thine altar stone, good Father?''

"Aye, that will I. If His Holiness would wish it, then thou
shalt have it. Come; I will lift it for thee."

They came out of the chapel a few minutes later, Father Al
holding the stone wrapped securely under his arm.

"That wasn't quite honest, was it?" Rod asked.

Father Al looked up, startled. "Why not? The letter's
genuine, I assure you! That *is* the impression of the real Papal
Seal, and the signature of the real Pope!''

"Yes, but not *his* pope."

Father Al frowned. "What do you mean? John XXIV *is*
Pope . . . Oh."

"Yes." Rod nodded. "In *our* universe."

"But he is not, in this universe?''

"How could he be?''

"Why not?" Father Al turned a beaming smile on him.
"This Earth is very much like the Terra of our universe; the
constellations are the same; the language is the same as that of

Renaissance England. Why might there not be people who are the same in both universes, too?''

"You don't seriously believe that, do you?''

Father Al shrugged. "I'm willing to consider it. But it doesn't really matter greatly. We Catholics believe that the Pope speaks for God, when he speaks *as* Pope, not just as himself—*ex cathedra*, we call it.''

Rod stopped dead still, ramrod-straight, eyes closed. He counted to ten, then said carefully, "Father—doesn't that strike you as a little medieval?''

"Have you looked around you lately?''

"Cheap rejoinder, Father.'' Rod fixed him with a gimlet eye. *"Our* universe isn't medieval—but your belief is.''

"Not really,'' Father Al said earnestly. "Spiritual beliefs really can't be proven or disproven by physics or chemistry, any more than theology can deduce the formula for a polymer. It comes down to faith, after all—and we believe that Christ gave Peter the power to speak for Him, when He told that first Bishop of Rome, 'I give to you the keys to the Kingdom of Heaven. What you bind on Earth, it shall be bound in Heaven; what you loose on Earth, it shall be loosed in Heaven.' We also believe that Peter's 'keys' descended to his successors, down to the present Pope.''

"Very interesting, but I don't see . . .'' Rod broke off, staring. "Oh, no! You don't mean. . .''

"Why not?'' Father Al smiled. "Did you think there would be a different God for each universe? I can't prove it with physical evidence, but I believe in a God who existed before anything else did, and who created everything—one God who began *all* the universes. I've noticed that the people here are Christians—Roman Catholics, in fact. So, if it's the same God for both universes, and the Pope speaks for Him, says what God wants said, surely the Pope in this universe will give the same answer to any given question as the Pope in our universe would.''

"So your Writ from your Pope says what the Pope in *this* universe wants that old priest in there to do.'' Rod gave

Father Al a sidelong look. "Doesn't that sound just a teeny bit lame to you, Father?"

"Of course," said Father Al, with a disarming smile. "Because, when my Pope wrote this letter, he wasn't speaking *ex cathedra;* so he was speaking as John the XXIV, not as Pope. Nonetheless, I've no doubt the Christians here hold basically the same beliefs as Christians in our home universe; so I don't doubt the Pope here would want me to have this altar stone." He frowned, gazing at the sky.

"Pretty problem, though, isn't it?" Then his face cleared. "Well, I'll tell the Jesuits about it, when we get back. Shall we get down to business?"

CHAPTER TWENTY-ONE

Gwen brought her broomstick hovering over the ledge, a hundred yards from the Tower, and brought it slowly to ground. Rod and Father Al dismounted, just as Magnus and Geoff popped into sight beside them.

"What're *you* two doing here?" Rod demanded. "I want you up on top of that crag!"

"Aw, Papa! Do we *have* to?"

"Yes, you do! I want you watching from a safe distance, ready to teleport me out of there if it looks like he's really apt to kill me! And where's Elidor?"

Magnus's eyes widened; then guilt rose in them. "Uh— we left him atop the crag."

"Uh-huh!" Rod nodded grimly. "So what's to stop a spriggan from hopping in and snatching him again, huh? Now, you two get back there—fast!"

"Yes, Pap . . ." They disappeared before they finished the syllable.

"And that goes for you, too." Rod glowered at the witchling who hovered before him on a makeshift hearth-broom. "Stay out of the fight, Cordelia! But help your Mama, and be ready to drop a few rocks on the meany!"

"Oh, all *right*, Papa!" Cordelia huffed, and wheeled her broomstick up and away toward the top of the mountain.

"You, too, dear." Rod caught Gwen's hand. "Out."

"I will." Tears stood in her eyes. "Take care of thysel'."

"I will," Rod promised. "You take care of me, too, huh?" And he gathered her in.

Father Al turned away to study the local geology for a few minutes.

Rod turned back to him with a happy sigh. Air whooshed

behind him as Gwen swooped back up to the top of the mountain.

"Some very interesting stratification, here." Father Al pointed to the rockface. "At a guess, I'd say this was a seabed a few million years ago."

"I'm sure it was—and thank you for your delicacy, Father. Come on, let's go meet the monster."

They strode down the rock ledge, Rod saying, "Now, I want this clear. I go in first, to draw his attention; then, while I've got him occupied, you sneak up behind and brain him with the stone."

"I think a touch will suffice," Father Al murmured.

"What happens if he knocks you over the ledge, and still turns around in time to brain me?"

"Wear a crucifix, don't you?"

"Not ordinarily; but it's a good thought." Father Al pulled out a rosary and slipped it over his head. "Now! The crucifix will protect me—because he'll have to look away from me to avoid seeing it."

Rod nodded. "Right."

"And since I'm protected, *I* should go in first."

Rod stopped dead.

"You must admit, it's more logical."

Rod sighed. "Well, I never did have too much luck against logic. All right, Father, you win. You first, into the lion's den—but I'll be right behind you."

"Your reference was to Daniel," Father Al mused as they started up again. "I wonder—is your soul in as good a shape as his was?"

Rod was quiet for a few paces. Then he admitted, "I *was* raised Roman Catholic . . ."

"And how long has it been since you took the Sacraments?"

Rod sighed. "My wedding, Father—nine years ago. And you've got a point—if a lion's in there, I'd better be in top shape. Give me a few minutes to examine my conscience."

And they moved slowly toward Redcap, murmuring softly together.

"Ego te absolvo," Father Al said finally, making the sign of the Cross. "And I think you're about to meet your penance."

They rounded a curve, and the Tower loomed over them.

The ledge around the tower was strewn with human bones and a few skulls. That almost did Rod in, right there. The fear hit, suddenly and totally. He paused, letting it wash over and through him. The tidal wave passed, leaving that old, familiar, clutch-bellied, knee-jellied feeling; but he could cope with that. He glanced at Father Al; the priest looked to be feeling it, too. His face was drawn and pale, but his lips firmed with resolve. He unwrapped the altar stone and held it out with both hands. "Are we ready, then? . . . Good. 'Then into the Valley of Death.' " And he strode forward before Rod could say anything, chanting:

" 'He who digs a pit may fall into it,
And he who breaks through a wall
May be bitten by a serpent!
He who moves stones may be hurt by them,
And he who chops wood is in danger from it!
If the iron becomes dull,
Though at first he made easy progress,
He must increase his efforts;
But the craftsman
Has the advantage of his skill!' "

With a roar, the Redcap was on him.

It bolted out of the tower, crusted with filth and crazed with hatred and loneliness—about five feet high; shoulders as wide as a barrel; greasy, grizzeled hair flying about its shoulders, huge eyes afire with bloodlust. Its tunic and leggings were stiff with grease and covered with dirt; its iron boots rang on the stone and crunched through bone. It whirled a pikestaff high with one hand, like a hatchet; then its rusty edge sliced down at the priest.

Then Redcap saw the altar stone, and clanked to a halt.

They stood frozen for a moment, the priest holding out the

stone like a shield, the monster glaring at it balefully.

Rod drew his sword and came running.

Father Al began to chant again:

" '. . . a live dog is better
Than a dead lion. For the. . .' "

Redcap roared and slashed out with his pikestaff.

The flat of the blade slammed into Father Al's side; he went flying, landed ten feet away, the altar stone jarring out of his hand. Redcap grabbed a small boulder, still roaring, and heaved it at the stone. It swerved aside at the last second, narrowly missing Father Al's head.

Then Rod leaped in, shouting, " 'Oh ye dry bones, now hear the word of the Lord! . . . I heard a noise; it was a rattling as the bones came together. . .'' and lunging full-out for Redcap's belly. The sword shot into the monster's smock with a CLANK! that shocked through Rod's arm and into his body. The blasted critter was made of rock!

Redcap brayed laughter and swatted out at Rod back-handed. Pain flared through Rod's side, and the cliff and tower tumbled past him. Then, with a crack that exploded through him, he stopped, and got a close-up view of a rock wall sliding upward past him. He realized he was sliding down the cliff face and turned, frantically, as he jolted to a stop on the ledge. He was just in time to see two small figures appear right next to Redcap, inside his guard, and start chopping at his legs with small swords. "Boys, no!" he tried to yell, "Get back to your mother!" but it came out more like a chorus from a frog-pond. He could scarcely hear it himself, anyway; Redcap was roaring loudly as he reached down toward the mites. . .

A boulder slammed into the back of his head.

Redcap jolted forward, and tripped over Magnus, went sprawling. Small rocks bombarded him; then a boulder crashed down, just as he was getting up to his hands and knees. It crashed into his back, flattening him again.

Magnus and Geoffrey ran to finish him off.

Panic surged as Rod scrambled to his feet, lashing over him like a coating of fire. He had to get his boys out of there! He stumbled forward as Redcap heaved mightily, shaking the rock off his back, and rolled to his feet just in time for the boys to carom off his legs. He laughed wickedly, and bent toward them, then straightened suddenly and reached up to catch a boulder. He swung around following its inertia, and hurled it back up toward the mountaintop.

The bastard! If he'd hit Gwen or Cordelia . . . Boiling rage surged up in Rod, seeming almost to come from somewhere outside himself, flaming hatred at a monster who dared injure *his* child! He slammed into the back of Redcap's knees, and pain howled through his shoulder; then a small mountain crashed down on his back. Dimly, he heard Magnus howl, and fought his head up just in time to see Father Al, on hands and knees, reach out toward Redcap, who lay fallen backward across Rod. The stone was in the priest's hand; it touched the monster's forehead. Redcap howled, his body bucking in agony—

And disappeared.

Rod stared, not believing.

Then the whole scene turned dim; stars shot through it, a cascade of stars, leaving darkness in their wake. . .

". . . three broken ribs. That nosebleed is stopped? Then the flow's from his mouth."

"Oh, Father! His lung. . . ?"

"Pierced? Could. . ."

The sound faded out, then faded in again. ". . . shoulder's broken, and the collarbone. How . . ." Roaring came up like the surf, then faded. ". . . on his feet again?"

"His back is broke?"

"No, but I think there're cracked vertebrae."

Rod felt awfully sorry for the poor slob they were talking about. Who, he wondered?

Then an inspiration hit: Look. Just open the eyes, take a look.

Who was that, crying in the background?

Trouble was, there was this sandbag on each eyelid. And pain, that blasted pain, all through him! But he could do it; he'd done tougher things. He just fought a giant, hadn't he? A five-foot giant. . .

"Please, Magnus, staunch thy tears, and comfort thy sister and brother! Elidor, canst not help with Geoffrey? I must work!"

Agony seared through his shoulder. His eyes snapped open, and he bawled like a dogie who'd bumped a branding iron.

A lovely face hovered over him, framed with flaming hair. "He wakes! Husband! Dost hear me?"

Reason returned for an afterthought: Gwen was trying to mend his shoulder telekinetically. "Stop . . . please . . . Pain. . ."

"It will take time." She nodded, tense-lipped. "But it must be done. Oh, Rod! So many wounds. . ."

"It won't work; there're too many, and it'll take too long." Father Al's face slid into view as Gwen's slid out. "High Warlock! Hear me! Wish, as you've never wished before! Wish, with all your might, all your being, for your body to be whole again, completely mended, as it was before you ever were wounded!"

"I do," Rod croaked. Now that the priest mentioned it, he did! Oh, how he wished! If anything could stop this agony, let it happen! He wished, fervently, for total health, for an unmarked body, for the wounds to go away, and never come back. . . !

And the helping spirit was there again, sliding inside, up, and all through him, kindly, reassuring, healing, absorbing the hurt. . .

Then it was gone—and so was the pain.

Rod stared, unbelieving.

Then he lifted his head, slowly, and looked down at his body. He was covered with blood, and his clothing was torn to rags—but the blood was still, there was nothing new running. And he felt well. In fact, he felt wonderful.

"Uh . . . Gwen. . ."

"Aye, husband." She was there, her hand cradling his head.

"Just to be on the safe side, I'd better not move. Check the shoulder, will you?"

He felt her fingers probing—rather pleasant sensation, really. In fact, more than pleasant. . .

" 'Tis whole, Rod." There was wonder in her voice.

He relaxed with a sigh, letting his head fall back. "Thank Heaven for that! Was there anything else wrong?"

"Quite a bit," Father Al admitted.

The children had hushed.

"Check it out, would you? I'd hate to move if I'm going to start hurting again."

"I will, husband." He felt her fingers probing his side, his collarbone, his nose, rolling him a little to test his back.

"Thou'rt whole, husband." The wonder gave way to rejoicing. "Oh, thou'rt healed!"

"Well, then, let's get back into action." He sat up and gathered her in. She clung to him as though he were a rock in the rapids, sobbing. "There, now—there, love," he murmured. "I'm okay now. There, be a good girl, don't cry, we'll go find a haystack as soon as the kids're asleep, and I'll prove it."

She smiled up at him, blinking through her tears. "Well, if I'd any doubts, they're resolved. Thou *art* healed."

"Papa!" shrieked three jubilant voices, and the kids piled onto him.

He just barely managed to remain upright, patting and hugging. "There, now, children, don't worry. Papa had a bad time, but he's clear now . . . Gwen, watch Elidor, would you? We don't want to lose him again . . . No, now, there, I'm all right!"

"Aye," Gwen breathed, eyes glowing. "Father Al hath cured him."

"No—*he* did," the priest insisted. "I just told him what to do."

Rod stilled.

Then he cleared the children gently out of his line of sight.

"You mean *I* wrought that miracle cure?"

"Well . . ." Father Al spread his hands. "We'd already established that what you wished, happened . . ."

"Yes, we had," Rod agreed. "Ready to try a hypothesis yet, Father?"

"No-o-o-o," the priest pursed his lips. "But I *am* getting closer. . ."

"You and my robot," Rod sighed, getting to his feet. "He never would state a hypothesis until it was established fact. Hey, I don't even feel any of the aches from those faery pinches last night!"

"Interesting," Father Al breathed. "Have any old scars?"

"Hm—that's a thought." Rod glanced at Gwen. "We'll have to check that tonight, dear."

She blushed, and explained to the priest, "Some of them are where he cannot see them."

"I always did like a good Christian marriage," Father Al agreed. "Well! If we've picked up all the pieces, can we get back to the chapel? I have an altar stone to return."

"Yeah, I don't see any reason for hanging around here." Rod surveyed the scene, turning grim. "Hey! What're you doing, Magnus?"

"Picking up pieces." The boy straightened, holding up a long, sharp tooth. "Can I keep this for a trophy, Papa?"

"What—the monster left a tooth behind?" Rod shuddered. "Why would you want to remember *him,* son?"

"I do not know, Papa." Magnus's chin thrust out a little. "I only know that I think 'twould be wise."

Rod frowned down at him. Then he said, "Well, I've learned that your hunches generally turn out to be worth having. Okay, take it along—but wrap it up tight, and swab it down with alcohol first chance you get."

"I will, Papa." Magnus blossomed into a smile and pulled a rag from his wallet.

It *had* been a handkerchief, once. Rod turned to Gwen. "Ready to go, dear?"

"Aye." She picked up her broomstick.

"And I." Father Al came up, tucking the wrapped altar

stone under his arm. He looked up at the tower. "Whose army will garrison this place now, do you think—Duke Foidin's, or Lord Kern's?"

"Whichever gets here fastest." Rod turned away. "Frankly, Father, right now, I'd love to see the blasted thing fall apart." He looked up sharply at the gleam in Magnus's eye. "Don't you dare!"

They came out of the copse toward the back door of the church as the sun was setting. Rod looked around the town, frowning. "Little quiet, isn't it?"

"It *is* the hour for supper," Gwen mused.

"Well, it's been a strange day all around." Father Al knocked on the "rectory" door. "No doubt the good Father will explain."

The door opened a crack, showing an eye and a slice of beard. The eye widened, then so did the door. "Thou livest!"

"Was there any doubt of it?" Father Al smiled and held out the altar stone. "We had a saint on our side!"

The old priest took it gingerly, as though not quite believing it was real. "And the Redcap? Is he dead?"

"Well, vanished, anyway." Rod smiled. "I don't think he'll come back."

"Nay, they never return, once they've been routed; none of the faery folk do!" The old priest breathed a long, shaky sigh. "We heard thunder in the mountains, and hid our heads. I and half the parish are here, besieging Heaven with prayers for your safety."

"Well, that explains my quick recovery." Rod locked gazes with Father Al. "I had reinforcements."

"A very intense field to draw from, nearby?" The priest pursed his lips. "Perhaps. . ."

"Dost thou know what thou hast done?" the old priest burst out. "Caravans once did move through that pass above us—whole armies! None ha' dared venture there for ten years, since the King's army attempted, and lost!"

Rod stared, his eyes growing huge. Then he stabbed his

finger toward the mountain pass a few times, making noises in his throat.

"Milord?" the old priest said humbly.

"You mean . . ." Rod finally got his voice in gear. "You mean *that* was the monster that's been blocking Lord Kern from coming out of the Northwest?"

"Aye," the old priest said, " 'twas, indeed."

Rod clasped his hands tight to stop the trembling, then had to clench his teeth to stop the chattering.

The old priest blinked, bemused, then turned to Father Al. "Should I not ha' told him?"

"Oh, no, it's all right, it's all right!" Rod protested. "I'm just glad you didn't tell me *before* we went up there. . ."

CHAPTER TWENTY-TWO

They camped that night by a mountain stream. When the trout had been eaten and the bones buried, and the children and Father Al lay bundled up in blankets the villagers had been only too glad to contribute, Gwen cozied up to Rod with her eyes on the campfire. "Thou dost lead us northwest now, husband."

Rod shrugged. "Why not? Somehow, I think we'd better keep moving—and we *are* trying to get to Lord Kern. Though why, I don't know," he added as an afterthought. "We could just sit back now, and wait for him to come to us."

"Indeed. He will likely march down through the pass with all his army, to rend Duke Foidin from the seat of power." Her eyes strayed to the sleeping children. "There should be one more amongst them, husband."

"There should." Rod felt the aching longing for his baby. "But remember, dear—he's safer where he is. . ."

"Would I could be sure of it, with King and Abbot like to rend the land with civil war." Her eyes lost focus; suddenly, she stiffened. "I do hear his thoughts again!"

"Whose! Gregory's?"

"Aye." She clutched Rod's forearm, gazing off into space. "Aye, 'tis the touch of his mind. Oh, my bairn! . . . He seems alive and well. Be comforted, sweeting; thy mother and thy father strive to rejoin thee, as certainly as thou seekest us! . . . His touch is stronger now, mine husband."

Stronger? Rod frowned. Why should that be? The two universes couldn't have come closer together!

"And Fess—his words begin!" Gwen frowned, concentrating. "Still, I cannot quite discern the words. Summat

there is, about Dr. McAran, and the crafting of weird engine
. . . and the Crown and Church; the Southern barons do
declare they cannot, in all good conscience, fight against
their Holy Mother Church . . . The Northern barons have
sent men and knights to Tuan . . . And the Abbot hath sent
out a call to all the nobles, summoning them with men and
arms, to fight against the tyranny he doth say doth threaten
Holy Mother Church!''

Rod groaned. ''They're shaping up to start a civil war for
sure! Of course, the Southern lords see this as their big
chance to break their oaths of fealty to Tuan with some moral
justification, and without losing the support of their people!''

''Yet they have not declared allegiance to the Abbot, nor
defiance to the Crown,'' Gwen said hopefully.

''Only because the Abbot just got around to issuing the call
to arms! Mark my words, Gwen, there're futurian agents
showing their hands in this. Someone's gotten to the
Abbot—why else would he turn around to nullify his agree-
ment with Tuan, before he'd even arrived home at his
monastery? One of his entourage is a totalitarian agent, and
talked him into it on the road! The totalitarians would love to
have the Church take over the government; a medieval theocracy could turn into a very tight police state, if it were given
a few modern techniques! And the anarchists are probably
advising the lords again—they'd love to see the barons band
together under the Church's banner, just long enough to
topple the monarchy, then fall to bickering between themselves until the whole country fell into warlordism!'' He
slammed a fist into his palm. ''Damn! And I'm stuck here,
where I can't fight 'em!''

''I believe 'tis as they planned,'' Gwen murmured.

''You bet it is! And in the middle of all of that is *my baby!*''

''Peace, mine husband,'' Gwen soothed. ''We do come
nigh Lord Kern; quite soon enough, we shall return to our
own time and place; sweet chuck, doubt it not! Then shalt
thou make all things well.''

''You've got more faith in me than I do,'' Rod grated—but

he was calming down a bit. ''But maybe you're right. Okay, darling—you go 'talk' to baby; reassure him, tell him we're still with him, at least in spirit—and our bodies will be joining him, as soon as they can.''

"I will," she murmured, and leaned against his shoulder, eyes glazed. He sat as still as he could, gazing out at the stream, his thoughts in turmoil, worry about his baby son alternating with stewing about the war, and ways to avert it. He sorted through a dozen different plans for information he could send back to Fess through Gwen's telepathy, that might brake the conflict—but none of them could work. If he were there in person, his stature as High Warlock, and as the architect of the Crown's previous victories over the lords and the mob, would turn the balance; both sides would listen to what he said and, to some extent, would back off due to sheer intimidation. But that required his personal presence; there wasn't much string-pulling he could do, without at least being on the puppet stage.

But the scheming did dissipate the adrenalin; that, and maybe some spillover from Gwen's comforting of Gregory. He began to feel more relaxed. Then he glanced at his sleeping children, and let the warmth and security of the family seep in to calm him. He put his arm around Gwen, resting his cheek on her head.

'' 'Tis faded,'' she murmured. "Yet I think I left him comforted.''

"Me, too. You seem to have a wonderful effect on males.''

Gwen smiled. ''I would thou hadst thought of that ere we left the village.''

Rod frowned. "Why?"

"For that we could ha' stayed the night there—and mayhap found a chamber to ourselves.'' She looked up at him, eyes wide; and he felt himself being drawn down into them, down, down . . . He let himself go, but only as far as her lips. Still, it was a very long, and very satisfying, kiss.

Unfortunately, it was also very stimulating.

He pulled himself out of the kiss with a sigh. "Well, when we find Lord Kern, maybe he'll spare us a room for the night—alone."

"Aye." She smiled sadly. "Till then, we must needs bide in patience." She let go, and lay back, rolling her blanket around her. "Good night, husband—and wake me if thine eyelids droop."

He'd rather have waked for other reasons, but he only said, "I will. 'Night, love," and caressed her hair.

She smiled contentedly, and wriggled under his touch, then lay still.

The whole night was still. He sat beside the dwindling fire, watching the woods and thinking long thoughts. When the moon had set, he woke Father Al, and rolled up in his own blanket.

Then a small earthquake rocked him. He looked up blearily, frowning; he'd *just* managed to doze off. . .

"Lord Gallowglass, we've got company," Father Al informed him, "and it wishes to speak to you."

" 'It?' " Rod scrambled out of his blanket.

"Yes. In fact, it ducked back down under water at sight of me; it just barely had time to call for 'the wizard.' "

"I thought there were supposed to be *fewer* interruptions, at night." Rod glanced toward the east. "Mm. Not all that much 'night' any more, is it? Well, I'll take the call." He went over to the stream, and called out, "This is the wizard speaking."

A splash, and a gush of water, and a great, green, round head on a huge pair of shoulders, with a red cocked hat on its head (a feather in it, yet!) popped out of the stream. It was covered with scales; its nose was long, sharp, and red at the tip; it had little pig's eyes, and was covered with green scales. It held up a webbed hand, and grinned. "Good morn to thee, wizard!"

Rod squeezed his eyes shut and gave his head a shake, then looked up again. "Uh—good morning."

"Aye, I'm real." The water-man grinned. "Thou'st never seen a Merrow afore?"

" 'Fraid not, I wasn't quite ready for it. Uh—don't you

find that stream a little confining?''

''Aye, but we go where we must. I am sent with word for thee.''

''What word?''

''Word of the Redcap thou'st routed from the Tower of Gonkroma.''

Rod shuddered. ''I'm not really interested in where that critter is, thank you.''

''Then thou'lt wish to know where it ha' been—or so says the Grand Duchess.'' The Merrow rolled an eye at him. ''The fellow appeared out of nowhere, struck away guards, and stole a yearling child away.''

Rod stared, electrified.

Gwen rolled over and sat up sleepily. ''What moves, husband?'' Then she caught sight of the Merrow; her eyes widened.

So did his, and his grin turned toward a leer.

''Good morrow,'' Gwen said graciously.

''No, good Merrow,'' Rod corrected. ''At least, he'd better be.'' He let his hand rest on his dagger-hilt.

The Merrow held up both webbed hands and bowed its head. ''Ha' no fear o' me. I am nothing if not willing, and seek nought else in return. I only seek to discharge my message, nought more.''

''What message?'' Gwen frowned up at Rod.

''It seems Redcap wanted revenge,'' Rod said slowly. ''He's stolen an infant, and disappeared.''

Gwen gasped.

''I know,'' Rod said grimly, ''but we've got to get home; we've lost enough time playing Good Samaritans. I mean, I feel sorry for the kid and its parents, but. . .'' He ran down under Gwen's glare.

''Be shamed,'' she said severely. ''The child would rest securely, had we not routed Redcap.'' She turned to the Merrow. ''Who sent thee?''

''The Grand Duchess.''

''Then tell her we will seek out Redcap, and have the child back.''

The Merrow looked questioningly at Rod.

"All right, all right!" Rod threw up his hands. "I know when I'm beaten, between you and my conscience! Might be the same thing, come to think of it . . . All right, Monsieur. We'll do it. And if I know the Grand Duchess, she's got thorough information about the specifics. Who's the child?"

"Whose? Why, Lord Kern's, of course."

Rod and Gwen both stared.

Then Rod said slowly, "Does Duke Foidin know about this?"

"Aye. A troop of his men doth race hotfoot to seize the child—though, knowing Redcap's repute, I misdoubt me that they make quite so much speed as they might."

"I don't blame 'em," Rod said grimly. "But *if* they succeed, Foidin will have the best hostage he could hope for. He might even be able to make Kern surrender. Who told Foidin about the kidnapping?"

"Eorl Theofrin, who knew from a gazing-crystal, be-like."

"Theofrin?" Rod frowned. "Why would he suddenly be helping the Duke?"

"For the enmity he bears thee." The Merrow grinned.

Rod just watched him for a minute, trying to figure it out. Then he gave up. "All right, I'll ask the obvious question: How does telling Foidin about the kidnapping help Theofrin hurt *me?*"

The Merrow spread his hands. "I know not, milord."

" 'Tis a trap, mine husband," Gwen said softly.

Rod nodded. "They must be figuring we'll run to the kid's rescue—and they're right. Then the troops come in, and capture the kid *with* us. Well, I think we can have a little surprise waiting for them."

"But do we guess aright?"

"We'll know when we get there." Rod slapped his scabbard. "If we see a battle in progress when we get there, we've guessed wrong—in which case, we'll puzzle it out later. Did the Grand Duchess say where Redcap's hiding?"

"Aye." The Merrow nodded. "He ha' found an auld tower, at Dun Kap Weir."

"Yonder." Elidor pointed down at a ruined tower atop a mound in the middle of a plain. " 'Tis Dun Kap Weir. Foul deeds were done there, long years ago."

"Of course." Rod smiled sardonically. "What other kind of lair would Redcap choose? I don't like this coming east again, back into the Duke's country."

"We are warned against his troops," Gwen reminded him. "Hai! They are there!"

Rod peered down over her shoulder, at a battle raging in front of the tower. A dozen foot soldiers fought frantically, shouting, pikes flashing in the early sunlight. Underneath their clamor was roaring.

"I guess they weren't planning to ambush us," Rod mused.

Suddenly, two men went flying. They hit twenty feet downslope and lay still, among a score of their fellows.

"What a fighter!" Rod shook his head in admiration. "Redcap against thirty soldiers, alone! Too bad he's on the wrong side. . .''

"Do not think of converting him," Gwen said grimly.

Five more soldiers went flying. The rest drew back, leaving an open half-circle; for a moment, the stunted ogre stood at bay, facing his enemies.

Then he whirled up his pike and charged them, bellowing. They howled in fear and ran. Redcap followed them to the brow of the hill and stood, glowering down, breathing heavily, watching as they tripped over their fallen comrades and went rolling, scrambling back to their feet, then running on down the hill and over the meadow to the shelter of nearby trees.

Redcap tossed his head and turned back to his tower.

"What do we do now?" Father Al asked.

"Let me." Magnus suddenly disappeared.

"Magnus—NO!" Rod and Gwen shouted together, and the broomstick went into a power dive.

Redcap whirled, looking up at the shout—so they had a great view as Magnus appeared in front of the monster, holding up its missing tooth. Redcap just stared at it, frozen, wide-eyed. Then he began to tremble.

"My father comes, with the priest," Magnus warned.
"Begone, foul monster, and never come near human places
again!"

Redcap threw back his head with a shriek of dismay, and
disappeared.

Cordelia shot past Gwen on her broomstick, and darted
through the tower doorway.

"Cordelia! Thou knowest not what may dwell there!"
Gwen cried, and shot after her.

Rod leaped off five feet above ground and landed running.
He jumped up against the side of the tower to brake his
momentum, and rebounded to face his son.

Magnus was calmly picking up something from the spot
where Redcap had been standing. He held it up for his father
to see—another long, nicked tooth.

"Well—it worked out okay." Rod stepped up to his boy
and caught him against his hip in a bruising hug. "But don't
do something like that again, son—please! I could swear you
took five years off my life, and your mother's! What
would've happened if you'd been wrong? If the sight of his
own tooth *hadn't* banished him?"

"But it did," Magnus's voice said, muffled.

Rod sighed. "And I'll admit, I'll never question your
hunches—but couldn't *you* learn to?"

Cordelia appeared in the tower doorway. "Papa! Come
quickly!"

Rod ran.

He braked to a halt beside Gwen, saw an infant wrapped in
her arms. He sighed and relaxed, the ebb of adrenalin leaving
him weak. *"This* is an emergency?"

She turned an unfocused, faraway gaze up to him. " 'Tis
Gregory."

Rod stared down at the baby. Dark hair, big grey eyes—
and that look. That solemn, solemn look. "But—it can't be!
Not here!"

But it made sense—almost. If someone had thrown Gregory through the Gate, Redcap would have sensed he was Rod

and Gwen's baby, and have gone after him in revenge!

"The *child* is not." Gwen's voice was remote. " 'Tis almost more like him than himself—yet 'tis not him; I would know."

"Then what . . . ?"

"His thoughts." Her eyes searched for his face, but stayed far away. "This child carries Gregory's thoughts."

Of course! That was why they'd been able to hear Gregory's thoughts twice before—and why the second contact was clearer; they been further northwest, closer to this child!

"It could happen," Father Al said quietly. "In another universe, there *could* be a child that exactly corresponds to your own. And your Gregory has been searching, yearning outward, achingly, with every iota of his tiny strength—enough for his thoughts to resonate through another mind, exactly like his own. Then, once *this* child was stolen from *his* parents, his mind would do the same—and their thoughts would meld, so that Gregory's would become much more clear."

"So their minds form a link between universes?"

Father Al nodded. "If the two individuals are analogs of one another."

"Words come," Gwen said suddenly. " 'Tis Fess . . . '. . . attempted to turn off the transmitter and close the Gate, but I prevented them, and remanded them to King Tuan; they are in his prison. They admit to being futurian anarchists, but nothing more; and King Tuan, in accordance with your joint policies, continues to resist Queen Catharine's insistence on using torture. Brom O'Berin summoned Yorick . . .' "

Father Al started.

Rod cocked an eyebrow at him.

" '. . . Yorick, who identified the device as *not* being a time machine, and brought Dr. McAran, who tentatively identifies it as a mechanism allowing travel between alternate universes. He is currently working at fever-pitch, attempting to construct such a device of his own. He attempted to dismantle this one, but I would not permit him to turn it off. So, if you can endure, help should be forthcoming—

eventually. Meanwhile, in your absence, the Church and
Crown have moved toward war. The Abbot has issued a
formal declaration that the Crown encroaches so far upon the
authority of the Church that all folk of good conscience
should resist their King and Queen as tyrants. He has ab-
solved the barons from their oaths of fealty, and summoned
them to attack Their Majesties in force. Four Southern barons
have answered his call, with all their knights and men. Three
Northern lords have brought their armies to Tuan. The other
five lords claim the conflict is no concern of theirs, but is only
between the Church and Crown; they therefore stand neutral.' ''

"Ready to jump in and take over when the other barons
have torn each other, and the Crown, apart," Rod growled.

There was time for it; Gwen had paused, eyes glazed, lips
parted, waiting. Now she spoke again. " 'FCC robot number
651919, transmitting on human-thought frequency, near the
Gate through which the Gallowglass family disappeared, in
an attempt to contact them. Though I think it extremely
unlikely that the Gate will re-transmit my signal into another
universe, I must attempt it. Situation report: The agents
responsible for your exile attempted to turn off the transmitter
and close the Gate . . .' '' She blinked, eyes focusing
again. "He repeats himself."

Rod nodded. "Faithful old Fess, standing twenty-four-
hour watch at the Gate, trying somehow to reach us. He
probably doesn't even realize Gregory's his transmission
link. Just keeps repeating the message over and over, hoping
against hope—and updating the situation report, of course."

Father Al nodded. "I was wondering when you'd get
around to confirming that your horse was a robot."

Rod jerked his head impatiently. "No point in giving away
information, is there? Though I might as well have; you do a
very nice job of putting together comments I've dropped here
and there." He turned to Gwen. "Did you reassure him?"

She nodded. "As well as I could—that we still do live, and
will come home."

"But not when." Rod's mouth tightened. "Well, you do

have to at least *try* to be honest with a child.'' He looked up. ''And with ourselves. The situation at home just keeps getting worse, and here we stick!''

''Thou didst say, husband, that even should it come to open war, our babe will not be endangered.''

''Yeah, *probably* not—but even two percent sounds like too high a probability, when we're talking about our own baby! Come on, Gwen, let's get out of here and return this infant to his rightful parents, so we can get busy collecting the favor his father owes us—a quick burst of magic that'll send us back to Gramarye. If he can do it. Let's go.'' He turned away to the doorway, looking about him, frowning. ''Magnus and Geoff and Elidor stayed outside, eh?''

He stepped through the doorway, and saw his sons lying unconscious at the feet of soldiers dressed in the Duke's livery.

Then something exploded on the back of his head, and he just had time for one quick thought, before the stars wiped out the scene:

Of course. The Duke kept some forces in reserve for an ambush, just in case we did show up. . .

CHAPTER TWENTY-THREE

When he saw the light of day again, it was golden-orange, and dim. Turning a head that seemed as large as an asteroid and rang at the slightest touch, he saw the reason for the dimness—a tiny window, barred, and up near the low ceiling. Turning his head again in spite of the pain, he saw walls of rough-hewn rock, damp and splotched with fungus.

He levered himself up on his elbows. Consciousness tried to slide away again, but he hauled it back. Little Geoff huddled next to him, curled into a ball. Beyond him, Father Al sat gravely watching.

They were both shackled to the wall by four-foot lengths of heavy chain.

"Good afternoon, my friend," the priest said softly.

Geoff's head snapped up. He saw Rod's eyes open, and threw his arms around his neck. "Papa!" He began to cry.

"There, there, now, son," Rod soothed. Chains clanked as he wrapped his arms around Geoff. "Papa's all right. It'll be okay." He looked up at Father Al. "Where're Gwen and Cordelia and Magnus?"

"In a room like this one, I'd guess. The soldiers carrying them split off one floor up; I gather they've two layers of dungeons here."

"You were conscious."

"By then I was, yes." Father Al fingered a bruise in the middle of his tonsure. He had several more on his forehead and cheeks, and there was clotted blood around his nostrils. "It wasn't much of a fight. Your wife stepped out just as you started to crumble, and they caught her on the back of the head with a cudgel; she was out before she could do anything. Your little daughter and I made something of a try—the air

was quite thick with flying stones for a few minutes there, till
a soldier caught her from behind with a pike-butt. For myself,
I found a reasonably solid stick, and actually managed to lay
out a couple of them, myself.'' He sounded surprised.

''Which lost you your clergy's right to not get hit.'' Rod
found his respect for Father Al going up still more, while dull
anger grew at the bastards who'd struck his wife and
daughter—and clouted a priest, besides!

He took Geoff by the shoulders and held him back a little.
''Try to stop crying, son. I've got to check you over. Where
does it hurt?''

Geoff pointed to his head, and Rod fingered the spot
gently—there was a large goose-egg. Geoff winced as he
probed, but didn't cry out; and the bone didn't give when he
pressed it. Good. ''Look at me, son.'' He stared into Geoff's
eyes—the pupils were the same size. ''No, I think you're
okay.'' *Thank Heaven!* ''You'll have a headache for a while,
though. Now, close your eyes, and see if you can hear
Mama's thoughts.''

Obediently, Geoff sat back against the wall and squeezed
his eyes shut. After a few minutes, he said, ''She there,
Papa—'n' Mag'us 'n' 'Delia near. But everyone aseep!''

''Haven't come to, then.''

''*Big* sleep, Papa—bigger 'n' you just had!''

'Bigger?' Rod didn't like the sound of that—it smacked of
drugs.

A key clanked in the lock, and the door groaned open.
Duke Foidin stepped in, grinning, flanked by guards. ''Well,
well! The gentlemen wake!''

''Yes, we do.'' Rod glowered up at him. ''Gonna slip us a
sleeping potion now, like you did to my wife and other
children?''

The Duke couldn't quite mask the surprise. ''Well, well!
Thou dost have some power! And to think Eorl Theofrin
assured me 'twas the other three who were dangerous.''

''We operate as a unit,'' Rod snapped. ''What're you
planning to do with us?''

''Why, turn thee over to the Eorl, naturally—his help thus

far has been rather half-hearted, being solely concerned with capturing thyself. Thou must have offended him deeply.''

"I didn't exactly find him complimentary, myself.''

"Delightful, delightful!'' The Duke rubbed his hands. "He should be quite eager to seize thee and thine—eager enough to pledge full support. To assure it, I believe I'll give him thy family, but save thee till Lord Kern's defeated.''

Rod studied the Duke's face, deciding that his usual squeamishness about murder could be waived in this case.

"Oh, and thy wife! I had forgot!'' The Duke raised a finger. "I ha' not had time to attend to her properly—but I shall.'' A leering grin spread over his face. "Be assured that I shall.''

Rod held himself wooden-faced, but the anger and loathing condensed and hardened into iron resolve.

Footsteps clattered in the hall, and a soldier burst in, covered with dust and caked blood. He dropped to one knee. "Milord Duke! Foul sorcery! Lord Kern's troops filled the pass ere ours could come there! We battled to hold them within, but a horde of monsters turned our flank, and. . .''

"Be still, fool!'' The Duke snapped, with a furious glance at Rod. "Well, I must attend to this matter, wizard—but I'll see thee again, at my leisure! Come!'' he snapped to his guards, and whirled out the door. The messenger scrambled to his feet and stumbled after him. The guards clanked out and slammed the door; the key grated in the lock.

"I don't think he'll have much leisure for anything, now,'' Rod said, with vindictive pleasure. "Lord Kern'll come down like a whirlwind, and mop him up. Unless . . .'' his face darkened.

"Unless Eorl Theofrin joins him whole-heartedly?'' Father Al nodded. "But he has to buy Theofrin's support. I suggest we do what we can to eliminate his buying power.''

"Yes—and now, while he's busy!'' Rod turned to Geoff. "Try to wake Mama, son! She can get us out of these shackles. Try really hard.''

"I . . . will, Papa,'' the little boy said hesitantly. "But sleeps *real* hard.'' Nonetheless, he screwed his eyes shut, concentrating. His whole little face knotted up with trying.

Then he yawned.

"Son? . . . Geoff. Geoff!" Rod reached out and shook him. Geoff's head lolled over against him, with a little smile, and the boy breathed deeply and evenly.

"Damn! Whatever they put into her must've been *really* strong—it put him to sleep, too! What do we do now, Father?"

"A good point." The priest frowned down at his hands. "We are, as they say, thrown back on our own resources."

"Which means me," Rod said slowly. "Ready to try a theory now, Father?"

The priest sighed and straightened up. "I don't have much choice now, do I?"

"We *have* come to the crunch," Rod agreed.

"All right." Father Al slapped his hands on his thighs. "Try to follow me through this. First, the Gramarye espers could read your mind—until you fell in love with one of them."

"Hey, now, wait a minute. . ."

Father Al held up a hand. "It was your falling in love that did it. You can't remember the precise moment you became psionically 'invisible,' of course; but you weren't before you met her, and you were afterwards. What other event could have triggered it?"

"Mmf. Well, maybe," Rod grumbled. "But why? I want her to be able to read my mind, more than anyone!"

"No, you don't." Father Al waved a forefinger. "Not subconsciously, at least. She may be your greatest blessing, but she's also your greatest threat. A man's vulnerable to his beloved when he's vulnerable to no one else; because you've 'let her into your heart,' she can hurt you most deeply. You needed some defense, some way of keeping the core of yourself inviolate—which you couldn't do, if she could read your mind."

"It *sounds* sensible. But Lord, man, it's been nine years and four children! Wouldn't I have outgrown that by now? I mean, shouldn't my subconscious be convinced it can trust her?"

"Should," the priest agreed.

Rod was silent, letting the implications sink in.

Father Al gave him a few minutes, then said, "But that's beside the point. What matters here is that the ability to shield your mind from a telepath indicates some power in you, some sort of esper ability that you've never been aware of. Not the ones we ordinarily think of—I'd imagine there've been some rather desperate moments in your life, when you could've used such powers badly."

"Quite a few," Rod said sourly. "In fact, my subconscious should've dredged them up out of sheer instinct for survival."

"But it didn't; therefore, you don't have them. What I think you *do* have is the ability to use the psionic force that espers, and latent espers, leak into the general environment."

Rod frowned. "But there must've been plenty of that power leaking into the rocks and trees of Gramarye; in fact, the place must've been permeated with it. Why couldn't I use that?"

"Because you didn't know how. You didn't even know you could. You needed something to trigger it in you, to release it, and to teach you how to use it."

"So what did it? Just being in a universe where magic works?"

"Not quite." Father Al held up a forefinger. "When Redcap finished with you, you were so thoroughly chewed up that I doubt the most advanced hospital could've put your insides back together—but you wished for it, didn't you?"

Rod nodded slowly.

"And it worked." Father Al smiled. "That wasn't the doing of a neophyte wizard—it was the work of a master. And I suspect it took a bit more power than your own."

Rod frowned. "So where did it come from?"

"Lord Kern."

Rod looped his head down and around, and came up blinking. "How did you figure *that* one?"

"The child, the one we saved from Redcap. He's an exact double for your own infant son—and his analog." He stopped, watching Rod closely.

Rod watched back—and, slowly, his eyes widened. "Holy Hamburg! If the kid's Gregory's analog—then his parents have to be analogs of Gwen and me!"

Father Al nodded again.

"And if Lord Kern's his father—then Kern's my analog!"

"But of course," Father Al murmured. "After all, he, too, is High Warlock."

"And if he's my analog—then he and I can blend minds, just as his baby and Gregory did!"

"If you could learn to drop your psionic shield, yes—which, in a moment of great emotional stress, you did."

"At least for the moment." Rod frowned. "I never told you, Father—but each of those times I worked a 'spell,' I felt some . . . presence, some spirit, inside me, helping me."

"Lord Kern, without a doubt!" Father Al's eyebrows lifted. "Then perhaps there is something of the telepath about you—or about Lord Kern. For, do you see, whether or not you can hear his thoughts, you can apparently draw on his powers."

Rod shivered. "That's a little intimidating, Father. Well, at least he's a nice guy."

"Is he?" Father Al leaned forward, suddenly very intent. "What is he like?"

Rod frowned. "Well—from what I've felt when I was wanting some magic to happen—he seems kind, very kind, always willing to help anybody who needs it, even an interloper like me. But he's stern; he knows what he wants and what he believes is right, and he's not going to put up with anyone going against it."

"Hm." Father Al frowned. "That last sounds troubling."

"Oh, no, he's not a fanatic or anything! He's just not willing to watch someone hurt somebody else! Especially children. . ."

"Yes?" Father Al prompted. "What about children?"

Rod shuddered. "Threaten a child, and he goes into a rage. And if it's *his* child. . ."

"He loses control?"

"Well, not quite berserk. . ."

"It sounds somewhat like yourself," the priest said gently.

Rod sat still a moment; then he looked up. "Well, shouldn't it?"

"Of course." Father Al nodded. "He's your analog."

Rod nodded. "But where's *your* analog, Father?"

"Either we haven't met him, or he doesn't exist." The priest smiled. "Probably the latter—and that's why *I* can't work magic here."

Rod frowned. "But how come I'd have an analog, and you wouldn't?"

Father Al held out his hand with the fingers spread. "Remember our theory of parallel universes—that there's a set of 'root' universes, but any one 'root' branches? Every major historical event really ends both ways—and each way is a separate universe, branching off from the 'root.' For example, in our set of universes, the dinosaurs died, and the mammals thrived—but, presumably, there was another 'main branch' in which the *mammals* died, and the dinosaurs survived, and continued to evolve."

"So there might be a universe in which Terra has cities full of intelligent lizards." Rod gave his head a shake. "Sheesh! And the further back in time the universes branched off from one another, the further apart they are—the more unlike each other they are."

Father Al nodded slowly, gazing steadily at him.

Rod frowned. "I don't like being led. If you've got the next step in mind, *say* it."

Father Al looked surprised, then abashed. "Pardon me; an old teacher's reflexes. You see, this can't be the universe next to ours—we've skipped a whole set in which science rules, and magic's just fantasy. There should be a universe in which the DDT revolution failed, for example, and PEST still rules—and one in which the I.D.E. never collapsed, the old Galactic Union. And on, and on—one in which human-kind never got off of Terra, one where they made it to the Moon but no farther, one in which the Germans won World War II, one in which they won World War I and World War II never occurred . . . millions of them. We skipped past all of them, into a universe far, far away, in which magic works, and science never had a chance to grow.''

Rod stared, spellbound.

"Now, logically," Father Al went on, "since the farther you get from your 'home universe,' the more it changes—the number of people who have analogs grow fewer. For example, think of all the soldiers who came back from World War II with foreign brides. In the universe in which World War II never happened, those couples never met—so their descendants have no analogs in that universe, nor in any of the universes that branched off from it.''

Rod scowled. "Let me head you off—you're working around to saying that, by the time we get this far away, there're damn few analogs left.''

"Exactly." Father Al nodded. "Very few, my friend. You seem to be a very rare case.''

Suddenly, the stone floor felt very uncomfortable. "What makes me so special?''

"Oh, no!" Father Al grinned, holding up a palm. "You're not going to get me to make *any* guesses about that—not without a great deal more research! After all, it could just be a genetic accident—Lord Kern and yourself might not even have analagous grandfathers!''

"I doubt it," Rod said sourly.

"Frankly, so do I—but who's to tell? I don't quite have time to work out a comparative genealogy between yourself and Lord Kern.''

"But how many universes *do* I have analogs in?''

"Again—who knows? I'd guess you don't have any in universes that never developed *Homo Sapiens*—but I wouldn't want to guarantee it.''

Rod chewed at the inside of his lower lip. "So I might be

able to draw on the powers of wizards in still other, more magical, universes?''

''It's conceivable. Certainly you've got to have a great many analogs, to have come even this far.''

''That makes two 'I don't knows'—or is it three?'' Rod folded his legs. ''Time to quit speculating and get down to practicalities, Father. How do I control this gift? How do I go about drawing on Lord Kern's powers? I can't just wish—it's a little too chancey.''

''It surely is. But when you're wishing with great emotional intensity, all you're doing is opening yourself up—and there are techniques for doing that deliberately.'' Father Al leaned forward. ''Are you ready?''

Rod settled himself a little more comfortably, swallowed against the lurking dread that was trying to form in his belly, and nodded. ''What do I do?''

''Concentrate.'' Father Al held out his rosary, swinging the crucifix back and forth like a pendulum. It caught the remaining ray of golden sunlight and glittered. ''Try to let your mind go empty. Let your thoughts roam where they will; they'll settle down and empty out. Let the dancing light fill your eyes.''

''Hypnotism?''

''Yes, but you'll have to do it yourself—all I can do is give directions. Let me know when I seem a little unreal.''

''As of three days ago, the first time I met you.''

The priest shook his head. ''That kind of joke's a defense, my friend—and you're out to let the walls fade away, not make them thicker. Let your mind empty.''

Rod tried. After a little while, he realized that's what he was doing wrong. He relaxed, letting his thoughts go wherever they wished, keeping his eyes on the glittering cross. Words whirled through his mind like dry leaves; then they began to settle. Fewer and fewer remained—and he felt as though his face were larger, warmer, and his body diminished. The cross filled his eyes, but he was aware of Father Al's face behind it, and the stone room behind that— and he was aware of the ceiling and floor lines slanting together toward an unseen vanishing point, as though the whole thing was painted on a flat canvas. There seemed to be a sort of shield around him, unseen, a force-field, four feet thick . . . "I'm there."

"Now—reach out." The droning voice seemed both distant and inside his head. "Where's your mind?"

It was an interesting question. Rod's head was empty, so it couldn't be there. "Far away."

"Let your consciousness roam—find your mind."

It was an interesting experience—as though he were groping with some unseen extension through a formless void; but all the while, he still saw only the dungeon, and the priest.

Then the extension found something, and locked into place. "I've got it."

And power flowed to him—blind, outraged anger, a storm of wrath, that filled him, he could feel his skin bulging, feel it trying to get out of him and blast everything to char.

The crucifix filled his eyes again, and the priest was barking something, in Latin, Rod couldn't follow it, but it was a thundering command, with the power of Doom behind it.

Then the crucifix lowered, and the priest's voice was muffled, distant. "Whatever it is, it's not supernatural."

Rod shook his head, carefully. "It's human." His voice seemed to echo up through a long channel, and also be right there at his eardrums. It occurred to him that he should be scared, but he was too angry. Slowly, he rose to his knees, keeping himself carefully upright. "What do I do now?"

"Use it. First. . ."

A sudden shock shook Rod. "Hold it. It's using me."

"For what!"

"I don't know . . . No, I do. It's Lord Kern, and he's not a telepath, but I'm getting the bottom level of what he's going through. He just used me for a beacon, and he's drawing on me in some way, to teleport a chunk of his army in . . ." He convulsed again. "Another chunk of infantry . . . Cavalry . . . archers . . . they're all here now, very close by . . . Now he's done with me."

"Do you still have his power?"

Rod nodded.

"Wake your family."

Rod didn't try to slide into Geoff's mind; he just willed him awake, pushing a bit of power into him to throw off the effects of the drug. The little boy yawned and stretched, and looked up at his father with a sleepy smile. Then his eyes shot wide open, and he scrambled to his feet.

Rod reached over to grasp his shoulder. "It's okay, son. I'm still me. Now I've got to wake your brother and sister. Find them for me."

Geoff gulped, paling, and squeezed his eyes shut. It was almost as though Rod could see the line of his thought, arrowing off through the stone wall. He turned his eyes that way, glaring up at the ceiling, pushing power out to his family and willing them awake.

"They awake." Geoff's voice was hushed and subdued. Father Al gathered him in.

"Are they chained?"

"No, Papa. They were asleep."

"Then tell them to meet us at the stairwell. We're going to find Elidor."

"How, Papa?" Geoff held up his manacle.

Rod glared at the iron cuff, and it shattered. Geoff screamed and cowered back against Father Al. Rod glared at his other wrist, and the iron shattered again.

Slowly, Father Al held up his own wrists, side by side. The manacles shattered. The Rod pushed his arms straight forward, and his manacles crumbled. He stood up, very slowly, keeping his body very straight; he felt as though his head were swollen, his face two feet in front of itself. "Guide me, Father. I can't feel the floor."

And he couldn't—he could feel nothing but the tremendous, vibrating power that filled him, the towering rage that he fought to contain. He reached out to grasp the priest's arm, and Father Al gasped. Rod lightened his hold, and the priest guided him slowly toward the door. Geoffrey followed, eyes huge.

They paused at the huge oaken panel. The lock erupted in a cloud of wood-dust; when it settled, they saw the lock twisted half-out of the door. Rod kicked it open and staggered out into the hall. Father Al scurried along, holding him up, bracing him. Rod's head was beginning to ache now, with a savage throbbing. They moved toward the stairway.

There were a handful of guards at the iron gate. They looked up, saw Rod coming, stared, then caught up their pikes.

The iron gate suddenly wrenched itself out of shape, and the pikestaves exploded into flame. The soldiers shrieked and dropped their weapons, and spun toward the oaken door behind the gate—as it exploded into flame, too. They fell back, howling, as the center of the door blew out, scattering burning wood through the passage.

"I didn't do that," Rod croaked, "any of it."

And Gwen stalked through the door, surrounded by flame, eyes burning in wrath, coming to claim her man. Magnus and Cordelia leaped up on each side of her, faces flint, hounds of war.

She saw him coming, and the anger hooded itself. She came to him, caught his arm. "Husband—what hath thee?"

"Power," he croaked. "Lead me."

Up the stairwell, then, and through the halls. Soldiers came running, shouting, pikes at the ready. A huge invisible fist slammed them back against the walls. Courtiers leaped out with swords arcing down; something spun them aside and threw them down. The family stepped over their bodies, advancing.

They climbed the Keep. On the last step, Magnus suddenly screamed in rage and disappeared. Geoff yelled and disappeared after him.

"Where've they gone?" Rod grated.

"To the King's chamber!" Gwen's fingers tightened on his arm. "Hurry! Duke Foidin seeks to slay Elidor!"

Rod grabbed Cordelia's arm and closed his eyes, swaying, concentrating. The ache pounded in his temples; blood roared in his ears and, behind it, a singing. . .

He felt a jolt, and opened his eyes.

He stood in a richly-furnished room, with an Oriental carpet and tapestried hangings. A huge, canopied bed stood against the far wall, with Elidor huddled against the headboard. Near it, under a tall slit of a window, stood a cradle.

The Duke stood before the bed with his sword drawn. Between it and Elidor, Geoff and Magnus wove like cobras, fencing madly against the Duke. He roared, laying about him with huge sweeps of his sword, maddened at not being able to touch them.

Elidor uncurled and plunged a hand under the featherbed, snatching out a dagger.

A huge blue face appeared at the window, and a blue arm with iron nails poked through, groping toward the cradle.

Cordelia shrieked, and the hag's arm suddenly twisted. It bellowed, and Geoff looked up, startled, then whirled away to the cradle, to thrust up at the monster. With a howl of glee, it scooped him up. Geoff wailed, suddenly only a very frightened three-year-old, struggling madly.

"Aroint thee!" Gwen screamed, and the monster's arm snapped down against the window ledge with a crack like a gunshot. The hag shrieked, but her hold on Geoffrey tightened; his face was reddening too much. Then the blue face fell back, and the hand yanked Geoffrey out of the window.

Rod leaped to the window and bent out, looking down.

Below him, the hag scuttled down the wall of the keep, like a spider, waving Geoffrey in the air. Rod's eyes narrowed, and the cold rage that filled him left no room for pity. Suddenly, the hag's arm twisted, and twisted again, ripping free from her shoulder. Her screams drilled through Rod's head as she fell, turning over and over, to slam into the ground.

But her arm floated high in the air, with Geoffrey.

Then Gwen was beside Rod, staring at the huge blue hand. One by one, the fingers peeled back, opening, and Geoffrey floated up toward them, cradled by his mother's thoughts, sobbing.

Rod didn't stay to see the rest; his younger boy was safe,

but the oldest wasn't. He turned, deliberately, cold glare transferring to the Duke.

Duke Foidin still fought; but he fenced with a gloating grin, for Magnus was tiring. His parries were slower, his ripostes later. The Duke slashed at his head, and Magnus ducked—and tripped on the carpet's edge, falling forward. The Duke roared with savage satisfaction and chopped down at Magnus.

His arm yanked back hard, slamming him against the wall; he screamed. Then he looked up into Rod's eyes, and dread seeped into his face. Rod's eyes narrowed, and the Duke's body rocked with a sudden, muffled explosion. The color drained out of his face as his head tilted back, eyes rolling up; then he crumpled to the floor.

"What hast thou done?" Gwen murmured into the sudden silence.

"Exploded his heart," Rod muttered.

A scream erupted from the cradle.

Gwen ran over to it, scooped up the baby. "There, there, now, love, shhh. 'Tis well, 'tis well; none here would hurt thee, and thy mother shall come presently to claim thee." She looked up at Rod. "Praise Heaven we came!"

Father Al nodded. "The Duke's sentries must have told him Lord Kern was virtually at his gate—so he tried to kill Elidor, in spite."

"And would've gone on to kill the baby!" Suddenly, the anger soared up in Rod again, bulging him out, shaking him like a gale—and Father Al was there beside him, shaking his shoulders and crying, "The deed is done, the Duke's dead! Elidor's safe, the baby is safe, *your* children are safe! *All* the children are safe—and you are Lord Gallowglass, not Lord Kern! You are Rod Gallowglass, Rodney d'Armand, transported here from Gramarye, in another universe—and by science, not magic. You are Rod *Gallowglass!*"

Slowly, Rod felt the anger beginning to ebb, the Power to fade. It slackened, and was gone—and he tottered, his brain suddenly clouded; stars shot through the room.

"My lord!" Gwen was beside him, baby cradled in one

arm, the other around him.

"Yes, I know you are drained." Father Al had a shoulder under his arm. "That use of magic took every bit of reserve your body had. But pull yourself together—it's not over yet! Hear that?"

Hear? Rod frowned, shaking his head, trying to clear it. He strained, and dimly, through the ringing in his ears, he heard shouts, and the clash of steel. War!

"Lord Kern's troops are battling the Duke's," Father Al snapped.

Adrenalin shot its last surge, and Rod straightened up. "No . . . no, I can stand." He brushed away their hands and stood by himself, reeling; then he steadied.

And a voice thundered through the castle, coming from the walls themselves: "THY DUKE IS DEAD! THROW DOWN THINE ARMS!"

There was a moment's silence; then a low moan began, building to despair. As it died, Rod heard, dimly, the clatter and clank of swords, shields, and pikes ratttling on cold stone.

"That voice," Gwen murmured.

"What about it?" Rod frowned. "Sounded ugly, to me."

"It was thine."

"I believe your counterpart has come," Father Al murmured, "to reclaim his own."

"Good," Rod muttered. "He's welcome to it."

Mailed footsteps rang on the stone of the hallway.

"Quickly!" Father Al snapped. "Hold hands! Link your family together!"

Rod didn't understand but he reacted to the urgency in the priest's voice. "Kids! Children-chain! Quick!"

They scurried into place, Magnus and Cordelia catching Geoff's hands, Cordelia holding Gwen's hand and Magnus holding Rod's.

Just to be sure, Rod grabbed Father Al's arm. "What's this all about?"

"Just a precaution. Do you know what to do when you see your fetch?"

"No."

Father Al nodded. "Good."

Then the doorway was filled, and Gwen's exact double stepped into the room.

Well, not exact—her hair was darker, and her lips not as full—but it was unmistakably her.

The "real" Gwen held out the baby. "Here is thy bairn."

The woman gave a little cry, and leaped to scoop the child out of Gwen's arms. She cuddled it to her, crooning to it in the same tones Gwen used.

"My thanks."

Rod looked up.

The hair swept the shoulders, and he wore a jawline beard and close-clipped moustache—but it was Rod's face behind all the hair. "I give thee *greatest* thanks, for the lives of my babe, and my King."

Then Lord Kern's face darkened, and he bellowed, "What dost thou here, what dost thou here? Seekest thou mine end? Get thee hence! Get thee gone!"

And the scene exploded into a riot of color.

Swarming colors, sliding into one another and back out, wavering and flowing all about him. Rod couldn't see anything else; he was floating in a polychrome void; but he could feel the pressure of Magnus's hand within his, and Father Al's arm. And he felt yearnings and longings in different directions, like unseen hands trying to pull him five ways at once; but one was stronger than the others, and pulled him harder. He moved toward it; it was the direction Magnus's hand was pulling in, anyway. Gregory, he realized—baby Gregory, calling Mama home. And Papa, too, of course— but who's really important to an infant, anyway?

Then the colors began to thicken, blending into one another, then separating out again—brown stripes, and multi-hued ones, that coalesced into wooden beams and draperies; white, that bristled into stucco. . .

There was a floor under him. He let go of Magnus and Father Al and shoved against it, levering himself up, feeling dizzy—and gazed around the big room in his own home.

Near the fireplace stood a cradle, with Brom O'Berin bulking over it, scarcely larger than it was, staring.

Gwen scrambled up with a glad cry, and ran to catch up the baby.

Brom bellowed in joy and flung his arms around her.

"Uncle Brom!" the children shouted, and piled onto both of them.

"Fess?" Rod muttered, not quite believing it.

"Rod!" The voice cracked in his ear; he winced. "Is it feedback in my circuits? Rod! Are you real?"

"I'll have to admit to it," Rod muttered. "Never knew I'd be so glad to hear your tinny voice. You can shut down the transmitter, now."

"Oh, Papa!" Cordelia scampered up to him, disappointed. "Just one more time?"

"No! Definitely not! . . . At least, not today." He turned to see Father Al picking himself up off the floor. "If you don't mind, Father, I definitely prefer technology."

CHAPTER TWENTY-FOUR

Not that they made a practice of it, you understand—but this was one occasion when the Gallowglass family just *had* to have a horse for dinner.

Not that Fess ate as he stood at the end of the table—though he did stick his nose in a feedbag, to keep up appearances. After the mad flurry of greetings and rejoicings, Gwen had quickly parceled out victuals, and the whole family had sat down to their first meal in a day. Cordelia and Geoff had been packed off to bed (protesting), and the adults (and a bleary-eyed Magnus) sat down to tell Brom (and Fess) their adventures.

"The varlet!" Brom cried, when they were done. "Thou hadst oped his road to victory, slain his chief enemy, and succored his son—and what is his thanks? To bid thee get hence!"

"Oh, it's not as bad as all that," Father Al explained. "In fact, he probably *was* very grateful—but not so grateful as to be willing to die."

"To die?" Brom scowled at him. "What is thy meaning, shave-pate?"

"He thought Rod was his fetch."

Brom stared.

Then he slapped the table and threw back his head, roaring laughter. "Nay, o' course, then, o' course! What recourse had he, save spells of banishment?"

Rod looked from him to Father Al, then to Gwen; but she shook her head, as lost as he was. "Somebody wanna let us in on the joke?" Rod said mildly.

"A 'fetch,' " Father Al explained, "is your exact double,

and seeing it usually means you'll die in the near future. It's also called a co-walker, or in German, a *doppelganger*."

"Oh." Slowly, Rod grinned. "And in this case, the superstition would've proved true?"

"Well, we'll never know now. But it could be that, with both of you in the same place, that universe might've cancelled both of you."

"Wasn't room enough in that universe for both of us, huh? Not the original *and* the analog?"

"Perhaps. At any rate, Lord Kern took no chances. He pronounced the traditional phrases for banishing a fetch—and it worked."

"Banished me right back to my own universe." Rod lifted his wineglass. "For which, I thank him."

"Exactly," Father Al agreed. "No harm or ingratitude intended, I'm sure."

"Yes, nothing personal. So he gets to keep his universe—but do I get to keep his powers?"

"An interesting point." Father Al pursed his lips. "I'm sure he retains them—but the experience of using his powers certainly should've eliminated any blocks you'd unconsciously set up, freeing you to use whatever powers you *do* have—and we'd already established that you had *something* of your own before you went to that universe."

"Such as the power to manipulate the 'magic field?' "

Father Al nodded. "You may still have that. And from what you've told me of Gramarye, the population here should be providing a very powerful magic field."

"Then he is a warlock?" Gwen demanded.

Rod shrugged. "No way to say until I try, dear—and if you don't mind, I'd rather not, just now."

"Of course," Father Al reminded him, "you *could* always draw on the power of one of your analogs. . ."

Rod shuddered. "I'd *really* rather not. Besides, their powers couldn't work, in this universe."

Father Al got a faraway look in his eyes. "Well, in theory. . ."

"Uh, some other time," Rod said nervously. "Wait till it

scabs over, will you, Father? Somehow, I don't think any of us are going to be the same after this.''

He heard Gwen murmur, "Aye. I fear 'twill mark Gregory for life."

"Yes," Rod agreed somberly. "Going through this at less than one year of age, the effect could be massive. I just wish we could know what that effect will be." He turned to her, meeting her gaze with a smile that he hoped was reassuring.

But she was staring, shocked. "My lord. . ."

Suddenly, it was very silent. Brom frowned, perplexed.

Father Al coughed delicately.

Rod scowled, looking from one to another. "Would someone please tell me what this is all about!"

"Papa," Magnus said, round-eyed, "she did not speak."

Now *Rod* stared.

Fess cleared his oscillator. "Ah, Rod—I hate to trouble you at a time like this. . ."

"Oh, no problem!" Rod jumped at the shred of relative sanity. "Trouble? Yes, yes! Tell me!"

"We do have the matter of the conflict between the Abbot and the Crown. . ."

"Oh, yes! Been meaning to get to that. Thanks for your bulletins, by the way—we *did* receive them. I'll tell you how sometime, when you'll have an hour or so to recover. Your last dispatch said four Southern lords had answered the Abbot's call to arms, and three Northern barons had risen to the King's banner. . ."

"Precisely. Tuan marched his armies toward the monastery of St. Vidicon; the Abbot, hearing of his approach, rode out to meet him with four armies at his back. As of sunset, they were camped in sight of one another, and the King and the Abbot were exchanging dispatches."

"I'm a little too cynical to think they'll have reached a compromise." Rod glowered at the floor. "In fact, I'd bet that the final words of defiance arrived by special messenger before they bedded down for the night." He glanced out the window at the sun. "Think we can still get there before the first charge, Fess?"

"We can but try, Rod."

"Then let's get going." Rod headed toward the door, calling back to Gwen, "Sorry, dear—the boss just called."

Gwen jolted out of her stupor. "Oh, aye! I shall hold dinner for thee!"

"I *hope* we'll be done by then." In fact, if they weren't, they'd probably be in the middle of a battle. He bolted out the door, not a moment too soon, with the great black horse on his heels. Clear of the doorway, he swung aboard, and kicked his heels into Fess's sides.

Something jolted behind him. He looked back to see Father Al riding Fess's rump. "From what little I heard in that one-sided conversation, I thought I had better come along."

Rod shrugged. "Suit yourself, Father—but hold on tight; this ride's going to make a broomstick look cozy!"

Fess galloped over the meadow, extruding jet engines from his flanks, leaped into the air, and roared away.

CHAPTER TWENTY-FIVE

"There they are." Rod pointed downward.

Ahead and below, the trees gave way to a plain. In its center, two long lines of armored knights faced each other, two hundred yards apart. As Rod watched, the two lines seemed to lean forward, then began to move. The horses broke into a trot, then a canter. . .

"Hold on! They can't start, now that we're almost there! Buzz 'em, Fess! And make all the noise you can!"

The great black horse stooped like a falcon, and the engines' roar suddenly increased by half. Father Al gasped and held on for dear life.

The black horse shot down the alley between the two lines of charging knights, five feet above the plain, jets racketting. Horses screamed, rearing back and throwing their riders. Other knights reined in their mounts with oaths of dread. Behind them, the soldiers roared with panic and turned about, trying to scramble over each other to get away from the roaring spirit.

Fess climbed up, circling. Rod looked back over his shoulder with a nod of satisfaction. "That oughta do it. It'll take 'em a while to straighten out *that* mess." He felt a certain smug pleasure at the thought that, near the Abbot and near each baron, there must be a futurian agent who was gnashing his teeth in frustrated rage at the appearance of the High Warlock.

"We can't do much good up here," Father Al bellowed in his ear.

"Oh, I'd say we haven't done too badly so far," Rod yelled back. "But you're right; the rest of it's gotta be done on foot. Mechanization can only go just so far . . . Bring us in, Fess.''

The great black horse circled around, slowing, its engines lowering in pitch, then dove along the same path as its first run. Hooves jolted on the ground; shock absorbers built into his legs took up the impact. He landed at a full gallop, slowing to a canter, then a trot as he came up to the center of the line, and King Tuan.

Tuan snapped up his visor, staring in disbelief. Then a huge smile spread over his face, and he spurred his mount forward to grasp Rod by the shoulders. ''Lord Gallowglass! Praise Heaven thou dost live! But how comes this? We had heard that thou wert witched away!''

Rod grinned and slapped him on the shoulder. Then he winced; armor is hard. Something jolted behind him, and he whirled around, to see Father Al running across the plain toward the opposing line—and the Abbot! For a moment, anger shot through Rod. What was this—treachery? Then his anger turned into chagrin. Of course, he couldn't blame the man for adhering to the side he was sworn to.

''Who was that monk?'' Tuan demanded. ''And how wast thou ensnared in sorcery, with thy wife and bairns? Where hast thou been? How comest thou back? Nay, tell me who ensorcelled thee, who doth command those wretches in my dungeons, and I will turn these knights and men upon him!''

Rod grinned and held up a hand. ''One question at a time, Your Majesty, I beg you! But I'm very gratified by your welcome.''

''Thou dost not know how sorely we have needed thee. But what of the Lady Gwendylon and thy little ones?''

''Returned with me, and all well. As to the rest of it . . . Well, it's quite a story, and I think it'd be a little easier to understand if I told it to you straight through, from beginning to end. Let's let it wait a while, shall we?''

''It seems we must,'' Tuan said reluctantly, ''for there is this boiling coil to consider. Thou hast stopped the beginning of this battle, High Warlock—but I think that thou canst not prevent its end.''

"It's worth a try, though, isn't it? Reconciliation is always possible."

"An thou sayest it, I will try." Tuan shook his head. "But there have been harsh words spoke, Lord Warlock, and I fear it hath gone beyond all hope of healing."

"You're probably right—but I'd like a chance to prove it to myself." Rod turned about. "Let's call for a parley."

But they would have to wait. Across the field, Father Al stood beside the Abbot's horse, and the Abbot stared down at a parchment in his hand. Even across the distance, their voices carried.

"The *Pope?*" the Abbot cried, in shock and dismay. "Nay, but surely he is legend!"

"Thou knowest he is not," Father Al replied, politely but firmly. "Thou dost know how long the line of Peter did persevere, and know within thee that some few centuries' time would not obliterate it."

The Abbot lowered the parchment with a shaking hand. "And yet I think it cannot be. What prove have I that this is real, or that the Seal is genuine?"

"Thou hast seen it in thy books, Lord Abbot. Dost thou truly doubt its authenticity?"

They locked gazes for a moment; then the Abbot's face clouded with doubt. "Nay, not truly so. Yet for five long centuries, the Vatican hath forgot our presence here. How is't that, now, only *now,* do they deign to notice us, and then only to command?"

"This was a grievous omission," Father Al admitted. "Yet, did the founder of this branch of our Order seek to notify the Vatican of his intentions, or his presence here? And canst thou truly say that thou, or any of thy predecessors, have attempted to renew the contact? And tell me not that thou couldst not have done so; I have met thy monks."

The Abbot locked gazes with him, still trembling. Then, slowly, he nodded. "Nay, I must own there is omission on both sides. Yet how doth it chance now, when—*interference* is calamitous, that it doth come?"

Now Father Al's face softened into rueful sympathy.

"Milord—thou art a Cathodean; thou dost know of Finagle."

The Abbot folded. "Aye, certes, certes! 'When the results will be most frustrating. . .' Aye, aye." He sighed, straightening in his saddle. "Well, we must adapt to these vicissitudes, so that we can turn perversity back upon itself, must we not? Therefore, tell to me, Father, what His Holiness doth, through thee, command."

"If we might have converse aside, Milord?"

"If we must, we must." The Abbot climbed down from his mount, his breastplate and helm suddenly incongruous atop a monk's robe. They stepped out into the plain, between the two armies, muttering in low voices.

Tuan frowned. "Who is this shave-pate thou hast brought to our midst, Lord Warlock?"

"An honest man, and a goodly," Rod said promptly. "If it weren't for him, I'd still be . . . where I was. Or dead."

Tuan nodded. " 'Tis warrant enough. Yet goodly or not, in this fell broil, thou canst not be assured that he will not now turn against thee."

"No," Rod said slowly, "I can't."

"As I thought." Tuan squared his shoulders and sat straighter on his mount. "Well, we'll learn it presently. They do come, to parley." He touched his spurs to his horse's side, and rode out to meet the Lord Abbot, who was pacing toward him. Fess trotted after him. Tuan swung down to stand beside the Abbot—a good touch, Rod thought. There was no hope of reconciliation if you insisted on looking down at your opponent. Accordingly, he dismounted, too.

"Well, Milord Abbot," Tuan said, "Heaven hath interceded, and aborted this battle when all mortals would have thought 'twas far too late. May we not now discover some fashion of preserving this gift of peace, thou and I?"

The Abbot was pale and drawn, but his lips were tight with resolution. "An thou dost wish it, Majesty, I am not loath to attempt it. Yet we must consider deeply."

"I will," Tuan promised. "Say on."

The Abbot took a deep breath. "We must consider that the

Church and State must needs be separate in their powers and functions.''

Tuan blinked.

Then, slowly, he inclined his head. ''Even as thou sayest, Milord. Reluctantly I do admit it; but we must agree to the principle. We cannot claim authority in matters spiritual.''

The *Abbot* blinked, this time; he hadn't been expecting quite so gracious a response to his about-face. ''Ah—I own to great joy to hear Your Majesty speak so. Accordingly, following from this principle, we must own that Holy Mother Church can claim no authority in the distribution of State funds.''

Tuan stood, expressionless, still.

Then he nodded slowly. ''Even as thou sayest, Milord; yet I would hope that we may rely on your good counsel in this matter, especially as regards those areas within our domain whose needs are not adequately met.''

''Why—certes, certes!'' the Abbot cried, startled. ''My counsel is thine, whenever thou dost wish it! Yet. . .'' His face darkened. ''In like fashion, Majesty, we must insist on the authority of Holy Mother Church to appoint her priests to her own parishes!''

Tuan nodded. ''Of this, the Queen and I have spoken at some length, Lord Abbot; thou wilt comprehend that, to us, 'tis sore trial to give up such power.''

The Abbot's face hardened—reluctantly, Rod thought.

''Yet,'' Tuan went on, ''when we consider our adherence to the principle of separation that thou hast enunciated— why, there can be no question. The appointments of clergy must rest within thy hands; henceforth, we wish nought to do with such.''

The Abbot stared, speechless.

''We would ask that thou be mindful of thy pledge,'' Tuan said, somewhat severely, ''to inform us where and when aid to the poor is lacking, and to bring to our notice any devices for the better relief of the indigent that thou dost encompass!''

''With all my heart!'' cried the Abbot. ''Be assured, I shall advise thee of all good knowledge we gain, and all ideas we may devise! Indeed, I shall set my bretheren to meditating upon such means as soon as I am arrived again at mine abbey!''

"Oh, come, 'tis not needful!'' Tuan protested. "Still, an' thou wouldst. . .''

There was more of it, in the same vein; in fact, they virtually swore to a mutual crusade against injustice and poverty right there.

And, after the Abbot had disappeared within his own ranks, wobbling with relief and fairly glowing with good intentions, Tuan rounded on Rod. "Now, warlock! By what wizardry hast thou brought about *this* sea-change?''

"Why, I had nothing to do with it,'' Rod said virtuously, "except to bring along Father Uwell—and you wouldn't expect *him* to tell, would you?''

"All right, Father, let's have it,'' Rod shouted over the roar of Fess's jets.

"Oh, come now!'' Father Al roared back. "Can't I claim a professional privilege?''

"You showed him that writ from the Pope, didn't you? And he *did* recognize the signature!''

"No, but he knew the Seal. Beyond that, all I did was explain the Holy Father's policy on relations between Church and State.''

"Which he proceeded to quote, chapter and verse.'' Rod nodded. "Even so, I wouldn't've expected him to cave in *that* quickly. How'd you do it?''

Father Al shrugged. "Probably shock, mostly. They haven't heard from Rome in more than 500 years.''

CHAPTER TWENTY-SIX

Finally, he was able to close the bedroom door (an innovation, on Gramarye) and shuck off his doublet. "What's the matter with the kids?"

"Why, nought, I should think," Gwen answered from the pillow. "They have been perfectly behaved, all afternoon!"

"That's what I mean. What's wrong with them?"

"Oh." She rolled over on her side with a cat-smile. "They do fear thou'lt hear their thoughts."

"Oh." Rod grinned. "So they can't even think about being naughty, huh? Well, I do sort of hear them—but so far, it's only a mutter in the background. Of course, I haven't been trying." He stripped off his hose and slipped into bed.

"Thou'st forgot thy nightshirt," Gwen murmured.

"I haven't forgotten anything." Rod reached out, caressing; she gasped. "Hmmmm, yes, just as I remembered. Sure that's all that was bothering them?"

"That, and the memory of thine aspect as thou slew the Duke." She shuddered. " 'Twould shake a grown man, let alone a child."

"Hmm, yes." Rod frowned. "I'd like to say I'd never even try to do that again, dear—but you know occasions are bound to arise."

"They are indeed." Her voice was hushed; she cuddled close. "I doubt not thou'lt be enforced to draw on such powers again."

"If I can," he agreed. "And if I do, dear—well, I hate to say it, but, as wife, you sort of have signed on for the job of keeping me sane while I do it, of being my link with who I really am."

281

She only smiled, but her words murmured inside his mind: *Have I not always done so?*

He grinned, and agreed, his words wrapping themselves in her mind, while his arms wrapped her in a much closer, much warmer embrace than she'd ever known.

MORE SCIENCE FICTION ADVENTURE!

ACE
SCIENCE FICTION
SPECIALS

Under the brilliant editorship of Terry Carr,
the award-winning <u>Ace Science Fiction Specials</u>
were <u>the</u> imprint for literate, quality sf.

Now, once again under the leadership of Terry Carr,
<u>The New Ace SF Specials</u> have been created
to seek out the talents and titles that will lead
science fiction into the 21st Century.

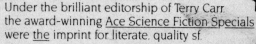

__ THE WILD SHORE	88871-2/$2.95	
Kim Stanley Robinson		
__ GREEN EYES	30274-2/$2.95	
Lucius Shepard		
__ NEUROMANCER	56958-7/$2.95	
William Gibson		
__ PALIMPSESTS	65065-1/$2.95	
Carter Scholz and Glenn Harcourt		
__ THEM BONES	80557-4/$2.95	
Howard Waldrop		
__ IN THE DRIFT	35869-1/$2.95	
Michael Swanwick		

rices may be slightly higher in Canada